The more she knew her, the harder it was to realize she'd never know her. She could only love her.

Leaving Nirvana

an account of love and oppression
race, gender, honor

JuliAnne Sisung

Copyright 2017

ISBN-13: 978-1544260136
ISBN-10: 154426013X

This is a work of fiction. Characters and incidences are the product of the author's imagination and are used fictitiously.

Published March 2017 by Julianne Sisung

Books by JuliAnne Sisung

The Hersey Series

Elephant in the Room
a family saga

Angels in the Corner
a family saga

Light in the Forest
a family saga

Place in the Circle
a family saga

The Idlewild Series

Leaving Nirvana
an account of love and oppression
race, gender, honor

The Whipping Post
a story of oppression, enlightenment and
redemption of those who tied and were tied
with ropes seen and unseen

Ask for the Moon
a tale of love, growth and acceptance
as Idlewild comes of age

Acknowledgement

The Idlewild Series takes place in Idlewild, Michigan, a village rich with history and flamboyance. Research left me in awe of the people who were brave enough to take first steps into the Idlewild Resort for Colored People. My heartfelt first thanks go to you, and the second is for the folks who remembered the history and told it.

Idlewild is a stone's throw from Hersey, where my first series takes place, and Reed City where I grew to adulthood. I want to thank my classmates for telling me stories they recalled about Idlewild and making me eager to find out more.

Thanks to my brother, Mark Jessup, for telling me the story wasn't finished when it wasn't. It is now. Thank you, Mark.

And thank you to my editor, Larry Hale, for his painstaking work. We didn't even fight much.

As always, thanks to my family for their continued encouragement. I know I couldn't barricade myself at my desk for months without their understanding.

Cover image by Mark Jessup

How it All Began

1912

"Ratty, you told them we'd stay for three years. You promised, and you can't go back on it. You keep your word." Flora sat at the polished maple table he'd brought from their home in White Cloud, Michigan. It didn't look like it belonged in the rustic, one-room cabin, and neither did she. Her dress was crisp, and the back bustle was stylish. Her hands were soft and manicured. So were Ratty's.

Erastus Branch, known as Ratty to his friends, hadn't built the cabin. He'd hired laborers to do that, and it was just enough of a home to be truthful with the government authorities when they came calling to check on their homestead agreement.

He was going to have a tough time enduring its primitive condition, but Flora was hardier and could be happy anywhere as long as she was part of Ratty's life.

He toed a new pine wall and mumbled.

"I know we have to stay here, but... we're gonna freeze this winter."

Flora left her chair and wrapped an arm around him. He always needed settling, and she knew how to do it. She stood on her tiptoes to nuzzle his cheek and whisper in his ear. Her words made him smile.

"If that's how we'll keep warm, I may have come out the winner after all. But that's the fourth time in a row I've lost the flip."

"What did you call?"

"Tails."

"Del probably used a two-headed coin."

He chuckled, his mustache tickling her cheek. Even at forty-eight, he could still make her shiver with anticipation.

i

All the Branch men had charisma, big smiles and full heads of hair. They were naturally athletic and lean, and when they walked into a room, heads turned. They expected it. But they didn't demand it because they all knew better. That wasn't the way to make friends.

Ratty and Del, Adelbert to his mother, were two of four hard working brothers. Together, they had built a realtor's empire headquartered in White Cloud, a few miles from the resort they planned to build on twenty-seven hundred acres. They and two other couples from Chicago had purchased the land from the federal government.

Wilbur Lemon and A. E. Wright, their partners, couldn't be expected to leave their Chicago homes and businesses, so Ratty would fulfill the three-year homestead requirement. Besides, the partners were needed in Chicago to create interest and excitement in America's largest cities by way of vigorous advertising marketed to middle and upper class Negros.

In Michigan's beautiful northwest, amidst national forests and pristine lakes, the Idlewild Resort would be a playground where marginalized colored men, women and families could come and find peaceful relaxation in a place of their own.

"I have things to do," Ratty said. "They can't expect me to stay in this one room shack twenty-four hours a day."

"I don't think they do, but we have to show improvements, like we mean to stay put. And we do what we say we're going to."

He squeezed her, lifting her off the floor.

"My sweet, honorable wife. What would I do without you?"

"Probably go to hell when the angels come and take one good look at you," she said. "But I'd come to your rescue, just like always."

"I have to go into the land office. Want to go?"

"Absolutely."

They picked up brother Del and his wife, Isabelle, in the automobile Flora called *His Liz*, a new model T Ford. Flora climbed in the back seat with Isabelle and left the men to discuss securing rights to the sections they wanted, ones that sidled up to the Manistee National Forest and Lake Idlewild and were over and above the purchased acreage.

They left the land office in Baldwin with the land rights all but secured and drove east, going right past Idlewild.

"Where are we going?" Isabelle asked. "Thought for sure we'd wander around Idlewild for a while. Plot and plan and scheme on how to grow a city from a wheat field."

She smiled with her words, but Del felt the spike of her disapproval in his back.

"We're not taking money from babies, or is that candy?" he said, rubbing his chin.

"Candy. You sure?"

Ratty turned his head and looked at her for as long as he could without driving off the road. He didn't like the sound of discontent in his sister-in-law's voice.

"We're not doing anything people don't want us to do. These folks need a place to play, and we're giving it to them. Well, selling it to them," Ratty told her.

Flora patted his shoulder.

"Where *are* we going, dear?"

"To Nirvana."

"Why. What's in Nirvana?"

"Absolutely nothing, anymore," he said.

"Then why are we going there? I'm confused."

"Don't bother," Isabelle said. "You'll never figure out the Branch boys, and you probably don't want to."

"I do, Isabelle. Want to, that is, and I've been trying to for thirty years."

Del took pity on her and half turned in his seat.

"There's a hotel there with an owner we'd like to invite to Idlewild. I've heard he's the best. If the town is dying like we think it is, we'll talk to him about moving. We have a hotel waiting just for him."

"We do?" she said, eyes wide.

"Not yet, but we will."

When they pulled up to the Aishcum Hotel, a curly headed man was sitting on the porch. He had a stick in one hand and a knife in the other, and he stared at the shiny Ford parking in his yard.

Ratty and Del got out and talked with the man, one foot each on the bottom step. They smiled as they left him.

"He'll come," Del said. "Lumber's moving out faster than the Pere Marquette in spring run-off, and there won't be a lumberjack to be found around here soon."

"We build. He buys?" Flora asked.

"Sure thing."

"And how do we build when the trees disappear?"

"With eleven mills around Nirvana, many will have stock piles of white pine waiting to be planed into building lumber. They'll have it for a long time."

They drove to White Cloud to have drinks with William Sanders. He was going to head up the IRC, the Idlewild Resort Company.

Flora was meeting him for the first time and had a few questions about his principles and preconceptions. It was Del and Ratty who owned the company, but she had control of Ratty, and everyone knew it.

"Pick his brain, sweetie. See if he fits your vision of fitting and proper," Ratty said to her, before they stepped inside the restaurant.

"You can bet I will."

He grinned when he shook her hand, holding it longer than the others, and Flora was satisfied, knowing the man's heart was gentle and mind was open, if flamboyant.

"Did I pass?" he asked, patting the top of her tiny hand.

Flora blushed.

"Was I that obvious, William?"

"Bill, please, and yes, you were, but I appreciate your concerns. They're mine also."

Once in the Model T, they teased her about her new beau with the beautiful clothes and shiny gold watch chain.

State of Grace

I have no conscious wish to fly
No one who pushes from my nest
No harm inflicts
No hate exists
And yet I cry.

I cry for freedom of the sky
For full use of opened wings
To play with clouds
Uncertain winds
I have a need to try.

No distant treetop beacons me
With lure of spring's new bud
No one to blame
Not gold nor fame
For this need have I to fly.

My wings in some unspoken trust
Have opened wide without demand
No will creates
This restless state.

Fly I must.
I Must.

By JuliAnne Sisung

Chapter One

1915

Nirvana died. It didn't even give a last gasp before crumbling to dust. The few lumberjacks in town slammed their empty glasses on the bar and lunged around it. They hefted a woman onto their shoulders and paraded her around the room, singing slurred words of adoration. They claimed their love for Abby, their love for her whiskey, and their sorrow in leaving her – all night long. But nothing was left in Nirvana. It was a ghost town.

"Put me down, please, gentlemen," she commanded with a smile. "I can't fill your glasses or cook your breakfast if my limbs are broken."

Her auburn curls came loose from the jostling ride and fell past her shoulders and down her back. Her skirt rode up slender calves, showing sturdy black shoes and plenty of ankle.

"She's showing off her pretty legs, Irish," Bear said to her father.

Abby grinned. "Da would say it's the arse sitting on yer shoulder I should be concerned about, not showing a little leg."

"Come with us, Abby. Marry me. We'll all take good care of you," Yancy pleaded. "I can't leave you here with that weasel, Frank. He ain't good enough for you."

"And I love you, too, Yancy. Frank is a good man. Now, please put me down."

They lowered her to the floor, and she smoothed her skirt and tried to put the curls back into the ribbon at her nape, but the abundant hair refused to be corralled, and she gave up.

"I like it down, Abby. It's pretty like that," Shorty said, his whispery voice making people look around to see where the sweet, melodic sound had come from. Shorty was a giant, six foot five and three hundred pounds, with hands the size of hams on a boar and legs larger than some whole adults.

"Thank you, Shorty." She hated the blush growing on her ivory cheeks, and it happened without reason.

Yancy pushed his way to her side, shoving plaid, flannel shirttails neatly into his waistband and drawing himself up as tall as his frame allowed. He lacked a good inch from meeting her eye to eye, but Abby was tall for a woman, five nine without her large shoes.

"So, you're really closing the place down and moving?" he said, a whine of complaint making his feelings clear. "Not sure about you going to Idlewild. Not at all."

"We are, Yancy. A hotel needs customers. A bar, too. When you're all gone, who'll keep me company here? Who'll buy drinks and a bed to sleep in?"

"We'd stay if there was work," Bear said, meaning it. He turned his scarred face to Abby, and moisture thickened her throat.

Bear had come by the name after a fight with one of his namesakes, during which the animal had nearly come out the winner. He'd been mauled and was barely alive when the lumberjacks brought him into town. Doc had patched him up as much as he could and sent him to the hotel to recuperate.

Abby tended him for days without knowing if he would live or die. When he came to, he thought she was an angel, and he was in heaven. He still called her Angel when he was in his cups and, drunk or sober, treated her like she wore white wings and sat on clouds near heaven.

Abby touched his bearded face and felt the paths and craters where hair wouldn't grow. Affection trickled from her eyes.

God, I love these men. I don't want them to go.

They were her family, and she was sorry they were leaving, sorry they were closing the Aishcum hotel and saying goodbye to Nirvana.

Patrick poured another round for them all and began the Irish ballad he loved to weep over when he was melancholy. Shorty grinned, slung an arm around Abby's shoulder and shook his head.

"Your papa's a good man, but . . . Well, he'd better take care of you or . . . or you know. He'd just better."

Phantom, Abby's white tomcat, leaped from the bar to the landing at the top of the stairs and streaked down the hall and back. Shorty blanched, spun around to watch its path, and made the sign of the cross over his massive chest.

Abby grinned seeing the big man tremble over a little white cat, and Phantom leaped to the railing to do a tightrope walk along it, flicking his tail, his blue eyes glaring at Shorty.

"Don't tease, Phantom. It's not nice," she told him.

Patrick and the lumberjacks drank until the wee hours, and Abby heard stories she didn't want to remember, blushed as she did and hoped the men who told them would forget they'd shared. She didn't want to curtail their fun, so she just turned her head away and pretended she wasn't there when they got bawdy. They were good men, and they were her friends. Eventually, they found beds in the empty Aishcum Hotel and slept until long past sun up.

In the morning, she fed them breakfast and waved goodbye from the front porch, feeling like she was losing family, like they were a bunch of treasured, crazy brothers.

Tears gathered and she swallowed hard, turning away as soon as she could so they wouldn't see them fall and calling "Bye, bye, see you later," like she did every day as they went off to work. She pretended that was the truth of it, but it didn't work.

A few years back, eleven saw mills surrounded Nirvana. Diners, general stores, barbershops, bars, and merchants offering to fulfill every need or desire littered the downtown streets. But the town had boomed early during the lumber era, and it died – early, too – with shocking suddenness.

Without trees, there was nothing to do and nowhere to work. Families packed and left before bellies grew hungry.

Now, Abby and her father were moving to Idlewild, and the idea was overwhelming even though it was only five miles away. She'd been there a few times, so it wasn't a complete unknown, but Nirvana and her father's hotel was all she'd known since birth, and she loved it.

She leaned against one of the four columns holding up the portico roof. Paint peeled from it in big greying flakes and stuck to her dress. The hotel had suffered from a lack of attention in the last few years as the lumber boom crashed to a close, but it was still a substantial building, two stories with big windows, one in each of the guest rooms. A long front porch held white, wooden rocking chairs for relaxing on summer evenings and watching the sun set, listening to the crickets and counting fireflies.

She looked around at the nearby white pines still standing green and tall . . . untouched by the saws and axes of lumberjacks. She'd fought her father to save them more than once when the hotel needed money for repairs.

Patrick would have sold them for the ready cash, but she'd threatened to leave if he did, and she was his free labor. He always conceded with a devil's grin, knowing she'd never leave and knowing he'd never cut her trees for money.

The copse was her sanctuary, and it had been her mother's.

Abby turned her face away and sucked in a breath. There was work to do. It was packing day. She picked paint scales from the sleeve of her dress and snorted. She didn't have time to be sentimental over things that tugged at her heart. She had to put one big, durable shoe in front of the other and point them both in the direction of Idlewild, her new paradise. For the moment, those shoes took her inside.

Abby heard her da moving about in his room at the top of the stairs and called to him. He opened the door and poked his dimpled face out. Patrick's worn work pants sagged from his hips, and his chest was bare. He scratched at the sparse gray hair covering it.

He was a bandy-legged Irishman with broad shoulders and fire in his belly. He feared nothing and no one – except his daughter, which was strange because she was soft spoken and sweet, even if she could grab a lumberjack by the ear and drag him to the door, with ease when provoked. What she wanted was to please, and perhaps that was why Patrick feared her. It scared him that she was so tender.

"Put some clothes on, Da. Please. Are you packing?"

"About to, Daughter."

"You missed breakfast with our friends, but I saved some. It's on the stove."

"They're no friends of mine – drinking all my whiskey and running off."

"I'm going to my room to pack. I'll do the kitchen next, so please eat and get your stuff ready."

It didn't take long to crate up her clothes and the few personal things she owned. She carried them downstairs and stacked them just inside the door in case of a sudden downpour, grabbed a few more crates and headed to the kitchen.

Patrick was finishing his breakfast and beamed at his daughter.

"You look lovely as usual, lass. Thank you for the victuals. I'm ready to take on The Pottawatomie Giant. I could, too. Look at your da. Strong as a wee bull."

He raised his arms in a boxer's stance, scowled and pursed his lips, and Abby laughed at his antics as she always did. He expected it. Enjoyment was his gift. Whether it was the dimples or the sparkling emerald eyes, no one could be ornery around him for long. It wasn't allowed.

"Your beau comin' around today?" he asked.

"Frank said he'd be here this afternoon to help load up and unload when we get to Idlewild. But beau is a funny word. I don't think I like it."

"Every man in the county would be your beau if you'd look their way."

Patrick stretched, grabbed skillets from a shelf and packed them in a wooden box. He shoved utensils in the spaces around them and stuffed it with a half dozen stove mitts.

"That's silly, Da. You loving me doesn't mean they would."

He grabbed the strings of her work apron, tugged them loose, and laughed as she slapped his arm and grinned.

"And so does Shorty and Bear and Yancy and Bob and Bill and Boy Howdy and . . ."

"Get to work," she said, retying her apron. "We have a lot to do."

Frank pulled up behind Manny Watkins who was delivering their borrowed farm wagon. He leaped from his mare and took the steps two at a time, boots thumping hard on the wooden porch. He burst into the kitchen, wrapped an arm around Abby and squeezed.

"Ready?" he said.

She recoiled from the abrupt transition from *getting ready to go* to *going* and nodded, swallowing the suddenness and thrusting back her shoulders.

"I . . . guess we are."

Frank Adams was tall and lanky, willowy, but muscled through the shoulders and thighs and filled any room with energy when he came through the door. He grabbed a crate, raised it to his shoulder and wove his fingers through the handle of a second one. Glass clanked together as he lifted it, and Abby cringed, seeing her mother's china in pieces even before making it to the wagon.

"Glass," she said. "I packed with as much paper as I could find, but . . ."

"Oops," he said, ducked his head in silent apology and grinned.

Between the four of them, dozens of crates and furniture they wanted to keep for the new place were loaded on the large hay wagon and ready to go in no time.

"I'll ride along," Manny said. "Then I'll just bring the wagon and team back. Save you all a trip."

"That's kind, Manny. Right neighborly. Bet you could use a sip for the trip, right?"

Manny gave a sheepish look – like he'd been caught behind the barn with Grandpa's calabash– and nodded.

Patrick ambled to the carefully packed crate of whiskey bottles stashed in a convenient and accessible corner of the wagon and took one from it, handing it to the farmer. Manny removed the top, lifted it in salute, and took a sip. His burly head shook, his shoulders shivered, and he closed his eyes.

"Good. Thanks. Ready?"

"Let's get this wagon rolling," Patrick said.

"I'll follow shortly," Abby said. "If you'll ride in the wagon with Mr. Watkins, Da, I'll take Phantom and Cleo in the buggy. I want to take a last look around."

"You need me?" he asked.

"No. I won't be long. I need to find the cats, and they won't come out with all this commotion. Please, go on ahead."

Frank tilted his head in question, and she answered it with a wave. Abby watched until they were out of site, the wheels making dust devils in the road.

She poured the rest of her sunflower seeds into the birdfeeders and stuck ears of corn on nails pounded into stumps. She hauled the last bag of shelled corn and apples to the deer feed pile and dumped it out.

"Hope it lasts awhile," she said.

She walked a well-worn path just inside the copse of pines and oaks, the same trek she had made daily as she escaped the noise of the hotel and bar for the solitude of her small, private woods. The animals were used to her and stopped their busy work only briefly before continuing their labors. Her mother had walked the same path long ago, at least that's what her father told her. She'd died shortly after Abby's birth, so what she knew of her had come from him.

"You look like your mother," he'd said. "Tall like her, brown eyed and auburn haired. Bonny lasses, both of you."

Abby asked about her often as a girl. She had been eager to know the woman in the picture who looked like her.

"Tell me again, Da. Tell me about her."

"You just want to hear me say how beautiful you are. I'm onto you, lass."

"No, I'm not. My nose and teeth are too big. My feet, too," she'd said as a twelve-year-old who needed her mother in the flesh and blood, not in her da's memory. She had questions without answers and problems without explanations. About that time, she had quit searching for her through her da. It was easier.

But she did wonder if her mother would still come to her after they moved. Would she still feel her presence? Leaving Nirvana felt like she was abandoning her, and the thought brought pain, like a hand reached inside her chest, grabbed her heart and squeezed.

"I'll be back, Ma. Maybe Sunday. Don't leave."

She made a tour of the rooms, pretending to look for things they had forgotten, touching the scarred table and old, worn sofa in their private rooms, and looking for Cleo and Phantom. She called their names, offered bits of meat she'd tucked in her pocket and worried they would hide until she had to leave.

"Come on, kids. We need to go. I have a nice, soft bed waiting for you."

Cleo, the black cat, crawled out from under the sofa, grabbed the piece of meat and leaped on Abby's lap, purring and rubbing her head against Abby's hand.

"Where's your buddy, Cleo? Where's Phantom?"

Cleo's green eyes blinked and looked straight into Abby's. She hunched her back and offered it up for scratching.

"Come on. I'll have to come back for him. He's a bad cat."

She said goodbye to her home of twenty years, tucked Cleo into her basket, took a last quick look for the white Phantom and left.

8

Abby let the old mare mosey through what was left of the town. She took mental pictures of the empty buildings: the diner where lumberjacks had lined up early to scarf down Georgia's famous pancakes after a night at one of the many bars; the two competing barbershops sitting next to one other, each with a red and white painted barber pole, now gray where the paint had peeled; the church that no longer had a reverend; the saloon that no longer had drinkers, it's half doors open to the elements.

"It's sad, Cleo. Such a sudden death."

She mewed and bumped her head against the confining lid of her basket.

"You can't come out, girl. Sorry."

Mew.

Abby opened the basket lid enough to put in her hand, and Cleo purred so loud the mare turned to look for the strange noise.

When Abby rode up, the sun was low in the sky and burning into the water of Lake Idlewild. Sparks of red shot from a gull's splash as it dove into the water for a late dinner. She was going to love front-porch-sitting with this view. It was breathtaking.

She jumped from the buggy and peeked inside the basket where Cleo dozed. She was curled in a fuzzy ball, without caring her world had changed.

"So much for worrying about taking you on a scary ride," she said, and headed for the hotel with a basket full of cat.

"You're late," Frank yelled, lifting a small sofa over his head and carrying it through the open door in front of her.

"Sorry. Wait and I'll help with that."

"Nope. Got it."

"Okay," she whispered, watching him climb the stairs. "You're going to hurt tomorrow."

Cleo leaped from the basket, scooted across the room and flew up the stairs, running in between Frank's legs. He stumbled. The sofa tilted. He somersaulted down the stairs, cursing, and the sofa came to a stop on his back. Cleo

9

screeched to a halt at the landing and sat, washing her paws and watching the fun at the bottom of the stairs. Abby dropped the empty basket and ran to Frank.

"Why in hell did you do that?" he said, moaning.

"Do what?"

"Let that darn cat go running off and almost kill me."

"I didn't mean to. She just went. I'm sorry. Are you alright?"

Frank hunched the sofa off his back and stretched out his legs, testing for broken bones and bruised muscles. He flexed his arms and made fists of his hands.

"Everything seems to be working," he said. "Let me try this again."

"Wait til I get Cleo, Frank. We don't want to test the fates."

The cat stayed put, waiting to be picked up, and calmly snuggled into Abby's arms, purring as she was carried to a room at the end of the hallway.

"Stay in here out of trouble, Cleo. Be a good girl."

She curled up on the bed and watched with wide innocent eyes as Abby shut her in.

Frank was half way up the stairs and again refused her offer of help. Abby led the way into the room she and her father would be using as a small parlor. She winced when the sofa bounced off the door frame.

What made some men want to do it by themselves instead of taking help from a woman?

He groaned as he stood and held a hand to his back.

"Are you alright?" she asked. "Does your back hurt?"

"Well, I did take a circus ride down the stairs thanks to your damned cat, but I'll live."

He grinned and ran a hand through blond hair that was a smidge too long and hung over his collar, just the way she liked it. He tugged her to him in a fast embrace, kissed her before she knew he was going to and was out the door before she could unpucker.

It was dark by the time they finished unloading, and candles and oil lamps glowed in each of the downstairs rooms. With the last crate plunked by the door, Patrick declared work done and Irish whiskey time so his friend Manny could help launch the new bar before his ride home. He pulled a bottle from its safe haven in a box filled with torn up newsprint and shouted for them to meet him at the bar.

"A bar is like a ship," he said, his thumb hooked in one of his suspenders, "and it needs to be christened properly. But I'll be damned if I'll break a bottle of good whiskey on it. Maybe I'll just pour a wee bit. A drop."

Manny sidled up to the slab of glossy wood that ran almost the length of an entire wall, and Frank joined him. Abby rummaged around looking for the glasses.

"Come on, Abby girl. We need glasses, cups, anything. We're parched," her father said.

"They're here. I know they are."

"Hey. You in there?" a voice bellowed from the lobby of the hotel.

"In the bar," Patrick shouted. "Come on back."

He glided into the room, his hand held out to shake the first one he came to. His white hair was slicked back, comb ridges still stiff and wide. His suit was crisp, and a shiny, gold watch chain hung from pocket to button hole over the belly of the vest. He was something to see.

"William Sanders," he said. "IRC leader and welcome wagon."

Patrick rolled the man's way, his short legs curved as if he was riding a horse and turning his walk into a waddle. He extended his arm for an eager handshake.

"Glad to see you, Sanders. Heard a lot about you."

He turned to Abby.

"Set one up for Mr. Sanders, Daughter."

"Bill to my friends, and likewise."

Abby found the glasses, wiped them on her apron, and lined them up on the bar. She tipped generous portions in each and waited to hear the words.

"*Slainte*! May the hinges of our friendship never grow rusty," her father said, his words tinged with an Irish burr that grew when he gave a toast and became even heavier with each one.

11

He slammed his empty glass on the bar, and the other four followed.

"A bird with one wing can't fly," Sanders said. He pulled a wad of money from his pocket and peeled off a few bills.

Patrick grinned at the Irish toast coming from William Sanders' lips and pounded him on the shoulder.

"Put that away, man," Patrick said. "Your money's no good here today. This day is for friends. Give us another wing, Abby. You heard our friend."

"IRC? What's that?" Manny asked, stuck on Sanders' first words. "Some secret clan thing?"

Bill pulled back his suit jacket and stuck his fingers into the backside of his trousers' waistband, a proud stance that emphasized his substantial trunk.

"Idlewild Resort Company. That's what it is. The biggest thing Michigan will see in this century. And this man," he said, slapping Patrick on the back, "will be part of it. We're gonna make a fortune and names for ourselves. The entire country will know about Idlewild, William Sanders, and Patrick Riley. Yes, sir, they will."

"But what *exactly* is it?" Manny asked, his palms out and shoulders hunching.

"This lake, these forests. It's all prime land for colored people who have no place to go. No place to play. That's what it is. We'll have cabins and clubs, music and comedians, a place for swimming and hunting and horseback riding. Every pleasure they could possibly want at their fingertips. We've bought up over twenty-seven hundred acres of paradise, and we're selling it off in little chunks to coloreds from Chicago and Detroit. Hell, from all the way down south. Dr. Dan – the famous Chicago heart surgeon – is buying in. You've heard of him."

"Why here?" Frank asked, a skeptical frown creasing his brow.

"Because we're inviting them . . . and because they don't have anywhere else to go. But mostly because they're invited. We want them here, and we have real estate men in Chicago, Cincinnati, all the major cities, even in Canada,

selling lots for a dollar down and a dollar a month."
paradise
He sipped his drink and looked each person in the eyes
before continuing.

"This is a utopia for colored folks who have money to
spend and no place to spend it. We'll invite the best Negro
entertainers and set them up in hotels. Think about it," Bill
said, pausing and tilting his manicured head sideways.
"They'll have a great place to have fun – for the first time –
ever. This will be their Eden."

"I don't know," Frank said, chewing the side of his lip.
"This is farm country. How are people gonna take all this?"

Bill ignored Frank's negative comments and stuck to
the reason for his visit. "This is where you come in, Patrick
Riley. We need you and your hotel. You in?"

"I am. Wouldn't miss out for nothing," he said. "It's just
what the Branch boys told me, and that's why we're here,
isn't it? To run a hotel and fill it with people." He sipped,
and a confused look wrinkled his bushy brow. "What
exactly is it I'm needed for?"

"Rooms for the entertainers at first. At least until we're
established, and then they'll pay their own way, happy just
to be here."

"Guess I can do that. It'll bring in paying customers
who just want to be near celebrities, so . . . what the hell. We
can help out, can't we, girl?"

Sanders tipped back the last of his whiskey, licked his
lips and thanked Patrick for his hospitality.

"The missus will be wondering if the hobgoblins got
me. It's a yeller moon night."

"And that means . . . what?" Patrick asked, cocking his
head and contemplating his new friend with interest.

Bill laughed. "Don't ask," he said.

Patrick followed him to the door, slapped him on the
shoulder and walked with him down the steps of the front
porch.

Outside, the night was warm, and the early *yellow*
moon cast shadows on the lake. A loon sang its mournful
hymn, and both men stood silent until it ceased, respectful

of the bird's lament. The night belonged to it and the other nocturnal creatures that left daytime to mankind. A bullfrog croaked, boasting the size of its prominent, bulging throat, and a barred owl questioned the night.

Hoot, hoot, hoot, hoot-a-hoot? he asked. His only answer was the yip of a neighborly red fox.

"This is a paradise," Patrick said. "I'll miss my place in Nirvana, but..."

"Frank family?" Bill asked.

"Not yet, but he and my lass are spoken for. Why?"

"No reason. Just wondered." He scuffed a shoe on the wooden step, his face grave and thoughtful. "I'll be off. Thanks for the drinks. Appreciate it."

Chapter Two

Patrick stuck his head into Abby's bedroom where she was hanging dresses and filling drawers with small clothes. She grinned at her father's wild reddish-gray hair. "I'm going to the island with Adelbert Branch and his wife. You're gonna have to meet with the other Branches. Sounds like a tree coming to town, all these Branches," Patrick said. "Can you handle it?"

"Of course, but comb your hair. You look like a Kerry bog pony."

He ruffled his longish mane and grinned.

"What do you know of the Kerry bog, lass?"

"Everything. You spent my first ten years telling me all there is to know about your Ireland."

He grinned, and the dimples excavated his cheeks.

"I've heard Flora Branch is a sweet woman, and Erastus is a gentleman. We'll have tea," Abby said.

"A spot a tea," he mocked, his pinky finger pointed into the air. "Erastus might want something a bit stiffer than a cup a tea. Offer it, lass."

Abby nodded and went on with her unpacking.

"You good with all this?" he asked.

"Fine, Da. I'm fine. I have to go back home and find Phantom soon, though. I'm worried about him."

"This is home, Abby. But I understand. Want me to go with you?"

"Nope. And go away, now. Let me get my work done."

From her bedroom window, Abby watched a flawlessly dressed couple climb from their shiny black touring auto. She'd heard it coming a long way off, and her brow wrinkled. Like many, she wondered if the day would come

15

when earsplitting horseless carriages filled the roads, and fumes and obnoxious noise filled the air.

Patrick met them on the porch and led them to the small boat that would take them to the island.

"I thought you were building a footbridge, Del," Isabelle said, looking from her high heeled shoes to the boat and back again.

"For now, it's swim or row. I'm told the bridge is in the works. Should be done by winter," Del said.

"If you want to wait here, have some tea with my daughter at the hotel . . ."

Isabelle slugged Patrick on the arm and harrumphed.

"Course not. I came to see our wilderness, and I aim to do just that. *I* invited *you* along," she said, grinning underneath her scowl.

"Don't be impertinent, woman," her husband said, taking her arm and settling her in the small rowboat.

"That you did, Isabelle. You invited me. May I call you Isabelle, Mrs. Branch?"

"You may, Patrick. And this old goat is Del."

On the island, they walked directly to the cleared space Del indicated was the acre he wanted Patrick to buy for a new club. It bordered the lake, which was shallow and sandy in the cove, perfect for swimming and playing in the water. The inlet area was a prime piece of property.

"You could buy a fleet of fishing boats to rent out, build a dock and a boat house, make a fortune."

Patrick visualized the area full of singers, dancers and musicians – celebrities, vacationers from Chicago, Detroit, and Cleveland, staying for a week or two and heading back to the city and jobs, their working lives. Young people out of college for the summer would flock in, looking for fun, to be entertained.

It was easy to see. They were already there in his mind. He kicked the sand under his feet and squinted.

"I sunk a load into the hotel we just left. I don't know if I can manage this, too," he said.

"Dr. Dan already bought up a bunch of acres, and he's ready to develop. We're gonna have a hotel and club on the island, maybe more, and I wanted to give you first shot at it," Del said. "Didn't want you blindsided by someone else coming in and running you out of business just because you're on the mainland."

"I appreciate it. I do. I'll just have to think on it."

Del turned to view the island and cleared his throat.

"It might not sell right off, but we've got crews in all the major cities advertising a magical resort. One of a kind. A place all their own. I don't think it's gonna take long to catch on."

"I know. I'm sure you're right."

They walked around the island, poked into wooded areas, peered into the clear water and headed back to the boat. It was a quiet ride back to the hotel, and Del broke the silence.

"It'll be there a while, Patrick. No rush."

Erastus and Flora Branch pulled into the driveway just after Patrick had pushed the boat away from shore and Del picked up the oars. Abby met the couple at the registration desk.

"We need a room, young lady," he said, his voice booming in the small lobby.

"Ratty, say hello before you order people around," Flora said, her voice minutely above a murmur.

"Sorry."

He extended his hand, grabbed and squeezed Abby's in both of his, and pounded it up and down.

"I'm Erastus Branch. Ratty. This is my wife, Flora. We'd like a room for the week if you're ready for visitors."

Abby introduced herself and grinned. She liked this brusque man, but knew right off who wore the pants, even if the visual said otherwise.

"Bill Sanders told us you'd be coming, so I have a room prepared. We just got here, so we're not fully staffed. I hope that'll be okay."

"Don't want to cause trouble. Anything with a bed is going to be fine," Flora said. "We've been homesteading for the last three years, and this will be a palace."

"I've made tea. Will you join me in the dining room? It's really the bar, but that's where we'll serve food."

Abby led the way and left to get the tea tray. They were wandering the room, looking at the wall hangings and out the window at the view of the lake when she returned.

"Isn't it marvelous," Flora murmured.

"It is. I do love it, even though I miss our old hotel and our lumberjack friends."

Abby poured tea and offered the small sandwiches she'd made.

"This will be different for you," Flora said, taking a cucumber sandwich wedge and nibbling at it. "A much different group of people from your lumbermen. Are you prepared for that?"

Abby watched Ratty fumble with the small handle of his teacup and smiled, remembering her father's words that morning.

"Could I offer you a glass of whiskey, Mr. Branch, instead of the tea?" She wanted a moment to consider Flora's question. It was obvious she was probing for something, and Ratty was struggling.

He beamed and thumped the cup down, splashing brown liquid into the saucer. His wife winced.

"You certainly could, young lady. You certainly could."

Abby brought whiskey in a wide glass, one he could wrap his large fingers around.

"You were saying, Mrs. Branch?"

"Flora, Dear. Just, well . . . your clientele will be much different than you had in Nirvana. They'll be fairly well off, not necessarily rich, but comfortable. Some will be entertainers and celebrities, of a sort, and . . ."

"Dark skinned?" Abby said, the truth hitting her like a bolt from a stormy sky.

"Well, yes." A blush rose to Flora's face, and she patted her neck trying to cool her own pink skin.

"I don't think that makes them so different," Abby said, "just darker. Wouldn't you say?"

"Yes," she whispered. "I would. I would say so. We agree."

Ratty leaned back in his chair and sighed. "Happy now, Flora?"

"I am." She picked up her cup and sipped, a smile warming her eyes. "Yes. I am," she repeated. "And thank you for the tea, Abigail. It was a lovely thing to do. Let's go find our room, Ratty."

"I'll take your bags," Abby said, "and show you to your room."

"Just point and tell us the number, Abigail. Ratty's twice as wide as you and can easily carry both our bags – and me, should I choose," she said, leaning to run a hand down his arm.

In the kitchen, as Abby chopped vegetables for the night's stew, she considered Flora Branch's pointed words. She had assumed skin color was something Abby would care about. Why would she make that assumption? She pushed the troubling thoughts away and threw herself into dinner preparations.

Abby's days were spent trotting from one chore to the next, from changing linens and cleaning rooms, to cooking meals, to tending the bar. She knew she had to get some help soon, or she'd collapse into a babbling heap. Her father would resume the evening meal preparation at some point, but that point hadn't arrived. She might have to emphasize it with the end of a cattle prod sooner rather than later.

She served the dinner meal, washed up, cleaned the kitchen, and went to the bar where Patrick was holding court for all four Branch brothers and their wives. Frank was at the end of the bar, nursing a glass of whiskey and looking happy to be out of the conversation.

"This is what I know," Patrick said. "This is what the leprechauns left to me instead of the pot of gold. I can run a hotel."

"Looks to me like little Abby is doing the running," Isabelle said, grinning. "And you're kissing the stone."

"And what do you know of the stone, lass? Is there a bit of the wee Irish girl in you?"

"My father was Paddy O'Donnell. Thought I might want to keep that name cuz Branch comes from those beastly English and wasn't Irish at all, but . . . Del didn't want a wife with a better name than his. Isn't that right, husband?"

Flora was stroking Cleo, who sat on the bar next to her drink and was soaking up the loving when a face appeared in the window and disappeared just as quickly. Flora's head spun as she glimpsed the image from the corner of her eye, and she stiffened. Cleo leaped from the bar and ran to the door howling.

"What on earth was that?" Flora thought, concern bordering on fear she didn't want to put a name to. The face in the window had been shadowed in gray, a female with wild, long hair and huge expressive eyes. She was speaking, or at least her mouth was moving, and she pointed off to her right like she was trying to say something.

"Did you all see that?" Flora asked when she found her voice, but her words were buried as the door blew open on a sudden gust of wind, and a fur ball streaked in, a massive, white blur. He leaped to the bar, walked serenely to the end of it and perched there.

"You came, Phantom! You came all by yourself," Abby said, running to the end of the bar where he sat washing his paws and face. The cat turned his head away, blinked his blue eyes twice, and went still, waiting.

"I'm sorry I left you. Really," Abby said, stroking his head, "and I'm glad you found us."

"I gather this is Phantom," Isabelle said.

"Yes. How'd you know?" Abby asked, surprise widening her eyes.

"You just said it."

"Oh . . ." she said, laughing. "I did. He got left in Nirvana a few days ago, and I've been worried sick. He hid when we were packing, and we had to leave. I planned to go back this weekend to find him. I missed you, Phantom."

She crooned the last part to the sphinxlike cat who had succumbed to her strokes and was purring. Flora sipped her sweet drink and looked back and forth, from midnight ebony Cleo at one end of the bar to pure white Phantom at the other. Bookends. She smiled and nodded. It couldn't have been more fitting.

"So, you found your way here," Frank said. "Didn't know cats could do that. Dogs can. They're smart and good trackers. Fetch, too."

Phantom turned his wide eyes on Frank, tail twitching, and stared unblinking until Frank turned away mumbling something about creepy, sneaky cats.

"Cats are smarter than a lot of people I know," Isabelle said. "They're misunderstood."

"Gotta go. Early day tomorrow," Frank said.

Abby followed him outside and hooked an arm through his.

"Nice night," she said. "Listen to the frogs. They're crazy tonight."

"You're crazy," he said, with a smile to soften his words. "You run your Pa's place single handed. What's he gonna do when you get married?"

"What do you mean?"

"Well, when we get married and you move to the farm. How's he going to get along?"

Abby's grip on his arm loosened, and she gazed at the moon's silhouette across the water, a tadpole with a yellowish long tail and a water bubble at the end. She waited for him to explain or say he didn't mean it, that he was kidding, but the silence continued.

He spun her around and crushed her to him, kissed her hard and released her just as quickly. His breath came in spurts.

"I can't wait, Abby. I need you. Let's set the date."

"We need to talk about this, Frank. I don't know that I'm ready. I can't leave Pa here alone. He needs me, and running a hotel is what I do."

21

Her words were rushed, without calculation, but real. She hadn't even settled in yet.

Frank glared at the tadpole on the water, his brow creased.

"What about me? I need you. You're my wife. Well, not yet, but soon you'll be."

Abby dragged him to the chairs lining the porch and sat, crossed her arms and tilted her head.

"You still want to get married, don't you, Abs?"

"Sure, I do. I love you, Frank."

"Then what's wrong?"

"I told you. Pa needs me. You have your whole family at the farm. Your mother and father, your brothers and Cecily. Your nephews. You don't need me there, and I need to be here."

"Well . . . what about me?"

Abby was quiet for a moment, watching the stars blink on and twinkle in the dark, wondering if the cities had such spectacular skies. It wasn't possible.

Someone let Phantom out, and he leaped on her lap, curled up and closed his eyes.

"Couldn't we live here? At the hotel? My room is plenty big enough for two, and I could bring in a small sofa." She smiled. "Maybe the one Cleo dumped on you?"

He took her hand and was quiet, stared hard at her and swallowed.

"As long as I can be married to you, sleep in the same bed with you," he said with a knowing smile. "When?"

"When what?"

"When can we get married? I'm tired of waiting, Abby."

"January. After the Christmas rush," she said. "Is that okay?"

"That'll work and, if you'll dump the cat, I'd like to kiss my bride."

The bar was quiet when she went back in. She looked for her father, wanting to share the news with him, to tell someone, celebrate, talk about it, but they'd all gone to bed. She turned the lamp off and made her way through the lobby, up the dark stairs and down the hallway to her room.

"I'll be Mrs. Adams soon. Mrs. Abigail Adams. Sounds nice. Has a classy ring to it. What do you guys think?" she asked Cleo and Phantom who had beaten her to the room and were waiting by the door.

They leaped on the bed, four eyes watching her, two deep cobalt and two bright jade. Round orbs with vertical, pointed black ovals in the center, eyes that followed as she moved about the room. But they didn't answer her question.

Abby fixed breakfast for the hotel guests and said goodbye when they left. She began unpacking the shipment of goods that had come that morning, new sheets and blankets, dresser scarves, pitchers and bowls for each room, and wall hangings. She had dragged all the boxes upstairs when she heard Cecily, Frank's sister-in-law, calling her name.

"Upstairs. Second to last room on the right. Get up here and help me."

She hugged Cecily and grabbed the two boys who squealed when she kissed their cheeks.

"Yuk," Chunk said, wiping his face with the sleeve of his shirt. He was anything but chunky. He was tall for a five-year-old and as skinny as a long-handled hoe. "Don't kiss," he added.

Bailey just grinned. He didn't talk much, and he liked girls kissing him, especially pretty ones, so he held on to Abby's arm hoping for more.

"Want help?" Cecily asked and tossed a long black braid over her back.

"Do I look like a fool?" she said. "Yes, yes, and yes. Grab that sheet and help me make the bed. And there's more where this one came from."

Cecily shook out the sheet and let it float down on the mattress, tugged it tight, and made hospital folds at the foot.

"Your mama taught you right, Ceci. Nice corners."

"You bet. I can really make a bed," she said, her round, olive cheeks creasing in a grin.

They worked in silence until they went into the next room.

"You ever gonna tell me?"

"Tell you what?" Abby said.

Cecily propped two fists on her ample hips and made a face.

"What?" Abby repeated. "Do I have a secret to tell?"

"Abigail Riley, you are not like any other young woman I know. Not any. They'd all be busting to tell people. If they were getting married, they'd be running around town shouting the news."

Abby stuck her finger over her lips, tucked her head and rolled her eyes up, a grin of conciliation on her face.

"Sorry? I forgot."

"How could you forget? That's not something a person forgets."

"I got busy. So . . . okay. Hey. Frank and I set a date. We're getting married in January. How's that?"

Cecily grabbed her friend in a bear hug.

"I'm so happy, Abby. Finally, I'll have another woman in the house. Someone to talk to besides Terry's mother. She's so crotchety, and I can't . . . What? What's wrong?"

Cecily put a hold on her tongue and stretched up to her scant five feet.

"I'm not moving to the farm, Ceci. I have to stay here. With my da. He needs me."

"But you're getting married. Women go with their husbands. They live together." She poked Abby in the side and wiggled her dark brows. "That's how you get these things," she whispered, pointing at her boys.

"We know were babies come from, Ma," Chunk said, giving her a disgusted look and wrinkling his nose. "We live on a farm, remember?"

"I know it's different," Abby said, "but . . . It's what I need to do. And we will live together. Here."

Cecily didn't have a response. She wrapped an arm around the much taller woman and squeezed. "Sure. Okay. Let's do the next room. Come on boys. Grab a crate."

Chapter Three

Indian summer was in full swing, and the blue jays were going crazy, jeering, mimicking hawks and fooling us with their liquid, whispering song amidst the jeers. Canadian geese were taking advantage of a warm layover and settled on Lake Idlewild far enough away from the white swans to not aggravate the beautiful, but obnoxious creatures. Goose honks competed with the jays, though, and Abby saw irritation in the graceful curve of several swan necks.

"Look out, geese," she said. "You're treading on thin ice. Well, it's water you're treading now, but it won't be for long."

Abby walked from the hotel to Jesse Falmouth's office just a hop and a spit down the dirt road. Phantom followed her, much to the distress of the birds, and Abby wondered if his presence, not the gorgeous day, was the reason for their wild, exuberant cries.

"Jays are insufferable birds, Phantom. Listen to them. You can't even hear the songbirds with them around."

Phantom didn't respond.

Jesse met her at the door, had it open before she walked up the steps to the small porch.

"You have an escort," he said, stretching a long arm to shake her hand.

"It seems I do. Since we moved here, and he had to search for us, Phantom doesn't let me out of his sight. He can wait outside."

"No need. He's welcome. Come on in."

Jesse motioned to one of the chairs positioned in front of his desk, and Abby took it. Phantom took the other, and Jesse smiled.

He was a striking man, slender, with a captivating, toothy smile that settled in his eyes and skin of burnt umber. He wasn't wearing a jacket, but the burgundy satin vest was immaculate, and the white shirt was crisp. Abby felt underdressed next to him and ran her hands down her cotton skirt in a futile and unnecessary effort to remove imaginary wrinkles.

"I came from work," she said lamely, as if it was important for him to know she could have dressed better.

He nodded and smiled again.

"Well, thank you for seeing me." She was uneasy and confused by her attack of nerves.

"It is my pleasure. To what do I owe the honor?"

"Right." She threw her shoulders back. "I'll just lay out my idea. I'd like the Idlewild town fathers, like you, to support holding a Chautauqua. Several of them, in fact. With speakers and music, dances, whatever we can come up with to bring people to Idlewild. To celebrate the arts, intellectual activities, and simply have fun."

She paused and watched Jesse process. His head lowered, and he was silent for long moments.

This is unsettling. He could have said something, anything, a 'hmmm . . .' or an 'I see' would have been appropriate.

"Um. Not that you're old, like sometimes town fathers . . . well. Did I say something wrong?" she asked when it felt like too much time had gone by.

He looked up at her like he was surprised to find her sitting in his office and gave her the full force of his enigmatic grin.

"I'm sorry. I sometimes get lost in ideas. Edna, that's my wife, is used to it, but it's disconcerting to people who don't know me."

"It's quite alright. I just . . . wasn't expecting it. The silence, I mean. What do you think?"

He looked confused. "About silence?"

"Oh, my. Maybe I should go out and come in again."

Phantom stood up in the chair, watched and waited.

"Let me try this again. What do you think about holding a Chautauqua in Idlewild this spring or summer?"

"I love the idea. Where?"

"The pavilion?"

"What pavilion?"

"Oh. I got ahead of myself."

Abby blushed and tugged at her braid.

"I'm really sorry. I don't know what's the matter with me. We need to talk with everyone about building a pavilion where we can hold the Chautauqua and services. Church services. Except in the winter. A place bigger than the private homes where they hold them now. Big enough for us all."

"All of us?" he asked, the grin back in place.

"Sure. Why not all of us?"

"Colored and white?"

Abby lifted her chin. Her eyes widened. "Are you saying you wouldn't want a mixed congregation? You wouldn't want to go to church with me?"

"No. I'm not saying that." Jesse shrugged, unwilling to spell it out if she didn't want to recognize color differences in church services. "Let's get back to the Chautauqua. I like the idea. Let's walk one step at a time."

"Good. Let's do that," she said, miffed but uncertain why or why it should matter what he thought of her ideas. This was a perplexing man, for sure, and she'd been on a lame horse ride since she'd arrived at his office. She didn't know what to do about it.

"We need a committee of people, as usual. Can we hold a meeting at your hotel?" he said.

"Sure. Good idea. I'll post notices around town, and we'll see who we get."

This time his smile erupted into laughter.

"Around town. Oh, you are a rose-colored-glasses kind of woman, aren't you, Abby Riley? Where would around town be?"

Her back stiffened again, melted, and eventually she laughed with him.

"I see what you mean. The hotel, here, the grocery store, and maybe get Bill Sanders to let all the Idlewild lot owners know we'd like their ideas at the meeting."

Jesse stood. "I like your plans, Abby. You're going to be good for Idlewild. See you at the meeting."

Phantom, who had settled into a ball of white fur, stood again and was at the door in a lightening movement. Waiting.

"What do you think about William Jennings Bryan?" Abby asked on the way to the door.

"Smart man."

She stood with one hand on the knob and the other rubbing the back of her neck and laughed.

"I really need to learn clarity if I'm going to be allowed out in public. I meant as a speaker. Bryan as a keynote speaker. I understand he does Chautauqua events."

"I like it. And you're alright, Miss Riley. I like you, too."

She stopped by Joe's Grocery and searched for the list she'd made that morning. The bell over the door clanged, and Joe Foster came from the back room, rubbing his eyes like she had awakened him from a nap.

Dust swirled as the door shut, making Abby's eyes water and a sneeze threaten. It was a tiny store. One small room with floor to ceiling shelving packed tight with goods. A counter ran the length of one wall, and a six-foot-tall shelf stood in the middle of the room. Phantom sneezed, and Joe peered over the counter and spotted him.

"Get the cat out. This is a grocery store."

Abby nodded and opened the door. Phantom tilted his head to stare at Joe, hunched his back once and ambled out.

"I'm Abigail Riley, Mr. Foster, from the hotel."

"I know who you are. Heard about it."

Joe didn't look happy about whatever it was he'd heard. Either that or he'd gotten up on the wrong side of his nap.

Abby pulled back the hand she'd been about to offer and went for her grocery list instead.

"We need a few things. Should I gather them myself, or would you like. . .?"

Joe grabbed the list from her hand and turned away. *Well said. At least that was clearer than I've been all day. No doubt about what he means.* "I'll just wait here," she said, plucking at the skirt of her work dress. She heard him mumbling but didn't know if it was in response to her words or to himself, and she didn't want to get close enough to him to ask.

He stirred up more dust moving around the room and slapping packages down on the counter. She tried to hold it back, but, just as he stopped in front of her and pointed at an item on the list, she let loose the monster of all sneezes.

"Excuse me. I'm so sorry," she said, pulling a handkerchief from her handbag and wiping her nose. "It's the dust, not a cold or anything."

"What's this?" he said, ignoring her apology.

"Oyster crackers."

He peered at her.

"Oyster crackers," she repeated, as if saying it again would help him understand, and, when his eyes continued to roll up to the corner of the room, she added, "You know, little round crackers for putting in bisques or chowders."

He shook his head and moved his finger to the next item.

"Bisques. Huh. No woman to clean," he mumbled.

At least, that's what Abby heard. She wasn't sure, nor did she know why he would tell her he needed a woman to clean.

Clean it yourself was on the tip of her tongue until she bit it.

When he finished gathering and everything was laid out on the counter, he pulled a broken pencil from over his ear, licked the lead, and scratched numbers on a yellowing pad of paper. He added on his stubby fingers, carried the numbers over on top of the columns, and did it again to check his figures. When he finished, he took her money, counted back the change and silently piled her groceries in a box he took from a stack in the corner.

"Where's your man to carry this?"

"I can handle it, Mr. Foster."

"There's men's work, and there's women's. Carrying is men's."

"I carry heavier bags at the hotel," she said. "I'll be fine, but thank you."

"Wasn't lookin' for to help. Was saying I don't hold with women working . . . less it's cleaning and cooking for her man. Not doing men's work. That's all."

Abby stepped back, surprised, not by his words, as she'd heard them before, but by the fact he thought he had the right to say them to her.

What's so manly about stocking shelves and putting groceries into a box?

"And while I'm at it," he said. "If your hotel is catering to them Idlewild resort people . . . well, you might want ta not."

Dead silence filtered through the dust motes.

"Are you threatening me, Mr. Foster?"

"Hell, no. I don't threaten. If I think something needs to get done, I just do it. That's all. Now git, girl."

"Mr. Foster, please don't order me around." Abby jerked the box off the counter and headed for the door. She was so angry it was feather light. She braced it on a hip and held it with one hand, grabbed the brass knob with the other, and slammed the door open, clanging the bell hard.

"That's a stupid, stupid man, Phantom."

Mrow wah, he said, blinked, rubbed her ankle twice, and led the way back to the hotel.

"I agree," she told him.

Mrow.

Abby was in the kitchen chopping bacon, carrots and potatoes when Patrick stuck his shaggy face in to say she had a visitor.

"Who is it? And you need a shave, Da. Badly."

"Don't know her. Pretty colored woman and her little girl."

"Tell her I'll be out in a few minutes. I have to finish this, or we won't have any supper tonight. And Frank's coming."

Her father nodded, scratched the gray stubble covering his face and grinned.

"Tomorrow, lass. I'll make myself pretty tomorrow morning." He dunked his head up and down and skedaddled before she could scold him.

"She'll be out presently," he told the woman and proudly introduced himself. "Patrick Riley. I'm the owner of this fine establishment. Perhaps I could treat you to a wee drink? A brandy before dinner? I have Jules Robin."

Patrick held his arm out for her to take, which she did, and he escorted her into the bar where she lifted her daughter to a stool and took another herself.

"Jules?" he asked.

"I would love one. Thank you, Mr. Riley."

He went behind the bar and poured two hefty tots of the fine cognac, a root beer for the youngster, and set them on the counter.

She sipped and smiled.

"Nice. What a treat. I'm Edna Falmouth, and this is my daughter, Daisy. Say hello to the nice man, sweetie."

Patrick shook the little girl's hand and told her he had a daughter, too, almost as pretty as she was.

"It's a pleasure to know you both. Is Abby expecting you?"

"No. My husband, Jesse, sent me over to help her with the Chautauqua planning meeting. She doesn't know anything about me."

"Chautauqua?" Patrick said, clearly puzzled.

Edna grinned again, her eyes crinkling at the corners and settling in Patrick's heart.

"And it sounds like you don't know anything about that," she said.

"No surprise. Abby tends to do stuff on her own. She'll let me know when she's ready or she wants my help. Independent wee cuss." The dimples confirmed his words were affectionate, not angry. "So, tell me about this Chautauqua."

They were on their second brandy when Abby found them. She took Patrick's seat while he went behind the bar and poured one for his daughter. With Daisy busy scribbling on paper, the women put their heads together and shared ideas about creating a poster designed to encourage Idlewild folks to attend their meeting. Abby said she'd deliver them, but her new friend said it would be more fun if they did it together. She named some places the signs needed to go, and Joe Foster's was one.

Abby flinched and described her earlier trip to Joe's grocery store. Edna shuddered.

"That man . . ." Abby said.

"Mmmhum. I agree, but I think *man* is way too complementary for that rodent. Not even sure he qualifies for the term," Edna said, with a nod and a wink.

"He surely has nothing good to say about women," Abby said.

"Or colored folk. He's made that inordinately clear," said Edna, waving a manicured hand in the air, dismissing Joe Foster as an insignificant entity, a gnat in a world filled with wrens who would soon have dinner and clear the air of irritating insects. Her long, graceful fingers spoke with eloquence.

"I'm sure he doesn't know the word *inordinately*," Abby said, and slapped her thigh at her own humor.

Edna wrapped an arm around Abby's back and pulled her closer. They stayed that way, head to head, whispering, and Patrick grinned.

Contentment streamed around him, and he knew a bit of peace. His girl hadn't grown up with female friends, had no mother to learn from, no girlfriends to giggle with. She'd lived in an isolated world of lumberjacks and him. Her learning had come from their harsh but loving ways, and this sight filled his heart with joy, his Irish eyes with tears.

Daisy squealed and pointed at Phantom who'd suddenly appeared on the bar in front of them. She whipped her head around and squealed again. Cleo was perched at the end, her black coat glistening in the light of the lamp Patrick had just lit. Her emerald eyes were two glowing spheres, ears laid back and twitching.

"Where'd they come from?" Edna asked. "They just appeared out of nowhere."

"They do that. It's actually kinda spooky."

"Kitty," Daisy said, and Phantom reached out a paw and let it lay on the girl's arm.

"Claws in," Abby warned.

Mrow wah.

Edna laughed and gathered up their scribbled notes, lifted Daisy from her stool, and gave Abby a last hug.

"You can't know how happy I am to have you in town," Edna said.

"That sentiment is echoed. Really. You don't know." She bounced on her toes, eagerness lighting her face. She had found a friend, and it felt good.

As she walked with Edna, out of the blue, she said, "Where do you go to church? I mean, if that's not too nosy."

"Course not, but you know we don't actually have a church yet. Hopefully your new pavilion will work til we build one."

"I guess I thought you might attend a church in a nearby town."

"No, and Jesse told me you wanted to build a place for all of us. He can't keep anything to himself. Especially stuff he's excited about."

She shoved one long leg out and planted Daisy on a hip while she watched Abby's face. "By the way . . . I don't think it's crazy for coloreds and whites to worship the Lord together. He's a Neanderthal. Jesse, not the Lord," Edna added with a nudge and a giggle.

It began to snow on Sunday morning, big, fat flakes that filled the sky and lay on the branches of the trees surrounding the lake. The island turned into a fluffy cloud in the middle of the dark water. Abby threw on a warm coat and took her coffee to one of the chairs on the porch. It was protected by a roof, and, with no wind, she was comfortable as she watched the island grow into a feathery pile of white.

A buggy pulled into the driveway, and Abby sipped her coffee and watched. When it drew up to the porch, Edna leaned out and waved.

"Come on. Let's go mix up the Gerard's church service." Abby's face lit. "Really? Should I? I mean *we*?"

"Yes. Go tell your father you're leaving."

Abby flew through the door, found Patrick in his room and told him, checked her hair in the entry way mirror, and was back out in minutes.

"Thanks . . . I think," she said as she climbed in the small back seat beside Daisy.

"Hello, again." Jesse flicked the reins and leaned back.

"Good to see you. Surprised."

"If you're thinking about building a pavilion or a church for all of us," Jesse said with a grin, "maybe you ought to see how this goes first."

The buggy left the resort area and pulled down a two-track road that ended at a small, gray house tucked into the trees. Smoke spiraled from the chimney, and several buggies stood in the yard, the attached horses covered with blankets in an effort to keep them dry. Feed bags hung from them, and reins were looped around various tree branches to keep them from wandering off.

Abby jumped down, reached behind the seat for the horse blanket, and busied herself while waiting for her friends to attach the feed bag and get Daisy. She wanted them beside her when she went in.

Edna grinned. "Your eyes are like two dinner plates. You afraid?"

"Not really afraid. It's more like . . . um . . . uneasy anticipation."

"Hah! That's fear, my friend. No goblins or witches in this makeshift house of the Lord. And no one here eats young white women that I'm aware of."

Abby snickered. "What colors do they eat?" She giggled again and straightened her shoulders to get hold of herself. "Sorry. I know. It's just that I *don't* know if they'll want me here, now that I'm actually standing in their yard, uninvited. And remind me to ask you about a witch. I mean, she's probably not a witch, but a very strange woman I saw the other day."

"*I* invited you. Let's go." She turned a quizzical face to Abby. "Probably?"

Abby's was the only white face in the small room, and it was not white at all at the moment. It was bright pink in embarrassment. Chairs and benches had been brought from somewhere and were lined up facing one direction. They were all inhabited, and one man rose to offer his to Edna. Another to Abby.

Before sitting, she shook her neighbors' hands and introduced herself, told them she was the daughter of the hotel owner and was happy to be there. Children were gathered in one corner on the floor, and their unguarded eyes showed surprise which the adults made varying degrees of effort to disguise.

Abby stood when the hosts, James and Mildred Gerard, and their daughter, Betty, stopped by her chair and welcomed her, meeting her eye to eye with confidence. Almost all the folks grew outwardly comfortable, if not completely joyful, to see a white face at their church service. Edna nudged her back into her seat and pulled her own chair closer as Reverend Jenkins began by welcoming her. Being singled out made the color of her rosy cheeks flame red.

When they sang, Abby forgot where she was and got caught up in the music. She loved it, harmonized where it was suitable, and raised her voice with contentment, lost in the song. Heads turned her direction during the singing, some with nods of appreciation. Abby smiled when their eyes caught hers. That's what music did. What it was all about.

Peace fell around her, and, at that moment, it didn't matter where she was or whose home she was in. It all felt good. She missed her own home in Nirvana. She missed Shorty and Bear and Yancy. She missed her other life, but she was making a new one, and it was with these people.

Hang on Idlewild. I'm here.

Following the service, the door to the kitchen was thrown open and a crowd of hungry people flooded into it, following their noses to the aromas coming from an assortment of covered pots, pans and casseroles. She was self-conscious once again. Of course, she didn't have a dish for the potluck; she hadn't known she was coming.

"It's alright," Edna whispered, poking her in the side.

Abby's stomach growled as succulent scents made their way to her nostrils. Chicken pot pie, boiled beef and potatoes, green beans and ham, stewed chicken, corn bread, hot cabbage salads. She was hungry and couldn't take her eyes from it.

A man walked up to her, one she hadn't met prior to the service. He didn't extend a hand to shake, and he moved too close, invading her space. She took a step backwards, bumping into the door frame.

Abby didn't offer her hand, either. She was disconcerted and uneasy. He was good looking, slender with smooth, perfect skin. A narrow black mustache lay like a line drawn between his nose and mouth. White teeth showed when he offered a smile that didn't reach his eyes. Nothing on his face moved except his lips, and Abby tried unsuccessfully to maneuver away from the doorjamb and him.

"Samuel Moore," he said. "And you are Abigail Riley."

"Yes. Nice to make your acquaintance," she whispered, unable to find a smile. Her face had frozen with her lips in a grimace.

"I will not be foolish enough to say the same."

She stiffened. "I'm sorry to hear that."

"That I'll not be a fool . . . or that I won't repeat inane, social prattle?"

Abby pushed herself out of the corner she'd been trapped in, forcing Samuel to move, and she gloated.

That's right, your turn to step back.

"You won't find Uncle Tom in me, Miss Riley. I won't apologize for the color of my skin."

"I wouldn't expect you to, Mr. Moore. Nor would I wish you to," she said, echoing and emphasizing his formal tone.

"I'd never apologize for mine, either, but I don't know why you feel it necessary to express the sentiment."

He pulled wire rimmed glasses down his nose and peered over them at her as if she was a bug he was preparing to stomp on, but something flickered beneath the mustache. She stiffened under his scrutiny, and he walked away. Abby fumed, and her appetite fled.

Who in hell did he think he was?

On the ride home, she only half listened to Edna's chatter. Responses to Samuel Moore, perfect, scathing ones, ran through her mind and stuck on her tongue where they usually did. She alternated between the high road, ignoring his arrogance, and the gutter where she stomped his face into the ground. The latter was more fun, but she knew she'd never do anything so blatantly corporal. She was more *turn the other cheek* even if she'd like not to be.

She wondered if she chose to turn her cheek because she was afraid not to. And just how many times should it be slapped before she hit back? She didn't know. She'd just keep on turning until she spun out of control, got dizzy and fell over.

She chuckled at her own little joke, and Edna looked back at her.

"I miss something good?"

"Nope. Just me being silly."

Chapter Four

Christmas

Jesse and Edna continued to stop by for Abby on Sundays, and she got to know many of her neighbors by being in their homes. Most were gracious, if initially tentative, and as much as she enjoyed the services, she loved the homey potluck meals. Food paved a direct and resolute pathway toward the creation of bonds.

Abby asked Cecily to attend services with her one day and was given a wide-eyed stare in response.

"At the colored homes?" she asked.

"That's where services are, until we build a place for Reverend Jenkins to hold them."

Cecily lifted the corner of the mattress they were fitting with sheets, folded the fabric and tucked it in. Abby watched her sister-in-law, knowing her mind was running amuck, derailing.

"Well?" she asked.

"Oh, Abs. You know Terry wouldn't like that."

"Why ever not? That's silly. And you could offer to hold a service at the farm, too. Everybody takes turns. I'm going to offer the hotel."

Cecily picked up the bright patchwork quilt and flipped it in the air. It landed in a heap in the middle of the mattress, and Cleo made a dive to tunnel under it.

"Come on out, Cleo. No time for play today."

She poked her head out, green eyes glowing in her black face.

"Boys, take the cat downstairs, will you? She's being a pest," Cecily said.

When Chunk and Bailey were gone, Cecily tossed her black mane and faced Abby, feet planted, arms crossed.

"There's been talk at the farm about you going to church with Jesse and Edna Falmouth and about the work you're doing with the committee and the resort people. The Chautauqua stuff."

"What about it?"

"Terry and George don't like it much. And they're Frank's brothers. Their Ma and Pa don't have much good to say about your doings right now, either."

"And you, Ceci? What do you have to say?"

Abby's hands were jammed into the pockets of her apron, her shoulders hunched forward. She thought about the people she'd met and the homes she'd been in. They were humble places, three or four rooms and a few just two, but all were clean and cared for, and the people were proud, hardworking and spiritual.

"You know what I think. But Terry's my husband, and it matters to me what he thinks."

Abby shook her head, her auburn curls bouncing in unconstrained abandon. She grabbed a fistful and tugged, pulling her head back until she stared at the ceiling, her eyes rolling.

"Chautauqua are delightful intellectual and musical events. How can anyone disapprove of them? Or censure the people working to make them happen. Anyway, it'll be Christmas soon, and everyone will be invited on Christmas Eve. *All* my friends and family. Soon after that, we're having a wedding – mine, and I'm going to be Mrs. Adams. Sounds great, doesn't it? Maybe I'll have a son and call him John Quincy. Why didn't you call either of your boys John?"

Cecily knew her friend running around the problem, feet kicking up dust, and was glad. She didn't want an argument with her. She liked Abby, even admired her, but couldn't say so in the sweet arms of her critical family of in-laws.

The last Sunday service before Christmas was at the Parkers. They arrived earlier than usual, and Abby found Bunny Parker in the kitchen where she went to see if she could help. They were acquainted from prior services, and Abby moved in to hug the slender woman at the sink.

"Tell me what to do, Mrs. Parker."

"Bunny," she said, "and you can pile the plates and silverware on the table, please, from that cupboard. Then stir the hearth beans and shove the kettle to the back to just keep warm."

They worked without words until Abby finished and leaned against the cupboard looking around.

"Your kitchen is lovely."

"Mighty plain, but it works."

"I'd love a kitchen."

Bunny's head spun around, her wide brown eyes curious. She was in her fifties, but her skin was deep russet satin, unlined and unblemished. She was stunning, but aloof and contained.

"You must have one," she said, "else, how would you feed your hotel guests?"

Abby chuckled. "We do. A big one. I meant a kitchen like this, like in a home. It's so . . . homey. It's pretty and comfortable. And I didn't say homely."

She laughed again, and Bunny smiled. Abby didn't know why she needed this woman to like her, to understand her desire for a real kitchen, but what this beautiful, peaceful woman thought of her was curiously important. The connection between them bloomed in the warmth of her kitchen.

Edna came into the room and looked around, feeling like she'd interrupted an intimate moment, like waiting words would hang in the air until she backed out of the room and left them alone.

She spoke just to hear a sound crack the air.

"Uh, I was just remembering, Abby. You never told me any more about the witch woman you saw. Did you find out who she is?"

"Witch?" Bunny asked. Her face stiffened, and the warmth in the room cooled.

"I was joking. I'm sure she isn't a witch," Abby said, aware of the abrupt change in the air.

"Describe her," Edna said. "I'm betting Bunny knows the sorceress and can clear up your dark fairytale."

Bunny patted her close-cropped hair and wiped the beads of sweat from her forehead. She dried her hands on a towel and leaned against the counter next to Abby. "Well then. Let's hear what Abby saw."

"Just a woman. I . . . uh . . . think she lives down a wooded pathway in between the hotel and Joe Foster's store. I saw her one day when I was walking home."

"Why did you call her a witch?" Bunny asked through flattened lips.

Abby flinched. She saw Bunny's rigid expression and felt the barbs of her displeasure.

"I don't know. I was being funny, I guess. She had long . . . very long, gray hair and strange clothes. She talked to herself, and a bunch of cats followed her down the road. It was strange."

Bunny grew taller and her shoulders wider as she stared back at Abby. Her black eyes were pools of knowledge.

"Don't make assumptions about people you don't know, Miss Riley. And don't go around talking about them like you do know. Is she colored? White? Does she have children? A husband? Is she educated? Is she happy, sad or broken hearted? Is she lonely?"

Abby felt the flush grow from the collar of her dress up to her scalp where it prickled. Her cheeks burned.

"I'm sorry. Really. I wasn't . . . I didn't mean . . ."

Bunny turned away from Abby and left the room, leaving her apology hanging in the air without acknowledgment.

After the service, Reverend Jenkins read the announcements, asked who would host next Sunday and if anyone had other news. Abby stood, nervous and afraid her voice wouldn't cooperate with her tongue.

Well, damn.

Afraid she'd said it out loud, she peered at the nearest eyes to see if they registered shock and saw only curiosity, so she stumbled on.

"My father and I would like to invite you to a small celebration on Christmas Eve at the hotel. Just snacks and a drink or two. Around six. To ... uh, thank you for letting me attend your services."

She heard surprised comments and stayed standing, waiting for questions or something; she didn't know what. Nothing. "Bring your friends," she added and sat, her face flaming.

She knew her father would be surprised to hear he'd invited the neighbors in, but ... he'd love it eventually. And since she'd told them to bring friends, she wouldn't have a clue how many would be there.

I'm a mess.

She hoped those were silent thoughts. She wanted these people to accept her; however, and the invitation was a start. She smiled and felt better about the day.

Abby sat on the window seat wrapped in the warm afghan her mother had made just after she and Patrick were married. It was one of Abby's treasures, and she used it sparingly, usually when she was feeling down or ill. The crocheted cables ended in yellow flowers on spring green squares. She traced the design with her finger, feeling the warmth of a mother's love she'd never known except in the words and eyes of her father.

Phantom and Cleo stretched out on her legs and purred, enjoying her attention as she stroked their heads.

She had a cold, and Patrick had sent her to her room. Told her to get in bed and rest. She had undressed and put on a flannel nightgown, but it was hard obeying his order to rest in the afternoon. It wasn't even dark. She was trying; however, and she even had a book she *wasn't* reading lying open on the seat next to her.

Beyond her window was the frozen lake, and snow lay on it in drifts where the wind had piled it, making late afternoon shadows and pictures in the landscape. Without too much trouble, you could believe it was the Sahara, and the drifts were parched, arid sand dunes. The lone ice fisherman dragging a sled of supplies was an Arabian sheik, and the sled was his camel. Abby let her imagination wander.

Two snow covered riders ambled down the road, stopped in front of the hotel and stared, nodded at each other and dismounted. They wrapped their reins around the hitching rail and brushed the snow from their hats, shoulders and legs.

Abby leaned forward to watch, her forehead pressing against the cold pane.

"More sheiks?" she said. "Who do you think they are, guys? An Arabian prince and his menial slave?" The cats stared, blinked slowly, ready to get back to their naps and making a clear statement about her nonsensical chatter.

"The big one has a familiar walk, and they ... Shorty ... and Bear!" she shrieked, and the cats flew off her lap and halfway across the room. They landed on the bed, their backs raised in defense position, fur standing on end down their spines.

"Sorry, babies. I didn't mean to frighten you. But it's Shorty and Bear," she said, as if that should be justification enough for scaring them.

Oh. Well, of course, Phantom said, but his blue eyes claimed otherwise.

She grabbed a robe and was out the door and into the hallway before she had it on and tied. The bell over the door jingled as they came through, and they looked up to see Abby sprinting down the stairs toward them, two steps at a time.

She hooked arms around them both and hung on.

"What are you doing here? Where have you been? I'm so happy to see you. Where are you heading? Oh, my God, it's good to see you."

Tears threatened, and she held the men tight until she could dry her eyes. She blinked a few times and sniffed.

"Which do you want answers to? Or are you just blathering?" Shorty whispered.

"Some blathering, some not. Come in. Bring your saddlebags. Let me take you to your rooms."

She dragged them toward the stairs.

"Wait. I'm so confused." She grinned up at them. "Your horses. Take them to the barn first, back of the hotel, and bring your saddle bags in. I'll go get dressed."

"Speaking of that," Shorty said, raising his bushy eyebrows and running a gloved hand over his bald head. "Why are you in night clothes in the middle of the afternoon?"

Concern was written on his face. In all the years he'd known her, Abby had never been a lay-about. She was a work horse, and everyone knew it.

"Oh, Da was being bossy and sent me to bed."

"Without supper? Were you being bad?" he asked.

Abby giggled. "I haven't been bad in way too long."

"Gonna have to fix that," Shorty said, and the giant man picked her up in a hug that hung her feet a foot off the ground. She squealed, protested the indignity and was blissful.

"Put me down, you big oaf. You go take care of the horses, and I'll get dressed. Meet me upstairs."

She left her door ajar so she'd hear them return, threw on some clothes and checked on two rooms to make sure they were ready for guests. She straightened a picture, hung clean towels from the washstands, and ran down to get water for the bowls and pitchers. She was gasping for air when they found her.

"We can share a room, Abby," Bear said. "We don't need to take up so much space."

"Nonsense. You're my guests, and one of you takes up a lot of space."

"For tonight, then," Shorty said.

"Wash up and meet me in the bar. Da will be glad to see you."

She found Patrick in the kitchen cooking up his infamous Irish stew. His dimples deepened when she came through the door.

"What you doing out of bed, lass? Although you do look a mite better. You get some sleep?"

"Nope. Something better."

Abby hadn't bothered to straighten her tousled curls, and she looked windblown or like she'd just climbed out of an amorous bed. Her father's eyes crinkled at the corners; she looked so like her mother did in the morning.

"What has you looking so beautiful and shiny-eyed all of a sudden?" Patrick asked.

"Not beautiful, Da. Don't say that. And that's the surprise. Guess who's here?"

"Old Santy come early?" he said.

"Try again."

He scratched his stubble and pondered.

He heard Bear shouting for whiskey from the bar, and his eyes opened wide.

"I'll be damned. That old maggot."

"Two maggots," Abby said. "Shorty's here, too."

He shoved the kettle to the back of the stove and ran to the door, his bent legs jerking him from side to side like a ship in a squall.

They stood in the center of the room, taking it all in.

"Mighty fancy, Irish. Didn't know you were gonna go posh on us," Shorty said.

Patrick bobbed his head and blamed Abby.

"It's the girl. She likes things nice."

"She deserves things nice," Bear said, taking his friend's words literally. "She should have only the best, and introduce me to the man who says otherwise."

She waved an arm over her head. "I'm right here, fellows. Right here listening. Don't talk about me like I'm a wall hanging."

Patrick clapped him on the back and walked behind the bar. These two lumberjacks were like the sons he'd never had, and he had missed them.

"What'll you have, boys? Whiskey to warm your cold hearts?"

Bear pulled a pouch from his pocket, and Patrick put his hand over it.

"On me, friend."

"That's why you're always broke, Irish," Shorty said.

Abby squeezed in between the two men who both put arms around her back at the same moment. She felt Shorty push Bear's arm away and Bear do the same to Shorty. Back and forth they went in a silent battle to give and get affection, and Abby smiled.

"Don't fight, boys. I love you both."

Patrick poured several hefty shots of his finest and lifted his glass. "May the cat eat your enemy, and the devil eat the cat."

"Da! Don't say that! I hate that stupid, Irish salute."

He grinned and asked where the men were heading.

"Right here. It's as good a place as any to *not* be working," Shorty said. "You grew on us over the years, kinda like moss on a blarney stone."

"No lumbering?" Patrick asked.

They shook their heads and shrugged their shoulders like they had timed it, and Patrick laughed.

"You two have been together too long. You're like an old married couple who starts to look like each other and talk alike. Even finish each other's sentences."

Bear looked over Abby's head at Shorty and smiled. "That'd be one big, damned wife."

"If anybody's gonna be the woman, that'd be you – simpering and primping all the time. Trimming your beard just right, folding your shirt so it doesn't wrinkle. Yup. You're the woman."

Patrick let out a howl. "Listen to you! Damn, didn't know how much I missed you!"

He topped off the drinks and pulled up a stool on the other side of the bar from them.

"So, no work where you been?" he asked.

"Don't think there's a pine tree worth cutting left in the state of Michigan," Shorty said.

"Stay here," Abby said. "Something will turn up. You'll meet a bunch of people from the area on Christmas Eve. We're having a gathering. Someone will have work."

A black streak landed next to Bear and climbed his leg. She curled around his neck, front and back legs hanging over his shoulders and down his chest, and closed her eyes.

"She missed you," Abby said. "I'm jealous."

Mew, Cleo said, but it was a tiny sound and muddled with her purring, so Abby wasn't sure.

The next day, Abby talked Shorty and Bear into going with her to cut a Christmas tree for the hotel. They saddled the horses and went into the forest. Snow muted the sounds, except for the occasional woodpecker or squirrel, and silence shadowed their trail. They were content to soak in the landscape, dark green branches laden with snow and sunlight streaking through periodic breaks in the canopy of trees. A forest crystal palace.

"Fishing?" Bear asked.

Abby nodded. "We're near the head waters of the Pere Marquette River."

"Good?"

"Trout, I'm told. Steelhead."

Bear nodded and went quiet.

The stillness and tranquility surrounding them produced brevity of talk, an unwillingness to scar nature with voices. They all felt the pull toward silence.

Abby halted Marie and slid down. She pointed at a small pine, and Shorty hauled a saw out of his saddle bag.

He tried to crawl under the low branches and yelped when he dumped snow down his back. Bear laughed, sat on his horse and watched with satisfaction as Shorty wiggled and wormed his way under the tree and close to the trunk. When he got there, he couldn't raise his arm to move the saw.

"If you weren't Paul damned Bunyan, you wouldn't be fighting that tree. You'd be sawing it."

"You want this saw?"

"You're already soggy. Say thanks and get to it. You're supposed to be a lumberjack."

"Thanking the tree?" Abby asked.

"I do. And not that I care, but why isn't your man here doing this with you?"

"He's farming," she said, watching a squirrel scratch at the base of a scraggy oak.

They dragged the tree back, and Shorty picked it up and shook it free of snow.

"You're handy, Shorty," Abby said. "Help me with the sand bucket?"

They stood it on an old rug to dry while they set about making the decorations and were hard at it when Frank showed up. He watched with a half grin on his face as Shorty stabbed repeatedly at the cranberry he was trying to string. His thumb was bleeding, and he periodically stuck it in his mouth to suck off the blood.

"Damn needle. You gave me a defective one, Abs," Shorty said, his voice so soft she had to lean in and ask him to repeat it.

"Notice I'm not bleeding," Bear said, peering up from his work through dark lashes. "And why you don't speak up is . . . I don't know. You afraid someone will actually hear you?"

"String the popcorn, Shorty. It's easier," Abby told him.

Frank whooped and hollered, slapped his knee. "How did she sucker you two into this? You should be down at Cousin's making friends."

"Whose cousins?" Bear asked.

"Uh . . ." Frank's skin took on the color of a sailor's sunset as he realized he'd blundered into something he didn't want to elaborate on with Abby nearby.

"You got cousins we should visit?" Shorty said.

Abby let Frank shuffle his feet, chew his lip, and rub his neck as long as she could. She stood and tucked her arm in his, stared up at him with wide, innocent eyes.

"I didn't know you have family I've yet to meet, Frank. Who?"

"Well, they're not really my kin. But they are cousins – to each other."

"Why should Shorty and Bear meet them but not me? That doesn't seem real neighborly."

He shuffled again, shoved his hands in his pockets and glared at the men like they'd started this conversation.

"It's just a place to go. Something to do. You know, get a drink. It's like a saloon."

"*Like* one?" Shorty whispered.

"Yeah. It's like one."

Abby giggled and hit herself in the head as if she just figured out what Frank was talking about.

"Oh! I know. The really colorful place a couple miles down the road, sort of in the woods. It's pretty, painted yellow, purple, green, all kinds of great, bright colors. Lots of men like to go there . . . for a drink and . . . company. I think that's what they say."

Shorty guffawed. Bear's ears and face turned red above his beard, and Frank spun away and cussed.

"You describing *the house*, Daughter?" Patrick, said, coming in on the tail end of Abby's description of Cousin's.

"Yes, I am, Da. Frank is trying to get our guests to visit the house of pleasure."

Frank choked, and Abby got up to slap him on the back. "You alright, Frankie? Breathe."

When he could, he asked what she knew about houses of ill repute.

"I hear things, Frank. I listen." She smiled and knew they had a lot to learn about each other. *Soon*, she thought and twisted the promise ring on her finger. *Soon*.

The tree was decorated and pine boughs lay on the hearth mantle in the bar area. Red holly berries nested between the deep green, aromatic branches. Abby bustled around, adding finishing touches to the festive room and cussing out Joe Foster for coming early.

He was nursing his third glass of ale, one eye on her and the other on the door. Two of the Tatum brothers flanked him, drinking on Joe's dime. They needed haircuts and baths, the layers of dirt making their skin look ashen, and Abby wondered why their mother didn't show then the bathtub.

Shorty was helping Patrick in the kitchen, and Bear had gone out to take care of the horses for the night. Abby was wishing one of them would show up. The threesome at the bar made her uneasy.

But she was excited, too, hoping for the kind of Christmas Eve of her dreams; friends and family with arms around each other, smiling, singing, and laughing; children with awe in their eyes when they looked at the brightly decorated tree, their squeals when she handed out the small sacks of candy she'd made for them.

You're mushy and maudlin, Abby. Stop it.

Anxious, she peered out the window for the tenth time, saw the last of the sun's rays tinting the snow in glorious shafts of color and wished someone would arrive.

She went to light the lamps and candles she had placed around the room. The door jingled behind her before she had the first one lit, and she cussed gratefully hearing Edna's voice, a gentle curse, not one that would send her to hell.

"My glass is empty, girl. Can't you see that?" Foster shouted.

Edna's eyes went wide and she came to a shocked stop in mid hug.

Abby shrugged and wrapped her arms around both Edna and Daisy before heading toward the bar to refill his glass, hoping this would be his final one of the night. The last thing she wanted to see today was Joe Foster, and even beyond that would be a drunk Joe Foster.

"Where's Jesse?" she asked heading back to her company.

"Taking care of the horse. He'll be here."

"I'm glad. Soon?" she said, with a laugh and a glance toward Foster. She hung their wraps and pointed to the buffet. "Help yourself to some refreshments; red is for kids and lightweights."

Edna grinned and headed for the eggnog bowl. They were admiring the tree when Bear came in, stomping off the snow and whistling a carol.

"Bear," Abby shouted. "Get rid of your coat and come meet my friend, Edna."

Bear ducked his head, his typical friendly greeting, and Daisy asked why he had pictures on his face. Edna gasped and apologized. Bear picked up the little girl and, with her hand in his, traced the lines of his scars.

"What does this one look like?" he asked.

"A duck," she said with a giggle. "You have a duck in your beard."

He followed more of the scars, and she named more animals, enchanted to know someone with a farm on his face. Both Edna and Daisy were in love. Jesse came in, and Abby began to relax.

Flora and Ratty Branch, along with Isabelle and Del Branch, showed up next. Frank and his two brothers, Terry and George, followed, with Cecily and the boys trailing behind them. Manny Watkins, James and Mildred Gerard, and Jackson Parker all came at once as if they'd planned it. Others came, people she didn't know and people she knew only second hand.

When she saw Jackson Parker, her eager eyes looked for Bunny, his mother. She'd hoped she would celebrate Christmas with them all. Disappointed, she turned to the folks who were there, and pleasant confusion ensued.

Abby yelled for her father to get out of the kitchen. He did, leaving Shorty in charge of his food. When everyone had a drink in their hands, Abby peered out the window one last time, hoping to see Bunny.

She circulated and picked up on snatches of conversation around her. As always, there was talk of the lot owners' organization and people who had bought land on the island and would be building in the spring. Other voices bemoaned the solitude that would be lost when all the people and workers came. She heard the word Chautauqua and her own name, the pavilion and her name, church services and her name. She felt a prickle of heat down her neck and wondered if she was getting sick or if it was a warning.

The door opened and all conversation ceased. Eyes widened. In walked Sally and Sue, the cousins.

They nodded around the room, proudly introduced themselves, and Patrick, who was nearest the door, took their wraps and led them to the bar.

"What'll you have, ladies?" he said, his arms spread wide, his grin matching. "Punch, eggnog, or something a little stronger?"

"Look at those dimples, Sally," Sue said, standing on tiptoes to poke at the side of Patrick's face. Sue was one of the shortest people he'd ever seen, like an elf only rounder. Perhaps she was even as wide as she was tall.

Sally grinned and looked down at her cousin from six feet of long, skinny body that led up to her long, narrow face.

"You can't really be cousins," Patrick said, still grinning. "Why, you're no more alike than cookies and cabbage."

"We're all cousins, children of the Lord, brothers and sisters. Isn't that right, Joe Foster?" Sally said, glancing at the man next to her with glee in her eyes.

Joe grunted and stared at her.

"I'm no cousin to a colored, woman or man."

Patrick sucked in air and wondered if he'd have to toss Foster out this night.

"You never know who your kin might be," she said, mystery in her voice.

"I know mine. You likely don't."

"Enough, Foster. I think you need to leave," Patrick said, putting his hand on the man's glass and preparing to take it away.

Sue touched Patrick's arm. "Let it go, Mr. Riley. It doesn't matter."

"It does to me," Patrick said, anger firing his eyes.

"Let it go," she repeated, picked up her glass and floated away into the middle of the mass of people, her cousin trailing behind.

They worked the crowd, drinks in hand, Sue's bosom bursting from the deep vee in her dress, catching the most reluctant eye, and Sally's nonexistent. But Sue got lost in people's belly buttons, so Sally kept a running monologue about who was in attendance. Who was talking to whom and what they wore.

Abby corralled her father and, with Shorty's help, they brought out the buffet food and spread it on two long tables she had moved to the side of the barroom.

People automatically gravitated there, and Abby was finally able to meet the cousins. She grinned as she introduced herself, thinking about Frank as she talked and deciding to track him down. She wrapped her arm around his back and kissed his cheek.

"Having fun?" she asked.

"I'd rather it was just us somewhere quiet," he said, and pulled her tight to his side.

"Be good and pretend to like my friends, Frank," she teased, but meant it, too.

"Are all these people your friends?" he asked. "Really?"

She tilted her head from side to side and rolled her eyes to the ceiling. She squeezed her eyes almost closed and pursed her lips.

"Yesss?" she said.

"How about Samuel Moore?" Frank asked, knowing him and thinking he knew how Abby would react to the haughty, intimidating man.

Her eyes widened. "Why do you ask?"

"Cuz he just walked in."

Her head sunk into her shoulders, and she swiveled so she could see the door.

"Aw, damn. And everything was going so well," she said, more to herself than to Frank.

"Really?" He asked, eyebrows raised in question. "With Foster and the cousins getting into a scuffle?"

"They are?"

"They were. It's over."

"Well. I was about to pass out the children's gifts and get them to sing some carols, so I'm just going to do that. Samuel Moore doesn't matter. Neither does Mr. Joe Personality."

Moore moved through the crowd, nodding and smiling like he owned the place and hadn't a care in the world, like everyone here was his best friend. He helped himself to eggnog and walked to the bar, put one foot on the foot rest a short distance from Joe Foster, and watched the festivities. He pulled a gold watch from his vest pocket, checked the time as if he had some place to be and put it back.

Phantom leaped on the bar near him and rubbed against Samuel's shoulder, leaving a trace of white hair along the arm of his black suit jacket. He glanced down and tried to brush it off and rolled his eyes at the cat who took a walk to the far end and sat, lifted a paw to wash his face while he watched Samuel watching him.

"Slumming, Samuel?" Joe Foster said and moved closer to Moore with his drink in his hand. "Just hanging with us regular old folks?"

Moore tipped his head back so he could look down at the grocer, crossed his arms and leaned back against the bar.

"Just keeping my eyes open. Who let you out of your cage?"

"I'm not the animal. I don't need a zoo keeper like some of the folks I'm lookin' at."

"You could get into some serious trouble with that mouth of yours," Samuel said, and turned away.

Foster put a hand on the man's arm and tried to turn him back. Moore moved so fast, Foster didn't see it coming. In an instant, his shoulder was squeezed between Moore's fingers, and his whole arm was burning and going numb. Before Joe could collapse, Moore released him and leaned in, his smile white brilliance, his eyes black venom.

"Don't touch me."

Shorty got there just as Moore released Foster. He stood as close to both men as he could without stepping on their toes and looked down at the top of their heads.

"I'll walk you out," he said.

"No need," Samuel said. "I was just leaving. I have a prior engagement."

"Let's go, Foster," Shorty said, and trailed him to the door. He watched the man walk away until he was out of site. "Bad news," he murmured.

The Tatum brothers poured the remainder of their drinks down and followed Foster.

When Shorty closed the door behind them, Abby was trying to lead the group in a carol, but her worried eyes had followed their walk. She smiled when he nodded and let her alto find its own path to harmonize with the rest.

"It's downright pretty," Shorty said and leaned against the door to watch and listen.

Chapter Five

Early 1917

Greenery filled the hotel lobby where they were to marry. Edna and Cecily were in her room, fussing with the blue ribbons she'd woven through her auburn curls.

"What I wouldn't give to have your hair, Abby," Cecily said. "Hold still while I tie this last one."

"I don't even want to hear that," Edna said. "I'd take either one of yours."

Edna patted her short, dark hair. She had straightened it for the occasion, and it was slicked back showing off her classic beauty, a regal queen straight out of Africa

"You're both beautiful. Kind of remind me of Phantom and Cleo, different ends of the color scale and both exactly right. Am I ready?" Abby asked, turning in a slow circle.

"I don't know," Edna said with a smirk. "Are you?"

Abby's stomach flipped. "What do you mean?"

Edna took a couple of steps backwards. "I don't suppose you had the talk with her, did you, Cecily?"

She shook her head, hung it, and hoped Abby's pa had.

"The talk?" Abby asked, looking whiter than her gown.

"You know. The birds and bees. Usually mothers tell brides about the wedding night. What to expect and all," Edna said.

Cecily regained her equilibrium and opened the door. "You're gonna love it. Just have fun," she said, and walked out. "Come on Edna. They're calling for us."

Bear was strumming his guitar, and his fingers on the strings made the wedding march sound sweeter than any church organ could have. Abby waited on the landing until her friends were at the bottom of the stairs. She nodded to her father who stood at the door of his room, and he held his arm out to her, tears in his eyes, his smile a lie.

"You are your mother, lass. You are so beautiful I couldn't describe you if I had a thousand years and a thousand words."

"You're kissing the blarney stone, Da, and thank you. I love you."

"You love him?"

"Of course."

"I'll kill him, you know . . ."

"I know."

At the makeshift altar, next to Frank and Reverend Jenkins, Patrick kissed her cheek, and Abby hugged him, afraid she couldn't let go, afraid she didn't want to.

What am I doing?

He took her hands from his shoulders and clasped them together, his green eyes holding hers.

"I will always be your father, and I will always be here with you, for you, til the good Lord parts us," he whispered.

She nodded, blinked to stem the tears, and Patrick put her hand in Frank's.

The ceremony was brief. They threw rice and poured drinks to toast the couple. Manny brought out his fiddle, and, with Bear's guitar, they made music to dance to.

Frank didn't like dancing much, but he shuffled around the floor enough to call it a bride and groom's dance, and the rest joined in.

"Mrs. Adams," he said in her ear. "I wish we could have a proper honeymoon. Maybe this summer we can get away. Just us."

"That would be good, Mr. Adams. When we can hire some help for the hotel. Where do you want to go?"

"A little cottage in the Upper Peninsula? We could fish and lay around. The U.P. is great in the summer."

"Hmmm. We could."

The song ended before she had to tell him it didn't quite sound like the honeymoon of her dreams. But she was married now, and if that's what would make her husband happy, it would make her happy, too. She smiled and squeezed his hand.

Patrick tinkled a fork on his glass and raised it high. When it was quiet in the room, he looked around and began, first in Irish.

"*Slainte agus saol agat. Leanbh gach bilian agat.*"

"Speak English!" Frank said. "You don't live in Ireland anymore."

"Health and life to you. A child every year for you."

The last was met with guffaws and slaps on Frank's back, winks at Abby whose face burned, and she tried not to turn away. Frank patted her bottom, and the blush burned hotter.

"Folks, refreshments are in the bar area. Please help yourselves," she said, trying her best to deflect embarrassing conversation.

She didn't know why she was being so sensitive. She'd never been before, and she was used to bawdy lumberjack talk. Why now? But her stomach rolled.

She wanted to run, to saddle Marie and gallop off to Nirvana, sit on the old porch and talk to the critters. Walk in the woods. Talk with her mother in the quiet of her pines with the song of the forest around her. Ask her what to expect. How it would be?

It wasn't long before it felt like she had always been married to Frank. She got used to the snores as soon as his head hit the pillow and to being awakened by his heavy tread when he needed to get up in the night. At first, she'd been startled and thought intruders had come into the room, but that quickly disappeared.

The days and nights became routine.

She rose while dark still claimed the world in order to make him breakfast before he left for the farm. It wasn't far, but he liked to be there before his brothers made it to the milk parlor. It was a point of pride. And he liked mornings.

Sausage was sizzling in one pan and potatoes in another when he came into the kitchen. He reached around her side and cupped a breast.

"Your coffee is poured," she said, and turned to the stove so his hand fell away. "I love you, too."

"Busy day today," he said. "We're fitting up fields, so I don't know when I'll be back."

"I'll be here waiting. Wish you didn't have to work so hard. You want me to wait supper, or you plan on eating with your family?"

"Probably there. I'll be hungry."

Abby put his breakfast on a plate and set it on the table in front of him. She put her arms around his neck and kissed his hair while he shoveled in the food.

She grinned and lay the side of her face on the top of his head.

"I can hear your jaws working through your skull. Powerful."

"I am all power," he said, throwing his fork on the plate and standing. He wrapped his arms around her and squeezed. "Gotta go," he said, and was out of the room before she realized he was leaving.

Phantom and Cleo slipped in as soon as the door opened and Frank left.

"Where have you two been? I missed you."

Mrow wawah awah, Phantom said.

Cleo opened her mouth as if sound would surely come out if she opened it wide enough, but nothing did. It usually didn't, but she always tried. Maybe she figured Phantom made enough noise for both of them.

Abby patted them both, let Phantom curl around her neck and hang there.

"I have food for you, my sweeties. Eggs and milk. How does that sound?"

Mrow wawah. No mice?

Cleo stared, her big green globes getting the point across.

"You'll have to catch them yourselves," Abby said.

She started on breakfast for the hotel guests. Besides Bear and Shorty, three other rooms were occupied, and all were expecting to eat. She liked doing kitchen duty in the morning, letting her father sleep. It was quiet, and her hands knew what to do from years of practice. Her mind could meander elsewhere.

Bear strolled into the kitchen, poured a cup of coffee and started slicing potatoes. He did it every morning.

Abby threw sausage in the huge cast iron pan and loaded the stove with a couple more sticks of wood. She picked up her cup and sipped, leaned against the table and watched Bear work.

"You good?" he said.

"Sure. You?"

"Uh huh."

"Work on the cabins going good?"

"Yup. Nice to find work right here. Hope it lasts a bit."

"The way Sanders talks, it'll just get busier. They're making quite a splash in the cities. More tours coming every week."

"War's coming. Soon."

Abby swung around, spatula in hand as if she could slap his words from the air.

"No. President Wilson won't involve us. He said so."

"Politicians don't always mean what they say," he said, shaking his head at the ridiculous absurdity of an untrustworthy person at the head of the country. "Cept, I think this one tried."

"You won't go will you, Bear?"

He sat, stretched out long legs, and leaned back in the chair.

"I've been mauled by a bear, had both legs broken by a white pine, and I like whiskey more than some. They wouldn't want me."

"What about Shorty?" she asked.

"They won't like him either," he said and went back to sipping his coffee.

Within moments, Shorty lumbered in, grabbed a cup and slumped in a chair.

You didn't talk to Shorty in the morning. Or if you did, you needed to be prepared for a growl in response. He didn't do morning until his first cup of coffee was finished.

Abby and Bear knew it and left him alone. Patrick hadn't come to terms with that fact or his mouth didn't obey his mind, and Abby tried to ban him from the kitchen until Shorty finished his first cup of coffee.

One early morning, shortly after the two came to stay, Patrick danced into the kitchen smiling, dimples happy and deep, chattering away in half-Irish blarney. Abby darted her eyes toward Shorty, trying to let her father know he was dancing with a gorilla, and Bear nodded in that direction, too, trying to get him to stop talking. But when Patrick ignored their signals, they gave up and stepped back to watch the fun.

Shorty stood, put his hands in Patrick's armpits, raised him into the air and set him on top of the high cupboard, his legs swinging sideways, his eyes wide. Patrick hunched down, his chin on his fists, and did his best to appear wretched. It didn't work well on his face. It wasn't in him. He looked like a gnome, friendly, elfish and not to be trusted, not completely.

The kitchen went quiet. Shorty finished his coffee, stood, lifted Patrick down and patted his head.

"Sorry. Didn't hurt you, did I?"

"No, lad. It was a good view from there. Thanks. Got coffee, lass?"

Abby finished setting out the buffet breakfast just as the real guests were coming down the stairs, and Jesse Falmouth came through the door with Bill Sanders and several people she didn't know.

"Let's meet in the corner so we don't disturb their breakfast," she said.

Jesse sniffed and smiled. "Smells good. You do know how to treat your guests."

"I do."

"Bear and Shorty still here?" Jesse asked. "We have some questions for them if they could join us for a few minutes."

Abby got them from the kitchen, and they settled down to discuss the coming Chautauqua. Of main concern was the pavilion. Would it be ready in time?

"As long as you keep the materials coming and the weather holds, it'll be done. Gives us three months, so there should be no problem," Shorty said.

They left and the meeting continued. Jesse said William Jennings Bryan had confirmed he'd be keynote speaker, and Carnegie's philosopher, Wayne Andrews, responded positively, as well. And the best news, according to Abby, gospel blues musician Buddy Black was eager to play for them.

Bill had a list of community residents who agreed to provide food at outdoor buffets and help serve. They also had several tents in reserve in case some folks hadn't brought one – even though the literature had said it was a necessity because the hotel was booked full with regulars, the speakers and the entertainers.

"I want to hire some help before then. Any ideas?" she asked.

"What kind?" Jesse asked.

She sighed and pondered, tugged on the braid she'd plaited that morning in an effort to control her rampant curls.

"Someone to help with the rooms and another to help at the desk and in the bar. Or the kitchen. I just don't know where the most help will be needed. But definitely the rooms. I can't keep up."

"White?" Jesse said with sincerity and no angst or disrespect intended.

"I don't care as long as they want to work. I won't tolerate laziness in any shade."

Jesse laughed, and Mildred Gerard spoke up.

"Then my Betty could use a job. She finished high school last year and hasn't come up with work. Things have been tight here, and we thought she might have to move away, but . . . she'd be grateful if you'd give her a try."

"So would I," Abby said. "Send her over and we'll talk."

"There's Jackson, too. He's same age as my Betty."

"Jackson Parker? As in Bunny Parker's son?"

"The same. He was at your Christmas party, so you know him."

"Hmm," Abby said, rubbing her bottom lip and swallowing.

Bill tapped her on the shoulder and peered through thick glasses at her.

"You look like a four-legged lemon crawled into your mouth and sat on your tongue."

"Sorry. It's just . . ." She couldn't finish because she didn't know what to say.

"He's a good boy," Mildred said. "He got good grades in school. Never got in trouble. He's clean . . ."

Abby put a hand on Mildred's arm to slow down her praise of the young man.

"I'm sure he is. Here's the problem. I don't know if his mother will let him work for me."

"Why ever not?" Jesse asked.

"I may have said something that offended her, but I don't know how. I mean . . . I do. I said a woman I saw could be a witch, but I didn't mean anything by it. I can't imagine why that would make Bunny . . ."

Abby babbled on, without a clue where she was heading with her words or why she was telling all, baring her breast to these people.

"The woman lives down a path between here and the store, looks kinda scary and just stares at me with something like loathing, but not really that, more like ardent apprehension. And I don't even know how one thing could look like the other. Blast the bog! I don't know what I'm saying."

The others giggled and guffawed, punched each other on the arms, and wiped the tears from their eyes, and Abby ceased talking to look each person in the eyes, growing affronted.

"What? What did I do?"

"That's Bunny's sister. She's a clairvoyant, a diviner, and you called her a witch."

Abby's head jerked back and her mouth fell open.

"You . . . she's . . . No, I was only joking, kind of."

Jesse told more about the woman and how Bunny had tried to distance herself from the rumors plaguing her family since she was a child.

"She never accepted the fact that her sister had the gift of sight. She saw it more as a curse," he said.

"Then why did she get mad at me?"

"It's one thing when *she* says witch. Another when someone else does, especially one of . . ." Jesse searched for the right words. "Your shade," he said, grinning.

Abby nodded. "Ghost white? I get it. But I don't think she'll let her son work for me."

"Let me suggest it to her," Jesse said. "Or Edna. That's it. I'll send Edna and Daisy to do my dirty work. They're so good at it."

Frank made it home for dinner, and, afterwards, they escaped to their room early, taking advantage of a little time alone. She was eager to tell him about the Chautauqua meeting, the big names who were coming to their little town and the young people she hoped to hire.

Frank ran his hand over her body and leaned to kiss her neck. She recognized the moves and reminded herself she could tell him later. He'd had a busy day and was eager to love her. She was lucky he was eager.

When he rolled from her, she snuggled on his chest, ran a foot down his leg, and kissed his neck as his heartbeat settled.

"Have a good day, Frank?"

"Uh hum. It was okay."

"What'd you do? Tell me about it. More fields?"

"We did. The south fields. West ones tomorrow. The hills are drying up good."

"I'm glad. I had a good one, too. We had a Chautauqua meeting today. I'm really excited about the guests and entertainers coming."

He didn't respond, so Abby went on.

"And I might hire two people to help at the hotel. Maybe you know them."

"Probably not. I've got work that keeps me busy. You thinking about moving out to the farm yet?"

"I can't do that, Frank. How could I?"

Her spirits deflated. She'd wanted to share her excitement over the Chautauqua plans. It was something big. Something that was her idea— that she'd been a part of creating. She chewed the tip of her pinky finger, listened to the beginning rumbles of the snore she'd come to expect and told herself he worked hard.

Farming takes it out of a man. A good wife understands.

The next morning, Abby slipped out of bed while the moon was still casting its eerie glow across the room. She slipped into her work dress and left Frank sprawled, taking up most of the bed, his legs wide, one arm flung to the side and the other across his eyes. She shut the door and tiptoed so he wouldn't be disturbed.

Bear was already in the kitchen and had the stove rekindled and coffee percolated. Phantom was curled around his neck, and Cleo lay on his lap.

"Are they keeping you warm?" she asked.

"They're my bed partners."

"I miss them."

"Some adjustments are hard. Maybe Frank will get used to them."

She shook her head.

"He just doesn't care for cats," she said, wondering how anyone could not like an animal. But some folks didn't. She knew that.

"Aw. That can't be true. Look at them," Bear said, rubbing Phantom behind the ear and stroking Cleo. "Ancient Egyptians believed cats capture the glow of the setting sun in their eyes and keep it safe til morning."

"That's beautiful," she said, pouring two cups of coffee. "Any other cat tales?"

"Well, the Chinese say cats were originally in charge of the world. They gave it to humans to keep and went silent so they could laze about. Now, when they see the mess we make of it, they wear this supercilious expression like they could do a much better job. It's the cat and the canary look."

"Bear, you are a surprise. How do you know this stuff?"

"I'm full of feces," he said, grinning and sipping his chicory coffee.

"Mmmm. You do make a good cup of coffee."

She fed Frank and kissed him out the door. She stripped the beds. Swept the rooms and dusted the furniture. Washed the dirty linens and hung them on the line, hoping for a sunny day so they'd dry before nightfall. She needed to buy more when she went into Baldwin just in case rain and a full house happened two days in a row.

The door tinkled and suddenly the room was filled with people, all talking, telling jokes, laughing, carrying suitcases, and stopping in front of the desk. They all wanted rooms.

"Oh, my gosh. How many rooms do you need?" she asked. I'm limited."

The man in front turned to the group and started pointing and counting.

"Twelve," he said.

"I'm afraid I only have ten available. Can some of you share? A few of them have several beds."

"Hey, Barbie baby, you get to sleep with me."

"You've been saying that for years, Jack, and it hasn't worked yet. You got something new and different to offer today?" she said.

Jack's back got a pounding, along with some good-natured ribbing.

"I'm determined. You gotta give me that," he said.

"I can bunk with Mayme. And you share with Willie," Barbie said, sorting out the roommates. "How many did you say you have, sweetie?"

"Ten. And how ever you want to do this is fine, just sign the register right here, and I'll go get the rooms ready. I just stripped them."

She was about to race up the steps when she spotted a young woman coming through the door. She peered through the crowd, saw Abby, and pointed to herself and upstairs. Abby nodded and fled to the steps, meeting her at the top. She was quick.

"I'm Betty Gerard," she said.

"You're hired. Grab a pile of linens from that shelf and follow me."

They no sooner finished making a bed when folks came in and good naturedly took over the room. She had never made up rooms so fast, and she'd been doing this all her life. Betty knew what to do before she'd been told and was a tornado without the damage.

All ten rooms were finished, people were making themselves at home, and Abby asked Betty to follow her to the bar. She poured coffee for them both and plopped into a chair. The frantic pace had exhausted her.

"So . . ." she said, her head thrown back and braid swinging. "You sure you want to work here?"

She laughed, and Abby aimed big, friendly teeth at her new employee. Betty liked the smile. She could get used to seeing that every day.

A young man came to the doorway between the lobby and the bar while they were still chatting and having their coffee. He stood, held his cap in his hand and turned it round and round and stared in their direction.

"That's Jackson," Betty said. "I thought he'd show."

Abby waved him over, and he sauntered in their direction.

"I'm here to see Mrs. Adams," he said, still spinning his hat.

His handshake was firm and so was his jaw. It jutted out as if he expected a problem or an attack.

"Sit, Jackson," Abby said.

He nodded at Betty and said, "Hey," took a seat and finally put his cap on his lap.

"Coffee?" Abby asked, and, when he said he'd like some, she went to the kitchen and came back with a cup.

Jackson stood when she returned to the table, and she smiled.

"I appreciate it, but you don't have to get up every time I leave and come back."

"Sorry," he said, and twisted his cap again.

"Sit, Jackson, and stay put."

"Sorry," he said, again, "I'm not used to a white woman waiting on me."

"I'll try to remember that," she said, her eyes squinting in mischief, "and let you wait on me, instead."

His face blanched in agitation, and he cleared his throat. "I don't do that."

Abby sat back in her chair, puzzled about the direction this conversation had taken. She didn't want to offend him, especially since she'd already done that to his mother. But she also needed to be able to speak directly if she was to be his boss.

Phantom strolled into the room and leaped on his lap. He stiffened and held his hands in the air, his eyes wide.

"Push him off if he bothers you, Jackson. Don't you like cats?"

He shook his head. "My aunt has cats. Lots of them."

Betty picked up Phantom and let him climb her arm to lay over her shoulders.

"You're a baby, Jackson. It's just a cat," she said.

"Sure," he said.

Abby figured it was time to get to the point of his visit and asked him why he'd come.

"For work. Mrs. Falmouth talked to Ma, and she said it was alright."

"I'm glad," she said, and looked him in the eyes. "Are you?"

"Sure," he said, but he didn't look it. He looked about as edgy as a dog who'd figured out the raccoon he was about to catch had quills.

"Do you know what you'll be doing here?" she asked.

"I can go find something to do, Mrs. Adams," Betty said, uncomfortable with the tension in the air.

"You're fine right here. In fact, it's perfect because this is a small business, and all of us have to learn to do just about everything, from cooking to washing dishes, making up rooms to helping wash linens, from carrying luggage to waiting on guests, together, like we're a team. Are you willing to do that work, Jackson . . . even waiting on people?"

Abby stopped talking and watched his face register a waterfall of emotions, each one building and bubbling over and into the next, beginning with irritation, changing to belligerence, fear, and finally acceptance.

"Do you have a problem with me, Jackson?"

He shook his head.

Abby was growing frustrated with the taciturn young man and wanted to light a fire under him – find out now, before she was committed, what pricked his sensitivities and how his mind worked.

"I'm going to be blunt with you. I don't give a darn what color your skin is. Do you care about mine?"

"No."

"You sure? Because it seems that way to me a little."

"No, and don't tell me you're color blind," he said. "That's bull . . . never true."

"I didn't say that, Jackson. I can see colors just fine. My eyes are good. I simply don't care about it. And I'll ask you again; do you?"

"No," he repeated.

"Well, good. Betty and I haven't had a chance to talk about this, yet. We've been too busy. But I don't believe we need to, do we, Betty?"

"Good Lord, no. You're white, and I'm colored. So are you, Jackson, in case you didn't notice," she said, turning to him. "You gonna be an ass about it? I don't want to be around you if you are."

Abby burst out laughing, feeling affection for the blunt girl sitting next to her.

"I like you, Betty."

"I like you, too. And Jackson will, too, as soon as he gets his head out of his . . . well . . . The lower extremity of his trunk."

"I get it." She leaned forward and looked hard into his eyes. "Jackson, do you want this job?"

He sighed and slumped in his chair, rubbed a hand over his freshly shaved face and gave her a hint of a smile, his first since he walked in. He looked much younger than before, boyish and pleasurable.

"Yes, ma'am. I want the job."

"You'll happily wait on people?"

"I will, and I'm sorry. I don't know what got into me. I'm not like that ... I mean ... sorry," he added, not knowing where else to go with it.

Abby held her hand out, and he took it. Shook it with strength.

"Then you're hired, and please call me Abby, both of you. Ma'am makes me sound really old. Can you be here around four thirty today, Jackson? I think we're going to be slammed in the bar, and I could use the help. Betty, can you be here early tomorrow, around seven for the breakfast hour?"

They left, and she sat back and slumped in her chair. She hadn't realized how tense she'd been. In all the months she'd been in Idlewild, she hadn't come up against such raw skin color issues.

You need to think about this, Abby. This is important, and you need to be more aware, stop walking around with blinders on.

Chapter Six

The bar was full of excited property owners by the time four-thirty rolled around, and Abby was waiting tables and tending bar at the same time. Patrick was trying to help and went back and forth from the bar to the kitchen where he was trying his best to get supper ready for the guests.

She swiped stray curls from her forehead, picked up the watch hanging from her shirt and glanced at it. She was mouthing a silent curse when Jackson came into the room. She handed him a pad of paper and a pencil and told him he was a waiter.

"I'll be behind the bar," she said.

"Just write down what they want?"

She nodded. "Then lay it here, at the order station. I'll get the drinks and put them next to the order sheet."

"Where do I start?" he asked, looking around the busy room.

"Look for empty glasses or a table with people and no glasses."

"Gotcha," he said, and took off for a table in the far corner.

He was a quick learner, and people liked him. She could tell by their expressions during the brief conversations he had with them at their tables. Some of the ladies openly flirted, and he blushed red under sepia cheeks, smiled, and moved on.

He was a good looking young man, slender with broad shoulders. His hair was short, his clothes pressed, and his fingernails clean. Abby had checked them out during the interview. She watched him work, happy to see Jackson was going to be good at his job, an asset.

She smiled at him when he handed off the order. He grinned back, and Abby wondered what had prompted his attitude earlier in the day. Whatever it had been, it had vanished.

Jesse sat with Bill Sanders and a group of new lot owners who had gathered around several tables shoved together in the middle of the room. He twirled his finger in the air to indicate another round for them all, and Abby tried her best to remember everyone's preference. She tilted her head to look at their glasses and saw Frank enter the room, head straight toward her, and stand at the drink station.

"Hi, honey," she said. "I'll be with you in a minute."

"I'll take a beer," he said.

"In a sec." She leaned around him to check out the end of Jesse's table.

She piled the last of the order on a tray, and Jackson came to get it but needed Frank to move.

"Excuse me," Jackson said.

Frank looked up and shifted slightly, but not enough for Jackson to grab the tray.

"Sir?" he said, hoping Frank would vacate the work area, but he didn't.

Abby pushed the tray down the bar, away from Frank and turned to him with his beer.

"I'm glad to see you." She smiled at him, but didn't feel like it. He was being obtuse.

Frank didn't return the smile.

"Who's that?" he asked.

"Jackson. New employee, and he's doing a great job, especially for his first day."

Shorty and Bear came in with several friends from the construction crew and stood at the bar. She lined up whiskey glasses and poured. She knew their choice of drink and didn't need to ask.

Phantom appeared and walked the length of the bar, stopping periodically to rub his head against a few chosen patrons and perched where Bear and Shorty stood. He dipped his white head into Bear's whiskey glass, flicked a pink tongue at the liquid a few times, said *Mrow wah-wah*, and walked up his arm. In seconds, he was wrapped around

Bear's neck, one eye on the crowd, the other closed in sleep. He could do both.

Jackson reached around to give Abby a drink order. She filled it and placed the tray in front of Frank, wanting him to take the hint and move, and turned her back to wash glasses.

Jackson saw the tray, saw Frank blocking it and rubbed his face. From the corner of her eye, Abby watched. She nodded approval when she heard Jackson ask Frank to please move, and pointed to an open space.

"This is a work station, sir, and we need it for the drink trays."

Frank stiffened and glared at the young man before picking up his glass and heading down to the end of the bar where there was available space – where he'd been directed to stand.

He swore under his breath, not liking any of it. He wanted his wife, not a barmaid. He wanted his farm, not a hotel. And he didn't want to share Abby with every man in town who wanted a drink.

Abby grimaced. She should have asked Frank to move, but she didn't want to hurt him and . . . she wanted to see Jackson handle it. He was just another customer to Jackson, and he'd done it right. Not angrily. Not impatient. Just said what needed to be said.

And that was all twaddle and a lie. She'd been a chicken leaving it to him, letting someone else upset Frank instead of her for a change. She had to fess up and let Jackson know what she'd done.

They were busy through supper, and after they'd washed dishes and only a few stragglers sat in the bar, she invited Jackson to sit with her. Frank had gone upstairs. Patrick poured a cognac for her, a whiskey for himself, and gave Jackson a root beer. They all slumped in their chairs, happy to give their legs and backs a break.

"You okay, Daughter? This was one hell of a day for you, right since sunup."

"I'm fine, Pa. How about you, Jackson?"

He grinned, happy with his work. He'd asked her what to do with the tips people had given him and was ecstatic when she told him they were his to keep.

"That means they like you," she said. "It's a testament to your skill and personality."

"We might need more help," Patrick said.

"Don't frog leap there, yet. This doesn't happen every day. It might end up this busy, but we need to wait and see." She sipped at her drink and turned to Jackson. "I need to confess," she said.

Jackson widened his eyes. "I'm not a priest," he teased, and leaned forward, deep brown eyes alight in anticipation. "But what did you do?"

"I left you to deal with my husband."

"Excuse me?"

Abby cleared her throat and took too long to answer.

"What'd you do, Abby?" Patrick said, his voice accusatory.

"Frank was in the way and wouldn't move voluntarily, so I left Jackson to handle it, which he did beautifully, I must say," she added before either of them could scold her.

"That was cowardly," her father said. "He's your husband."

"I know."

"Well, now I know who he is . . ." Jackson left it there. "So, I did alright?"

"You did better than alright. You were splendid the whole night. See you tomorrow? Three okay?" she asked, rising and waving goodnight.

She opened the door to their room quietly, not wanting to wake him if he was asleep. The room was flushed with moonlight, and the scent of spring and lilacs sifted through the open window. She sat on the window seat and watched the soft glow stream across the sky, sit on the water, and dissolve into it. It was only a half-moon, but she could see the rest of it hanging in the dark, a waiting shadow.

A cat crept along the edge of the lake, poised to pounce but perched like he was tiptoeing so his feet didn't get wet.

He stopped for a drink, and moved on, and Abby wondered if he belonged to the witch woman, Jackson's aunt who had a bunch of cats.

Shouldn't call her that. But I don't have a name to call her.

She sighed, not a tired sound, but a yearning breath that gazing out the window or at the moon frequently caused. It twisted and teased something within her.

"You coming to bed?"

Abby jerked and almost fell off the window seat. Her hand flew to her chest.

"My God! You startled me."

"Sorry."

"I didn't know you were awake."

"Been laying here thinking."

Abby undressed and pulled her nightgown over her head. She poured water into the bowl, dampened a cloth and scrubbed at her face.

"Mmmm. Feels good." She groaned and wiped the cool cloth over her neck. "What have you been pondering, honey?"

"We should move out to the farm. Your father can hire someone to do what you do."

Abby was silent. This again. Just when she thought they had it worked out, it came back to prick like a thistle in a finger. She wanted to do what Frank desired; she was his wife, and she wanted to be a good one. It concerned her that she wasn't everything he wanted. She tried, but her father needed her here, working at the hotel. She was all he had.

"He couldn't hire someone to take my place, Frank."

"Why? What's so hard about making a bed? Or pouring whiskey in a glass?"

She bit her lip and rubbed hard with the washcloth at her forehead where it was beginning to throb.

"That isn't all I do. It's a lot more complex than that, and I not only work here but with community to build it and the hotel into something better, something to be proud of."

"Yeah, and that's another thing," he said in an offhand way. He wasn't being mean. He simply didn't get it. "This is farm country. Not everybody wants a bunch of strangers camping out in town, people like were in the bar tonight."

She hung her towel and watched Frank stretch his long arms over his head and yawn. He rubbed his tousled blond head and scratched his chest.

"All those people won't be strangers long, especially when their cabins get built over on the island. It's exciting."

"Not everybody wants em here, Abby. That's all."

"Are you trying to say something, Frank?"

"Nope. I just did. Come on and get in bed." He flung back the covers and patted the bed.

She did as he said, and he rolled toward her, but her mind was elsewhere. Frank didn't notice, though, and when his pulse returned to normal and a small snore rumbled from him, she slipped from bed, grabbed her mother's afghan and left the room. The door closed with a whisper, and she crept down the stairs on tiptoe and went out to the porch.

The moon had risen higher in the sky, and stars, like brilliant gemstones, winked on and teased the earthbound with hints of space and other worlds. Abby wrapped in her afghan and settled in the rocker. Phantom joined her, and soon Cleo nudged him to find lap space by his side.

"Thanks, my friends. It's a wondrous night, isn't it?"

Mrow wawah wah.

A bat zigged across the sky, and Cleo's head followed it. The trees rustled, and her ear twitched; her eyes slanted. Abby heard the *hoo hoo hoo hoo* of a great horned owl and looked for its yellow eyes in the shadowed trees.

"It's a wild critter night, babies. Don't go gadding about and get yourself picked up an owl. You'd make him a good snack."

A movement caught her eye at the edge of the lake, and Abby quit rocking. The cats sat up, alert. They were motionless until Phantom hunched his back and hissed, and Abby saw what had moved. It was witch woman, poking along the edge of the lake with a stick in her hand and several cats following like ducklings in a row.

She walked a few feet, poked her stick into the sand at the edge of the water, bent to retrieve something and put it in a sack hanging from her arm. She repeated the process, moving, poking, retrieving and moving on. She had gone thirty feet along the edge of the lake when she turned to stare at the hotel porch. At least, in the dark, that's what it looked like to Abby. She stood motionless, feet wide and firmly planted, a mythical image, her stick in the air, her bag on her arm, and her eyes unblinking spheres burning in the moonlight.

The hair on Abby's neck stood up, her skin prickled, and the peaceful night was a cold memory. But she didn't go into the house. She wasn't going to be frightened away from her own porch. She watched until the woman walked back the way she'd come and was out of sight, trailing a long line of cats.

Abby laid her head against the back of the chair and shoved her toe against the porch floor, rocking once again. Phantom settled back in his curl, and Cleo slipped up to Abby's chest and lay there.

What a day. I don't know anything anymore. I really don't.

Come Monday, the throng of people had gone home to their cities, and the hotel was quiet. Abby put Chunk, Bailey and Daisy at a table and gave them paper and pencils to keep them occupied while she and her friends talked about choir.

"Quiet children get root beer later," she said.

Chunk put a finger over his lips, and Bailey punched him. Daisy scooched her chair to get away from the obnoxious boys, and Cecily walked behind Bailey and pulled on an ear. He howled, and she kept pulling until he quit howling.

"Aunt Abby said quiet. What exactly don't you understand about that, boys?"

"I punched him quiet."

His mother rolled her eyes, mouthed *boys* and thumped him gently on the head.

"How's this as a reward for good behavior? Good boys don't get spanked. Hmmm?"

"Ma," Chunk yelled. "I didn't do anything."

"I know . . . yet."

She turned and pulled out a chair between Bunny Parker and Flora Branch. Isabelle Branch and Edna Falmouth were already jotting notes with their heads together, ignoring the kid chaos. Abby came out of the kitchen with a tray of cups, coffee and coffee cake.

"Okay, I'll pour and you guys get started," Abby said.

"Who's gonna lead this choir, and what we gonna sing?" Edna asked.

"We haven't decided yet to have just a single service," Bunny said. "I'm not convinced it's a good idea."

"Why not?" Edna said. "Why would we have two small ones when we could have one big service with all the plate money in just one pot? Doesn't make sense."

Bunny scowled and sat back in her chair. Her beautiful skin revealed anxiety in the two furrows between her eyes, lines of irritation marring perfection.

Flora leaned forward, her ample breasts spreading out on the table. She moved her cup and cake plate to make room for them.

"Why, Bunny? You can say it here. We're your friends," she said.

Bunny glanced at Abby whose neck showed the beginning flame of embarrassment.

"White folks and coloreds don't think the same. And they don't need to," Bunny said, looking around the table. "But church is important. We maybe want to praise the Lord in the ways that work best for each of us, and some believe that might be separate. There," she said, pushing her chair back from the table. "I've said what I came to say. You can do whatever you want with it."

Bunny got up, grabbed her wrap, and headed out.

Abby followed, meeting up with her at the door.

"Bunny," she said, taking her arm to stop her headlong exit. "I think I've offended you, and I'm sorry. But you're right about one thing, church is important to all of us. That's why we should all be together. We're a community, a family."

"No, we aren't family. We're not kin. Don't be foolish, young lady."

Bunny stood tall, her shoulders thrown back, her eyes hard, her lips straight, determined lines.

Abby pointed to the chairs against the wall.

"Would you sit with me for a minute, please?"

The woman gave a barely discernable nod and sat on the edge of the seat, her behind a foot away from the back of the chair.

"Let me retreat a bit," Abby said, trying to relax in her own chair and take a clarifying moment. "First, thank you for letting Jackson work here. He's amazing, a good worker. You raised a fine young man."

"Of course," Bunny said, not giving an inch toward a conversation.

"I like him a lot."

Bunny crossed her arms and waited.

Abby tossed words and ideas around in her head, tried to make them come to her tongue, but they all stuck somewhere in the rear of her throat, back by her tonsils.

Nothing was right – except for Bunny.

She *was* foolish. What did she know about her neighbors, about being Negro? A silly white girl with no experience at all. Before coming to Idlewild, she didn't even know any colored people. Not really, and not well, anyway. But she wanted to.

She dove in head first without holding her breath.

"Tell me about you, Bunny."

That wasn't what the woman was expecting; Abby could see it in her eyes. Bunny looked out at the lake, watched a flock of Canadian geese come in on a tattered V-shape and settle on the water, honking. She turned to Abby, her eyes black and penetrating.

"My grandfather was a slave in South Carolina. His body was emancipated by Lincoln, but funny thing about being freed . . . It doesn't wash away the whip scars on your back and in your mind and in your soul. He became a sharecropper, and my father was, too. Did you know a freed Negro could be whipped just like he was a slave? They don't own themselves."

Abby was silent. She'd heard the tales of horror and believed, like many, that it was all over. Lincoln had settled it. It was done.

Bunny's eyes half closed, looking back.

"After the war, plantation owners hated my daddy cuz he wouldn't be whipped, so they beat him. Poor whites hated him cuz he worked hard and took their jobs. They beat him for it. Near to death. That's how we ended up here, in the middle of nowhere. Now, here you are, pushing us again. Is that enough about me, Abigail Adams?"

"Am I pushing you, Bunny?"

Bunny's head raised, and her pointed chin jutted out. Abby was struck again by her regal beauty.

She nodded. "You would. But only if I let you, and I won't."

She stood and walked down the steps without another word. She never looked back, and Abby felt tears well in her eyes.

"Damn," she said. She sniffed, filled her chest with fresh, spring air and, after a moment, went back in the hotel.

"Am I pushy?" she asked as she approached the table.

"Sure," Flora said.

Abby sat and picked up her coffee.

"I have to be firm . . . here . . . at the hotel. That's how I get things done."

"We know, dear," Flora said, patting her leg like it was a dog's head.

"I mean that," she sputtered. "I have to get a little . . . you know, assertive, but not with my friends or my family."

"You don't know assertive," Edna said with a laugh. "Hang around me, and I'll teach you what it really is."

Betty came down the stairs and joined them.

"Rooms are dusted, Abby," she said.

"Thanks for finishing up, Betty. Join us, okay? By the way, am I pushy?"

"What?"

"Pushy," she repeated, waving her hands in the air like she could conjure understanding out of it. "Assertive, forceful."

"Right now, you are, and it's a little scary," Betty said, grinning. "Not usually, though."

That broke them all up, and Abby let it go.

"Who's gonna lead this group of misfits in song?"

"I'll do it," Edna said. "There. Now that's assertive."

"We need more people. Men, too," Isabelle said. "I can get my Del. He loves to sing. Flora? Will Ratty join?"

Flora nodded.

Abby pulled at her lip. "I don't know about Frank. I'll try.
And I need to go to Baldwin shopping. Anyone want to go with me?"

"Yup, if I can get a sitter for Daisy. When?"

"Tomorrow, if I can get a sitter for my father," she said, laughing and looking at Betty who gave her a nod.

She drove by the pavilion site on her way to pick up Edna and was thrilled to see the progress. It would be done by now if they didn't keep taking the crew away to work on the cabins and footbridges.

Edna was waiting outside when she pulled up, and they were off.

"I feel like a kid playing hooky," she said. "It's a gorgeous day, and I am footloose and downtown."

She gave a whoop and Abby laughed.

"What do you need to buy that crabby old Foster doesn't have?" she asked.

"Linens and, uh, things like that," she said, being evasive.

"You can order from the catalog, you know."

Abby looked away, caught in a fib.

"Okay, I need food supplies – and linens," she said, glancing sideways at her friend who raised her eyebrows in doubt.

"I do need them. I just can't tolerate that man. He gives me the creeps and makes me mad. I know I should patronize a town store, but..."

"He's something, for sure. It's okay, Abigail Riley Adams. It's a beautiful day for a jaunt, and I'm happy to be childless for a couple of hours."

They shopped, browsed, talked and laughed. Abby treasured this new experience of female friendship, had longed for it even though the need had never jumped up and smacked her in the face. Her father had always been her best friend, and the lumberjacks who came to the hotel and bar. She hadn't known any women, not more than just to say hello and call them by name, anyway.

Shopping done and rumble seat full, they climbed back in the buggy and took their time going home. The sun was warm and the breeze sweet scented.

"We'll have to do this again," Abby said. "Would Jesse mind?"

"No, heavens, no. He doesn't own this brown body or care what I do as long as I take good care of his baby girl – and him, feed him and keep his bed warm at night. But the man is a good lover, so I'm not minding that part," she said with a poke to Abby's side. "I am sure enough lucky."

Abby didn't respond, caught up in thinking about what Edna had said. She'd meant it, that she was lucky.

"How about Frank?" Edna asked.

"I don't know. I don't think he'd mind."

"I meant is he a lover, too? A good one?"

"I guess so." She gave her friend a half laugh, uncomfortable with the conversation, but curious, too.

"You guess?" Edna shouted. "I think you'd be the only one who'd know for sure, and if you don't know..."

"Yes ... yes, of course he is."

Edna slanted her head and looked sideways. Abby chewed her bottom lip, and a frown creased her forehead.

"You alright?" Edna asked. "I shouldn't pry. I'm an old busy body. Ignore me."

"You're not. You're fine and so am I. Everything is fine." She flicked the reins, and Marie picked up speed. "Let's have a drink at the hotel before I take you home. Want to?"

Edna lifted her brows. "You looking to corrupt me?"

"Yes."

"Okay, wicked woman. You're on."

When Frank came home, she asked if he'd had supper. When he nodded, Abby wrapped her arms around him and led him upstairs. His eyes lit up, and he slid a hand around to her breast.

Abby was in the kitchen frying up breakfast sausage and potatoes when Bear came in carrying Cleo, with Phantom draped over his shoulder. She didn't hear him. Her mind was elsewhere, and she dropped the spatula into the greasy pan when he touched her arm.

"Darn," she said, wiping grease spots from her arm with the corner of her apron.

"You burned, Abby?" Bear asked. "Put cold water on it, not more grease. That's an old wives' tale that doesn't work. Sorry I startled you."

"Not your fault. I was wool gathering."

"And now you have bare naked sheep?"

"Yes," she said, smiling and pouring coffee for them both. "Hope it doesn't snow on them. You're early."

"Want to get that damned pavilion done today. The whole town is coming to help."

"It's exciting. I can't wait for the Chautauqua: famous speakers, musicians, lots of new people."

"You got something against old people?"

He rubbed the paw dangling over his chest and grinned at Abby's enthusiasm. Her eyes were on fire and sparkled with eagerness. She danced on her toes as she talked about it.

"Well? You excited?"

"Sure. I'm excited," he said in the best monotone he could deliver, sounding like a foghorn on a Lake Michigan barge.

"If you weren't draped in a cat shawl . . ." She threatened him with a towel. "And speaking of my cats, why are you stealing them from me?"

Mrow, Phantom said and added *Wawah a wawah* for good measure. Abby scratched his chin. He flicked his tail. It tickled Bear's nose, and he sneezed, sending both cats flying. They landed on the floor side by side, and glared, two blue and two green unblinking orbs.

"You did that on purpose," Bear said. "You evil, jealous woman."

"Evil? I think I might be."

"Definitely."

She gave him a wicked grin and called to the cats. "Breakfast babies. Come get it."

Chapter Seven

Spring 1917

The bar was packed with strangers. Abby and Jackson filled whiskey glasses, mixed drinks they hadn't heard of before and laughed. People they didn't know recognized them and called their names from across the room.

"Jackson, you young pup, I need a drink. I'm gone dry."

The young man smiled, waved, nodded and came to the bar to order it, but Abby had heard and the Iced Sidecar was waiting on the bar.

"Sure glad for the inside information about their drinking habits," she said. "Who'd have thought to stock up on orange liqueur and cognac? Who'd have thought to have any at all?" she said as he scooted between customers and grabbed the glass.

Patrick pushed through the swinging doors with a tray of bowls and called for Jackson.

"Arms are going. Help please," he yelled.

Shorty made it in two long strides and grabbed the tray. "I'll take it. I know where it goes."

Patrick gratefully gave up the heavy load and headed back into the kitchen with a hand rubbing his sore back muscles and groaning. Maybe he'd hire more help. A girl just for the kitchen. A young, strong one.

Bill Sanders' voice boomed as the kitchen doors swung against the crowd.

"War," registered in Patrick's brain, and "United States."

Abby's hands stilled in the soapy water, gripping the whiskey glass she'd been washing, and she stared, not believing. Heads turned, chatter ceased, hearts beat – drubbing against chest bones faster than before the words had been uttered. Dread saturated the air in acrid perspiration and toxic fear.

Bill's eyes traveled the room like a weary drifter's. He hadn't wanted to be the one to tell them, to let them know death would come to town trailing behind the Chautauqua, the event intended to bring people together, to raise philosophical and spiritual awareness.

Frank, sitting at the end of the bar, stood with his glass in his hand. He raised it high and waited for quiet.

"It's about damned time. Drink to victory."

He threw it back, swallowed and slammed the glass so hard on the bar it should have cracked. She ran to fill it, eyes wide with fear and a trace of tears she wouldn't allow. She blinked, and the liquid dried into brackish sand. Her eyes itched in the aftermath, but she didn't have time to dwell on the events of tomorrow and the days after – on the war. She had drinks to pour. Orders to fill.

Jesse Falmouth raised his glass to the men in the room.

"I'll be here," he said, when they were listening, "but many of you'll be in the trenches with bullets screaming over your heads. I'll be here," he repeated in a chant-like voice, "working for the Idlewild you protect while shells burst around you. My job may sound easy, but it won't be. I'll be here . . . praying for you."

"Here, here," unknown voices said.

"You better pray double hard for the brothers fool enough to fight in this white man's war," Samuel Moore said. "Take your shovel with you, boys." He brought his glass to his mouth and stared hard over the edge of it.

"What are you talking about, Samuel?" Jesse asked.

"You want to run point and take the bullets, you go right ahead. Our illustrious armed forces will surely use colored troops for that. For bullet bait. Or maybe to dig their trenches for them. That's what I'm saying."

"Maybe not," James Gerard, Betty's father, said. "There are colored troops now, especially in France."

"James is right," Jesse added. "France appreciates our efforts. Colored troops fight right beside the rest."

Samuel scoffed, looking like he knew something about soldiering no one else did. But he tended to look that way about everything. He peered over his eyeglasses and let his gaze roam around the room, taking in the entertainers and speakers here for the Chautauqua, the Idlewild people in all shades of black and several shades of white.

"Fools are everywhere," he said, his words dripping with sarcasm and the knowledge of generations. He drained his drink, stood and strolled to the door, not bothering to acknowledge anyone as he left.

Abby watched from the bar. She'd heard Samuel's words. Everyone had, and discomfort was on their faces, in the set of their lips, the tilt of their shoulders. What he'd said was true, at least partly. She knew it and hated to admit the man was right about anything. He was hateful and made no effort to be anything else. But he might be right about this.

"What do *you* think, Abraham?" she asked a quiet man hunched over his drink at the bar.

"About what, girl?"

"What Samuel said. Would a colored man be a fool to enlist in the war?"

Abraham's head hung while he pondered. His close-cropped hair and beard were silver threaded, and his shoulders curved with age. He'd been born in Idlewild some sixty years ago, had farmed a few acres and been left alone his whole life. He didn't mind the solitude, and he stayed put in Idlewild or on his farm. Didn't seek anything else. After the stories his parents had told him about escaping southern slavery, he was satisfied to have a safe place of his own.

He was silent for so long, Abby wondered if she'd offended him or he'd nodded off. She bent down to peer up at his face and saw that his eyes were still wide open, so she waited.

"When you ask questions, you might get answers you don't want to hear," he said.

Abby pulled her bottom lip between her teeth and wiped at the bar, fixed a tray of drinks for Jackson and came back to Abraham.

"I want to know the truth," she said.

He rubbed at the huge knuckles on his twisted hands and looked hard at Abby.

"Since long before Lincoln's war, white armies been using colored men in their fights, and the colored men been doing it and doing it and dying. They keep on, thinking when they're done with the fight, if they survived, they'd get looked at different. White people would give them some respect, not expect us to look away instead of into their eyes. They'd get a job and could go into a restaurant for a bite to eat, a drink of water."

He paused and stared at her.

"You see that happening?" he asked.

"But we're all together here," she said, hoping she didn't sound stupid. She wanted it to be otherwise, wanted what was right to be real and true.

He nodded and glanced around the room, looking at all the dark faces interspersed only sporadically with the white ones. Even in this room, segregation existed, and Abby followed his gaze around the tables and knew it. Abraham's eyes came back to hers.

"You see it, too, don't you? Even here. And here's a difference. In Idlewild, we're inviting you. Did you even know that?"

She covered his knobby hand with hers when she saw the trace of a grin on his lips.

"I didn't, but I know now, and I appreciate it. Thank you, Abraham."

"Go on," Betty said. "I know you're dying to get out there to hear him. I'll finish up."

"Thank you, thank you," Abby said, hugged the girl and flew from the room. She found her father in the kitchen, told him where she'd be and was out the door. The pavilion was near, so it didn't take her long to get there. She heard his strong voice long before she saw him. She heard loud applause and then more words.

". . . and I hadn't planned to talk about the war, not about your part in it, about your hopes and dreams, but change is a consequence of conflict."

She came in near the end of William Jennings Bryan's speech and stood at the back of the crowd trying to hear the treasured words of one of her heroes.

What about their part in it? Who is they? What of their dreams and hopes?

"You may be conscripted," he continued, "and go where they send you. Or you may enlist and try to get into the 93rd division, even the 369th regiment. There, you will fight hard shoulder to shoulder with other soldiers, with trust for one another, with regard for one another. And you may die, but you will die with dignity. In France."

Bryan paused to search the faces turned up to him, the eager eyes, trust evident in most of them. He continued.

"And while I understand Mr. Moore's words and sentiments from last night as having a basis in truth, stand strong and proud, embrace your opportunity to protect our nation and create change, look to the future for your children, and know that France has suffered greatly during this time of tribulation and will praise you for your aid. As I do. As we do. Bless you all."

Applause erupted as Mr. Bryan left the podium, and Abby wished she could have been there for all of his speech. She'd read and reread his words, and recognized him as a wise, compassionate man, one who was renowned for his struggle to create the very change he'd talked about in his speech.

Buddy Black's trio was setting up on the makeshift stage before Bryan walked down the steps, surrounded by folks wanting to continue the dialogue. The refrain to *Old Woman Blues* sang from Black's guitar strings and was accompanied by the mournful strains of a harmonica. Bass riffs kept the rhythm and soon, folks were tapping their feet and humming.

They didn't miss a beat when the tune was finished and swung right into *Miasma,* a lament about a man who didn't know his woman at all. Abby hummed along and wondered if husbands and wives ever understood each other. Perhaps it was just the way of the world, the differences in the sexes.

She listened to a few more songs and headed back to the hotel to get ready for the lunch crowd. Joe Foster was already at the bar waiting. She nodded his way and tried to smile.

"You missed out on some good music, Mr. Foster."

"I didn't miss out. Didn't want to hear it."

Abby ignored his irritable words.

"Too bad. It was really good," she said, not letting his sour face infect her mood. "If you're waiting for some of Father's Irish stew, I can get it for you."

He nodded, and she fled to the safety of the kitchen.

"God, Joe's an ornery old coot," she whispered in her father's ear.

"Aye, he's the Blue Hag's son, her and her carrion crow. Should a stayed in Hebrides. Here's his stew, and blast him if he finds fault with it."

"Thanks. I will, Da. I'll blast him if he does. Jackson here yet?"

"Nope."

"Hope he shows. We're gonna be swamped."

She saw Jackson at the head of a large group of folks who were laughing and talking as they came through the door. She handed Joe his stew as they began shouting orders.

They were so busy Abby did double duty on the floor and behind the bar. She knew most of the new folks by name, and their interactions were light and teasing, like they'd always known each other. During a brief slow moment when they'd all been served drinks and meals, she paused behind the bar to survey the crowd. Old Abraham's words about the segregation in her own hotel came to her, as well as the fact that colored folks had invited them to Idlewild, not the other way around.

Even after Bryan's beautiful speech, most tables held people of a single color. She didn't know why, but it wounded her. If she was hurt by it, how did it feel for Jackson, for Betty, for all of the colored people in this room, people she cared about? This was her place. Well . . . her father's. She didn't want segregation here and didn't know what to do about it.

She meandered through the room checking drinks and clearing away dirty dishes. At every table, the discussion was war and enlistment or conscription, and every once in a while, it seemed her presence halted conversation.

They didn't want to talk around her, and it made her want to run to her room and sit with her mother in the window seat. She made a face at her foolishness and shook her head, losing some of the pins that held her auburn curls. She snarled a mild expletive, dropped the dishes on the bar, and pulled out the rest, tangling her fingers in the auburn mass and pulling strands out by the roots.

"I'm being dumb. I am. I know it."

"Don't say bad things about my tall, skinny friend," Betty said, walking up and grinning.

"Well, sometimes your friend is silly."

"You being pushy again?"

Abby laughed. "Don't know. I'd like to be."

"Who would you be pushing and what for?" Betty asked.

She thought about Betty's question. Perhaps she had hoped for too much from the Chautauqua events. Perhaps she was seeing folks realistically for the first time, or maybe the war intensified behaviors. The good and the bad. Maybe Bunny was right. They could never be family.

Abby didn't know and said so.

"I'd push to be friends with these people. I think I'm disappointed were all not better friends."

"Did you think all of us were friends?"

Abby regarded the room, and her gaze settled on many of the small groups, some in animated conversation, some watching others and eavesdropping on the talk at other tables. She stretched her neck, trying to work out the kinks, tilted her head sideways and sighed.

"I guess not," she whispered, feeling like she was younger than the girl standing next to her. Abby's five foot nine inches towered over Betty, and she had a few years on her, but sometimes it didn't feel that way.

Like now.

For whatever reason, Betty was old. Maybe she'd been born old. Maybe it was the way she was raised. It could be she had generations of wisdom mixed into her morning porridge. Abby wished she could ask her questions. But the time wasn't right. The temperament in the room wasn't right. At some point, she would ask everything she wanted to know.

The rest of the day and all of the next left no time for pondering friendships. By Sunday night, the hotel emptied as carriages hauled Chautauqua revelers back to various trains and to various cities. Rooms were vacated, and, in the lobby, her voice echoed against the walls. It seemed a vast empty space.

Patrick wandered through, looking lost and tired.

"You okay, Da?"

He ruffled his hair, his green eyes sparkling.

"Going to pour a tall one and take it to the porch. Gonna watch the swans devil the loon as the moon rises. Join me?"

"Sure. I'll get Frank. Pour us one, too."

Frank was stretched out on the bed, a pamphlet in his hand. He laid it down when she entered and patted the bed beside him.

"In a while," she said, with a small smile. "Papa's pouring us a cold drink. Join us on the porch? We need a bit of a wind down."

"Sure. Be right down."

Abby found her father and took the tray of drinks from him to carry to their favorite rocking chairs. Patrick wobbled like a toddler when he was overly tired, and the bow of his legs grew wider. She worried he was working too hard, but he wouldn't stop, wouldn't have it any other way. Once he got started, she'd have to tie him to his bed if she wanted him to rest.

He groaned as he fell backwards into his chair, and she flinched as it creaked under his weight. She handed him his drink, and he sipped and sighed.

"Thanks, lass." He sipped again. "We found the end of the rainbow this weekend. Your Chautauqua brought more than a pound of silver and pot of gold."

"It did, but it was overshadowed by war. Even Mr. Bryan's speech changed to talk of conflict."

"I'm sorry that happened to spoil your event, Abby."

"The Chautauqua doesn't matter. Think of the men who'll go to fight, who might not come home, or will come home a different man. I hate it."

She turned, hearing Frank's heavy footfall on the wooden porch and pulled his chair closer. He took the drink she held out to him and sat, his head resting against the back of the chair, his eyes on the silhouette of the moon on the water.

"Did you like the music today, Frank? Buddy Black can sure make a guitar sing."

"It was okay. I like songs more upbeat."

"Blues is blue, that's for sure," she said, her low voice a soft caress in the dark remembering the soulful strings of Buddy Black.

Frank didn't respond, and they rocked to the sounds of night growing around them, the creak of their chairs an accompaniment to cricket chirps and tree frog chatters, both making determined, loud efforts to call mates.

"I'm gonna enlist," Frank said.

Abby turned to look at his face, to ensure the joke was meant to be funny. But it wasn't funny, and it wasn't a joke.

"You're not serious, Frank."

"I am."

"Why? You're a farmer. You're needed here to feed the soldiers and all the rest of us."

"The farm's fine without me. I have two brothers and Pa to work it."

"But . . . you're married."

"So is Terry – with two kids, and George is a kid himself. One of us should go, and that's me. It won't be so bad," he said, leaning back into his chair again.

Patrick rose, saying he'd give them some privacy, but Frank told him to sit back down, that he was part of everything.

Abby sat back, too. What could she say, should she say? She put a hand on his arm and left it there, hoping her touch would tell him what she didn't know how to.

"I've never been out of Michigan. Never would get to Europe any other way, so . . ."

He left the thought unfinished and watched Phantom slip quickly past him and leap into Abby's lap, his blue eyes glowering at Frank, black pupils widened by the dark and looking wicked.

"You could die," she said.

"But it could be an adventure, too. Your friend Bryan said conflict brings change, and change is good. Remember?"

"I don't think it was exactly like that, but, yes, some change is good. The right kind."

"My decision." Frank squeezed her hand, drained his glass and rose. "I've got some reading to do, so I'll see you upstairs."

Critters mocked the silence, their chirps, hoots, and chatters growing louder with each stretching minute, overcoming the creak of chair runners on wood, the slow intake of breath, the light sigh of distress neither was aware they made.

"Why do you think he wants to do this?" she said.

"Maybe it's just as he said, lass. Maybe he wants to go across the big lake and see Europe."

"During war? That makes no sense."

"Then maybe he thinks it's his duty. Lots of men do. I would've fought for wee Ireland."

"So . . . damn. I need to say nothing, smile and say goodbye?"

"You wouldn't be the first woman to bite her tongue and wear the smile of trickery."

She said goodnight to her father and went toward the stairs practicing the falsehood.

He had the pamphlet in his hand when she walked in, but it had fallen to his chest, and he stared at the ceiling instead of it.

Abby washed up and took her long white nightgown from the armoire.

"Leave it off," he said.

Her eyes widened, and she held the gown in front of her, stilled.

"But..."

Frank tossed the pamphlet to the floor and patted the mattress beside him.

"Come here, Abby," he said, not unkindly. "Leave the flannel thing."

"Don't you want to talk about joining up?" she asked. "I do."

He shook his head and patted the bed again.

She was uncomfortable getting into bed naked. It didn't feel appropriate. She knew he'd remove her gown if he wanted to, but that was different. This was ... unseemly. It felt decadent. Not wholly depraved, but the sense of it was there, lurking behind her eyes, in the flutter of her nervous fingers.

When he put his hand between her legs, she tried to block out thoughts of war, tried to sense the pleasure, the things Edna had hinted about, but her mind didn't have time to make her body behave accordingly. Or maybe it was other way around. There wasn't time for her body to let her mind know it was pleasurable, and just as she started to relax, to think desire was beginning with stirrings of passion, it was over.

Frank rolled to his side, his breath coming fast, his heart beating hard. She could see it thumping under his skin.

"Hmmm," he groaned. "You good?"

"I'm fine," she answered.

What else could she say? What more *should* she say? His feelings would be hurt if she tried to explain that she didn't feel anything when they made love, nothing at all, unless it was used, like a thing he briefly needed – before sleep.

Something was wrong with her. There must be, because Frank knew what he was doing. She didn't.

Her husband was contented, and that was the important thing. He fell asleep with his hand on her breast and one leg thrown over hers.

She wanted to don her nightgown, wrap in her afghan and sit on the porch, but her father would likely still be there. He'd question her with his eyes, if not with words, and she didn't want to answer or even ponder the answers. She didn't know them. She didn't even know the questions.

Chapter Eight

Witch woman stood surrounded by cats at the end of her long driveway and pulled Abby toward her with a wave as she was passing. Abby tried to keep walking, but the woman called to her and flapped her hand again with greater determination.

"Abigail Riley," she yelled, her voice a scratchy bark.

Abby's heart thrummed in her chest, and her nostrils flared. She'd like to run, but thought that would be ridiculous. She was just an old woman who loved her cats. That's all. Right?

She paused, and the woman reached out to grab Abby's sleeve. Her hair was long and wiry, hanging down her back and over her shoulders. Her cheeks were hollow, eyes black and piercing. She wore a shapeless long dress of several vibrant colors, and a purple shawl covered her shoulders. If this was Bunny's sister, they came from different parents because they were nothing alike.

"Come," she said, and Abby followed her down the long path to a tiny, grayed shack. One look at the broken steps made her halt, thinking her weight would surely break through the splintered boards.

"Come," the woman repeated and tugged again at the sleeve she still clutched.

"Mrs. . . . I don't know your name, but I don't think I should walk on your porch. It doesn't look safe."

"Bah. Come along, girl. Don't be a ninny."

"What is your name?" Abby asked. "You know mine, but it's not Riley anymore. It's Adams. Abby Adams."

"We'll see."

Abby had no choice but to follow where the woman led. It was that or forcibly yank her sleeve from the veined hand gripping it.

Inside, Abby stopped in shock. The room was a haven in pastel colors. Beautiful rugs covered the floor and walls, dried flowers were artfully displayed in earthenware vases on the cupboard and on the small table in the middle of the room. A fainting couch at the far end of the room was draped with a quilt in colors even brighter than her dress. Bunny's sister liked colors. And cats.

Abby's head spun as she looked around the room, finding more surprises each time her eyes landed.

"Beautiful," she said, her word soft and in praise.

"Sit," the old woman said, pointing at the table.

Abby made a curt nod, and her cheek muscles tightened.

"I will if you tell me your name. If not, I'm leaving."

"Cassandra."

"As in the Greek soothsayer Cassandra?"

"Mother had humor. She also had the sight. Tea?"

"Thank you. That would be nice." Abby figured she was here, so why not satisfy her curiosity. The woman *was* interesting, and Bunny couldn't accuse her of not learning who her sister was anymore.

The tea kettle was about to whistle, but hadn't when Cassandra reached for it, poured boiling water into a small pink pot and brought it to the table. She moved the flowers aside so they wouldn't interfere and reached for Abby's hand.

"It needs to steep," she said. "Meanwhile . . ."

Abby let Cassandra take her hand and watched as she studied it. She stroked it in places, tilted it to the light of the window, turned it over and flattened it against the table. Leaving it there, she hummed as she poured the tea.

Abby sniffed the steam coming from her cup and smiled.

"Whatever is this? It smells divine."

"No toad warts. I promise. It won't poison you."

"That's not why I asked. It simply smells wonderful."

"Lemon balm and dandelion. Grows right in your yard. All you have to do is pick it. Lots of good things in your own yard without going into somebody else's."

Abby sipped and sighed in pleasure. She let her eyes roam the room again, looking for the next interesting thing she had yet to spot.

"Why am I here, Cassandra? Not that I don't want to be. I do."

"I wanted to look at your hand. To see for myself."

"And did you?"

"Yes, it confirmed what I knew."

"Are you going to tell me?"

She closed her eyes and her breath slowed. Her shoulders moved sideways rhythmically.

"The rose is not asleep. It only waits, anticipates a full awakening."

Abby waited for more, something to help her words become magically clear. When nothing came, she asked what it meant and received more confusing verse.

"Don't step into water that has no bottom. Learn how to float in liquid space. Ask first if the drowning man wants your help. You may place weight on his back, and you may walk in quicksand, laughing."

"Cassandra, I don't understand," Abby whispered.

"I know. Be mindful, girl. Be sentient."

"I'm trying. I really do try my best."

"I know that, too. Fertilize and water. Some live, some die."

Cassandra tipped up her cup, drained it, and pushed back her chair. Abby rose, too, guessing the woman's moves meant it was time to leave.

"Thank you for having me," she said. "May I stop again?"

For some reason, she needed to return, maybe to get answers to the woman's riddles, maybe to soak in the wonderful room. Whatever the reason, she wanted to come back. She knew she would and also that visiting here held both joy and angst.

Cassandra nodded and walked with Abby to the end of the driveway.

Edna was looking for her when she got back to the hotel, and Abby's eyes lit up.

"I'm so glad to see you. You'll never guess where I've been?"

"You got me. I haven't a clue."

"Cassandra's."

Edna's eyes were blank, her hands in the air, palms up.

"Still no idea," she said.

"Cassandra . . . Bunny's sister."

Edna's face scrunched, but it became obvious she didn't know Cassandra by name or relationship.

Abby leaned to whisper in Edna's ear, looking around to see if Jackson was anywhere close. "Witch woman," she said.

Edna's eyes widened, her deep brown irises vivid in a perfect white setting, like children's playing marbles.

"You didn't.'

"I did. Well, actually, she did. She grabbed my sleeve and wouldn't let go till I went in with her. Scared me a bit, but it's lovely, really lovely. Her house, I mean, and she isn't so scary. She's nice. Strange, but sort of nice, and I'm rambling, aren't I?"

Enda stepped back, pulled her chin down to her chest and peered over her bifocals.

"Did that woman cast a spell on you?"

Abby laughed, her hand flying up to cover the big white teeth that embarrassed her.

"No. I enjoyed it." She leaned toward Edna, nudged her and took her arm. "Have a small glass of wine with me? Or tea. But I think wine for me."

"I'm going for the wine."

Abby led her into the empty bar, her arm entwined in Edna's, relishing the rapport she'd found with her. She poured the wine in delicate, stemmed glasses, and they sat at the bar shoulder to shoulder, head to head.

"So? Tell me everything."

Abby explained the strange encounter.

She described the dilapidated exterior of the shack-like house and the beautiful interior, the rampant color and the peaceful pastels. She told her about Cassandra's study of her hand and the verses that didn't make sense. About not going into another person's yard, thorny branches and deep water and helping a drowning man. Or not. Whatever she remembered of the woman's words.

"That all sounds strange and spooky," Edna said with a shiver.

"And she told me to fertilize and water, that some live and some die. That did get to me a little. Oh, and to be sentient."

Edna stared up at the ceiling and pulled at her bottom lip.

"Huh. I don't even know what sentient means. You?"

"Lots of things, I think. But I took it to mean be sensitive and responsive. To whom, I don't know."

"Listen to you with your 'whom' word," Edna teased and giggled.

Abby got up to pour more wine and watched her friend pull at her lip again. It was pink inside, just like her own. Odd, when her outer skin was midnight.

After she sipped from her glass, she mentioned it. Edna's eyes grew round.

"Were you born under a rock, girl? Sometimes you are the dictionary definition of stupid." She drew out the word making it sound like 'stooooopid.' "And I don't know *sentient* but you're just dumb."

Abby chuckled. "I am not. I just think it's odd. That's all."

"Okay. Not stupid, but definitely sheltered. Have you *never* been around colored folk?"

Abby shook her head, and Edna rolled her eyes.

"Just don't go out in public talking about how Negros and whites are pretty much the same. Even inside their mouths, see," she mimicked. "That'll get you an empty hotel or ridden out of town."

"Why is this so hard, Edna? I don't get it."

"I know you don't. You don't get us. Don't try cuz you can't."

"Then how can we be friends?"

Abby pulled back, afraid she'd blundered into a place she didn't want to go, a lonely place where she'd be without her friend.

"We are, aren't we?" An instant film covered her eyes, and she turned away. Maybe it was the wine or maybe too much happening . . . with Cassandra speaking riddles and Frank wanting to go overseas, and now this.

Edna slung an arm around her shoulder.

"We're friends. I don't have to know you inside and out for that. You're alright, and that's good enough. I'm not going to dissect you or cut you up in little bitty pieces to find out if I should like you or not. Or look inside your lip."

Abby wrinkled her nose and made a face. She tapped a fingernail on the bar.

"Maybe that's what Cassandra meant by the water with no bottom. I'll never find it. I'll just get sucked into quicksand. Probably by talking too much."

"Or Cassandra really is just a crazy witch woman, plain and simple." Edna's head whipped around like someone might be sneaking up on them.

"Looking for Bunny?" Abby asked.

Edna laughed and slapped her leg.

"I have to go. Jesse's going to think I got lost."

She was at the door before she remembered why she came in the first place.

"Sing a duet!" she said, stomping her foot. "That's why I came. I want to sing for the next Chautauqua, and I want you to do it with me!"

They settled on a couple of songs to practice and Edna left Abby pondering their conversation and wondering if it was true she would never really know a colored person, not inside where it counted. It bothered her. She'd wanted to talk with her friend about Frank and her, at night, but she couldn't get the words out. They stuck on the back side of her molars like they were glued there.

She found her father in the kitchen getting ready to make supper and told him about Cassandra, not in detail, but the shortened version. His eyes lit up and dimples deepened.

To an Irishman, witches and fairies were part of the natural world. They simply existed as facts of life. Cassandra belonged with the blarney stone, rainbows, pots of gold, and leprechauns.

Abby was still in the bar serving drinks when Frank got home. He took a stool at the end of the bar and sipped on a beer.

"You want dinner, Frank?" she asked. "Or did you eat with your family?"

"I'm starved."

Phantom leaped to the bar and perched near Frank, eyeing him.

"Can't you get him off the bar?" he asked.

"Sorry," she said, lifting the cat down to the floor. He loped off, and looked back at her like she'd betrayed him. Abby sat squarely between the cats she'd loved for years and demands of the man she loved and married.

Why couldn't they at least tolerate each other? Like each other just a little?

She brought him a large plate of meatloaf and mashed potatoes just as Bear came in wearing Phantom over his shoulder. He grinned, and the scars deep in his beard winked through the bristles.

"Gotch'er cat," he said.

"I see that. You wear him like an exotic fox stole."

"Set one up for Shorty, too. Quiet tonight."

"Feels good for now . . . as long as it doesn't last long.

"I wouldn't worry," Frank mumbled through his meatloaf. "You've made sure of that."

"I've tried to," she said, grinning at him and hoping he meant it as a compliment. "Guess who I had tea with today?"

"I wouldn't know," Frank said.

"Witch woman," Bear said.

"How'd you know?"

"Cuz I'm a warlock," he said, scratching Phantom's ears.

"Well, I did. Have tea with her, I mean, and her place is amazing, beautiful, and she's . . . strange, but, I kinda think she sees something the rest of us don't. Her name's Cassandra, like the Greek seer."

Frank snorted. "That's all bull, stuff they make up to scare sane people."

"But don't you think it's interesting, Frank? Fun to think about?"

"Nope. I don't. Why waste time pondering things you can't know?" he said, mopping up the gravy on his plate with a crusty piece of bread. "If I can't see it, touch it, or hear it, it doesn't exist and it's foolish to think it does."

"You forgot two," Bear said, watching Cleo leap to the bar, a glistening, black streak that perched at the other end like an effigy, her jade eyes glowering.

"Two what?" Frank asked, but he didn't stay to hear the answer. He shoved back his plate and stood. "Early day tomorrow. Need to be in the field by sunup. Breakfast by five?"

"Senses. Guess that meatloaf you just ate isn't real," Bear said to the air.

Frank didn't want an answer to his question. Hadn't been looking for it.

"It'll be ready. You going up now?" she said, walking around the bar to give him a hug on his way out. "Be there soon. Need to finish with the supper folks first and help Da clean up in the kitchen."

He squeezed her, slapped her bottom, and left. When she came back, her throat was clogged with moisture. She turned away from Bear and tried to shout to Shorty coming in the door, but her voice was throaty like she was getting over a cold. She busied herself getting Shorty's drink and wiping down the bar.

"What's wrong, girl?" he asked over the top of his foamy glass of beer. "You sick?"

"No. Nothing's wrong, why?"

"Liar."

Cleo moved down the bar and stretched out in front of him, opening herself up for a belly scratch. Shorty obliged and stared at Abby. He'd gotten over his fear of felines.

"Really. I'm fine."

"If you were any better, you'd be butter?" he said, his soft voice sliding over her like silk. Shorty always knew what to say. Or how to say it.

"Right," she said. "I'm butter."

Bear harrumphed, and she couldn't help the small giggle that wiggled its way out.

"Frank wants to go to France," she blurted.

Both men had the good sense to try and hide their surprise.

"He wants to see the world or save ours. I don't know. Maybe both."

She planted her elbows on the bar and sunk her chin onto her fists.

"If we're going to war, we have to have soldiers. Can't do it without them," Bear said.

"But he doesn't need to. He's a farmer."

"True. Doesn't mean he feels any less obligated to do his share of the fighting, farmer or not," Shorty said.

"Maybe. But if I had moved out to the farm with him . . ."

"What? How would that change anything?"

"Don't know, but it's too late now, anyway."

"You could move out there and let Patrick do this by himself?"

She threw her hands in the air, frustration wrinkling her brow.

"I know. I can't. And I don't want to live there. They don't need me. Da does."

Chapter Nine

Word came out in glaring black headlines on the front page of the Osceola County Herald. Only thirty-two thousand men volunteered to join the armed services, adding up to a total of one hundred forty-two thousand American soldiers, total, not even close to what was needed overseas.

President Wilson had tried to make an army out of volunteers, but it wasn't going to work. Three weeks following American entry into World War I, conscription began. Any man between the ages of twenty-one and thirty had to register for the draft. Frank's desire to join up was made concrete. Without a word to anyone, he did.

One week later, just one month after Wilson joined the war effort, Idlewild gathered to say goodbye to nine men.

Abby helped Frank pack a duffle and tried to act like it was any other morning. She didn't know what to say. She didn't want him to go, but she wanted him to do what he wanted, what he needed to do. She pressed her fingers over her lips to stop them from trembling.

The conflict within was a tight, burning knot in her stomach. Maybe she should have been more resolute, should have put her foot down or cried. But she hadn't. She'd done what she supposed wives should do, silently, and now he was leaving, and now she wanted to wail and do the last few months over again. She wanted him to *not want* to go.

He pawed through the armoire looking for the canvas jacket he needed to pack, cussing and tossing clothes because it wasn't in his hand where he wanted it to be.

"Let me, Frank," she said. "I can find it quicker."

He backed away and gave her space.

"Do you have your toiletries?" she said, pulling out the jacket and laying it on the bed to fold.

"Just give it to me." He grabbed it from her and crammed it into the bag.

"Frank," Abby whispered. "Are you alright?"

"I just want to get going."

She pulled him to her and laid her head on his shoulder, fighting the tears she knew were lying in wait behind her eyelids.

"Just hold me a minute, please. Here, before we have to go down and be with the others."

He tightened his arms around her, and they stood motionless for long minutes, feeling the other's heartbeat, holding onto the flesh and blood person, the muscle and bone under their hands, the reality of here and now that would only be memory and shadow for the next . . . who knew how long. That was a thought neither of them wanted to consider. Until when? Or if.

Patrick said goodbye on the porch, and Frank's family waited by Jesse Falmouth's coach. He and Bill Sanders had volunteered to drive the recruits to the station. The boot and top storage areas were already loaded with suitcases and duffle bags, and several men and boys stood by waiting to leave.

Watery eyes blinked as though the sun was too bright and they'd looked directly at it. Half smiles came and went. They told old stories to have something to say and laughed too loud at the punch lines, the laughter brittle and cutting into already broken hearts like shards of glass.

Mothers and fathers hung onto the arms of the boys they loved, who loved them, and the men jabbed biceps because they wouldn't cry. The women knotted their fingers, tears welling behind red eyelids and finally falling, the blinks ineffectual against the tide that would not soon ebb. Brothers and sisters punched arms or kissed cheeks, and wives kissed with quivering lips and ran.

Abby tried not to look. It seemed invasive to witness their raw emotion, the pain that would be stored safely inside but couldn't be when the body turned inside out and the soul was bared.

She turned her face from their tears and watched Frank's family as they jabbed *his* bicep, told *him* jokes, and blinked *their* eyes against the sun.

His mother moved next to her, and Abby tried to take her hand, but she pulled it back, anger flashing in her eyes.

"He shouldn't be going," she spat. "He should be having babies at the farm. With you."

"I'm sorry, Mrs. Adams. I wish he was staying, too, but he wants this."

She didn't respond, but walked to her son and took his face in her hands. She kissed him, walked to their buggy and climbed in, her back stiff, her face a weathered stone.

Abby stood alone watching the goodbyes. She was inside out, too. Nerve endings on the outside of her skin, heart hanging by tendons from her ribs, exposed and left to dry in the sun, beating and beating.

A few feet away, a woman stood erect, her sobs fearless, her tears unchecked, and Abby wanted to be her. She wanted to yell for Edna to show her their tears were the same. They ran in rivers down white and brown and black and freckled cheeks. All alike. Tears had no color.

A vivid procession moved down the center of the road toward where they waited and was led by several cats of a variety of colors. Cassandra, dressed in flowing yellow, purple and green, followed the cats, with Bunny, Jackson, and a young man who looked a lot like Jackson bringing up the rear.

"Nice bunch of cats," Abby said to Cassandra as they drew near, just to hear her voice, to have something to say.

"A clowder," Cassandra said. "A clowder of cats."

"Clowder," Abby repeated, eyebrows raised. She nodded to Bunny and looked at the duffle bag. "Your son?" she asked.

Bunny nodded, tears forming but not falling. Not yet.

"Lincoln. Knew he'd go with the draft. Thought to beat it."

"He looks like you and Jackson. Nice looking young man," Abby said, wishing Frank's family would leave and give her some time with him instead of strangers.

She held out her hand to Lincoln, and he grasped it and pumped it up and down briefly before heading on down the road, eager to be with the other soon-to-be soldiers.

"Be safe," she shouted.

"Boy'll be fine," Cassandra said. "No trouble."

"I'd like to be as assured as you are," Abby said, more to herself than to Cassandra, but she answered anyway.

"Your man be fine, too."

"I hope you're right."

Abby touched Bunny's shoulder, a butterfly landing because she couldn't do more, and left the odd group. She was going to push through to Frank's side if she had to shove somebody out of the way to do it.

Jesse hollered to load up, and last hugs and kisses broke the dam of held tears. Goodbyes choked out in voices that didn't sound like their owners, and every soul there wanted it to be over. Wanted them gone so they could hide somewhere, stop the charade that everything was the same today as yesterday. It wasn't.

When he was gone, she stood planted in the road, her spine rigid, chin high, watching the back end of the coach get small. Hands had long since quit waving from it, and Abby's arms dangled from her shoulders like limp wash on a line. She wanted to be angry, but couldn't. At who? At what? At the moment, she was lost. Even mad would be better. She turned back toward the hotel and saw her father come down the steps to greet her.

"You okay?"

She nodded.

"Shorty and Bear want to buy you a drink. Figured you could use one. They're waiting."

The bar was quiet and dim, and it was appropriate. Shorty lumbered around the counter and poured a hefty, foamy beer in a tall glass. He gave Patrick a short whiskey and raised his high in salute.

"Here's to the soldiers," he said, and they all repeated his words.

Patrick lifted his glass. "Until we meet again, may God hold our boys in the palm of his hand."

"Amen," Abby said, just as Bunny and Jackson came through the door, followed by many of the folks who'd said goodbye to their soldiers.

"I asked Ma to come," Jackson said. "And Aunt Cassandra told her she should have a drink with you." He grinned and waved a hand at the rest. "They followed."

"You working?" Abby asked. "Cuz I'm sitting, and Shorty is bartending."

Jackson took over, and Abby nodded to Bunny, patting the seat next to her.

"Sister said you had tea with her," Bunny said, sipping at a small glass of wine, her eyes following Jackson as he waited on the folks who had followed them in.

"I did. I'm glad I did, too. Her home is lovely."

"She says you're not mean spirited, just kind of stupid." Bunny gave her a sideways look, and Abby saw fine lines spread out from her eyes. They weren't there the last time she'd seen her. Perhaps Lincoln put them there when he'd decided to become a soldier. Or maybe they'd been there, but Abby hadn't noticed. Maybe there was much she hadn't seen.

That thought didn't feel good. She chuckled. Maybe she *was* stupid. That's what her friend, Edna, had called her, too.

"You're lucky to have a sister," Abby said.

"I have seven and three brothers."

"Good Lord. That's a clowder!" she said with a hollow laugh.

"Cassandra's been at you with her cat words," Bunny said. "But I guess the term's appropriate or would be if we were feline. Do you have any?"

"Two, Phantom and Cleo. In fact, I'm wondering where they are. They usually hang out if Bear and Shorty are around."

"You have a brother named Phantom? Or sister?"

Abby spit wine as she laughed, a full laugh this time, shook her head and tried to answer.

"Cats. Those are my cats' names. I have no siblings."

"Oh. Sorry. It must be lonely."

Abby shrugged it off. She'd not known anything else so had nothing to compare it to, but felt a loss, nevertheless. She had her father and the lumberjacks – and her cats. Now, Frank. Well, she'd had Frank.

Bunny finished her wine and rose to leave. She touched Abby on the shoulder as Abby had done to her when they said goodbye to the soldiers. Like hers had been, it was a light, feathery touch, a hint of a hand grazing the shoulder. It didn't presume but was meant to communicate.

"If you're lonely . . . with Mister gone . . ."

Her kindness made a lump in Abby's throat that words couldn't find a way around. She nodded and swallowed, and the other woman got it. She didn't wait for a response, but waved to her son and left.

She and Betty finished cleaning the rooms early and were having tea in the corner of the bar and discussing the next Chautauqua bringing new folks to town, along with famous entertainers and speakers. Abby was to sing the practiced duet with Edna, and she was already queasy with fear.

The outer door swung open, letting in shafts of light and the cousins. Abby had only seen them from a distance since the night of the Christmas gathering, and curiosity widened her almond eyes. She went around the bar and waited.

"Good to see you, Ladies. What can I get for you? Lunch? Tea? Something stronger?"

"Heard you have black chicory coffee. I'll take that. With cream," Sue said in between huffs and puffs resulting from her efforts to climb on the bar stool.

"Don't know why we can't sit at a table," she groaned to Sally. "My feet dangle off the stool, and then my legs go to sleep. Probably gonna tip over when I get down off it."

"I'll stand you back up."

"Hah! You and who else? You see anybody here strong enough to lift me?"

"And for you, Sally?" Abby asked, trying to hide her grin.

"Sherry. It's almost noon."

"Put some whiskey in my coffee, then, for my throat."

"What brings you ladies to the hotel. Just out enjoying this beautiful day?"

Sally nodded her long face and looked around as several lunch customers came through the door along with Jackson. She heard him tell the folks to have a seat and he'd be right with them, so Abby left him to it. It had been a smart move when she hired him, Betty, too. She brought her attention back to Sally and Sue.

"You have good day-business," Sally said.

"It depends. Some days, yes. My father's lunches are getting to be well known."

Abby knew the cousins' restaurant-bar business was primarily a front, but she'd never let on and played along with their pretense. "How about yours?"

"Pretty slow during the day. Nights are better," Sue said.

Abby nodded, not knowing where else the conversation could go. She thrashed around for a safe topic and came up with the Chautauqua.

"You know we have some great entertainers and speakers coming in for the weekend, don't you? Be prepared to be busy," she said.

"I think we can handle it," Sally said with a sly smile.

"Why not join us for the Sunday service?" Abby said.

Sue rolled her eyes.

"You trying to save this old colored woman from her sinful ways, Abby Adams?" Sally asked.

"N . . .no! It's just . . . we have a guest minister, and Brandon Helmuth, from Chicago, is speaking about the war effort, and I thought you might . . . ah, hmmm . . ."

She let her ineffectual stammering fade out and bit the tip of her pinky finger.

"And we might not. Just take us as we are," Sally said.

Sue shoved her teacup to the back edge of the bar and swiveled her stool around, looking like she was getting ready to leap to the floor.

"What on earth you doing, Sue?" Sally asked.

Sue pumped her wide legs back and forth and wiggled her black booted feet in small circles.

"I told you my legs would take a nap. They're sleeping all the way from my behind to my toes. Now they're tingling, and pretty soon I'll have needles stabbing me. You don't know what it's like, being so tall and skinny like you are, Sally. You just don't know. Help me down."

Sally grabbed an arm, and Sue slid. As soon as her feet touched the floor, she let out a yelp and melted like a pile of butter sitting in a hot pan. Abby ran around the end of the bar to see the corpulent woman lying on her back with her legs in the air, pumping up and down. Her skirt had ridden up to show pink pantaloons, and matching pink garters held up her stockings.

Sally stood back to watch, and when the full display registered, Abby rushed to yank Sue's skirt back down to a more modest place. The lunch guests were silent, eyebrows raised in amusement. A couple of them had lifted from their chairs for a better view.

"Are you alright, Sue?" Abby asked, concerned she had broken a bone in her fall.

"She's fine," Sally said, beginning to be bored by her cousin's histrionics. "She does stuff like this all the time. Blames it on being short. I think it's just her bushel that's short . . . a few apples. You know? Like she's one egg *short* of a dozen. One goose *short* of a gaggle." She laughed at her own cleverness, tapped a long, painted fingernail on her temple and rolled her eyes to the ceiling.

Abby covered the grin working at her lips, and patted Sue's arm. When Sue recovered the feeling in her legs, she got up, straightened her clothing and, holding on to what dignity she had left, headed for the door.

"Think about coming to the Chautauqua," Abby said, watching them stroll away, owning the room.

"We're never gonna be silk purses," Sally said, without a backward glance. "I'm more the satin and lace kinda bag, and Sue's flannel. She's cuddly."

When the last customer left, Abby looked around the empty room and saw Frank in the dim light at the end of the bar, waiting for her with a gleam in his eye. The scent of fresh cut hay wafted her way, and she heard his low chuckle. In the split second it took for her breath to leave her body, he vanished. The bar smelled like ale and was silent. She ran to the stairs and shouted for Bear and Shorty.

She dragged her father and friends out to the porch to watch the last rays of the sun dip into the lake. The orange globe perched where the sky and water met. It was momentary, so transient and fleeting as if someone snatched it from the sky. In that last instant, it sent a bright flash across the mirrored water of Lake Idlewild, and its searing rays sizzled and burned out.

"Didn't like having to leave Nirvana, but this picture is sure something to have right in our front yard," Patrick said.

"Truly is," Bear said, and grimaced as Cleo made a nest on his lap.

"I'd make some hot chocolate if anyone wanted a hot drink to help you sleep," Abby said, and made a face at their expressions of distaste.

"Backbreaking work helps me sleep," Bear said, and Shorty grunted agreement.

"A clean mind and good heart help me sleep," Patrick said. "Never had trouble nodding off."

"You have your blarney stone in your pocket, Da? Sounds like you're kissing it tonight."

She looked at the men in her life. She'd been blessed the day Shorty and Bear came home, and she'd do everything in her power to keep them with her . . . or near.

"I guess I'm it. Whiskey?" she said.

She came back with a tray of short glasses half filled with Patrick's best Irish whiskey. When she sat, four rockers clicked in rhythmic movement, heads tilted back, and eyes watched the mesmerizing water.

"What is it about water?" Bear asked. Rock, creak, rock.

"The cousins were here today," Abby said. Rock, creak, rock.

"Cousins?" Bear said. "Oh, not your relatives, but *the* cousins."

Abby nodded in the deepening dark.

"Why?" Patrick asked.

"I guess why not," Bear said. "They go where they want."

"Didn't mean they shouldn't. Just, did they have a special reason for visiting?" Patrick said. "I must've been in the kitchen and missed em."

"You surely did miss it." She told them about Sue's display of undergarments, the needles and napping legs, and watched laughter light their eyes.

"I invited them to church," she said.

Chairs stilled. Shorty choked on his drink, and cleared his throat.

"You did what?"

"Invited them to services this Sunday . . . and to the Chautauqua."

"Well, that, maybe. But church?" Bear said.

"You do understand what they do for their livelihood?" Patrick said.

They all heard her neck crack as she twisted and tilted it, stretching out the kinks.

"What does their work have to do with going to church?" she said.

Shorty laid a huge hand on her forearm, covering it from elbow to wrist. It occurred to her that he could snap it in two without moving from his chair or even changing the rhythm of his rocking – if he had been rocking, but he wasn't at the moment. He was staring at her.

"What?" she said, drawing out the word and feeling defensive.

"You trying to create paradise all by yourself?" he asked.

Abby's eyes glowed in the dark, huge black pupils with green circles surrounded by white clouds.

"No. I'm not doing that. It's just . . . they're lovely women, and . . . I like them."

"Lovely?" her father said, rotating his shaggy head to peer at his daughter's face. "You bringing Cassandra, the witchy woman, too?" he asked, not at all unhappy with his daughter. He loved it that she collected people like stamps and knickknacks.

Abby straightened and stiffened her spine as if she was under attack. Her chin lifted, and she did her best to look down her nose at all of them.

"Maybe. Maybe I'll pick them all up for church on Sunday. Harrumph! I would if we had a bigger buggy. It might do you all some good to go, too. I'll be singing," she added, with a toss of her head.

That stopped the rockers. Again.

"Well, hell. I'll be there," Shorty whispered, slamming his hand on the arm of the chair.

Bear agreed, and Patrick went in for refills to celebrate singing, or sinners, or owls. Didn't matter. Could've been unicorns and leprechauns.

The hotel filled on Friday afternoon, and it felt like a festival. Jackson and Betty came early and pitched in with everything from carrying bags, to giving directions, from serving drinks to helping Patrick in the kitchen and washing dishes.

The porch was packed with eager faces, reluctant to leave the view, yet eager to settle in and make Idlewild their home for a few days. They stood in the warm, fresh air and gazed out at dark blue water and tall pines, awe and anticipation a bright glow in their eyes.

Yet, the hope some wore was laced with hesitance. They fought against apprehension that crept in around the boundaries of joy and recognized their own learned and practiced skepticism in the faces next to them.

Abby showed them to their rooms, told them where they could swim or fish, where the row boats were docked, and how to find the footbridge to the island. Smiles stretched and crinkled their eyes.

She slipped out to listen to the speakers and music in brief moments when the guests were all occupied at Chautauqua events, but she could hear the music from the porch, and she opened windows to let in the sounds while she worked.

They left Jackson and Betty in charge on Sunday morning so Patrick could hear Abby sing. Folks stood shoulder to shoulder under the pavilion; it overflowed with worshippers.

"I think they came just to hear you," her father said as they approached.

"God, I hope not. Wouldn't want to disappoint them."

"Nervous?"

"My heart is banging like a kid is in my chest playing with a kettle and wooden spoon."

He hugged her, told her she'd do fine, and passed her around to Shorty and Bear as they walked up, just in time for the reverend to announce the duet.

It was a hopping song, and the choir clapped and swayed from side to side. Abby and Edna's voices rose above the choir, and soon the congregation joined in on the chorus, stomping their feet and clapping their hands, too.

Patrick's face glowed with pride. Shorty, standing a full foot above Patrick, said, "She's a beautiful girl, your Abby, and sings like a whippoorwill. Can you see her? Want to get on my shoulders?"

Patrick gave him an elf frown.

"Nope. I know what she looks like, and I can hear her."

After the service, the visiting reverend said he'd baptize any who were so inclined in the beautiful waters of Lake Idlewild, God's baptismal, according to Reverend Hammond.

He led the crowd to the water's edge and saw Cleo sitting at the end of the dock, washing her black paws with a pink tongue. Her tail flicked as if she was dancing in time with the music of the fiddle and guitar. The reverend stopped the procession to watch, turned to the group and told them Cleo was baptizing herself as we all should, every day.

"But not with your tongues," he added, with an unpastor-like grin. He went on and on about the black cat with the green eyes until a group gasp froze his words, and the crowd went silent. He turned to look for the cause.

Sally and Sue, in matching red, silk dresses flowing down to their ankles, strolled through the crowd, parted it like Moses did the sea, and walked directly up to the reverend. Sue tugged at the neckline of her dress, trying to cover her breasts. Sally patted her hair and tugged at Sue.

You could hear whispers move among the congregation, but in between the hissed words was stunned, awestruck silence. It was a dead yet electrified sound, like lightening had just cracked across the sky, and they were waiting for the next one to split the heavens.

Heads craned. Mothers drew their young children closer as if proximity to the cousins might taint them, and, like a plague, they might catch some horrific disease they'd all heard stories about. Some covered the eyes of their sons. Who knew why. Maybe they were expecting the women to strip naked before their eager eyes.

"We came to be baptized," Sally said to Reverend Hammond. "Never been. Isn't that right, Sue?"

Sue nodded, but the fear in her eyes would drive a stake through the heart of Satan.

The reverend opened his mouth to speak, but closed it again when Sue crumpled to the ground. He bent to her, pulled her lids open and peered in, put a finger to her neck to find a pulse. He shook his head and lifted his shoulders in confusion.

"She does this," Sally said, pulling the reverend upright. "She'll be fine. Isn't that right, Mrs. Adams?"

Every head in the congregation turned toward Abby as if the group was a wave on the ocean. Abby waited, expecting the tidal surge to crash upon the shore. Her eyes grew huge, eyebrows raised, mouth opened with no sound coming out. Her face turned red, like she'd spent all day in a July sun.

She didn't move forward to help. She froze, a single, silent voice hiding in the shelter of the pavilion in plain view of many. She nodded.

"I'm just saying . . ." Sally continued, "that she kinda did this the other day at Miss Abby's, so she saw it. That's all." She nodded at the crowd, expecting them to understand the simple explanation.

"So . . ." the reverend said, "did she swoon in religious fervor?"

"Oh, no. Because her legs were napping at Abby's bar. And she's afraid of water . . . because she's really short and well-fed. That's all."

Titters came from the first half of the congregation, those who could hear Sally's words. The back half stood, so they could see, and were mumbling to each other that these women shouldn't be here. Their chosen professions should preclude baptism, or something like that.

Sally turned to look at the crowd, kicked her cousin gently with the toe of her boot, and then scanned the crowd for Abby. Sue woke, groaned and grunted as she tried to sit up, and Sally gave her a hand, actually two hands. She leaned back, her body at a forty-five-degree angle as she pulled while Sue got to her feet. Once up, she nodded briskly to Reverend Hammond and said she was ready.

More vociferous objections came from the rear, but the reverend held a hand high into the sky, at least it felt that way to the sinners in the back. His voice thundered as if coming from the overhead clouds, white cumulous next to stratus, looking like a storm might burst straightaway.

"Jesus would wash her feet," he roared. "Are you without sin?" And the congregation grew silent. Eerily silent. Must have been a lot of sinners in the crowd.

He held out his hand to Sue, and she grabbed it, tugged it to her voluminous breast, and he let her. They walked to the water's edge, and Sue looked up at the sky. She kept her face turned to heaven as he led her in, all the way up to her waist. He turned her so he could tilt her backwards into the water, and she let him do that, too. Her back grew wet, her shoulders, her head, then her abundant breasts. All the way in he pulled her, and still she let him.

When he'd left her there long enough for the bubbles to stop and for the congregation to become concerned he was drowning her, most likely due to her sinful ways, he pulled her up. Her face was radiant, glowing, smiling and wet.

She blinked water from her eyelashes and threw her chubby arms around his waist.

"I'm not afraid of water!" she said.

"And you are saved," the Reverend added.

"And I'm not afraid anymore!" Sue insisted. She pounded the water with the flat of her hand sending spray over several of the closest viewers. "I'm pretty light in the water. I'm gonna learn to swim!"

Chapter Ten

With autumn, Idlewild emptied of visitors, and the village grew quiet, except for sounds of wildlife. From the hotel porch, bundled in warm coats, they watched ducks and geese land in crooked v-formations, their honks and cackles setting up a brouhaha. They splashed onto the water and rested for a day or two, feeding on minnows and foraging in nearby grass before moving southward.

At night, they watched raccoons busily fattening up for the winter, catching crawfish at the water's edge and pouncing on night crawlers and grubs after Cassandra and the cats slithered by. The raccoons' silent speed was bewildering and menacing to their prey as they moved from place to place.

And they listened to the yodel and tremolo of the loons marking territory, letting their brothers and sisters know they'd be back. The island region still belonged to them even in their winter absence – because it was theirs. They'd fought for it. The young loons who had ridden on their parents' backs in the spring were ready to make the long journey to the coast.

Their mournful wail accompanied Abby's sorrow as she waited news of Frank. A long time passed between letters.

She said goodnight and went to her room. She washed up, donned her long flannel gown and got into bed with Frank's last note. By the light of her bedside lamp, she read it again, as she'd been doing every night since she'd received it two weeks before.

It was full of the business of living – what he'd done during the day, who he'd been with, what the mess hall had served, what the town looked like. The details brought his world to life. It gave her a sense of his day, what it was like to be in France during wartime, but left him out. What it was to be Frank, her husband.

She held the paper to her nose hoping to smell his fingers or the hand he'd held it with, some scent of him, but it was paper. That's all. Cheap army paper that had flown across the ocean and smelled more of salt water than him.

A tear slipped from her eye to the pillow, and she swiped at her face, annoyed it was there.

Phantom attacked the envelope lying on her lap, knocked it to the floor and leaped on it. Cleo, who was hiding under the bed, ran out, grabbed the corner of it and tugged. It was tattered by the time Abby saved it from their tug of war game, full of holes from their teeth and shredded by long claws.

"Look what you did, Phantom. Naughty Cleo," she said with a grateful chuckle. "Thanks."

She put it with the letter and back under her pillow where she kept the most recent one until the next came in. The rest were in a box under her bed, lined up by order of date. She prayed the last date would be soon and she would have room in the small box for them all, that she wouldn't need a second container, or a third.

Hammers and saws accompanied fall days that skidded into winter, and the shingled roofs of cabins continued to sprout into view around the lake and in the center of it on the island. With cold weather, many of the rooms at the hotel were frequently empty, and Abby breathed a well-earned sigh of relief. It was short lived.

"I need help," Edna shouted from the door as she stomped snow off her boots."

Abby poked her head from one of the guest rooms upstairs where she'd been waxing the pine floor.

"You? With what?"

"Soldiers' care packages. I need knitters and bakers and candy makers."

"Sounds like a nursery rhyme," Abby said, slapping her thigh and giggling. "Do you already have a butcher and candlestick maker?"

"Funny girl. Do you know how to do any of those things?"

"I do a mean job of cutting a chicken apart. Does that count?"

"That *is* mean. I never would have thought it of you." Edna planted two fists on her plentiful hips and tilted her head to out-stare Abby. "Hmmm?"

"Okay. I know how to crochet, and Da bakes. Does that help?"

"Yes. Come down her."

"Bossy, aren't you?" Abby said, with a twinkle.

She taught young ladies to crochet scarves in the corner of the bar and had groups of women in the large hotel kitchen making fudge and fruitcakes to send to the soldiers. Patrick supervised the kitchen work, and was in his glory working with all the women. His Irish charm was in full bloom.

After several days of work, they met in the hotel bar to pack the goods for distribution and shipment.

"Who's running this to Baldwin?" Abby asked, packing newsprint around boxes of chocolate fudge and fruitcakes. "I'm worried we're already too late for Christmas arrival."

"I can't tomorrow. Jesse's mother is coming in."

Bunny shook her head, and Cassandra said she'd have to ride a cat.

"What about you, Betty?"

"Daddy needs me tomorrow."

The other three women said their men wouldn't like it if they took the buggy to Baldwin.

Abby grimaced. She'd hoped for a day off, but . . . the soldiers didn't get one, did they?

"I'll go with you, honey," Flora said. "Keep you company."

"Thanks, Flora. I'll have Marie hitched and the buggy packed by eight."

"Ouch. Early bird, aren't you?"

On the way back to town, Reverend Jenkins wildly waved his arms at her until she pulled the buggy up close to see if he was having a seizure or just being obnoxious.

"You alright?"

"I am, young woman," he said, but the three lines between his eyebrows said otherwise, and Abby wished she had kept on going, pretended she hadn't seen him.

"But I need your help," he said.

"With what, Reverend?" Abby asked, considering a flick of the reins to accidently get Marie galloping down the road.

"Building baskets for the area needy."

Abby made funny shapes with her lips, told herself she'd wanted to be involved in the community and be part of the Idlewild family. Now she was.

Okay, I made my bed. I'll pay the piper. Hmmm. Mixing clichés.

"When and where?" she asked when her lips were back in place.

"Well, I don't quite know. We haven't collected the goods as yet." He hurried on. "So, if you could canvass homes and get the ladies to making mittens and things, that would be great. Thank you so much, Mrs. Adams. Let me know if you need anything."

He nodded his bushy head up and down several times as he backed away from her, still talking, and getting out of there before she could protest.

"But . . . Damn it," she said, and whipped her head around to see if the minister had heard. If he had, he also knew he had a good thing going and didn't look back. His little feet were moving down the road double time.

Flora laughed nonstop all the way to her house, and Abby wanted to shove her to the ground, not help her down.

"It isn't funny," she groaned.

"If you'd seen your face, you'd think it was. Downright pissed off, it was. Never thought I'd see that look on sweet Abby Adams," Flora said, still chuckling. "The girl who can't say . . . well, never mind cuz I can cuss with the sailors."

"Thanks for coming with me, Flora. I appreciate it."

"You're welcome, and I'll help with the needy baskets, too. Just let me know what and when. And thanks for the laugh. I can always use a good one."

She stopped to see Edna before heading home, told her about Reverend Jenkins and chewed her pinky tip while her friend sniggered and pointed.

"What is it about me that makes people point and laugh?" she asked, jamming her hands in the pockets of her dress.

"You're such a chump," Edna said with a grin. She bent to hug Daisy and pretended to whisper. "Abby is not a role model, my sweet, smart daughter. She's a good person, but she doesn't understand the word 'no.'

"I do," Abby said. "It's just that he startled me, waylaid me, ambushed me out in the street. I could have run him over. I should have."

"Yes. Do that to the next person who asks you to do something for them. Or for anyone."

"Will you help with this new project?"

"No."

Abby gasped and her mouth fell open. She shuffled back a couple of steps and stared at her friend.

"No?"

"See? That's how it's done. And okay, I'll help. I'll just *help*. That's all."

Abby swatted Edna's arm and looked at Daisy.

"Your mother's not a good role model. She's a brat. I'm leaving now, but I'll expect you at the hotel tomorrow by ten."

During the week before Christmas, the hotel filled with people taking advantage of time off from work. Some of them were checking on the progress of their cabins and talking with contractors. Some simply liked staying at the hotel and enjoying the friendships they'd made with others during the summer.

They decorated a pine tree near the pavilion and gathered there on Christmas eve. Each hand held a lit candle, and torches flamed on each corner of the pavilion.

125

Snow had fallen during the day, and the ground lay pure and white around a nativity scene. Reverend Jenkins gave a brief sermon, and the children participated in a reenactment of the birth of Jesus.

Patrick held his daughter's arm, squeezing it every now and then when he saw her eyes mist over, and his voice was pure Irish tenor when he joined her in song.

"Did you ever think our savior could be dark skinned?" he whispered as the three wise men moved toward the baby lying in the manger.

Abby shook her head.

"But until now, I never gave it a thought." She slanted her head sideways, as if she could better know the scene in front of her, discern the color of Jesus' skin from a different perspective. "Guess it doesn't really matter. Does it?"

"Not for me."

Shorty's whispering voice said, "Nope. Can't think it should."

Bear nodded, caressing Phantom's arm draped across his chest, and the cat's purr grew in decibels. Abby caressed her father's arm much the same and sent a prayer out to Frank and the rest of the soldiers, all of them . . . on both sides.

"I don't purr," her father said.

Abby smiled.

I miss you, Frank. Please come home.

Stars burned bright in a dark winter sky. There was no moon glow to lessen the brilliance of each, and Abby rested her head against Shorty to gaze up at the astrological magic.

"Do you know the stars?" she whispered.

"Some."

"Can you use them for direction?"

"A bit. But you have to know where you want to be first."

She pursed her lips and scrunched her face. Shorty was in her brain, could see where her thoughts had been and where they were heading.

"True. Maybe I need to learn to navigate."

The children's nativity finished to great applause from parents, kinfolk, neighbors and friends. They sang more rousing renditions of old carols, finishing with multiple, heartfelt amens and halleluiahs, and dispersed, many heading back to the hotel where they were staying. Patrick and Abby, with Bear and Shorty beside them, headed the group.

They saw the paint on the door, gasped and stepped back, their heads spinning as they looked at it and each other with confused dread. An infamous white cross on a red background scarred the wooden hotel door in fresh, wet paint.

Every head turned to peer into the darkness as if the artist was skulking in the shrubbery, turned back to the cross and finally to their neighbors. Eyes questioned and hardened as they saw their dream resort go up in Ku Klux Klan flames.

Abby moved forward and touched it; her fingers came away dripping in red. She yanked the door open and asked the guests to go in.

"Patrick is going to offer you a drink on the house. Please go in while I take care of this."

"Get water, please, Shorty, Bear. I'll get rags."

They brought up several buckets of lake water and began scrubbing.

"Who would do this?" she said. "Who would ruin this night with hatefulness?"

"Many would, Abby," Shorty said. "Too many, and I worry about you."

"Why me? What did I do?"

"Upset somebody's status quo. Their singular place in the universe. I don't think this was a note meant for Patrick."

Shorty's voice was soft, making his words sound like a caress in the dark, but what they expressed was chilling, and she shivered as they crawled down her back.

"I didn't take anything from anyone," she said, rubbing harder on the paint and spreading it into a blob of blurred pink instead of the hateful Blood Drop Cross.

When they were finished and the door looked fresher than before, Bear and Shorty tossed the buckets of pink water into the road, and the three of them went on to the bar, watching faces and reading suspicion.

Heads turned toward them, talk quieted, eyes looked away, and Abby's heart sank. She hadn't done this terrible thing, but it seemed she'd earned their mistrust because of it.

She hoisted herself onto a bar stool and asked her father for a sherry. Bear and Shorty joined her, one on either side as if flanking her for protection in case the disquiet and uncertainty in the room combusted into flames.

Phantom perched at the far end of the bar, and Cleo strolled down the middle and stopped in front of her. She reached out to Bear, climbed his arm, and curled around his neck. Abby's lips formed a sad caricature of a smile.

Thank God for my cats.

She kept her back to the guests, and before long talk resumed, a semblance of comfort settled in and her shoulders returned to their normal position.

"Ignore it," Bear said. "Let it go away."

"I will. I am."

Chapter Eleven

Spring 1918

Abby pushed aside the hair tumbling into her face, smudging her cheeks with dirt and cussing as the locks fell back over her eyes. She slammed the hoe into the ground, and it shimmered and shook in her hand, stinging her knuckles. She was turning new earth for a vegetable garden, but it was hard work even in the loamy soil. She stretched and gave herself a minute to look around.

The air was full of the sounds of spring, and Abby turned her face to the sunlight and let her eyes scan the budding trees. A robin flew past with a blade of dried grass in her beak and headed for one of the nearby pines. They and the warblers had returned from the south and were building their nests. Flocks of ducks and geese settled on the lake with squawks and honks heralding their arrival.

"We heard you," Abby yelled back, laughing. "Everyone knows you're home."

She missed winter's tiny, dark eyed juncos and pale brown snow buntings. They'd disappeared with spring's warmth as they migrated north for colder climates.

She loved the slush that meant winter was ending, the crocus tips that peeped through early and survived snow, sleet and hail.

But spring brought more work, more people checking into the hotel, drinking at the bar and eating meals. Rooms needing to be cleaned and linens to be washed. She needed time to buy supplies, work up the kitchen garden, and her back ached.

She groaned and rubbed at her lower spine. If she could come up with an excuse to stay home from the soldier's group tonight, she'd take it.

Hah! Not a chance, she thought. Cecily was holding this one at the farm. Well, she was going to be late as usual. She couldn't leave while the bar was still full of drinkers.

Her father yelled at her from the porch.

"Rest your back at bit, lass. Take a wee break."

He sat with his feet on the railing, his face tilted up to catch the sun.

"And if I rest, who'll fit up this garden?" she yelled back. "The leprechauns? The fairies?"

"Aye. Maybe they'll come this night, and by morning we'll have tomatoes and potatoes and corn!"

"And you're Rumpelstiltskin, too," she said, laughing at her father's dimpled grin. She couldn't help it, and neither could he. His innate charm couldn't be escaped.

"Come on. Sit with your old da a bit."

Abby leaned her hoe against the side of the building, brushed the dirt from her hands, and trudged up the steps. She fell into the rocker next to him and tipped back with a sigh of delight.

"Feels way too good," she said.

"It's a good day to sit in the sun."

"But not when there's work to be done."

"You're a poet, Daughter. And when you're resting, there is no better labor than rest. You work too hard."

"I wanted to get the ground worked up before the dinner crowd, and then I have to go to the farm. The women's group is tonight – for the soldiers."

"Let Shorty or Bear drive you. I don't like you out alone at night."

"Since when do I need a chaperone?"

Patrick's eyes clouded, and he watched Cleo tightrope walk the porch railing, tail flicking, eyes narrowed, ears drawn back in stalk mode. It was the way Patrick felt, too. He'd like to track down the man who'd violated his property.

"Since the cross on the door. You know that was some kind of warning."

"I do. But I don't like changing my habits because of that cross, or because of idiots."

"Calling me an idiot? Do it anyway. For me."

Abby jabbed her foot out as if she was kicking someone. "That's what I think about them." She was miffed that she agreed with him. "I'll see if either is available. Maybe they have dates."

It was a light night at the hotel, and as soon as Shorty had cleaned up and eaten supper, they drove to the farm.

"What will you do while we're working?" she asked him.

He leaned against the seat back and turned to her.

"What is it you do?"

"Knit, crochet, quilt, cook things that will keep. Package stuff up when enough is ready."

"Then I'll knit, crochet, quilt, cook candied peel or package."

"Candied peel? What do you know about that?"

"My ma used to let me help her in the kitchen. I did it lots, especially at Christmas."

Abby considered his profile. It embodied strength, and she felt safe in his company.

"You miss your family, Shorty?"

"Got one right here," he said, so lightly she wasn't sure of his words, but didn't want to ask him to repeat them.

Frank's mother, Emily, met them at the door and summoned them to the parlor. Shorty rolled his eyes behind her back, and Abby giggled. Mrs. Adams glanced back in time to see Abby's eyes staring at the ceiling corner, all innocence and sweetness.

She punched Shorty in the side and whispered, "Behave."

"Mr. . . ."

"Shorty," he said, cutting her off.

"Mr. Shorty," Emily said, tilting her head back to look him in the eyes. "I don't know if you want to wait here in the parlor or . . . I don't know why Abby couldn't have come on her own."

"I could have, Mother Adams, but my father has been anxious since the door painting."

Emily pursed her lips, a triplet of deep lines running across her brow, and murmured something unintelligible.

"And it's no trouble," Shorty said. Mrs. Adams found herself leaning in to hear his words. In fact, all the ladies in the parlor were silent, listening.

"She can ride back with me, Shorty," Edna said. "There's room with Bunny, Betty and me. Isn't there, Ladies?"

He shook his head.

"I brought her. I'll take her home. Told her Pa I would. Sides, no reason I can't help out here."

Abby's smile wavered, and she pulled at her ear.

"It's okay," she said. "Let's just get to work. What would you like to do, Shorty?"

"Whatever works for you ladies. I'm at your disposal."

"Nice, Abby. Wish I had a Shorty," Edna teased.

"What?"

"Someone to carry me around and do my bidding."

"I . . . he doesn't. It isn't like that."

"Not so sure your husband would appreciate that, Mrs. Falmouth," Emily Adams said. "Not many would be so understanding as my Frank."

Abby's neck reddened and her hands clenched.

Cecily dragged Abby to the quilting frame and told Shorty to help pack boxes for shipment in the dining room. Abby's face flamed, and she wasn't sure why. She saw Frank's mother's eyes follow the big man as he left the room and bounce back to her. She turned her back so she wouldn't have to see the woman's curious glare.

Her hand shook when she picked up the needle, and it took several stabs through the layers of fabric before her stitches were even and straight. Cecily's chatter helped as she and the others settled into the activity.

Quilting was usually restful, providing a way to communicate without the starts and stops that obligatory socializing caused. When you quilted with a group, you didn't need to talk – or you could. If you weren't a chatterer, you could listen, provide an occasional *um* or *uh huh* to remain part of the contented group. This time it took a while for the quilting harmony to be real.

Mrs. Adams eyes rarely left Abby, who felt as if she was the one in the middle of a war zone. She should ask them to make a soldier's goody box for her. She snorted at the nonsense in her brain, and the quilters glanced at the odd quacking noise she'd made, raised their brows and went back to stitching.

The footbridge from the mainland to the island in the middle of Lake Idlewild had been completed the summer before, and this spring it was full of people walking back and forth just for the simple pleasure of it. Many had taken the Pere Marquette or other trains to Reed City or Baldwin, and carriages from depots to Idlewild.

They'd heard of Dr. Dan Williams and came to look at his home, get a glimpse of the famous man and maybe buy a lot of their own. Jesse Falmouth and Bill Sanders were everywhere, showing prospective buyers around, renting out row boats and setting up guided horse treks.

Idlewild was a beehive of activity. Several year-around homes were finished or in the works, and one couple had moved into a tool shed to wait for the completion of theirs. According to them, they were never leaving Eden.

Trees were toppled to make room for construction, and a line of small one-room cabins grew up overnight, called dog houses due to their size. Guests could rent them by the day, week, or for the entire summer and shared outhouses set back by the tree line. They drew their water from a communal hand pump, packed cold lunches to eat in the sunshine or had their meals at the hotel. Patrick never left the kitchen trying to feed them all.

"I'm gonna put out notices to find a kitchen worker," Abby told him. "You need help."

He wiped sweat from his brow and grinned. "I could use some in the summer. It's a wee bit busy."

"Can you think of anyone we know who could use the work?"

"Nope. Put up some signs, and we'll see what we get."

Abby posted notices one day and had a caller the next, a young woman who didn't look old enough to leave school, but claimed she was. Blonde hair hung down her back to her waist, she had freckles sprinkled over her nose, and her slender body looked as though she had yet to hit puberty. She appeared too frail for heavy kitchen work, and Abby asked her if she could lift the massive kettles.

"I throw cows," she said, "and I slaughter hogs. I think I can move a kettle of soup."

Abby straightened and felt she'd just been chastised.

"I see. Well, do you know how to cook?"

"My ma died when I was young and I have four brothers. I do it every day."

They sat at a small table in the bar, and Al Tatum laid her hands in front of her. Her nails were chipped and short, but clean. Her shirtdress was too small for even her slight frame, but it was clean, too.

Abby couldn't think of many things to ask her other than what would her family do without her during the day.

"I'll get up early," she said.

"You're hired, then. Let's go meet my father. You'll love him, I'm sure."

"Mebbe," she said.

"By the way," Abby said. "Al is a different name for a girl. Is it a family name?"

"I should've been a boy."

"Four boys and they wanted another?"

"Guess so."

"I'll bet your mother was happy it turned out the way it did."

"Don't think so."

Abby let it go.

Patrick showed her around the kitchen, said he'd see her in the morning, and tracked Abby down in the lobby.

"She's a bit strange, don't you think? And a wee mite," he said.

"She is, but she needs work and she's tough. I think she'll be fine."

Cecily came through the door dragging Chunk and Bailey along with her.

"I just saw the Tatum girl leaving. What's she doing off the farm? Didn't think that was allowed."

"Really? Why do you say that?"

"Just the way it's always been. It was the same for her ma when she was alive. Those Tatum men worked her to death."

"Come on. You're not serious," Abby said.

"I am. To a Tatum, a female is nothing. She's free labor is all. Has a passel of brothers that use her as a slave. That's what I hear."

"Well, she's working for us now," Patrick said. "In the kitchen with me."

"That's a surprise," Cecily said. "I wonder they'd allow it. Now I think about it, maybe they need money. The men sure don't want to work for it."

"That's harsh," Abby said.

"And true. I've known them forever. They come from my neck of the woods."

Patrick ambled off to the kitchen, and Cecily sent Chunk and Bailey out to play.

"Where you headed? Want some iced tea?" Abby asked.

"Sure. And I'm headed right here. I wanted to talk with you."

"Something the matter?"

"Sort of."

They went into the dim, cool bar, and Abby poured two tall glasses of tea. Her face settled into a frown as she put them on the bar and sat at one of the stools. She didn't like the queasy way she was feeling or her sister-in-law's expression.

"Spill it," she said.

Cecily took a sip and grimaced.

"That bad? I thought it was pretty good."

"No. It's good. Sorry. I just don't know how to say what I came to tell you."

Abby stirred her tea and squinted.

"Just say it."

"Okay. It's this. Our mother-in-law has been going on and on about you and your friends, Shorty and Bear, and you and practically everyone else in town. But especially Shorty. She doesn't think you act like a married woman, and she thinks you're too involved with all the colored people in Idlewild. Like doing the Chautauqua and all. There. That's it."

"That's it?"

"Isn't that enough?"

"Plenty."

"Actually, there's more. She says you're not a good wife or Frank wouldn't have gone to war, and if he dies, it's your fault."

"Now, is that all?"

"And you should live at the farm with the rest of the Adams clan. Now, that's all."

Abby tugged the ribbon holding her curls at the nape of her neck. It came away in her hand, and the hair fell over her shoulders in a glowing auburn mass. She shook her head trying to rid herself of the growing anger and buried her face in the strands.

"So, does the whole Adams clan sit around at night discussing my marriage and my activities?"

"No, but sometimes Terry and George talk about it. Frank's their brother. They worry about him," she added, as if that made their conversations appropriate and accurate.

"And your husband, Terry. Does he think he should choose my friends, too, like their mother does?"

"It's not like that."

"It *is* like that, Cecily. And I'm sorry I don't fit in the Adams' book of life. Shorty and Bear have been my family since I was young. And I don't adjust or control friendship by skin color."

Cecily finished her tea in silence and got up to leave. Abby regretted speaking harshly to her, regretted the whole conversation, and reached for her hand.

"I'm not mad, Cecily."

"I just thought you should know, Abby. That's all."

Abby nodded and tried to smile.

"I know. I'll think about what you said. I really will. And I appreciate you coming to see me."

"I did it because I like you, Abby. And I want things to be okay with you and Frank."

Abby hugged the shorter girl and rested her chin on Cecily's head.

"I like you, too. I do."

She was too busy to think of anything except serving drinks for the rest of the day, and the happy chatter and laughter boosted her spirits. She got to know some of the folks who had bought lots and were ready to build. Their eyes were lit with the eager spark of ownership in the nation's first resort for colored people, and Abby envied them their single-minded goals.

Jackson raced around the room, balancing trays of drinks, taking orders and flashing his toothy smile for tips. He'd learned how to increase his wage and was good at it. Abby couldn't help but smile with him as she watched. She hoped the new hire would be half as good as the first two.

Bear, Shorty, Cleo and Phantom perched at the end of the bar, one cat on broad shoulders and one curled on an arm soaking up caresses. Her family . . . and she was reminded of Cecily's words. A dark cloud settled in her eyes, and Bear watched as she fought it. He didn't know what caused it, but he knew it was there. He'd known Abby long enough to read her.

During a lull, he said, "You good?"

"Sure. I'm fine."

He nodded and knew she lied.

"Busy."

"Well, between running the hotel, and running the town," Shorty said, a slight grin crinkling his eyes.

"I'm not running it, but it *is* growing, and it's exciting! I love being part of it."

"Tell me about your next Chautauqua," he said.

"We're bringing Populist Party Reform speakers. You know about them," she said.

"I'll bet you're gonna tell us," Patrick said, coming up behind her to pour himself a drink

She poked his belly and grinned, getting excited again.

"They champion the rights of the common man, fight against domination by the rich and powerful, and battle political corruption."

Abby had a hand in the air like she was a warrior, and all three men laughed. Some of the other guests were listening to her small tirade and grew interested.

"But there's more," she said, eyes wide and intent.

"More?" Patrick teased. "Dinna say, couldn't possibly be more."

"You're joshing me, but, yes, over and above everything else, they support literature, music and philosophy. Don't you see? That's what Idlewild needs, those things that elevate us and separate us from the barbarians."

"I think she just called us barbarians, Shorty," Bear said.

"I'm offended. You?"

"You're a big piece of the Idlewild pie, Abby girl," Patrick said. "You keep on doing what you know how to do."

"I know nothing about growing a town," she muttered. "I'm just guessing what's good for the people of Idlewild cuz I want it so much, but I really don't know, and my in-laws don't like me much."

She cursed her silliness in blurting out that last part, and anger pinched her face. Thinking about helping the town had made her think of Frank and his family and how much they disliked her work.

"I didn't mean that," she said, trying to cover it up.

"I'm not so barmy about them, either, wee girl."

She turned to wrap an arm around him.

"I haven't been a wee girl since the womb, Da. In fact, I think I was big there, too."

In her room that night, after getting ready for bed, she lay in her pristine, white nightgown, snuggling with her cats. Alone. Her husband had left her for Europe. Adventure in a foreign land was an illicit affair.

And that's how I feel about it.

She didn't think Frank had gone to war for the good of the country, even though he'd do his part as a soldier and never shirk responsibility. She believed he went to see Europe, but she'd never say that to Frank's family – or hers, never say it out loud to anyone. It was one of those gut things that gnaw at you, though, a thing you just knew. Europe was the other woman.

The second gut thing was that it wasn't his fault; it was because of her. She was the reason Frank left. She hadn't been enough to keep him home.

She rolled to her stomach, squashing Cleo, who yelped and moved to her other side.

"Sorry, sweetie."

When Frank came home, maybe she would have to curtail her work in the village, concentrate more on the hotel and on being a wife. She could do that. She wanted children, a family and Frank's affection, more than anything. She wanted him to like her again.

"After this event, Cleo. I'll cut back. I'll be better."

Phantom slipped up to lay across her back. "You're heavy, boy. Let me turn over."

With a cat at each side and her hands rubbing their heads, she reviewed the coming Chautauqua.

Mrow wawah, Phantom grumbled as she scratched harder than she intended, and Cleo's mouth opened wide, without sound, but she was clearly complaining, too.

With the Populists in mind, she drifted off to dream in full battle dress, sword in hand, fighting savages for the right to make music. She woke, sweating with the nightmare combat, but smiling. It was still dark when she tiptoed to the kitchen to get an early start on breakfast for the guests.

Al showed up at six, and Abby threw her an apron and handed her a cup of coffee.

"Morning. Good to see you again," Abby said, smiling at the tiny young woman.

"Yup."

"You should tie your hair back, Al. If you need a ribbon, I can lend you one."

"Why?"

"Just to make sure no hair falls into the food. That's all."

"I've been cooking all my life and never had no one complain about that."

Abby bit her lip. Not off to a good start. She stuck the tip of her pinky between her teeth and removed it. Trying not to sound irritated, spoke again.

"I have a lovely blue ribbon I'd like you to use when you're in the kitchen. I'll go get it."

When she came back in, Al was scrubbing the potatoes Abby had put in water.

"I'll tie it up since your hands are all wet," she said and pulled back the girls long blonde hair, not giving her a chance to object. "It's really pretty," Abby said. "Like pale sunshine."

Al didn't respond.

"There. Done. I'll get the sausage going if you want to cut those potatoes for frying."

Al nodded.

Not another word was said until Betty entered looking for a cup of coffee. She came to an abrupt stop just inside the door and stared at the new employee. Neither spoke.

Abby poured coffee for all of them, handed Betty hers and said, "You know Al Tatum, Betty?"

"Surely do. Know all of em."

"Al is going to work with my father in the kitchen. It's getting too much for him to handle alone."

Betty sipped, her eyes never straying from Al's knees.

"Just kitchen?" she asked.

Abby looked back and forth from Al to Betty, tiptoeing through the charged atmosphere chilling the kitchen since Betty walked in. It was pure ice even with the heat of the cook stove and boiling water.

"That's the plan. Why?"

"Nothing. Take my coffee upstairs and get started," Betty said, and without another word, backed out of the kitchen leaving the door swinging behind her.

Abby followed.

"I don't think anyone's up and out yet. What's the matter, Betty?"

"Nothing. I'll just sweep down here then."

She put her coffee on the bar and grabbed a broom. She was sweeping, her eyes intent on her job as Abby shook her head and went back into the kitchen.

She put steaming bowls of eggs, potatoes fried with onions, and browned maple sausage patties on the buffet just as Betty finished cleaning the bar and went into the lobby area. People shuffled down for breakfast, sniffing appreciatively, and there was no further chance for talk. Patrick trailed them and went to the kitchen to begin the lunch menu, and she left him to deal with Al.

The weekend brought a full house, and Abby checked people in, ran up and down the stairs, carried bags, brought them drinks, gave directions, and welcomed them to Idlewild. She explained when the meals were, hefted heavy bags and groaned climbing the stairs. One burly man reached for his bag at the same time she did, yanked his hand back and scratched his neck with it, unsure what he should do.

"I'll get it, sir," she said, showing her big white teeth. "That's my job."

"You, skinny, little, white girl, are gonna haul my luggage up those stairs?"

"Yes, sir. And you only got one out of four correct."

He tilted his head and raised his eyebrows.

"Excuse me?"

"I'm not little, skinny, nor a girl," she said, grabbing his suitcase and heading for the stairs. He could do nothing more than follow. She waited for him at the door so he could unlock it, settled the bag on a chair and said, "but I am white. You got that one right. Welcome to Idlewild, Mr. Cassidy. Enjoy your stay."

His booming laughter followed her all the way down the stairs and caused a chuckle from her and others waiting in the lobby to register.

Sometimes that happened, and Abby was getting used to it. The regulars teased about having a white woman fetch for them. She could tell when it bothered someone and learned who she could tease and who she couldn't. She liked it better when she could.

Idlewild filled with folks, the Populist Party speakers, jazz musicians, poets, and people who were eager to be a part of it all. Buddy Black was back with his guitar, and Abby wasn't about to miss hearing him play. On Saturday evening, when the bar was empty, she sat on the porch listening, her head resting against the chair back, her feet tapping to the rhythm.

"That man can wail a blues," Shorty said, taking the chair next to her.

"That he can. Makes me want to sing the blues."

"Do it. You've got what it takes."

She looked sideways at him.

"First, I'd have to get a dog and then make him run away," she said laughing.

"I could steal your cat."

"Bear already did, but it's not the same thing. Did you ever hear blues lyrics bemoaning the loss of a kitty? My woman done left me and my old blue cat run off," she sang.

"I think you've got something there. Brandy new."

Shorty's smooth voice melted into the strains of music drifting from the pavilion and into the dusk settling on the lake. It became part of the loon's somber call. Abby's eyes watered and she blinked it away, berating herself for being a sentimental fool.

"It's so beautiful," she said.

"The music?"

"Everything. Sunset on the water, the sounds, the people. Why is it sad?"

"I don't know, Abby."

The screen door banged softly and Phantom strolled out, climbed in Abby's lap and curled up.

While Buddy Black was playing his last song of the night, an orange light flickered in the island. At first, it looked like a campfire close to one of the newly built doghouses until it grew larger than the cabin itself.

Flames and fear took hold, and people ran from the pavilion, found buckets, rakes and shovels, and carried them across the footbridge. Their feet pounded the wooden slats of the bridge, echoing urgency across the water.

It didn't take long to put out the fire with so many people helping, but the blackened walls were bleak and poignant reminders that it had happened, and unrest dropped over the crowd like a black shroud. They would see the charred building in their dreams that night, and some would picture the walls of their Eden crumbling even before it was built.

Unrest moved into their eyes and settled in the set of their shoulders. They were discouraged, and words weren't going to fix it. What could be said? It was an accident? It wasn't. It won't happen again? Why not? Bad things did. They knew it well.

Their shoes scuffed the ground, and they turned from the ashes to look at the lake, the shimmering of the moon on the surface, the concentric circles as a duck dove and surfaced, rippling the silver light.

But in some eyes, the flames brewed hunger, determination, and it showed in their bearing and their footstep. *This is ours, by God, and it isn't going to burn. This is ours.* The words became a silent mantra.

"I need a drink," someone said.

"Aye," Patrick agreed. "Abby'll set us up. Come on back to the hotel. Tis a dark night."

They descended on the bar like a swarm of hornets, their voices a low, constant buzz in her ears, filling the room, and Abby thanked God for Jackson. Notions concerning the fire darted from wall to wall, guesses about its origin, its intent. The men threw wild ideas across the tables, each one more preposterous than the last.

143

The lit match was held in the hands of opposition to the Populist movement, or an eager member of the KKK. Suppositions described a kid playing a prank all the way down to an angry, disgruntled lover.

A deputy sheriff showed up, his shiny badge causing some to try for an escape to their rooms, only to be halted by him. They obeyed, but irritation and distrust was in the set of their shoulders, the clench of their jaws, the deliberate vacant stare.

He made his way through the room quickly because no one had answers, only questions, and they wouldn't ask them of the deputy. He wouldn't have the answers. They'd known about flames and fear for generations. It was in their history, in their blood and breath. But they had no solutions.

Abby watched and waited her turn with the deputy. She was glad for Bear and Shorty at the end of the bar. The room held enough tension to eat with a knife and fork, and Abby knew tempers could flare, fists could fly. She'd been born in a lumberjack bar.

She kept an eye on the faces at all the tables, watching and gauging, but, so far, all was controlled. Jackson helped with his big smile and trays full of drinks. Bill Sanders moved around the room, soothing tempers, reassuring potential buyers with a smile charming enough to slide the skin off a porcupine.

It wasn't until after the deputy left, people relaxed enough to joke about the measly little fire. They did their best to make light of it and brush off the leftover mental ashes of the night. It had been a long day for them all, and Abby wished they'd go to bed, but there was comfort in community. Alone in their rooms, they'd have to face their anxieties and deal with the concerns of their wives and children.

Abby kept pouring, and they kept feeling better.

Al showed up before the morning coffee had percolated. She took the blue ribbon from her pocket and pulled her long hair back, looking at Abby as she tied it.

"Thank you, Al," Abby said, smiling, trying to warm up the taciturn young woman who nodded, washed her hands and reached for the slab of bacon lying on the table.

"Thick?" she asked.

"Yes. Thank you."

Bear and Shorty lumbered in, grabbed coffee, and slumped into chairs at the table where Al was slicing the meat. Both greeted her, and she kept her head down, focusing on her work.

Shorty rolled his eyes up to Abby and raised a brow.

"This is Al. Al, these are my friends, Shorty and Bear. They live at the hotel and help out."

She shrugged her shoulders and scratched her ear.

"Al is the new cook. Helping out Da most of the time and helping me in the morning for breakfasts."

"Welcome, Al. You'll like working for Abby and Patrick. They're good folks."

"Okay," Al said, and turned away to put the bacon in the pan. She kept her back to them until they ate and left with a kiss on Abby's cheek and a nod to Al.

"Strange," Abby whispered as she carried the dishes out to set up the morning buffet, and the girl was *Strange Al* from then on, but not out loud. She was surprised to see Betty sweeping up the bar.

"Morning. Don't you want your coffee?"

"Nope. Had some at home."

Betty swept, glancing at the kitchen periodically as if she was waiting for something to spill out through the doors and attack. She swung the broom in short, jerky movements, and the smile she gave Abby looked pasted on her face, never reaching her big, brown eyes.

"What's wrong, Betty?" Abby asked. "Something is. I know it."

Betty shook her head and continued sweeping.

"Nothing. Nothing's wrong. I'll just finish up here and head out to the lobby. See you upstairs when the folks rise."

"Want me to bring you some coffee when I come up?"

"If you want. Sure."

Abby shook it off. She wanted answers to her many questions but didn't want to meddle if the girl didn't want to talk.

She was finishing up the buffet, when a dramatically elegant woman came into the bar, looked around with intent, and selected a table near the window. She sat, folded her hands in front of her, and waited. Her back was rigid, and she stared straight ahead.

"Good morning," Abby said. "Breakfast is buffet style. You'll find eggs, fried potatoes, bacon, pancakes and coffee. Help yourself."

Abby went into the kitchen for the platter of pancakes, and when she came back out, the beautiful woman was still seated at the table, hands still folded.

Abby asked if she was waiting for someone, and the woman said, "For breakfast to be served."

Abby smiled and waved her hand at the buffet. "You probably didn't hear me. It's buffet style, Ma'am. You can serve yourself any time you like."

"My name is Mrs. Hamilton, and I don't serve myself, young woman."

"Oh! Well . . ." Abby said, stunned. "Would you like for me to bring a plate of food to your table?"

"I would."

Abby poured coffee and asked if she'd like cream and sugar. She nodded, and Abby fixed it and carried it to her table.   She went back to the buffet, filled a plate with breakfast food, took that and her silverware and spread it out in front of her.

Mrs. Hamilton sipped her coffee and frowned.

"There's too much sugar in here," she said.

"Oh, I'm sorry. I'll get another," Abby said, and ran for more. Put in less sugar and took it back to her.

"Maybe this will be better," she said.

She left the woman to eat and greeted guests as they started streaming in.

She smiled at Mr. Cassidy, the man who'd been surprised Abby would carry his luggage, and asked if he'd enjoyed the Chautauqua.

"I did, Abby. Until the fire, that is."

"I'm sure it was an accident," she said, hoping to lighten his mood.

"Sure," he said, eyes twinkling. "And I'm a skinny, little, white girl."

Abby chuckled and winked at him.

"I think you got all four wrong this time."

"Miss," a voice called from across the room.

"These eggs are too dry. I like mine a little on the runny side," Mrs. Hamilton said, pushing the yellow fluff around on her plate.

"Hmm. I'll see what I can do," Abby said, and managed not to roll her eyes until she turned away.

She quickly made more and ran them out to her on a separate plate.

"Anything else?" Abby asked.

"Not at the moment. I'll let you know."

She let her know frequently and persistently and kept Abby running back and forth through the entire breakfast period. She had little time left to refill the buffet bowls and trays, and she was getting more hurt and angry by the minute. She didn't know what to make of the woman or what to do about it.

She pinched her lips together and tried to keep from making eye contact with her, not wanting to give her any encouragement to ask for, or complain about, something else.

She went into the kitchen and threw herself into a chair, plopped her chin on a fist and tried to breathe. Just breathe.

"There's a woman out there who thinks I'm her personal servant," she said, more to the walls than to Strange Al.

"Colored?"

"Well, yes. What does that have to do with anything?"

"It's on purpose."

Abby straightened and stared at her.

"That's crazy."

147

She left the kitchen muttering invectives she hoped no one could hear.

Strange Al is wrong. But who did this woman think she was? She isn't the only guest in the hotel, and besides . . . this is buffet! Calm down, Abby. There's nothing you can do about it, and she'll probably be gone in the morning. It takes thousands of different leaves to make a tree. She's just one, and the tree is still magnificent.

Mrs. Hamilton walked out without a word, her head erect, her nose in the air, and Abby wondered if she stuck out her foot, would the woman see it before tripping and falling flat on her face? The desire was overwhelming. She restrained herself in the nick of time, and, when the door closed behind the cantankerous, bewildering woman, she wiggled her arms and shoulders like she could shake off the woman and evil thoughts like a dog coming out of the lake shakes off water.

The Chautauqua ended early since it was Sunday, and the hotel cleared out immediately after. Abby said goodbye to the guests, sad to see most of them go. Many of them had stayed at the hotel during each of the summer events, and they were beginning to feel like old friends. And some, like Mr. Cassidy, were instant friends.

"You'll be back, won't you?" she asked him.

"Sure will, little girl. I bought a lot yesterday, over on the island. Gonna build and move here as soon as I retire."

"You'll be back before then, though. You're nowhere near retirement age. Sorry about the deputy."

"Guess he was just doing his job. He does have a way about him, though."

"He questioned everybody, Mr. Cassidy. And he's brusque on his good days," she said, tugging the braid that lay over her shoulder. "He didn't single you out to be nasty to."

"And here I thought I was special."

He grinned, a big smile that crinkled his eyes and warmed her heart. She'd just met him, but it didn't seem that way. She reached for his hand and clasped it in both of hers with genuine affection.

"Come back soon. I'll tote your luggage any day," she said.

"That, my dear Abby, is definitely going to happen."

Toward evening, only Patrick, Shorty and Bear sat at the bar.

"I'm closing," Abby said. "Let's take our drinks to the porch. Watch the sun set."

When their rockers were in motion and the Chautauqua had been thoroughly dissected, she told them about Mrs. Hamilton. She was still stinging from the critical and obnoxious behavior of the woman. She couldn't let go of the hurt and thought maybe she'd done something to cause it, or, in the least, hadn't done anything to prevent it. She was confused and unhappy, even fearful of a repetition.

"Al said it was on purpose. She was treating me like her slave. Kind of saying it was because I was white and she wasn't."

"Could be," Bear said.

"Not all the nasty people in the world are white, Abby," her father said. "You've just been sheltered."

"I have not."

He nudged her foot with his toe. "Living in little bitty Nirvana all your life with just me and the lumberjacks around ye all the time . . . Aye, lass. You're my very own hothouse rose."

Abby saw Cassandra in the distance, poking along the road with a walking stick and her clowder of cats. The loon wailed, and an answering refrain echoed. It skimmed over the glass water, slid from shore to shore and back again, reverberating across the lake as if the water was only there for the evening song of the loon.

"I wouldn't treat anyone the way she did. It's like she hates me."

"Maybe she does, Abby. She may think she has reason to. Did you think only white people discriminated against others?" Bear asked.

"Long speech from you, Bear," Abby said. "You must mean it. I guess I never had reason to think about it before."

"What did you do?" Shorty asked.

"Whatever she told me to."

Abby gave a dark chuckle, and the men laughed, knowing she wouldn't have done anything else. At least, not the first time. Probably not the second time, either. Her cheek would've turned.

Maybe her father was right. She was a hothouse flower, oblivious to the world outside her own small one, ignorant of what it meant to be anything other than what she was.

Until now, it hadn't mattered because skin was a covering for the body to her. It kept the bones and tissues from falling apart. It wasn't a way of life, nor did it dictate life or you. But that was apparently a lie, and now she knew it.

She went to her room wondering if she could ask her friend, Edna, about it. Or maybe Bunny, who knew about sundowner towns. She'd been there. She'd seen the signs that proclaimed colored folks had to be out of the area by nightfall. But asking Bunny anything was tricky, and *that* was no lie.

On her knees, she prayed for Frank, for all the soldiers, and for Idlewild.

Chapter Twelve

Autumn 1918

Buddy Black's guitar strings wept. They bent across the guitar neck and the notes cried. They mourned. She could hear it from the porch. She didn't know the words, but they crawled under her skin and settled in her soul.

Everyone was at the pavilion, and the hotel was empty, so Abby skipped down the steps and ran to meet her father and friends at the Chautauqua. She could see the hotel from the grassy spot where they stood and would know if she was needed there.

They were at the back of the crowd, listening to Black's blues, swaying back and forth like an ocean tide surging in time to the music. The melody was haunting. It lingered in your soul long after the last note ended with a whispered prayer that the next notes would bring solace instead of sorrow. But blues knew no solace. It was grown from seeds of pain and heartache, nurtured on despair. Anguish *is* the color blue.

With an eye on the hotel, Abby watched Phantom streak from the porch, cross the yard to the pavilion, and leap onto Bear's shoulder.

"Phantom!" she whispered, chastising the cat. "Did he scratch you?"

"He never uses claws. He knows not to."

"I don't know who he loves more, Bear. You or me. You *are* cat man."

Abby draped an arm across Bear's back to rub Phantom and stayed there, moving in rhythm to Bear's swaying. It was comfortable, and before long Shorty was connected to her other side. She smiled and wrapped her arm around his back, too. So, she didn't have siblings, but she had Bear and

Shorty. Her makeshift brothers. Better than brothers because they chose her, and she chose them.

She ran to Foster's grocery after the breakfast crowd dwindled to pick up supplies for Patrick's lunch menu, wishing her father would plan ahead better so she could buy them in Baldwin.

She disliked the dusty little store more than ever, and she more than disliked the man who ran it. Joe always found a way to nettle her even when she promised herself to be charitable all the way from the hotel to the store.

He's alone and a pitiable, old man. A wretched person who harangues other people to make himself feel better.

"Wrong," she said to Phantom who trailed along behind her. "The man is just a jerk. But watch me smile and try to make his day."

She told the cat to wait outside, and he sat with a nod and a roll of his blue eyes, but before the door swung shut, he slipped inside and scooted around the middle shelving, out of sight.

"Bad cat," Abby whispered with a snicker.

Foster came out from the back room, running a hand through his hair and mumbling. Abby handed him the list and stood back. He shuffled around the room putting items on the grubby counter one at a time before scuffling back for another.

Abby wished he'd let her gather the things she needed and peered around the shelving to spot Phantom before he did. She was about to congratulate herself for composure beyond what should be required, when Foster bent to reach for a small bag of corn meal and Phantom, hidden between the bags, reached out a clawed paw and hissed. Joe fell backwards onto his back, and the bag flew across the room into a shelf and broke open. Flying cornmeal was everywhere, and Phantom leaped through the cloud of yellow. He paused at the door and sat there with regal nonchalance while Joe Foster screamed obscenities.

"I told you, no cats in my store," he yelled, turning purple in his anger. "No damned cats!"

"I'm sorry. He must have slipped in when I wasn't looking," she fibbed.

"You are foul! No good!" he said, pointing a knobby, shaking finger at her from his prone position on the floor.

Abby reached a hand to help him up, but he whacked it away.

"I don't need help. You do, sinner," he sputtered in rage. "You're the one's gonna need help. You and your galavantin with men. Fondling in public. You, a married woman. A disgrace. Disgusting."

Abby stepped back as if she'd been slugged, anger creeping in around disbelief.

"What on earth are you talking about?"

His eyes narrowed. Spittle grew at the corners of his lips.

"Don't need to tell you. You know."

Abby moved to gather her supplies, her face red with embarrassment and shock.

"And another thing," Foster muttered, getting to his knees and groaning as he stood. "Frank and his family ain't gonna like you turning colored and hanging around with em, specially that cat woman. She casts spells."

He was still grumbling and mumbling as Abby grabbed things off the counter and threw them into her bag.

". . . mebbe already did," Abby heard him sputter as she left the store.

Her feet pounded dirt, head down watching the tips of her work boots poke out from the hem of her skirt and hide again. Phantom raced ahead, stopping every now and then to look back at her and wait. His tail flicked back and forth at the tip, expressing annoyance and impatience. His eyes were blue slits.

"Coming," she said.

When she slowed her sprint down the road and looked up, she saw the pavilion where Buddy had broken her heart with his blues, the pavilion she had been instrumental in making happen. She'd helped bring the music and speakers, had been happy and excited to be part of growing Idlewild. Was it wrong?

She didn't know. She was beginning to think she didn't know a lot about most things.

She handed the groceries to Strange Al, said hello to her da, and went upstairs to clean rooms with Betty. This is what she did: feed people, clean their rooms, pour their drinks, feed them, clean up after them, make drinks for them. Her cycle of servitude. She usually didn't mind.

She found Betty in the second room, threw a sheet on the mattress, picked it up by the corner and shook it out. When it landed and the air had been pushed out, she yanked it straight, folded the corner, and shoved it under the mattress. She grabbed the top sheet and repeated the process with it and with the quilt, yanking it into place. When the bed was made, she shoved the dust mop under the bed, pushed it around the wooden floor and scooped up the dust to dump it in the waste can. While Betty polished the dresser and wash stand, Abby hung fresh towels, picked up their tools and left the room.

In the third room, Betty found her voice.

"Havin' a bad day? What's wrong?"

"Nothing."

The girl cocked one leg out and pursed her lips. Abby cracked a sad smile.

"You look like a fish."

"You ever see a black fish?" Betty said, one hand going to her ample hip.

"No. But you're not really black. You're kinda russet colored."

It was Betty's turn to grin.

"And you're pasty white."

"It's Irish white. I'm Irish."

"You ever see Ireland?"

Abby rested her chin on the top of the dust mop handle, her eyes going to the window as if she could see her father's homeland in the distance.

"No. I haven't, but I'd like to." Her voice was wistful, holding more sadness than her desire to see another land should have earned.

"I'd like to see Africa. Probably never will," Betty said.

She flipped the sheet onto the mattress, smoothed out the air, and tucked in her perfect hospital corners.

"Probably won't see Ireland, either," Abby said. "Took me a couple decades to get the five miles from Nirvana to Idlewild."

"You're kinda slow."

"Guess I am." She moved toward the window and pressed her fingertips on the chilly pane. "Thanks."

"For pointing out that you're slow?"

"No. Making fish lips."

Betty smacked her lips together to get Abby's attention and did a noisy imitation of fish kisses.

"Thank God for you, Betty."

On sunless days, fields of giant, angular sticks grow up out of the ground, like somebody planted crops of gaunt, useless, jagged things. Branches, like broken witches' fingers, were dark slashes against an angry, white sky. Cold winds had long since chased their leaves through the air, leaving them barren, trees without leaves, like mothers without children.

They were on the ground in a thick, rustling, orange blanket that moved from place to place on the whims of the wind. Brown whirligigs spun through the air and landed on the porch. She swept it every day, sometimes twice, but they came again and again, relentless in their need to find a place to propagate.

Squirrels scampered by with acorns between their teeth, looking for a burial ground for their booty. Abby promised to fill feeders with corn for them when the snow falls in case they forget where they'd buried their food. They liked her corn better, anyway. She'll make the trek to Nirvana to fill feeders for the critters there, too.

Ducks and geese flocked, arguing about who'll lead the formation south this year and when to go. Squawks ricocheted as they lifted off, wings splashing furiously against the water in their ascent, only to circle and splash down again. Waiting. They'll know when the time is right.

Wrapped in a thick shawl, Abby watched their antics from the porch, her hands around a hot cup of coffee. Phantom curled around her neck, and Cleo climbed onto her lap. She stroked ebony fur as she stared out at Lake Idlewild, eyes wandering aimlessly.

Two footbridges crossed over the water, the second one added late in the summer so folks didn't have to walk so far to get to the island.

Abby shivered feeling the effects of the sunless, cold day. The day and Joe Foster's careless, hurtful words still haunting her.

She'd spent some sleepless nights since he pointed his bony finger at her, and she needed to see Frank's family, link with him through them. But she was nervous, putting it off. What if they thought like the old man? What if they believed she was . . . doing things she shouldn't?

She rose, reluctant to make the trip to the Adams' farm and knowing she needed to. It wasn't just to reconnect with Frank's family, although that was the major impetus. She also wanted to arrange for shipments of food supplies, like eggs, milk and chickens. Unless she went into Baldwin twice a week, she was forced to do business at Foster's for perishables, and she was determined not to go there unless she had to.

She called to her father to say she was leaving, made sure Jackson knew he was taking over for her, shut Cleo and Phantom in the hotel, and left.

Old Marie looked sideways at her when she drew her out into the sunless day. *Not what I want to do*, the old girl said.

"I know. I don't like it much either." She rubbed the mare's velvet nose, touched her cheek to its softness and snuffled her pungent, dusty scent. "You're a good girl, Marie. A faithful friend. We'll go slow and take it easy."

It felt good to be away from the hotel, even if it was not the kind of day she'd choose for a jaunt or a place she wanted to go. Clouds made frothy humps across the sky, heralding snow, and Abby shivered.

156

She waved at Jesse, standing outside his office, and at Cassandra, walking down her long driveway. Ratty and Flora Branch passed her, heading in the opposite direction, and called out a friendly greeting. Everyone shouted acknowledgements like *stay warm* and *early winter this year*, all the salutations friendly folks use to stay connected. It was nice to be known in the community. Nice to be recognized.

She drove straight to the barn so Marie could wait in its warmth, tossed her some hay and walked to the house. At the door, she knocked quietly and opened it to call out. Frank's mother was kneading bread at the table. Her face blanched and eyes widened when she saw Abby.

"Come in. What's wrong?"

"Nothing, Mrs. Adams. I'm just visiting."

The older woman put a floured hand over her heart and left a dusty, white print there.

"So, you didn't get a telegram?"

"No. No! I'm so sorry. I wasn't thinking."

Abby walked around the table and put an arm around her mother-in-law's unyielding shoulders.

"Frank is fine. I brought letters for you to read." Abby rambled on. "Wanted to come before, but I've been really busy."

Emily Adams' eyes narrowed and glared, and she drew back her head and stiffened her spine.

"I don't believe that for a minute," she said.

"I have been, Mrs. Adams. Very busy, but it's starting to slow down now the weather's changed."

"That you wanted to come here before. Don't believe *that*, not for a second."

She dumped the dough into a bowl, wiped her hands on a towel and turned to Abby.

"From what I hear, you keep yourself busy in outlandish ways, Abigail Adams."

Terry Adams blew through the door with Chunk and Bailey hanging onto his arms. Their chatter gave Abby time to try to recover from Emily's verbal battering. She crossed her arms over her chest and backed away to consider what the woman was talking about. What did *outlandish ways* mean?

His head jerked up when he spotted Abby, and he gave her an angry nod in greeting. The atmosphere in the kitchen was more frigid than outside, and Abby feared she'd done some horrific deed. She cast about for the culprit but came up empty.

"Chunk, Bailey. Can I talk to your papa and grandma alone, please?" she said.

Terry pushed his sons into the parlor and turned back. "You have your nerve. What do you want?" he said.

"Why are you mad at me, Terry? What have I done?"

Mrs. Adams snorted and closed her eyes.

Abby uncrossed her arms, crossed them again and shivered in the cold.

Terry backed up to the cupboard and leaned against it, shoved his hands in his pockets and stared. His mouth was a straight line, his eyes slits. Abby had never seen him this way, and it frightened her. He no longer looked like Frank's handsome brother. This was a stranger, one she didn't want to know.

"Let's see," he drawled. "Your husband is off fighting a war, putting his life on the line for America. Right? Do I have that part dead-on?"

Abby nodded but couldn't speak. Her throat was too dry and her tongue was stuck to the back of her teeth.

"That's a start," he said. "He's hiding in filthy trenches while you . . . Mrs. Adams . . . are out in the open, not hiding at all, while you cavort with other men. Doing the dirty . . . in public."

Abby gasped. "No!"

His lip curled in disgust, and Abby pulled hard at the braid hanging over her shoulder and chewed at the inside of her cheek.

"Don't try to deny it. It's no use. I saw you. I was there."

"But what you're saying isn't true. I wouldn't. Ever!"

"You forget, Abby. I said, I was there, at the Chautauqua."

Abby shook her head, put her hands over her flaming cheeks, horror flooding her eyes.

What could he have seen? Nothing. There was nothing to see.

And then she recalled standing with Bear and Shorty, arms around each other, listening to the music.

"Oh!" she said, relief flooding her. "They aren't men," she said. "And we weren't doing the . . . anything. I mean, they're men, but they're my friends."

"I'll bet they are. Real friendly friends."

The kitchen door swung open.

"Abby! Didn't know you were here," Cecily said as she walked into the room. She looked back and forth at the angry faces and stood still. "Oh."

She knew. She'd already heard it all. The furious ranting by her husband and his mother. The accusations and indictments. Cecily hadn't believed their charges, but there was nothing she could have said to convince them. They had already convicted her.

"What are you doing here, Abby?" Terry asked. "What do you want?"

Abby's eyes swung to Cecily, to Frank's mother, to Terry, and then back to Cecily, the friendliest face in the room, trying to put together the right words, but every time she tried to speak, her eyes watered and moisture choked her words. Clogged her throat.

"Can't talk, huh?" Terry said. "I'll give you little bit of advice since you're supposed to be part of this family as much as I don't favor that particular idea."

He went silent, stuck a toothpick in his mouth and rolled it around like he was pondering.

"First, you might wanna remember you're a married woman – for now, anyway. And second, my friends tell me you're all gung ho about this colored resort thing."

He tilted his head down and looked up at her, eyes boring through her like ice picks. Abby shivered.

"Not everyone in this area likes the notion. Some want it just like it used to be. You remember that."

"Why?" she asked. Her voice cracked on the single word like a twig had been snapped.

"Just think on it."

Abby left without discussing the farm products, without sharing Frank's letters, without another word. She stumbled to the barn and didn't look back, maneuvered Marie out the wide door, and climbed in the buggy. She was glad she hadn't removed the harness. She didn't want to spend another minute at the farm. Didn't want to risk seeing Terry again should he have followed her to the barn.

Tears formed, but she wouldn't let them fall, not until she was down the driveway and on the road. She let Marie fall back into a slow walk as soon as they were out of sight of the house. She sobbed and gasped for air that wouldn't fill her lungs. She covered her face and let the tears fall, not even thinking about where the mare might take her.

She kept her head down and tried not to make eye contact all the way back to town so she wouldn't have to speak to anyone. She unhitched the mare and rubbed her down, talking to her as she brushed her shiny coat.

"Some people are just plain stupid. And mean."

Marie pushed the top of her head into Abby's chest, and Abby wrapped her arms around it, laid her face against Marie and hung on. "I should've been born an animal, Marie. They're nicer. Maybe a horse. Or a cat. I'd like to be one of Cassandra's cats."

She gave Marie some extra oats and promised her some carrots when she had some. "Maybe an apple, too," she added.

She let Jackson go early since the hotel was nearly vacant and few people were in the bar. Bill Sanders sat at the big table with several other well-dressed men she didn't know. Joe Foster and James Gerard took up stools at the middle of the long bar, and Samuel Moore took a stool as far away from Joe as he could get. Shorty, Bear and her father held down the other end of the bar.

Abby checked everyone's drink, refilled some, washed the glasses and wiped down the counter – anything to be doing something. She was filling salt and pepper shakers on the tables when Jesse Falmouth threw open the door and burst into the room like he was on fire. His arms went into the air as if he was singing hallelujah, praise the Lord, and his mouth opened in a wide grin.

"Today," he turned in a circle to include everyone. "On this day, November 11, 1918, we are victorious! The war is over!" he shouted. "Set em up, Abby. I'm buying!"

He wrapped an arm around her and swung her in the air, knocking a chair over with her flying feet. She didn't care. Nor did he. The war was over!

"Put me down so I can pour!" she cried, and saw Terry walk through the door as she spun in Jesse's arms. His face turned to stone.

"The good stuff, Abby," her father yelled. "Hello, Terry! Good to see you. Join us in celebration."

She patted her clothing back into place after the whirlwind ride and lined up the glasses on the bar. She poured some of Patrick's best Irish, and passed them around. Everyone knew there'd be a toast, so they waited.

Terry walked up and grabbed the last one, his eyes never leaving Abby. His scowl fierce.

"Thought you might want to know the news. Looks like your friends beat me to it," he said.

Abby blinked and tried to look away.

"Thank you," she said, and what she could find of her voice came out a whisper.

"Cecily made me come. But you don't need an Adams. You've got all these other men."

His voice was soft, but not kind, and Abby was glad her friends hadn't heard. Especially Bear and Shorty. They would've been hurt – or angry. This wasn't their fault, and they didn't deserve Terry's snide anger.

Abby turned away to see Jesse wrap a loving arm around Edna and Daisy. He held his glass high, and shouted, "To the end of all war!" and they sipped.

Afterwards, Patrick held his glass high again and waited for quiet before he spoke.

"May your heart glow with warmth like a turf fire that welcomes friends and strangers and soldiers. Blessings on them all."

They drank and cried, 'Hear, hear!' Even Joe Foster and Samuel Moore wore smiles, if not for each other or anyone else. It heralded better days.

"Happy, girl?" Bear asked, nudging her arm.

She looked at his scarred face, eyes tracing the roadmap nestled there.

"Don't be spilling my drink, Bear. And yes. I am very happy."

She glanced at Terry, saw him watching her with hawk's eyes and dropped her glass. It shattered on the floor at her feet, and Bear leaped to help clean it up.

"It's okay, Bear. I'll get it."

"Nonsense. I can help."

Terry slammed his glass on the bar and, without a word, spun around and stomped away. Every head turned to watch him go, with brows raised and questions in their eyes. No one spoke until Edna broke the uncomfortable silence.

"It may be a while before they come home, Abby," Edna said, seated on a stool next to Shorty. She either didn't note Terry's abrupt departure, or she was trying to cover it.

"It can't be too soon." Abby's eyes trailed off to a dark corner of the bar, and she heard Terry's march to the outer door and the slam of it behind him.

She cleared her mind and tried to see Frank and the other soldiers coming home. Imagined them hauling their gear from the trenches, loading it onto ships and heading to America. It was a strange image, so different from what she saw each night in her dreams and nightmares.

In this new vision, he was safe and whole, but worry straightened her spine.

"They're done fighting, right? No more skirmishes and battles?"

"Yup." Edna said. "That's what Jesse told me. They have to wait for the treaty to be signed, but they've pledged a cease fire. No more bullets."

"He's safe," she whispered. "I need him. I need him home."

She would have liked to close the bar and send them all away, or in some cases, to their rooms, but she understood the need to celebrate the end of war.

She wanted to as much as drawing breath. She smiled with the rest, but it was brief, and the corners of her mouth soon turned down. She laughed, but it was hollow cheerfulness. She wanted to dance and sing to the return of their soldiers, too, but Terry's vile words skulked from the back of her mind, where they'd rooted themselves, to the forefront, waiting to pounce and overpower her.

When Shorty hugged her in celebration, she saw Frank's mother's eyes watching her, judging her. When Edna patted the stool next to her, wanting Abby to sit and talk, she saw Frank's brother's scowl and heard his denunciation of her because she had colored friends.

She picked at a torn fingernail and winced as she ripped it off and watched blood seep from under it. Phantom left Bear's shoulder and strolled down the bar. He head-butted her several times and looked up. His blue eyes were round and wide, staring into hers.

Mrow wah-wah, he said, and when she didn't answer, he head-butted and tried it again.

"I know. I love you too," she said, running a hand down his back.

He flicked his tail, leaped over several glasses and landed on Bear's shoulder again.

"Sorry," Abby said to Bear and glanced at Joe Foster, glad he was a few feet away from them and it hadn't been his glass the cat flew over.

She wore lead in her shoes by the time they all left the bar and she could go to her room and be alone. Phantom and Cleo raced up the stairs and waited by the door, leaped on the bed and watched as she washed her face, put on her flannel nightgown and brushed her hair. She talked to them as she performed her nightly ritual.

When she was finished, she pulled the box of Frank's letters from under the bed and propped herself against her pillow. Starting at the beginning, she reread them all, looking for . . . what? An indication that he thought like his mother and brother about her? That he didn't like her relationships with the people of Idlewild? That he didn't trust her?

She slammed her head back into the pillow and stared at the ceiling, threw back the covers, grabbed her robe and went to the window seat, wishing it was warmer so she could sit on the porch. Outside, the moon's white glow lit the night like it was morning. In its reflection on the water, it looked warm and rich, falsely inviting. A few leafless trees at the lake's edge drew giant, bony shadows on the water, reminding Abby of the paths in Bear's dark beard.

She made a grumbling sound of disgust, and Cleo, curled on her lap, murmured an objection.

"So what if I love them?" she said. "And Edna is my friend."

She gently dumped Cleo from her lap, apologizing as she did so, and retrieved her tablet of paper and pen. She'd write to Frank and explain what some people were saying.

He'll understand.

She wrote half the night, but it was never sent. By morning, all hell broke loose.

Chapter Thirteen

Spanish Influenza

Joe Foster banged on the door before Abby was downstairs. She ran down and flung it open, fear for Frank painting horror in her mind.

"It's here. You have to close the hotel. We ain't lettin' no strangers into town now."

"What's here, Joe?"

She didn't give him the respect of using his surname. She was done with that. She *had* no respect for him.

"The sickness. That one that's killing everybody. Don't you know anything? Open up your eyes, girl. You got to close up."

Abby's heart banged in her chest. They'd been reading about it in the Herald, about the monstrous number of deaths, first overseas, then spreading to North America.

"Come on in, Joe. Let me put the coffee on," she said. As much as she wanted to tell him to go away, she needed to know what was happening. She turned and walked to the kitchen.

"Who is ill?" she asked.

"Ned Peach. His wife came to the store looking for something to help him. All I had was a jar of Vick's Magic Croup and a bottle of Chill Tonic."

"How does she know it's Spanish flu? Did Ned see a doctor?"

Joe scowled at her and rolled his eyes like she was just as stupid as he'd always said. She wasn't worth his time.

"You know better than that. They don't have that kind of money, and in case you didn't notice, we don't have a doctor in Idlewild. You might get one of those instead of a useless guitar player and an addle-pated philosopher. We could use a doc."

Abby stuck a fist on her hip and looked at him with a glint in her eyes, a fire that said, 'Eat muskrat, Joe.'

"We're going to have our own when Dr. Williams builds his house, and he's a famous surgeon. How do you like that, Joe?"

"Ain't he colored?"

"He is . . . and he's a brilliant doctor . . . coming to Idlewild." Her voice taunted him. She couldn't help it. He deserved every bit of ridicule she could lay on him and still maintain her own self-respect. She chuckled as she turned to the stove.

"Have a seat, Joe," Abby said, trying to move him away from her. The scent of his unwashed body made it difficult to imagine cooking breakfast, and he was crowding her against the stove. "So, how do you think closing the hotel is going to help us fight Spanish flu?"

Again, the eyes rolled to the ceiling.

"Sick people. We need to keep sick people away from Idlewild. We quarantine the town."

The door swung open, and Strange Al walked in, stared hard at Joe, and turned her back. She pulled her blue ribbon from her pocket and tied up her hair.

"Do you know Joe, Al?" Abby asked.

She nodded, grabbed the slab of bacon and asked how many.

"Forty or so. It's pretty slow."

"Gonna get slower when you shut down."

"We're not closing, Joe. Are you closing your store?"

He looked at her like she'd spoken in tongues.

"You crazy? People gotta eat."

"And how will you get food to sell if Idlewild is quarantined?"

"That's my business, girl. Ain't none of yours."

"And this hotel is mine." She handed him a cup of coffee and threw the cream and sugar in front of him.

"Mebbe. Mebbe not. Going to Sanders' next. He'll see to it."

He slurped down his coffee, stood and shuffled out. The door swung back and forth behind him, banging into his backside and hurrying him along.

Bacon sizzled in the cast iron skillet, and Abby breathed in the smoky maple scent, working for stability and balance in a teetering, off-kilter world.

"Everyone good at your house, Al?"

"Pa's got a cold."

"You sure it's a cold?"

"He said."

Later that afternoon, Jesse came into the bar, ordered a shot of whiskey, and tossed it down.

"You okay," Abby asked.

"Just dealing with the times, Abby, and a bunch of radicals."

"Like?"

"Like Joe Foster, Bill Sanders, Samuel Moore and Ratty Branch."

"I only hear two semi-lunatics in that line up," she said, grinning.

"Together, they're one colossal zealot puddle, and they're on their way here."

"What's going on?"

"They're talking quarantine. Do you know how impossible it would be to do that? To a whole town?"

"Jesse, Frank is . . . our soldiers . . . are coming home. We're not going to tell them they can't go to homes they've been missing for so long time. See their loved ones."

He put a hand on her forearm. The dim light of the bar highlighted their differences, and a smile formed on her worried face. She sandwiched his hand with hers. It was warm, comforting and easy.

"I wouldn't worry over it. We can't tell folks who've built cabins in Idlewild not to come to their own places."

"And who would stop them, Jesse? We don't have a constable."

"That's true, but if the town opted for a quarantine, some folks could – and would – make it mighty uncomfortable for owners and potential buyers. Might even make them think twice about our little piece of paradise."

Cold air gusted into the bar when they opened the door, and a shiver wanted to crawl down her spine. It started in the little hairs at the base of her neck and slithered. Cleo stood, fur spiking her back, and strolled the length of the bar, her eyes making narrow green slits in her black face.

Abby brushed her hand down Cleo's back when she walked by. "You're feeling it, too, aren't you, Miss Cleo? Where's your buddy?"

She served the odd group of men and tried not to listen to their angry conversation, but voices grew loud, toned down to whispers and grew loud again. Sanders' face was blotchy red, and he slammed his glass on the table when Joe insisted on stopping anyone from coming into town. Abby ran to wipe up the spill and brought him another.

"You can't do that, Joe," she said, setting Sanders' glass down. "You can isolate sick folks, but you can't stop life from going on in an entire town."

"I wasn't talking to you, girl. This ain't your business, and I didn't ask you your opinion."

"She's right, Foster." Jesse said. "People are working on their cabins and getting them ready for winter. You can't stop healthy owners from doing what they need to do."

"Hell, I can't." Joe said, and stood, glaring at the hard eyes around him.

Samuel Moore tipped his chair on its back legs, generating space between him and the rest of the men, distancing himself. Unreadable and silent, his head rotated from one speaker to the next. Everyone knew he wanted a black community, but that had nothing to do with this, and he knew it.

"Entire families are being wiped out," he finally said. "Don't you people read? And so many children are orphaned they overflow the orphanages. In the cities, garbage lays uncollected."

"That's nothing to do with here," Joe snarled, not seeing that Samuel's words were making his case for him.

"Michigan has over twenty-one thousand cases, and officials say that number's too low. They don't even report every death in northern places – like here – and people die in their beds in the Upper Peninsula, and they go unnoticed. If they're lucky, and if they have neighbors, they get buried in the woods."

He slammed his chair down on all four legs, shoved it back, and stalked out without another word. Joe followed at a distance.

"Set em up again, Abby, please," Sanders said, moving to the bar. "I need to settle down before I have a heart attack or go shoot somebody."

"Don't even say that, Bill," she said.

"She's right," Jesse said. "Tempers have flared enough around here."

"So, is there going to be a roadblock?" she asked.

Bill Sanders grinned and ducked his head, gave Abby a sheepish half grin.

"Flora Branch would skin me alive if I let any harm come to her resort, even a brief quarantine. I'm not going up against her, not for the Spanish flu. No sir. Not doing that. I'll take on Joe first. That bowlegged, red rooster," Bill mumbled.

They were finishing up the rooms when Abby heard the door open and Cecily's voice calling her.

"Go on," Betty told her. "Let me finish this up."

Abby went downstairs with concrete feet and wooden legs, unsure about her sister-in-law's feelings. She hadn't talked with her since that horrible scene at the farm and didn't know if she wanted to.

"Terry know you're here?" she asked as she neared the bottom step.

Cecily twisted the scarf hanging from her neck and shook her head.

"Can we talk?"

"Sure. My room?"

"I don't believe the things Terry said," she blurted out on the way upstairs. "Never did. He's just . . ."

"Come on in, Cecily. Have a seat. I guess I should have asked if you wanted something – coffee or tea or – anything?"

Cecily shook her head again and perched on the love seat. Her eyes scanned the room, and her mouth worked, trying to find the right words.

"Terry's not a bad man. He's just worried, Abby. About Frank, about the town. That's all. And he doesn't really hate you or anything."

Abby sat on the edge of her bed and looked from Cecily to the window, seeing the tops of the near pines and the vast lake. It looked cold in the gloom of the cloudy day, as cold as she felt.

"I didn't do anything wrong, Cecily."

"I know. But they've never seen a woman with men friends like you have. Good women, anyway. Maybe the cousins. And you're really close to them, your men friends," she said, turning to Abby with her palms out as if she expected a nod of support and agreement. Abby was silent and moved to the window.

"And he doesn't like it that the town is changing," Cecily added.

"That was fairly obvious the other day."

"It'll be better when Frank is home, and that'll be soon, now. When your husband is back in your bed, you won't want to be out stirring up the town with all that Chautauqua stuff."

She giggled, and Abby's eyes widened.

"How does having a man in your bed have anything to do with music and philosophy?"

"Maybe you'll be too busy with a baby."

"Maybe," Abby said. Could be Cecily knew more than she did. Maybe she had this wife thing down. "You could be right. But Bear and Shorty are my family, too. Frank knows that."

"I do, too."

Cecily joined Abby at the window and put an arm around her.

"If there's anything I can do, Abs . . ."

A late flock of geese left the water, splashing and honking as if they were in a hurry to get on with their long trip south. They aimed at the hotel and flew so close to the roofline it felt like they were coming in the window. Cecily involuntarily ducked, and Abby laughed.

"I think they do that on purpose just to scare me. One of these days I'm gonna open the window and end up with a goose in my room. Keep him for a pet. Do you think Phantom and Cleo will like him?"

"How about goose pate` instead of pet?"

Abby shivered. "Ugh. There is something you can do. I need supplies and don't want to get them from crabby old Joe's store. He gives me the heebie-jeebies."

"Like what kind of supplies?"

"Eggs, milk. Perishables. The kind I need more than once a week. I was going to the farm to ask the other day, but..."

"Sure, we can do that."

"Would you bring them in?" Abby asked with a sheepish grin. "I don't want to go to the farm right away."

"I can do that, too. Unless Terry has a fit."

"If he does, forget it. I don't want to cause trouble."

Cecily waved a hand in the air.

"I'll figure it out." She snapped her fingers. "I know. I'll tell him I'm keeping an eye on you!"

Cecily left with a hug, and Abby spent the afternoon in a fog of self-doubt. She moved through her work with haphazard attention because her thoughts were on Frank and his family. He wasn't going to like it if she was ostracized by the rest of the Adams clan, and she vowed to be the perfect wife when he came home. He'd see. She'd cater to his every whim, and he'd want for nothing. Because ... that's what good wives do.

In the meantime, she ran the hotel with perfection, guided Jackson, Betty, Al and Patrick, even though she tried to make it look like her father was the boss. He slept later and took longer naps every day, and Abby took over as much as time and her work load allowed.

No official quarantine was put in place, but she heard consistent grumbles and rumbles about it. Ned Peach recovered from his illness, but one of Al's brothers came down with what they believed was the flu, and Abby asked Al to stay at the hotel while he was sick. She didn't know if it was the Spanish flu or not, but she didn't want it brought to the hotel.

"Pa wouldn't like that," Al said. "Who'd cook for him and my brothers?"

"Don't any of them know how?" Abby asked, her eyes doubting Al's words.

Al shook her head.

"Well, you understand I have to make sure we don't spread Spanish flu to the guests, don't you, Al?"

She agreed to stay until her day off, and Abby wanted to hug the girl, actually reached out a hand and drew it back before she made contact. She didn't know what she'd do if she lost Al right now.

"Do you need to send a message to the farm to tell them so they won't worry about you?"

Al shook her head and chopped potatoes for hash browns, wielding a giant chopping knife that dwarfed her small hand.

That night, Abby was staring out her bedroom window, thinking about her day and Frank's homecoming, and saw Cassandra walking along the edge of the lake. She didn't see any of her stream of cats following and thought it odd.

On closer inspection, the woman in the moonlight skipped along the ground much quicker than Cassandra, and she didn't walk bent over. It wasn't the cat woman.

The moonlight caught long blonde hair, and Abby knew. It was Al, and she was heading in the direction of home.

Abby raced to the room she had given the girl and knocked on the door. She wasn't surprised when, after the second knock, no one answered. She turned the knob, and, of course, it wasn't locked. It was empty.

"Damnation!" she said. "Why did she tell me she'd stay if she didn't want to?"

Bear stuck his head out of his room.

"Problem?" he asked.

She swatted the air as if she could smack the offender and grimaced.

"Don't know. Maybe."

"Al's room?" he said, tilting his head toward it.

"Yeah. She left."

"Maybe she'll be back by morning."

"Probably. But that wasn't the deal. If her brother has the flu, I can't have her in the kitchen and taking care of her brother. Harsh, I know, but ... Damn," she repeated.

Bear leaned against the doorjamb and scratched his beard.

"Conundrum. I'll help make breakfast," he said. "And then you'll figure it out."

"You? Cook?"

He grinned, and the road map in his beard changed directions. His face was a forest with paths going to different destinations depending on his mood.

"I have many talents," he said.

"You have a deal. See you at five." She winked and went to her room.

Bear met her on the landing, and together they made their way to the kitchen. Al was there, slicing bacon and didn't even look up as they entered. Her hair was pulled back in the blue ribbon, coffee was percolating, and she acted like nothing was wrong.

Bear raised his eyebrows and backed out of the door.

"I'll be in the bar," he said.

Abby touched Al's shoulder. She flinched and kept sawing away on the thick slab of smoked pork.

"Told you Pa wouldn't like it if I stay here."

"And I said you couldn't work at the hotel and go home to Spanish flu at night."

"I need to work."

"Then you need to stay here or get a doctor to say your brother doesn't have that influenza. One or the other. Now wash your hands and go home, or tell me you'll stay."

Al pulled the ribbon from her hair and held it out. It was dirty and limp hanging between her thumb and finger, and Abby's eyes watered. She shook her head and pushed the girl's hand toward her chest.

"Keep that, Al. You'll need it when you come back to work, when your brother is well and the threat of Spanish influenza is gone."

Al headed out of the kitchen, and Abby followed.

"You'll come back, won't you, Al?"

She kept a steady tread toward the outside door, and Abby still followed.

"I mean . . . this isn't forever. Let me know when he's better, please."

Al's nod was imperceptible. Abby wished the young woman would talk with her, but she was gone, heading down the road, her determined gait not leaving any doubt about her intentions.

Bear joined her on the porch, laying an arm over Abby's shoulders.

"You know he may not get well," he said. "Some don't."

"Oh, God. I didn't even think of that." Abby teared up again. "I'm a terrible person."

"No. You're a woman with a heavy load. Let's make breakfast."

Bear continued to help cook breakfast, and together they learned to work in concert. He picked up Al's chores, and Abby no longer had to tell him what to do. She smiled, thinking she'd like to keep him in the kitchen. He was good company, and he wasn't nearly as taciturn as Al. He didn't talk much, but he would converse when she prodded him, and he wasn't cold and distant. He was Bear, her good friend, and life in the kitchen was running along on a smooth plane, even if the rest of it was off kilter.

Chapter Fourteen

A shiny automobile pulled up to the store, and she went in while her husband stayed outside fiddling with their belongings. They were the first property owners in the Idlewild Resort to bring an automobile to town, and it was loaded to the roof with boxes. He checked all the tires, wiped off the front and back lights and circled the auto several times, poking gently at the tires with the tips of his equally shiny shoes.

When he was satisfied, he ambled toward the store to join his wife. They collided as she slammed open the door and ran out, and he grabbed her arms in surprise.

"He says we have to leave, go home. That we can't go to our cabin!" she said, her face a stony mask of anger.

The handsome man stepped back in surprise and pulled his wife along with him. She didn't move easily. She was furious.

"Why on earth would we do that? We just got here," he said.

"This place is no different than any other. They don't want us here."

Her words were a blend of anger and bitterness painted with a lifetime of disappointment.

"Georgia, what are you going on about? You know better."

"No, I don't know better, Henry Piccard. What I know is that white man in there won't sell us groceries to take to our cabin. Says the resort is quarantined because of the flu or some such baloney."

"That's nonsense. The whole town can't be quarantined."

"Well, you go on in there and tell him that."

"We're here until the new year. Period. We're not leaving."

Henry Piccard's eyes glinted in the sun, narrow brown slits glared at the store his wife had been thrown out of.

Inside Foster's store, Terry Adams and Joe watched them through the grimy window glass.

"You know there isn't a town quarantine, Joe," Terry said, looking sideways and still watching the couple argue.

"I know that, but they don't. And I ain't gotta sell groceries to anybody I don't want to. I didn't want to."

"That's true. It's your store."

"Damn right."

Shoulder to shoulder, they watched him wrap his long arms around her, open the door to the auto and close her in.

"Where'd they get a fancy automobile like that?" Joe asked, ruts deepening his constant scowl. Envy warped his words.

"Good question."

Skunk Tatum and his brother loitered outside the store. He punched Moose in the arm and circled the car. He said something they both snorted over, pounded a fist on the trunk of the auto and drifted away like they hadn't a care in the world.

The Piccards watched, eyes wide and wary, while the men circled them like carrion amidst a flock of buzzards. Scornful laughter came in through the partially opened widows, and, as soon as the men left, Henry drove to the hotel. They parked and talked.

"They might not want us here either," Georgia said.

"They did the last time we stayed, and there's only one way to find out." He unfolded his legs and went around to help her out. "Come on, pretty lady."

Jackson met them at the registration counter and remembered them from the bar. He didn't know their names, but he pointed a finger and a grin at them.

"Scotch on the rocks and screwdriver," he said.

Georgia smiled and her shoulders loosened and settled, glad to see a friendly face, one like hers and Henry's.

"You have an amazing memory," she said, "and I sure could use one right now."

"I can help you with that," Jackson said. "Come on in."

He led them to the bar, and while he fixed their drinks, they told him what had happened at the grocery store. Abby came from the kitchen while they were talking and listened, stunned that Foster would actually refuse them food supplies.

"That old man is crazy," Jackson said, "and, from your description, it sounds like you met two of the town's favorite sons, two of the four Tatum brothers."

"The town isn't quarantined. We have a couple sick people, but we're isolating them, not the whole town," Abby said after welcoming them to the hotel. "And no one even knows for sure they have Spanish flu. They haven't seen a doctor, and we're just being safe."

"We need groceries," Henry Piccard said. "We're staying awhile. Can you tell us where to go?"

"Get settled and eat here tonight. You can go into Baldwin tomorrow and get what you need."

She leaned in conspiratorially and whispered in Georgia's ear. "Better stuff, too, and cheaper. Gotta get back to work. Welcome to Idlewild."

Her husband poked her in the side after Abby left.

"See?" he said.

"See what? I see just fine."

"It *is* different here. We're wanted."

He smiled and told her to drink up so they could get settled in their new cabin. They'd been looking forward to it for months and had finally taken an extended vacation from their law firm to enjoy it. The place was built and ready for finishing touches from the owners, the curtains and rugs, pictures and knickknacks that made a house a home. The light in Georgia's eyes burned brighter. Christmas in their new vacation home.

The hotel had grown too busy during the dinner hours. It hadn't been Abby's intention to run a restaurant, just feed hotel guests because they needed to eat, but people came from a distance to enjoy Patrick's Irish suppers. Sometimes, he should cook less well, cook just well enough to keep guests from complaining about the food. When she told him her plan, his lips turned down and he snorted.

"Can't be done. The Irish can't cook bad food. Leprechauns sneak in and sprinkle goodies in the pot. Where's your Irish soul, lass?"

"I think my tired feet kicked it out. I need to sit a minute."

"Climb up on a stool and let me fix you a toddy, Daughter. It'll make you spry as a sprite."

"Or knock me out," she said, and gave him a kiss before he walked around the bar.

"Ye didn't tell me about the shenanigans old Joe's been up to."

"No, guess I forgot."

"Hmmm," he said with a sideways glance.

He handed her the frothy green drink and sat next to her.

"Would ye be keeping things from your old pappy, like why ye have Bear working in the kitchen in the morn? And why you're doing Al's work and yours?"

"I'm not trying to keep things from you," she said, working on making honest eyes. "I just got busy, and it didn't seem important. Al will be back. I just don't know when."

Abby put an arm around her father's broad shoulders. He looked like a large man when he was sitting, the size of his torso inconsistent with the length and girth of his short legs. When he stood, people who didn't know him were shocked. Their heads moved up and shot back down when his face wasn't where they expected it to be. It always made him chuckle.

Patrick's dimple deepened when she hugged him.

"Buttering me up with a hug always works, doesn't it, Abigail?"

She had time to finish her drink, barely, before Shorty came in, followed by Bear with Phantom wrapped around his neck and carrying Cleo. Jackson was a second later, and just in time for the supper crowd. Abby was too busy to think about why she kept things from her father. She worried about him, though, and didn't want him to worry – if that made any sense at all. She'd do the worrying for them both.

She saw the Piccards, nodded to them and noted several other tables were occupied by cabin owners here for the holidays. Abby reminded herself it was almost Christmas. They needed a tree and some decorations for the hotel. Too damn much to do.

"We need a Christmas tree, Shorty," she yelled down the bar.

He shrugged his shoulders and looked in his pocket as if he might have one stashed there, put his palms up and shook his head. Abby threw a towel at him. It landed on Phantom, who had moved to his shoulders, and made Shorty look like a giant hunchback. Neither Shorty nor the cat bothered to move it. Most likely, responding to her childish behavior was beneath their dignity, but Shorty did grin and raise his eyebrows, and Phantom caterwauled a loud *Mrow a wah-wah*, drawing the attention of the drinkers and diners.

It was a fortunate yowl because when the diners looked around for the horrendous noise, they saw the orange glow on the island.

"Fire!" they shouted, bolted from their chairs and ran out, leaving drinks and food, forgetting coats and hats. But memories of other flames and burning cabins were more than enough to keep them warm.

"Not again," a deep voice moaned.

"Bring buckets!"

"Tools, rakes and shovels."

Feet pounded on the walkway to the island, and it trembled with the weight of so many, but held together. When they neared the fire, relief was immediate. It was only one of the outhouses, not a cabin. They doused the flames with buckets of water from the lake, thankful it was nearby, and stood in a circle staring at the charred remains.

Many remembered a fire in one of the doghouse cabins not long ago, and anger rippled through the small crowd. No one was there at the time, just like this one.

The deputy had asked a few questions, but no answers had surfaced, and it was left as accidental. Now, fire again.

Abby listened to the murmurs, the exasperation, the bewilderment and despair. An outhouse didn't start itself on fire. This was arson, and everyone knew it.

The flames were sending a message, and Abby hoped folks wouldn't hear the words or intent, that they'd ignore it as best they could, or fight it –somehow. But it was difficult to pretend it hadn't happened when the charred wood was a black and bleak reminder.

"Told you," Georgia Piccard said to Henry.

"This means nothing."

"Like hell it doesn't."

They raked through the few ashes to be sure no red sparks were left and turned toward the mainland.

"I need to settle up," Jesse said to Abby. "I'll walk you back."

Georgia said she was going to their cabin, and Henry gave her a hug and followed the rest back to the hotel.

"I'll be back after I pay for our meal. Put a light in the window. Your handsome husband will return," he teased, hoping to ease her anxiety.

They were on the footbridge when they heard the scream. It raced across the frozen water, streaked into the black sky and came back to earth louder and more alarming. The terror in its tenor bred shivers.

"That's Georgia," Henry said, his voice a harsh whisper filled with fear, and he shoved people out of the way to race in the opposite direction, back down the footbridge to the island. Several followed, and the rest stood planted, watching, their eyes glued on his back as he fled into the dark. The rest followed with a weary gait, not wanting to know, putting it off.

Lantern light flickered in front of their cabin and led them to her, but her sobs would have done so without it.

When they arrived, they saw the reason for her wail. The door was covered in red paint with a dripping white cross in the middle. Paint spread over the ground in front of the door and on Georgia's palms. She held them out in front of her as if they were blood covered and she was Jack the Ripper caught in the act of murder.

Tears streamed from her eyes, and her lips twisted in anguish, sobs heaving her chest.

Abby put her arm around the woman's convulsing shoulders and held her, watching the faces as they stared at the mess.

"Let's get this washed off your hands, Georgia."

She led her to the communal pump and placed her painted hands under the spout. Abby worked the handle and water soon spewed out, diluting the red and white paint into pink that washed into the ground and disappeared.

She started shaking, and Abby removed her shawl and wrapped her in it, but she shivered from more than the cold, and the violent shakes continued.

"Henry!" she shouted. "I'm taking Georgia back to the hotel. She's freezing. Bring some warm clothes for her to change into."

They warmed up with a hot brandy toddy Jackson made for them. Georgia began to relax and told Abby in greater detail what had happened at the store. For the first time, Abby heard there had been another man there when Foster tried to get them to leave town.

"Who was it? Did he mention his name?"

Georgia shook her head.

"Can you describe him?"

She gave a sardonic grin, and Abby was glad to see some grim humor bubble to the surface of her miserable day.

"What's funny?" Abby asked.

Georgia nudged her and her eyes squinted in tired humor.

"He was a white boy, and that's all I know."

"That's the best you can do? He was white?"

She nudged Abby again.

"All you white folks look alike."

Cold silence fell around Abby and surprise at Georgia's words. For a moment, she thought she'd misread her, and then she peered into the woman's face, saw the devil dance in her eyes. She began laughing and couldn't stop.

"Yes. I'm sure we do," she said when she could speak without choking on her words. "We're all white – but different shades and some with polka dots. What color hair? Eyes? How tall? Try those things."

Georgia sipped and sighed her pleasure.

"He was tall, maybe six foot three, give or take. Blondish long hair. Big guy. Didn't smile. I know they both watched us from the window. I saw them. He was little better than that troll who owns the place."

Abby nodded, picturing the man described to her. An uncomfortable portrait came to mind, and she immediately dismissed it.

"Joe definitely *is* a troll," she said. "I don't shop there if I can help it, and I can think of a whole lot of words that might better describe him, but I won't say them in polite company."

She grinned with growing fondness for the woman.

"I'm not so polite," Georgia said. "Ah, here come the masses and Henry with a ton of luggage."

"Good. You should stay the night, on me."

"Thank you, Abby. You're a good woman."

"I'm not so good," Abby said, and Georgia smiled.

"Guess we're both flawed."

"Thank God."

Cleo and Phantom leaped onto the bar and perched side-by-side, still and fearless. Georgia looked at the cats with interest.

"Deliberate?" she asked.

"What?"

"One black, one white?"

"No. They came that way. They found me."

"It's nice when that happens."

Abby took money from the people who'd fled the bar to help put out the fire and had returned to pay, made drinks, listened to the speculation, and tried to block out the idea that someone wanted to leave a harsh message through fire and the Blood Drop Cross, again. She blinked away the vision of flames and the cross and tried to pretend the night's work was done by a stranger, not a neighbor, not someone they all knew and maybe cared about.

They sent for the sheriff, but his deputy showed up and made the rounds of the bar, asking the same old questions. Getting the same answers. No one knew anything.

"Why are you here, Deputy? Where is Sheriff Hicks?" Abby asked. "Why aren't you out there looking for him? The person that did this? These people didn't start a fire. They were here. They didn't paint their own door."

Patrick patted her arm and watched the deputy bristle at her words.

"Little lady, I'm thorough. I talk to everybody, and I mean every person who might do this crime."

"Well these folks were here when it started. So, look somewhere else." She turned her head from him and muttered, "And I'm not your little lady, either."

Patrick chuckled and hoped the deputy didn't push her any further. This wasn't the night to do that.

"You let me do my job Mrs. Adams, and you tend to yours. Might want to let the men do men's work."

"What?" She'd had it. He was touching tinder with a live coal.

The deputy spun away, glared with intentional menace around the room and walked out, his left foot dragging across the wooden floor. An old military wound, according to him. But he only limped when he was tired or under the gun. Abby irritably and spitefully hoped it was both. Then frowned at her meanness.

Patrick hovered nearby, looking tired and saddened by the night and the rumors.

"I didn't think to find this when we came to live in Idlewild, Daughter. Maybe 'twasn't a good idea."

Abby ruffled his reddish gray curls and kissed his cheek.

"Sit, Da. Let me get you your Irish."

He slid onto the end stool and waited for his drink, watching all the faces in their anger and fear mixed with disgust . . . and tiny shreds of lingering enthusiasm.

He looked again. He was confused by the still eager eyes and said as much to Abby when she returned with the whiskey.

"Maybe you're mistaken," she said.

He shook his head.

"I know the look. The wide eyes, the glow in them. Watch. You'll see what I mean."

And she did. A few of the faces looked too enthusiastic. They scooted their chairs closer to the table and hunched their shoulders forward like they were ready to pounce.

"Hmmm . . . I wonder," she said. "I see what you're talking about."

Shorty and Bear strolled in and stood like bookends on either side of Patrick, their eyes roaming the room, judging the atmosphere, ready.

"Expecting something?" Patrick asked.

"Not so much expecting as pondering," Shorty said, and Bear agreed with a slight nod.

Patrick pursed his lips and wetted them with his Irish, licked them and turned toward Shorty.

"You're a contemplative kind a man."

"True."

"Bear, too."

Shorty nodded and Bear just watched in silence.

They continued to watch until after the crowd left or went to their rooms and the bar was empty.

It snowed during the night, and, when Abby rose and looked out her window, she saw flakes still coming down. The pines drooped with their white load, and the angular branches of the oaks were no longer barren and brown.

The first snow! It made her feel like a kid again, and she wanted to run outside and make angels, gather the clean stuff to turn into ice cream, do something - anything - to celebrate winter purity. After the harsh night, it felt right to be cleansed by a heavy snowfall.

Abby splashed water on her face, shivered and toweled dry, threw on a dress, and braided her hair. She wanted a Christmas tree and was planning to bribe Shorty and Bear into getting one – a giant one that would fill the corner of the bar. They'd have to move a bunch of tables, but . . .

Bear met her on the landing as he'd been doing since Al left, and they performed the synchronized work of cooking breakfast for the large group staying at the hotel. Sausages, bacon, potatoes, pancakes, and eggs.

He snitched bacon, and she glared. She tugged his apron strings, and he frowned. He danced when he flipped the pancakes, and she smiled. She wiggled her bottom when she whipped the eggs, and he wiggled his eyebrows. It was a concert, a dance, child's play they both enjoyed. Abby didn't look forward to the day Al returned. She'd miss the easy companionship with Bear.

A knock on the kitchen door startled them, and Abby peeked out.

"Yes?"

"Al says to tell you our second brother is sick now, and she still wants her job."

She stepped through the doorway.

"And you are?"

"Marcus. Her youngest brother."

His too long hair fell over the frayed collar of his thin coat, but it was the same color as Al's, wheat on a cloudy day.

"Are you well?" she asked.

"Yes."

"I'm glad you're well, Marcus. Thank you for stopping in, but you need to go since you've been exposed, too. I'm sorry. I'd like to send out some food later. Would that be acceptable?"

"Sure. I just won't say it to Pa."

Abby tilted her head and peered at the gangly young man. His pants were too short, showing bony ankles through thin grayed socks, his coat too big, gaping where it shouldn't. Dirt ground into his knuckles appeared to have been there forever – weeks at the least.

"Would he not like it, Marcus?"

He shook his head and shoved the cap back on, getting ready to leave.

Abby pondered Strange Al's strange family and reached to shake his hand, thought better of it and retracted her arm, folded it across her chest, protectively.

"Tell Al she'll have her job when you are all well. Will you do that, Marcus? And I'll send out some food. Somehow."

When she went back into the kitchen, Bear was getting ready to go to his real job, and Abby put a hand on his arm to stop him.

"I really appreciate you, Bear."

He shrugged and smiled.

"Will you and Shorty cut a Christmas tree for us? A big one?"

"Sure."

"Bear?"

"That's me."

"I'm a terrible person."

"What did you do?"

"All this time Al's been taking care of her sick family, and I haven't sent food out to her or tried to help. What a rotten person I am."

"Truly depraved, fetid and decaying. I'm surprised the buzzards haven't had you for lunch. Picked your bad bones clean."

"Get out of here. And leave my cats."

Phantom opened his eyes and looked up from his bed on a kitchen chair. His wakefulness was brief. Cleo pretended to be an ebony statue near the door. It was her job to guard the kitchen – or any place in or out of the hotel – and Abby. Her green eyes missed nothing.

Every time she heard an outside noise, Abby went to an upstairs window to look for her sister-in-law, but it was another guest coming or going. Cecily was bringing supplies, and Abby was getting anxious. She needed the potatoes, milk and eggs she'd ordered from the farm because Patrick was making Boxty and Colcannon. Irish potato pancakes and cabbage hash, Patrick always explained, for those who weren't blessed with Irish ancestors.

She peered out the window again, hoping to see the farm buggy, but the only conveyance in sight pulled up next to Foster's. She let the curtain drop back into place.

"Damn, I don't want to buy from that old bugger."

She turned back to making up one of the guest beds.

"Who you cussing at?" Betty asked, a glint in her brown eyes. She got a kick out of hearing Abby swear. It wasn't done in her home because her mother would box ears on the head that mouthed the curse.

"Didn't mean to say that out loud." She yanked her auburn braid and grimaced.

"Mad at somebody?"

"No. I'm waiting for supplies from the farm. We need them for the supper meal."

They finished making up the room, and Abby glanced out the window again before going on to the next one. As she turned away she glimpsed the buggy coming down the road.

"It's here, I'll be back."

"Need help?"

"Sure. Take a break from beds," Abby said.

She opened the front door expecting to see the buggy pulled up and her sister-in-law climbing down, but the street was empty.

"Odd. Where'd she go?"

Betty pointed down the road. There Cecily, stopped in front of Foster's store. Joe was outside, standing at the head of her mare and holding on to the harness. The mare stepped from foot to foot, sensing tension and wanting to be away, needing to move on.

Joe had one hand hanging from the brow band of the horse and the other on the rein terret, making sure the horse wasn't going anywhere. Joe's mouth opened and closed, his head shook back and forth.

Abby grabbed a coat and flew across the porch and down the steps. Betty followed.

"What are you doing, Joe Foster? Let go of that horse," Abby said as she drew near enough for him to hear.

Cecily's face was white, her eyes wide.

"Sorry. He says the town is shut down. I can't bring things in from the farm."

Abby planted her feet wide, set her shoulders in fight position.

"That's nonsense. It isn't shut down. Let go, Joe!"

"Ain't gonna, Abigail Adams. Too dangerous with the sickness and all." He smiled showing gaps where teeth were missing and yellow where they weren't. Abby shuddered.

"Let go, Joe," she said again, nostrils flaring, chest heaving.

Betty moved closer to her boss, afraid the man had evil intent and might hurt her. She didn't know what she could do about it if he did, but it seemed two might be better than one, and she was strong. Abby, while tall, was a slight thing.

Joe noticed Betty for the first time. His eyes narrowed, and he snorted.

"So, you still got the little brown slut working for ya. Might a known."

Betty blanched, and Abby moved forward to shove a finger in his face. It was just the impetus she needed.

"You watch your mouth, Joe Foster."

"Nope, ain't gonna do that either. Those Tatum boys'll tell ya about her. Ain't that right, Betty?"

Abby's anger took over and she shoved the man in his chest and twisted the fingers hanging onto the rein. He let go and made a fist as if he would punch her, and Abby yelled, "Go ahead. Hit me, you evil bastard."

Jesse, hearing the commotion, looked out his office door and came running.

"What in hell are you doing now, Joe? Let go of that woman's horse."

"None of your business, Jesse. This is between me and the women."

"Not anymore."

He stepped between Joe and the horse, put his back to the man's chest, forcing him to back step, took hold of the bridle, and pulled. Glad to be leaving the tension, the horse jerked forward and moved eagerly down the road. Joe was left behind, cussing Abby, Betty, Jesse, Negros, whites, hotel owners, Spanish flu, women, cats, America, and the Lord.

Abby tittered through her anger, listening to him rant all the way to the hotel. Jesse walked with them, making sure Joe didn't follow and create more havoc.

"What on earth was that all about?" he asked.

"He told Cecily the town was closed. Can you imagine that? Town closed?"

"Hmmm. He gets loonier by the day."

"She's bringing supplies from the farm for us. Guess he didn't like that."

He glanced at Betty who lagged behind them.

"You okay, Betty?"

She nodded, but Abby knew she was remembering Joe's ugly words. He'd made a terrible accusation, a malicious and vicious charge. He should be made to pay.

Jesse wrapped the reins around the hitching post and helped carry in the supplies, watching for Joe out of the corner of his eye.

Abby thanked him, and he left, telling her to stay out of trouble if she could.

"Glad the boys weren't with you, Cecily. They might have been frightened," Abby said.

"*I* was scared." Cecily twisted her wedding band, furrows etching her brow. "That man is creepy. He really wasn't going to let me go."

"He's nuts. Want some coffee?"

"No. I better get back. Ma Adams is watching Chunk and Bailey. You know how she gets."

"I do. Thanks for bringing supplies. I do appreciate it."

Cecily rocked back and forth and patted her hair, looked at her bitten fingernails. She pulled at her shirt cuffs and looked away.

"Something bothering you, Cecily?"

"It's just . . . I don't know if I can do this again. When Terry finds out what happened . . . he's not gonna let me come. You know how he is."

Abby shoved her hands in her pockets and looked at the wall. It was empty, sterile.

I need to hang a picture there. Maybe two or three. I need a nap. A really long one. Maybe two or three.

"Abby?" Cecily said, pulling on her arm.

"I'm here. And I understand. Don't worry about it."

"I'm sorry, Abby. I really am. Frank isn't here, so you don't have to worry about what he thinks."

She sucked in air.

"Right. He's not back from fighting a war. I'm really lucky."

Cecily bit her lip, and her eyes filled. "God, I'm sorry. I don't know what I'm saying."

Abby put an arm around her sister-in-law and led her to the door.

"So am I, Ceci. I shouldn't have said that. And it's alright. Everything is fine. I need to find Betty. Thanks for coming this time. I know it wasn't easy."

She said goodbye to her sister-in-law and waved wearing a labored smile on her face.

She found Betty sweeping the bar and asked her to have a cup of coffee with her.

"There's something I want to talk with you about," Abby said.

Betty's eyes widened, and her hand tightened on the broom handle.

"I do something?" she whispered.

"No. Not at all. Let me get the coffee."

Betty kept sweeping, her broom making wide, erratic arcs across the floor. She kept her face down, intent on her work, and Abby had to call her name to get her to stop.

"Come sit a minute, Betty. Want cream?"

"Yes. Please."

The young woman perched on her chair as if the seat was hot, sure Abby was about to fire her, that she believed what Joe had said.

God, she hated that old man. In fact, until Abby and her pa came along, she didn't like any white folks, but she was honest enough to admit to herself she hadn't really known any all that well . . . except the Tatums.

She knew *them*. Very, very well.

Abby stirred her coffee, taking in the young girl's anxiety. Betty looked like she wanted to be anywhere but having coffee with her. How to begin?

"It was a pretty awful day, wasn't it? And I want to thank you for being there for me. That was brave of you."

"Yes, it was nasty, and you're welcome." She sipped and stared over the rim of her cup.

Doesn't sound like I'm being fired.

"The other thing," Abby said.

Oh-oh. Here it comes. Betty's chin trembled, and she looked away.

"Well . . . I don't know how to say this."

"It's okay. I understand if you can't have me here now," Betty said. "I'll just get my things."

She lifted herself from the chair, and Abby grabbed her skirt and pulled her back down.

"Where are you going? What did I do?"

"You do?"

"Yes. Why are you leaving? We're having coffee."

"I thought . . . Weren't you going to fire me?"

"Heavens, no. I was going to ask you about the Tatum boys. Why did Foster mention them in connection with you? And are they the reason you won't be in the same room with Strange Al? Oops, darn, I mean Al."

Betty peered into her coffee cup. She knew them, alright. And she hated them all, loathed the day they forced their way into her life, into her. They were hateful, wicked men, and she'd walk miles out of her way to avoid them.

"I'm not a slut."

"Of course, you aren't. I know that."

"They're horrible men. They're filthy, evil and take whatever they goddamn want."

She choked out the last words, and they crackled with anger, burned with loathing.   After tense moments of silence, she apologized.

Abby's imagination played with a variety of pictures, none of which were tolerable. Knowing how they treated Al, guessing how they might treat a young, pretty, colored girl, her blood boiled for the second time that day.

"Can you talk about it?"

Betty shivered and pulled herself inward, ran her hands over her arms like she was cold and held them tight and hard, pinching her arms, protecting herself.

"No."

"Does anyone know? Did you tell someone what they did?"

"Why would I? What would that accomplish for me, for my ma and pa? If he knew, my pa would end up dead or in prison. And you know that, Abigail Adams."

Her voice was gravel, describing in those few words a picture of hatred and memory. Abby couldn't respond. She drank her coffee, and Betty's reality flickered like a candle struggling to hold a flame. She knew it was far from her own experience, and there wasn't a damn thing she could do about it.

It was Betty's past, and it couldn't be changed. But it could be acknowledged, and that was the best Abby could offer. That's all she had to give. She couldn't hold it in her arms or see it in her subconscious. She didn't have the memory.

Betty began the slow road to calm and picked up her coffee.

"So, I'm not fired?"

"No. Why would I fire you?"

"You're a good person, Abby."

She pursed her lips and blew out a puff of air. That was the second time in recent history someone had told her that. She had a response similar to the last.

"I wish I was. I wish I was better."

Chapter Fifteen

It was so cold her unyielding, frozen fingers refused to work and she kept dropping the harness. Her breath crystalized in white fog around her head, and she thought maybe shopping could be left for another day, but their guests would go hungry if she grew faint hearted and sneaked back into the warm hotel.

"Come on, Abby. You can do this."

She buckled the last strap and climbed the step. Once inside, she wrapped herself head to toe in a woolen blanket and warmed up. Body heat and warm breath brought up the temperature in the cocooning buggy, and she nearly stopped shivering.

She enjoyed going into Baldwin for groceries. She'd been doing it ever since her father thought she could handle it alone, way back when they lived in Nirvana, so she knew folks, and they knew her. They were friendly and always asked how the new hotel was doing and if she missed their old home. Sometimes it made tears hover at the rims of her eyes like an over-full cup that doesn't spill, and she fought nostalgia.

She was nearing the edge of Idlewild, passing a small grove of trees and lost in memory, when she glanced sideways to see arms waving frantically as if the person was drowning in midair. A bundled figure waddled out into the road in front of the mare. Abby jerked back on the reins, terrified Marie couldn't stop in time and prepared herself to leap from the buggy.

The bundle huffed around to meet Abby as she climbed down and recognized the person attached to the flailing arms. She wore a huge smile, a red coat, and a matching hat pulled down to her eyes. Cousin Sue.

"What's wrong, Sue? Is Sally sick?"

"No. Why would you think Sally is sick? She's always healthy, disgustingly so, and putting her warm clothes on."

"Then why did you make Marie almost run you down?"

"I wanted you to stop."

Abby laughed and shook her head, leaned against the buggy and took a couple of moments to calm her pulse.

"Okay, I'm stopped," she said, not sure her pounding heart wasn't still trying to leap from her chest. "What can I do for you, Sue?"

"We want to go to town and know you always go about this time. That's why I'm all ready and Sally is putting on her warm clothes – in a healthy way."

"Oh . . . well, I see."

"That's alright, isn't it? I mean, you're going anyway, and there's room if we squeeze."

"Sure, why don't I pull up next to the . . . uh . . . your house so I'm out of the road."

Sue hollered for Cousin Sally to get a move on and tried to climb into the buggy. She got one foot on the step, grabbed the pull strap and heaved, but the only thing moving was the buggy which wobbled back and forth in reaction to the unequally distributed weight. She tried several more times, and Abby got down to help, finally putting both hands under the woman's bottom and pushing upwards. Sue fell onto the seat, rolled, and righted herself, giggling with glee.

"It's always that way. They don't make buggies for short people."

Or really round ones, Abby thought, but kept it to herself.

Sally came out as Sue was catapulting onto the seat and said, "Or portly ones, Sue. They don't make them for the portly."

"Men like me, Sally, just as I am."

"I know they do. Most of them better than me, and I think I'm kind of svelte."

"You are. Nicely so."

Abby's mouth was frozen in an ill-mannered circle all the way to Baldwin. Nothing was out of bounds for the cousins, no subject taboo or too off limits. They discussed bodies and sex, breakfast and whiskey, breasts and penises, petunias and moonlight. Abby's head was spinning. She didn't need to respond to any of their chatter because they were used to talking together and didn't need anyone else. Besides, she couldn't. She was in a daze. Wouldn't know what to say.

"Where am I taking you ladies?"

"This little restaurant where coloreds go. There's a general store next to it, and we like to browse in it."

"It's a nightclub, Sue. Don't fib."

"Not in the daytime, it isn't."

"Okay, point me to it," Abby said.

She drove through to the other side of Baldwin and watched the houses get shabbier and smaller with each block. A stocky blacksmith in a stained, leather apron stood in the doorway of his shop. He wiped sweat from his brow and his head turned to follow the buggy with the white driver and two colored passengers, his expression neither hospitable nor hostile, but guarded.

Not much later, Sue stabbed a pudgy finger at a tiny building set off by itself. It was decorated in shades of purple and yellow, and music blared from an open door.

"Don't they know it's winter and colder than . . . you know," Abby said.

"It's hot in there. Always is."

She pulled up in front and went around to help Sally with Sue.

"Scoot to the edge of the seat, Sue," Abby said. "Now grab her arm, Sally. God, don't break a leg," she whispered in prayer as she pulled and hoped for the best.

Sue landed with a massive jiggle and a grin.

"Easy as peach pie," she said and adjusted her bright red hat that had been jolted over one eye when she landed.

"I'll be back in about two hours or so. Will that work for you ladies?"

"Jim Dandy, twice as randy," Sally said. "We'll be right here."

"What about the store you were going to browse in?" Abby asked.

"Nah. We'll be here."

The shopping went quickly, and it didn't feel like she'd been gone long at all. She checked the watch hanging from her dress front and decided to meet them anyway. She didn't have any place else to go, nothing else to do.

She pulled up in front of the brightly painted place and tied the reins to the hitching post, hiked her bag strap over her shoulder and went in. It was dark inside, and it took several moments for her eyes to adjust to the absence of light. She didn't find her friends near the door and moved further into the room to see if they were at a back table.

When her pupils dilated enough, it became obvious that every eye in the room was on her, and none appeared welcoming. She licked her lips, took a bite out of the bottom one and moved forward.

You're no stranger to a bar, Abs. Just meander like you've been bellying up your whole life, cuz you have.

"I ... uh ... um." She cleared her throat of the bullfrog nesting there and tried again. "I'm looking for some friends."

The bartender was a giant of a man, with arms as big as Abby's waist and no neck. He was the blackest man she'd ever seen, and she oddly wanted to put her arm next to his so she could measure the difference in their size and skin color, but she stopped in the nick of time, before embarrassing herself – or getting punched or thrown out.

His massive head swung back and forth like a pendulum as if he was moving in time to the music blaring from a small band in the corner, or he was telling her no.

Probably that.

"What you doing in here, white girl?"

She tried to stand taller and rolled her shoulders back in a show of confidence and strength.

"I told you. I'm looking for some friends."

He raised his eyebrows until it seemed they would crash smack into his hairline, and his eyes took on a macabre appearance with more white than brown showing in eyeballs riddled with red veins.

Abby took a step backwards and changed her mind.

"I'm Abigail," she said holding out her hand.

He shook his head again but took hold of her hand and moved it up and down in a slow, gentle hand dance.

"Well, Miss Abigail. I'm Gus, and I ain't sure you should be in here . . . looking for friends." He emphasized the last word as if it meant something different than what she'd intended.

"Not just any friends. Sally and Sue."

He smiled then, a wide, sweeping smile that took over his whole face, and he slapped the wooden bar.

"Why didn't you say so?"

"I did."

"I didn't hear anything about no Sally or Sue," he said, frowning.

"Well, I just said friends, and that's what they are," Abby said, backing down from a conflict, but not totally.

"They're here. In the backroom."

Abby froze, inappropriate visions pranced through her brain, all parading across her expressive face.

Gus slapped the bar again and guffawed.

"See that mirror behind me? Take a look at your eyes Miss Abigail. Did you ever see such eyes? Look like you saw spirits floating around in white gowns. Look like *I* would if I saw men in white sheets coming at me."

"I don't think it's so funny."

Abby asked for a glass of water, and Gus asked if she wanted anything in it.

"Make it a whiskey instead. I've earned it."

He raised those wild eyebrows again and brought it to her.

She sipped, looked at her watch and waited. Sipped again.

"Think they'll be done soon?" she asked

"They'll be done now if they know you're here."

He let her stew a bit just for the fun of it.

"They're playing poker. What'd you think they were doing?" he added in a sidebar whisper.

Abby choked on her whiskey and sputtered.

"You rat. You deliberately led me to believe . . ."

"What? What'd you believe, Miss Abigail? Want me to get 'em for you?"

"Yes. Please."

The ladies followed him from the backroom stuffing bills in the vee of their dresses and carrying their coats. They donned them, settled their hats and their drink tabs, and moved toward the door.

"Come on back, girls, anytime. It was a pleasure as always. You too, Miss Abigail."

He winked at her when she turned to wave, a lewd and playfully suggestive look flashing in his eyes, and she blushed a vivid shade of pink.

Gus is a rat. And that was fun.

During the afternoon, there was a peaceful hour – maybe two – when the upstairs work was done, the meals were made, and the bar was empty. They tried to take advantage of the quiet moments and rest their feet.

Her father found her at the corner table engrossed with the Osceola County Herald and a cup of hot coffee. He joined her and asked the news.

"There's a great article about Negro troops in Europe, how France treats the colored soldiers with esteem and gratitude for their loyalty and abilities. It's good to see."

"Doesn't happen enough," Patrick said. "Anything else?"

"Spanish flu is still rampant. Another twenty thousand dead."

"What have we done to earn God's wrath?"

"You don't really think that, do you?"

"No, by the seven saints, I don't. It's the saints work to keep us well. And our own efforts, or lack thereof."

She glanced back down at the paper, an idea forming for the next Chautauqua. A finger tapped a picture with the article, showing two soldiers of the 369th, the famous unit that fought so bravely alongside French troops.

"I want to honor the colored soldiers, Da. Here in Idlewild where they have a place that belongs to them. The spring Chautauqua."

Patrick didn't respond right away, but he watched his daughter process the newspaper article and the idea she was pondering.

"And, I want to bring them to the hotel for the two-day event, free."

Patrick sat back and rubbed his wild curls. His dimples deepened, and he crossed one leg over the other. The foot bobbed and his fingers thrummed on the table.

"Can we afford to do that?"

She wiggled from side to side in indecision, meaning maybe, maybe not, but she still wanted to do it.

"I think so. It's important."

"I can see by the fairies in your eyes that it is."

She bit at a cuticle and ran an explanation around her mind. The reasons she wanted to honor them were all around her, at Chautauqua and in the road on the way to Baldwin, at church and at the hotel. She squeezed her temples while she thought and put an elbow on the table, rested her head in her hand and closed her eyes.

When she opened them, boots were parked next to her chair and her head snapped up.

"I didn't hear you," she said.

"I'm a panther."

"You're a bear. Nice to see you."

"Everything alright?"

"Yes. No. Should be."

Patrick chuckled and his foot bobbed faster.

"That about covers all your possibilities. Playing it safe, Daughter?"

Bear held the cats, one on each forearm, and Cleo leaped to Abby's lap. She stroked her, and the contented sound of her rumbling purr eased the stiffness in her neck.

"You smell like catnip, Cleo. Where'd you find it in the winter?"

"In my window sill. I grow it."

"Harrumph. Cheater. No wonder they like you best."

She rolled the newspaper into a tube and beat out a soft, staccato rhythm with it, using the table as a drum.

"Have a good day?" Bear asked. He pulled out a chair and lowered his large frame into it.

She laughed, rolled her eyes and shook her head.

"You wouldn't begin to believe my day. Isn't that right, Da?"

"Tell him," Patrick said.

She did, and when she got to the part about going into the Negro bar to retrieve Sue and Sally, Bear scowled.

"You didn't go in a strange bar by yourself?"

"What do you think I should have done?" she said, piqued he would scold her.

Phantom howled and leaped from Bear's arms.

"Sorry. Didn't mean to squeeze."

"I'm perfectly capable of walking into a room, Bear, and asking for my friends. And what else could I have done?" She didn't tell him how uncomfortable she'd been or about the misunderstanding between her and the bartender.

"Nothing. I mean, you're right," Bear said.

Abby ran a hand through the loose hair at the back of her head and rubbed at her nape. She pulled her fingers through the curls and cussed as they tangled and her fingers came away with long strands hanging from them.

"God, it's a wonder I'm not bald. But the best part of the day is this."

She unrolled the newspaper and flattened it out for him to read about the 369th. When he was finished, she told him her plan to bring as many as she could to the hotel so they could be honored at the next Chautauqua.

"You gonna tell me why it's so important to you? Something special I don't know, lass?"

"I'm not sure I can put it into words, Da. It just is." She put her elbows on the table and leaned into them.

"I guess it's . . . I don't know if I can explain it. They get promises and more promises. Following the Civil War,

Negro soldiers were promised acreage and never got it. In the end, they had nothing and starved in their new emancipation. They thought they'd gain some level of respect with their freedom after putting their lives on the line, and ... that didn't happen either. That's what I've read, anyway."

"Tis true. I know it," Patrick said. "The Irish didn't fare much better."

"They fight and die and bleed just like white soldiers who have parades in their honor," Abby said. "I think they should have something. So ..."

"So, bring them. As many as you can fit in the hotel, anyway. But ..."

"But what?"

"Be safe, Abby. Remember the paint and the fires. Don't be getting yourself in the middle of something that gets you hurt."

"I will."

"I mean it."

"I'll be safe, but some things are important."

She thought about Frank, so far away and not being able to help him should he need it. She saw Bunny's eyes and the wounds reflected there when she talked about her family's struggles. And she thought of Betty, and helplessness filled her, but the Chautauqua honors she could make happen. She could do something to make things a little bit right.

"Aye. You're important ... to me, lass," Patrick said, bringing her back to her last words.

"And me and Shorty," Bear added.

Patrick left her to go check on the supper meal, and Abby flirted with an outline for the spring Chautauqua, forgetting Bear was even there. She made a mental list of people and needs and stopped to chew on a ragged fingernail.

If she took an active role in the next Chautauqua, would Terry and his mother be angry, would they think more terrible things about her? She saw Terry's angry face and Cecily's fearful one. The angry words came back to her.

"Shadows on your horizon, Abby?" Bear asked, watching her face.

"Yeah," she said with a sad chuckle. "Frank's family. Well, his brother and mother, anyway, don't think good wives should be involved with things outside the home."

She'd never shared what they'd said about him, Shorty and her, and she wouldn't. They didn't need to feel bad, too.

The white path of the scars in his dark beard flashed like lightening in a night sky as Bear's jaw clenched and unclenched. She put a hand over his.

"Do *you* have shadows, my friend?" she asked.

"No. I don't. What does Frank think?"

"About?"

"What good wives do?"

Abby leaned back in her chair and crossed her arms over her middle. She stared at her wedding band.

She didn't know the answer to Bear's question. She didn't have the least idea what Frank thought about most things, and she should. She wasn't a real wife, she guessed, let alone a good one.

I'm a fraud.

She coughed to rid her throat of evil frogs.

"I don't know, Bear. I don't know what he thinks."

"You'll figure it out."

"Maybe I'll just tell Jesse about my idea, and let him be the front man. Or Edna. Can't get into too much trouble that way, can I?"

After the supper rush and needing some peace, Abby left Jackson in charge of the bar to walk by the lake. It was frozen over and pristine white.

Traces of Eastern cottontails, their long back feet making distinctive paths, marked the snow. The solid plow of waddling porcupines and heart-shaped step of whitetails, all led toward the island where safety and plenty awaited them.

Dusk darkened into night, and Abby watched as an occasional star blinked in the unknowable distance. The night was soundless. Even her footfall was silent, and her heartbeat slowed, and her mind gentled, accompanying the stillness.

She needed this peace and solitude, and promised herself she'd make time for it more often. Make her needs come, if not first, at least somewhere in the count.

She bent to pick up a long stick and walked on, tapping it on the ground with each footstep. She snickered. If anyone was watching, she'd resemble Cassandra wandering the lake edge with her walking stick and cats. Phantom and Cleo sandwiched her, sauntering close by her feet, heads swinging at imagined movement, eyes perfect round orbs with huge black pupils.

Cleo hissed, flipped in the air, and landed with back humped, hair raised and legs stiffened in fight mode. Abby whipped around and saw Cassandra not more than a few feet behind her.

"Where'd you come from? I didn't hear you walk up."

"Shush," she said, talking to Cleo, and the cat laid down her fur and moved closer to Abby who noted Cassandra's many felines cared nothing about Cleo and Phantom. In fact, they looked bored. Cassandra, too.

"I thought I was alone," Abby said. "How are you, Cassandra?"

"My well-being is assured. Yours is the one in question."

"Excuse me?"

Abby frowned, disconcerted.

"I'm sure you heard me."

Abby fought between irritation and desire to know what the peculiar woman had to say. Why did she think she knew everything about her? What gave her the right to say anything at all?

Desire to know won out.

"Sorry. I did hear. Your words are . . . one big puzzle. I'm lost. Can you explain what you mean and why you think my well-being is in question?"

Cassandra turned to the lake, now stark white against the murky sky. Total darkness had overtaken the world and splashed its cold winter paint over them. Abby clutched her arms to her side. Phantom and Cleo pushed against her calves.

"You have no conscious wish to fly, no one who pushes from the nest, and yet you cry." She waved her arms, long purple sleeves flapping in the air. "You cry for freedom of the sky, for full use of opened wings. To play with clouds, uncertain winds, you have a need to fly."

Abby stared.

What on earth was this crazy old woman talking about? I'm not crying, and I don't have wings!

She snorted, wanting away from the woman and her clowder. She turned and said goodnight with as many pleasant words as she could muster, Cleo and Phantom hugging her legs as she walked.

She didn't know why she was so irritated. She liked Cassandra. Well, usually she did, but at the moment, she wanted away from her and her intuitions and premonitions – her crazy muttering.

At the hotel porch, she looked back, and Cassandra was staring. All her cats were, as well, lined up in a straight row, ears flat, and Abby heard a low growl from both of hers.

"Come on, babies. Let's go in. Let's go to bed early."

When she opened the door, they scooted in and raced up the stairs. They were sitting in front of her room when she climbed the last stair and rounded the corner on the landing.

In the morning, Strange Al stood at the door, outside in the cold. She was bareheaded and had tucked her hands in her sleeves for warmth. Abby saw breath fogging in front of her face before she recognized the girl in the window. She ran to unlock the door.

"Why didn't you go around back and come inside?" she asked.

Al shrugged, and it crossed Abby's mind that the girl was simple, but she didn't really think so.

"Come on in and get warm. Everyone well at your house?" she asked, shoving Al through the door to the kitchen and stoking up the fire.

Al nodded, pulled the blue ribbon from her pocket and tied back her wheaten hair. She poured water into the coffee pot, added grounds and set the pot on the stove where it was the hottest. She left the room briefly, returned with the slab of bacon and began slicing.

Strange Al settled back into the work like she'd never been gone. Bear stepped through the door, saw Al, and folded himself into a chair to wait for coffee. Abby made a face at him but didn't comment. She wouldn't want Al to know she'd rather work with her friend. Al might be strange, but she needed the job, and, as far as Abby knew, she was a decent person.

Betty bounced in and saw Al, grabbed a cup of coffee and, without a word, turned her back and headed out. It didn't seem odd to Abby now. She knew something had occurred between the Tatum boys and Betty, something so horrible the girl wouldn't talk about it. Betty wanted it buried, but it wasn't. It was fresh enough to cause her pain, harsh enough to cause her to avoid Al out of hate – or fear— or training.

Okay, Cassandra, I have a wish to fly . . . away. Far, far away.

But she grinned, finished the breakfast buffet and followed Betty upstairs to make up the rooms as guests vacated them, drawn by the scent of bacon and eggs, sausage and pancakes, and Patrick's special roast chicory coffee.

Chapter Sixteen

Before she finished cleaning the few rooms that held long term guests, four people were stomping snow from their feet and heading for the registration desk, a middle-aged couple with two young men in uniform.

"Welcome," Abby said, coming down the stairs and greeting them.

"Micah Chambers," the man said, extending his hand. "My wife Maggie, son Benjamin and his friend Bradley. They're fresh from France, and we thought celebrating Christmas here, along with a quiet week, would be just the thing. Bought a lot on the island last summer and can't wait to build."

The soldiers were handsome in their pressed uniforms. Clean cut, shaved and holding their caps to their chests deferentially. Abby admired them and thought of Frank, how he would look in his uniform. She'd never seen him in it, and that seemed odd.

She smiled at them.

"All the girls in Idlewild will be falling in love, Mr. Chambers. Better be watching out for your soldiers."

They were signing the registration book when Joe burst through the door.

"Thought you'd sneak by when I wasn't looking, huh? Well, you can just turn right around and go home! We're quarantined here!" Joe was loud, screaming, his face a blotchy red.

Micah Chambers bristled. His eyes widened.

"Is that true?" he asked, turning to Abby.

"No, Sir, it isn't. Joe Foster thinks he can make rules and enforce them all by himself."

Upstairs, Patrick's door crashed open, banging against the wall and smashing into the sconce behind it. He ducked his shaggy head out, pulling suspenders over the tops of his long johns.

"What in hell is going on down there?" he yelled.

"Your wanton daughter thinks she can flaunt the rules. Still taking in people even though we're quarantined!" Joe shouted.

Patrick came down the steps as fast as his awkward gait would allow and shoved his nose in Joe's face.

"What did you call my daughter?" he asked.

"I didn't call her anything. I said we're quarantined. Tell these people to get out. They're probably sick and we're all gonna get the flu and die!"

"Leave my hotel!" Patrick said. "If you don't move out that door fast, I'll move you."

Joe stuck out his chin and squinted his eyes nearly closed.

"I'll go when I'm good and ready. When these people get on outta here."

Maggie Chambers grabbed her husband's arm and held on tight, her eyes bulging. The soldiers spread their feet in a fighting stance, arms at their sides, hands flexing.

"The only place these folks are going is upstairs to their rooms and then to the bar where I'm gonna treat them to a drink in honor of them coming here to listen to an idiot like you talk nonsense. Get on out of here, Foster," Patrick said, pointing his knobby finger at the door.

Joe's jaw clenched and bulged. He grew rage-color purple, swung and landed a fist at the side of her father's head. Patrick went down, and Abby flew over the top of him, pummeling Joe, who pulled up his hand again, like he was going to punch her.

It never landed. Benjamin was there in a flash and had Joe's forearm locked in his long fingers. He was squeezing as hard as he could, delighting in the pleasure it gave him, until Joe's fingers weakened and unclenched from the fist they'd been making.

"If you lay so much as a finger on this lady, it will be a moment you'll regret for the rest of your life," he said.

He let go, and Joe cradled his hurt arm, glaring at the man.

Abby helped a sputtering Patrick sit up. When he was on his feet, he yanked his arm out of Abby's grip and headed for Joe, swung and connected.

"Never use your filthy, toothless mouth to talk about my daughter again. Let's go," he said, turning from Joe who sprawled on the floor. He grabbed two suitcases and dragged them up the stairs. He didn't look back to see Joe crawling to the door.

"So much for the quiet," Micah said, but he didn't appear to be upset. He grinned, shook his head, and followed Patrick.

They gathered in the bar later, and Patrick served them his finest, most treasured Irish.

"To your health and happiness," he said, his glass raised high. "The war's done. Are ye not? You heading back?"

"Bradley will be heading back as part of the cleanup. The 369th has a job to do yet," Benjamin said.

Patrick slapped his hand on the bar and a grin on his face.

"So, you boys are part of the Harlem Hellfighters? We're honored. I hear it's a crackerjack regiment."

"Thank you. We are, and it is," Bradley said, face split in a wide grin, pride showing in the set of his shoulders and the glow in his eyes. "Actually, it started out as the 15th Infantry assigned to the 185th Brigade. Later it became the 93rd, and we evolved into the 369th in March."

"See any action?" Patrick asked.

Benjamin tapped his buddy on the arm and gave him a warning look.

Bradley returned the look with a shrug of his shoulders. A message had just been silently delivered between the two of them and acknowledged.

"Not until we were passed off to another country," Bradley said. "Every man in the French 161st thought we were pretty good fighters. Liked having us there."

"You were given to the French?" Abby asked. "How can soldiers be given away like a pair of shoes?"

Benjamin ran a hand over his face and dragged it down to his chin. He rubbed his jaw where the muscles bunched, and he looked like he wanted to be done with the conversation.

Bradley sipped and peered at Benjamin over the top of his glass.

"Sorry, buddy. She asked the question." He turned to Abby. "The American military doesn't think Negro soldiers are good for much other than laborers. You know, give us a shovel or a potato peeler. That's it. No rifles and helmets. Afraid we might shoot them instead of the enemy."

He laughed, a hollow sound, as if he'd made a bad joke, looked around with his chin held high and settled back on his stool. His dark eyes peered into the distance for a moment. He didn't say *white* American soldiers wouldn't stand next to them in a fight, but it was true. They had refused, categorically, absolutely, and he kept that to himself.

"The French, now, they'd just as soon fight alongside us as next to one of their own. They trusted us. We were part of Lebouc's 161st Division in the Allied counterattack – over six months – the longest deployment in the war," he said, thrusting his chest out, his shoulders back.

"You don't need to tell the whole sordid story, Brad. It's history," Benjamin said.

"Yeah. And like most history, it'll be forgotten. Changed or never known. Except in France."

"Or maybe here – in Idlewild," Abby said.

Bradley tossed back his whiskey, and Patrick filled the glass again, touched his own glass to the soldier's and watched Benjamin' eyes.

A sorrow dwelled there, a mix of knowledge, grief and regret that softened when he heard Abby's words, and they settled on her.

"Why here?" Benjamin asked.

"We have several Chautauqua events from spring through fall, all with speakers, music and dancing. Lots of activities. This year, we want to honor our soldiers, especially our Negro heroes who go unrecognized in many parts of the country."

He nodded and fingered the cap on his lap.

"I hope to be back in France."

He ran his thumb over the front insignia, and longing decorated his face.

That evening, Shorty and Bear dragged in a giant white pine and stood it in a bucket in the corner of the bar. Abby danced in excitement as she poured liberal amounts of ale and whiskey for waiting customers.

"Popcorn," she said. "We need popcorn. Lots of it."

She sent her father into the kitchen with orders to return with bowls of the fluffy, white stuff and gave every customer a needle with long thread and a bowl of popcorn to string. They looked at her like she'd lost her mind, but she put her hands on her hips and threatened to take away their drinks if they didn't produce a few feet of tree decoration.

Edna sat at the bar chatting with Abby and enforced her warning.

"Do it. Get to sewing. You're not a man if you don't sew," she cajoled with a giggle.

"We'll be doing cranberries tomorrow, so by Saturday we'll be ready for the party," Abby teased.

"I'm not gonna sew," Jackson said when Abby handed him a threaded needle. "I'm no woman."

Edna cuffed the back of his head.

"What do you think a tailor uses? Glue? Does he glue those fine clothes together? Don't be a dope, Jackson Parker. I'll tell your mama."

He turned russet red, popped a kernel into his mouth and picked up the needle, jabbed it into one and slid it down to the end. It came off the thread, and Jackson held it and the needle in the air. Confusion took over his face.

"What'd I do?"

Edna showed him how to wrap the first pieced at the end of the thread as an anchor for the rest, and Jackson was soon making tree decorations. He got so engrossed, Abby had to remind him to wait on customers in between strings of popcorn.

"You turned into quite the tailor, Jackson," she teased.

"But I'm not a woman. Never."

"No," Edna said. "But if you keep practicing, you might – just *maybe* you *might* be almost as good as one."

Jackson wrinkled his brow and squinted his eyes, wondering if he'd just been insulted, but, because it was Edna, he wasn't going to risk saying anything.

Maggie Chambers joined Edna and Abby at the bar, her husband, Micah, having gone to sit with Benjamin and Brad at a table where Patrick, Jesse and Bill Sanders were rehashing the war effort.

"Bet you'll be sad to see them go back now you've got them home," Edna said to Maggie.

Maggie nodded, and her eyes strayed to where the men sat, saddened and melted into a puddle within a wisp of time.

"True, but we don't know if Benjamin will be going back."

"They might be stationed stateside? That's wonderful, but I thought Brad said they were heading back for clean up," Abby said.

"Probably not Benjamin, and the idea isn't wonderful to him."

"Then . . . I don't understand. Aren't they in the same regiment? Wouldn't they stay together?"

Red threatened Maggie Chambers black eyes, and she turned them away from her son.

"Benjamin still carries shrapnel in his chest. They couldn't get it all in the field, the pieces were so close to vital parts. They did what they could, but he's likely to be discharged."

"And I take it he's not happy about it?" Edna asked.

"No. He wanted a career in uniform."

"He certainly looks healthy," Abby said. "And you saw how he handled Joe Foster."

"What? What'd he do to that old fart?" Edna said.

Abby laughed and Maggie joined her.

"Strangled Joe's arm with the fingers of one hand just before Da punched him and made him crawl out on his hands and knees."

"Good for him. What else does he want to do with his life?" Edna asked Maggie.

"Make music. He's got music in his fingers, toes and all the parts in between. That's all. Be a soldier and play piano."

"Well, then that's what he's gonna do," Edna said.

By Christmas eve, a Baldwin piano sat in the corner of the bar, compliments of Jesse and Edna Falmouth, Bill Sanders, the Branches, and everyone who appreciated the work Abby was doing for the town of Idlewild. They trapped her in the kitchen while they wheeled it in, blindfolded her, and then dragged her out to see the surprise.

"You have to guess," someone shouted.

"I'm a terrible guesser."

"Try. Here's a hint. You want it."

"Gorgeous black hair. A bullfrog. Three wishes."

"She's right," Edna said. "She's a terrible guesser. Let her see it."

"Oh my, God. It's beautiful!" She ran her fingers over the keys. *Wish I played.* "Where's Benjamin? I need a Benjamin."

"Right behind you," he said, flexed his fingers and sat. He played Christmas carols, old Irish ballads, and war tunes; sad songs of longing – of wives for their soldiers, of soldiers for their fallen comrades, of lost loves and broken hearts, until Patrick filled glasses for a toast and demanded a drinking song.

When sleep called to them, Abby told Benjamin he was never leaving. He had a home at the hotel, and she was keeping him there whether he liked it or not.

"What's the name of this place?" he asked. "I don't think I saw a sign."

Abby scrunched her face.

"How odd. There isn't one. Just *Hotel*, and that's funny."

"We're gonna have to fix that, and I'll have to write a song about it."

The day was Rockwell-Christmas-card perfect. Enormous, white flakes hovered in the air before covering the abundant pines around the lake, sheathing them like a shawl over frail shoulders.

Everyone was invited: villagers, farmers, lot owners, anyone close enough to have heard there was a gathering at the hotel . . . even Manny who had helped them move to Idlewild.

Betty and Abby were rushing to finish the upstairs rooms, Strange Al and Patrick were in the kitchen, madly cooking an Irish stew, potato bread, and traditional plum pudding – which, oddly enough, had no plums.

Benjamin sat at the piano after devouring an astonishing amount of sausage and pancakes. The walls rocked with Christmas joy, and Abby hummed along with the music drifting up the stairs, not realizing it had been a long while since she'd hummed a tune for no reason at all.

"You sound happy, boss," Betty said, flipping a sheet so it landed in a flawless rectangle on the bed. It needed little tugging to get it into position for squaring the corners and tucking them in.

Abby straightened, dragging the dust mop from under the bed, heavy with the added weight of a fur ball taking a ride. She laughed and shook her off.

"Don't help, Cleo. I guess I am happy. Shouldn't I be?"

"You surely should. It's Christmas."

Abby hunched her shoulders and chased Cleo out of the room with her mop and a growl.

"Darn. Listen." She paused in the doorway. 'That man can play. I wonder if he'd stick around for a while. I'd pay."

"Make him an offer. I think he likes you."

"Betty Gerard. What are you saying?"

"Nothing, boss," she said, trying unsuccessfully to hide her teeth.

"And don't call me boss."

"Yes, Ma'am, Mrs. Adams."

"You're hopeless," Abby said, and threw the dirty towels at her.

"Thanks. Meet you in the next room. Take Phantom with you."

"Where is he?"

"In the dresser."

"Why?"

"I shut him in there."

Abby tilted her head, eyes wide.

"And you did that because . . .?"

Betty moved to the dresser and pulled open one of the drawers. Phantom, stretched out on a blue shirt, opened his eyes and scowled. "Kept him out of the way?"

Mrow a wah-wah, he said, and yawned and stretched.

"Oh, my God. You've got white hair all over his things. Get out of there."

Wah-wah.

"Don't sass. Go. Tell me again," she said, turning to Betty. "You shut him in, why?"

"I don't know. He opens the drawers himself and climbs in. I just shut them. He likes it."

"Oh, well. That explains it. Probably shouldn't do that."

She felt too great to be disturbed, even the littlest bit. Music did that.

Concerns about white cat hair on guest's clothing turned to mush when Benjamin began playing *America the Beautiful*, and Abby stood on the landing, listening.

He played it softly, each clear note a phrase in itself, of patriotism and heroism, of longing. When Benjamin built to crescendo on the words *in brotherhood,* her heart pumped wildly and banged against her breast bone. Her breath held in suspension, and the music stopped. *From sea to shining sea* stretched out in single notes like the words had been forgotten or were mere afterthoughts, the meaning lost to the phrase before.

She wanted to weep. He'd bared his soul, and Abby had no doubt what was in his mind and heart. She knew. She restarted her breath, her heart calmed, and she moved on to the next room.

Manny showed up early to help Patrick in the kitchen, he said. Since Benjamin wasn't at the piano, Abby could hear their happy voices singing Irish ballads while they cooked. The bar was filling up early, and she was glad to see Jackson's face peek around the door. He held his hands behind his back and danced into the room with a gleam in his eyes.

"You look like Cleo when she stole Phantom's mouse," Abby said. "Did you steal a mouse? From whom?"

"Nope. I have a surprise."

He held out a bright package and shoved it at her.

"Take it. It's a Christmas present."

"Jackson. How sweet. You shouldn't have done this."

"Open it."

He bounced back and forth like a little kid, excited and eager.

She laid it on a table, tore off the wrapping and held up an exquisite, white shawl. It was crocheted in a delicate shell design and was as soft as gossamer goose down and warmly thick. She put it to her cheek and her eyes went dreamy, as if she'd drifted away on a cloud. Jackson could tell she loved it. It was in her smile. It was in her eyes.

"It's beautiful. Where on earth did you get this?"

"Mama made it. I asked her to."

"Wow. She doesn't like me very much, you know. Sorry. I shouldn't have said that."

"No. You shouldn't have. You have a habit of doing that. Talking when you should be thinking. Guess Jackson didn't tell you I was here," Bunny said behind her.

Abby spun around, her face blanching as white as the shawl and beginning to grow red from the neck to the ears.

"Oh, my God. Why do I always say dumb things around you?"

"I don't know, young lady. But you do."

Abby held the shawl to her neck, feeling its softness against the warmth of her blush.

"This . . . uh, the shawl . . . it's gorgeous. Thank you."

Bunny waved a hand in dismissal, her regal bearing making Abby feel like a dunce, like an ill-disciplined child. Awkward and gangly, to boot.

"Jackson wanted it. It's his gift to you."

"But you made it. So, thank you both. I love it."

Bunny nodded and continued to stand without movement. Her stillness was disconcerting. It seemed she didn't even blink; her heart didn't beat. She was an alien being. Her face with its royal bones and flawless skin covering should have been a bust carved of mahogany, from the long, slender neck to the groomed hair that complimented a perfectly shaped head.

Abby found herself staring and an apology formed in her brain. She stuttered again and scratched her head, unintentionally pulling her hair loose from the ribbon holding it back.

"You've messed your hair, Abby," Bunny said.

"Uh . . . It's me that's a mess. Can I get you a glass of wine? I think you like a slightly sweet drink, right?"

"Yes. Thank you," Bunny said. Jackson pulled out a chair for his mother, and Abby was happy to see her move and sit.

She does move. She was real after all. Wow.

Abby ran to the bar to pour the drink.

"I asked Cassandra to come this evening," Abby said, when she returned and handed her the wine.

"She'll be here. She thinks you're quite interesting."

"Good. I mean, not good she thinks I'm interesting, but good she's coming. God . . ."

Abby fled to the safety of her place behind the bar and was glad to see Bear and Shorty come in, along with a large group of others. She hugged Bear, and Shorty lifted her off her feet and whispered words of affection, his voice like the rustle of dry leaves in the wind.

"Merry Christmas, Bear, Shorty," she said when her feet touched the floor. "Can you find a place at the bar or an empty chair?"

"Naw. Don't need one," Bear said. "We're helping tonight. I'll tend the buffet with Patrick and Shorty's gonna help you behind the bar."

"Aw. That's sweet, but it's Christmas Eve. You should celebrate."

"We are . . . by helping out," Bear said, his hand on Phantom's haunches as the cat climbed up to his shoulder. "Maybe we'll switch. Don't want Phantom hair in the buffet."

"Thanks, my friends. I appreciate it."

She didn't have time to think about how foolish she'd been with Bunny, or about anything except pouring drinks and making sure everybody was happy.

Shorty draped an apron over his head, and Patrick shoved a glass of whiskey at him in thanks. Bear threw a towel over the shoulder Phantom wasn't using and went behind the bar just as Cassandra glided through the room toward him.

"Cat man," she said.

"Do you two know each other?" Abby asked.

"Of him. I see him," Cassandra said.

"And I her. You have a great many cats of your own, don't you?"

"Well, Cassandra, this is Bear. Bear, Cassandra, just in case," Abby said and left them.

"Yes. I have a clowder. The ghost is not yours."

Bear grinned, "No, Miss Cassandra. Abby's, but he likes my shoulder."

"He is apologizing for his cousin, the misbehaving Ursa."

"And what do you know of bears and me, Cassandra?"

"Only the one who speaks on your face."

Bear scowled, not in anger, but confusion, and decided to leave it alone.

"What can I get you to drink, Ma'am?"

"I'll need to sweeten my voice for I'll be singing, so sherry."

She tossed it down in one sip and moved toward the piano, to stand by Benjamin who'd just sat down and was

JuliAnne Sisung

warming up, his fingers flying over the keys from one end to another, playing some melodic scales as appetizer to the piano entre` to come.

She finally tapped him on the shoulder, and he turned to her. His eyes widened when her appearance registered, the long stringy, gray hair, the purple gown hanging from her narrow shoulders, the black, piercing eyes. He closed his mouth, smiled wide, and opened it again.

"To what do I owe the pleasure," he said, breathing the words in a croon that was nearly a song, already in music mode.

"I'm going to sing," she said.

"Okay. What would you like me to play?"

"Swing Low, and play it as a lament."

Benjamin's fingers ran up to the end of the keys and slowly came back to the middle, and he nodded to her, his eyes squinting in joy.

When Cassandra started singing, folks were chatting and laughing, and the room was loud with people having a good time. Within the space of three vocal notes, not a sound could be heard except hers. Heads turned and eyes gaped, mesmerized.

The rich depth of Cassandra's voice was in such contrast to her appearance, it made you search the room for some trick. Who was really singing? Where was the owner of this ethereal voice? It was honeyed, plaintive, yet made you feel like going home to paradise would be the sweetest part of living. And every face in the room wore a satisfied, tranquil expression. Eyes melted in dreams of the celestial home.

On her last note, the room exploded with applause and Benjamin turned to her in reverence.

"I never heard anyone sing like that. You make leaving this world a thing of beauty, to be yearned for," he said.

"Isn't that Christmas?" she said, and when they demanded more, she shook her head and asked for a sherry.

"Cat's wait," she said, taking it with her.

Abby walked her out and thanked her for coming. Once outside, Cassandra watched her waiting felines,

218

sipped her sherry and stared at the frozen lake, her eyes narrow and searching.

"There, amid its thorny branches, standing guard, protecting, chaste petals sense the touch of dawn."

"Cassandra. What are you talking about? What do you mean?"

"It's plain as day."

The peculiar woman sipped again and licked her full lips, handed the glass to Abby and left.

Sally and Sue passed Cassandra on the steps and gave silent, respectful nods. Sue grabbed Abby in a fleshy embrace and released her only when Sally yanked her away for her own Christmas hug.

"Come on in before you freeze," Abby said. "And Merry Christmas."

"Sorry we're late," Sue said. "We had some visitors needing holiday cheer, so we gave them some. It's a lonely time of year for a lot of folks, and it was the Christian thing to do."

"I guess it was," Abby said, wanting to leave the topic as soon as possible. "You missed the most beautiful song. Cassandra has an unbelievable voice. You wouldn't imagine it was coming from her."

Sally pushed her hand against the door as Abby was opening it, effectively halting its movement.

"It doesn't," Sue said. "Come from her, that is."

Puzzled, Abby turned her back to the door and looked down at Sue.

"What do you mean? She was clearly singing. It was her, and it was great. More than great, it exceeded anything I've ever heard."

"What did it sound like this time?" Sally asked.

"This time?" Abby's forehead furrowed. "Like velvet and honey so sweet it made you want to lick the words or weep."

"Last time she sounded like bells. Made you think of dozens of churches, all ringing at once. She can do lots of sounds, but I don't believe it's really her. She borrows other voices."

Abby punched at Sally's arm and laughed.

"You ladies are pulling my leg. Nobody can simply sound like bells or somebody else just because they want to."

Sue grinned up at Abby.

"You sure 'bout that?"

Sally pulled them through the door and told Abby she'd hear some real singing now they were here. Real singing from real women. Bear poured for them, and they strode to the piano with purpose.

When Benjamin finished the tune he was playing, Sue leaned heavily against the piano, and Sally used a chair to climb on top of it. She sprawled on her belly, saloon-girl-style, her chin propped on one hand, her legs bent up at the knees, a sultry grin on her lips.

"Play *When the Boys Come Home for Christmas*, sweet man, and we'll teach you some carol singing you ain't never heard before," Sue said.

And they did. Applause was nearly as loud as for Cassandra, and the ladies nodded, pleased.

"We're good, cousin. What do you want to sing now?"

Chapter Seventeen

The week between Christmas and the new year was blissfully quiet. Bear and Shorty were there, of course, but other than Bradley Dempsey, Benjamin Chambers and his parents, the hotel was empty. They took long walks or read in their rooms, while Benjamin played quiet, sometimes melancholy tunes on the piano.

Abby didn't know how she was going to let him leave when the time came. She was growing dependent on his music. It filled the emptiness with heart and soul. She and Betty hummed along as they worked. It made the labor sweeter, the moments treasured.

Late one afternoon, everyone migrated to the bar where they were joined by Jesse and Edna. It was the perfect moment for Abby to enlist help for the spring Chautauqua, and two of the intended honorees were sitting right there at the table, so she folded her hands in front of her and did her best to appear angelic. That sometimes worked.

She described her imagined events to them, shaking her head at Benjamin and Bradley who blushed and objected saying he didn't need to be honored.

"I was just doing a job," he said, and Benjamin agreed, but his father thought otherwise and told Abby he'd like to be part of the planning.

She thanked her angelic posturing and plunged onward.

"Can you figure out how to contact others in the 369th and invite them to come for the April Chautauqua?" she asked. "The ones who are stateside, anyway. I don't have the foggiest notion how to do that, plus hundreds of thousands of men are still overseas, so they may yet be there and not able to come . . . or even get the invitation."

"Isn't your husband still there?" Maggie Chambers asked.

"He is. I can't wait for him to come home. But I bet all wives and mothers say that. And mean it."

"Every father, too," Micah said. "Don't forget us."

"Sorry, Mr. Chambers. Didn't mean to leave you out. Brothers, too. I know Frank's brothers miss him."

Micah glanced at his son and cleared his throat.

"Sorry. It'd be nice get Brigadier General Hoffman here for the ceremony. He's respected by both colored and white soldiers. And he's a good man," Micah said, glad to be back on solid ground.

Jesse clapped him on the back.

"All you can do is try. Write to his superior. Make it happen," he said with gusto. "Tell him it's good advertising for his troops."

Benjamin left the group for the solitude of the piano, and Abby watched while still trying to pay attention to the planning. Edna poked her with her elbow.

"Better quit making eyes at that young man, girl. He's the wrong color for you . . . and besides, you already have one." She grinned as she whispered, and Abby jerked her head back to the center of the group.

"I wasn't flirting. I was just watching him play. And my eyes are only for Frank."

"I know that, Abby. I surely do."

But she did enjoy Benjamin. He was calm and quiet, thoughtful and passionate. His soul was kept private but released in his music on the wings of every note. They rarely spoke, but Abby recognized that much about him and wondered if she knew Frank as well as the man at the piano.

She chewed her pinky and knew she'd be sorry to see the soldiers leave.

Bear and Shorty's boots stomped snow off on the rug just inside the door. Phantom flew off the bar and landed on Bear's shoulder when they entered the room.

Mrow a wah-wah.

"And to you my white, feline friend," Bear said.

Abby left the group at the table to pour their evening ale, glad to stretch her legs and move. Glad for the companionship of her best friends.

"Not much work today," Shorty whispered. "Looks like it'll be slow for a while."

"Just relax then. Take a break."

Cleo strolled down the bar to rub the top of her shiny black head against Shorty's broad shoulder, purring louder than she could speak.

"Noisy bugger, aren't you?" he said, nuzzling the cat with his chin. He'd gotten over his fear of felines since coming to Idlewild. "Gonna miss that piano player."

"Yeah," Bear said. "Nice hearing music. What's the matter, my friend?"

"Nothing. I wish he didn't have to go." She gave him a silly grin. "Make him stay, Bear."

After the Chambers and Bradley left, hotel guests were rare until March brought a few brave robins, some tiny crocuses poking through the snow with their purple and yellow heads, a false sense of spring, and a bunch of people eager to begin building. The warm infant sun brought life to Idlewild, and once again the sound of axes against timber rang out alongside shouts of warning and peals of laughter. They cleared just enough space for the size cabins they planned to build and traded the logs at the mill for seasoned lumber. They piled it at the edge of their lots, covered it, and waited, anxious for the ground to thaw enough to start digging foundations.

People filled the bar in early evening, and the guest register grew longer. It was good to be busy again.

Since the new year, Abby had spent too much time sitting at her window seat, staring out at the frozen lake. It had begun to feel too much like her heart, and she didn't know whether the chill and hollowness within was because she missed Frank . . . or because she didn't.

She should be crying for want of him. She should be antsy in anticipation of his homecoming, but she wasn't, and she was afraid of what she would feel when he came home

– or wouldn't. Longing had become too confused with fear. In a way, she dreaded his homecoming, and that hurt, too.

She put on her boots, called to Phantom and Cleo, and took a needed walk in the woods. She heard *rat-a-tat-tat*, looked for the master borer, and saw a crimson woodpecker hanging on the side of a tree, his sharp bill drilling for dinner. They followed a narrow trail and stumbled upon three whitetail deer standing on their hind legs, nibbling at the branches of a white pine. Seeing her, the buck snorted and slammed his front feet to the ground repeatedly in an effort to scare her away.

"I'm going," she told him, her voice hollow in the forest silence. "Come on, cats. Let's leave them to their dinner."

The buck tilted his head down as if he might charge. She laughed, and his chest muscles quivered. He cocked his antlered head, long-lashed eyes blinking.

"Sorry," she said. "I think I hurt his feelings. Come on, cats," she repeated.

She spotted coyote tracks and knew it led to a den they didn't want to disturb.

"You'd make her a fine meal, Phantom, with enough left over for her cubs. Wouldn't want that, would we?"

Turkey tracks led them for a distance and finally came to an end at Lake Idlewild where the fowl sipped water from thawed ice at the lake edges. Bare heads bobbing, and bristly, red beards flapping, they beat their wings in failed efforts to fly away. They finally ran squawking back into the woods, their ungainly bodies lifting and wobbling in awkward attempts to flee Abby and her cats.

Abby chuckled at their antics, brushed wet snow from a log, and sat, Phantom and Cleo sandwiching her.

"Nice, isn't it?" she said, closing her eyes and breathing in the scent of green and brown, pine trees and Michigan mud.

Mrow a wawah, Phantom said.

Cleo opened her mouth and blinked her jade eyes.

She stomped the snow from her boots on the porch and heard loud laughter coming from the bar as she opened the door and walked into the lobby. She cocked her head at the familiar voices, singling one out in particular. She shivered and smiled wide.

I'm happy to see him! I'm glad he is home!

Even more . . . she was jubilant recognizing it!

Abby ran into the bar and up behind where he sat, threw her arms around him and squeezed. He stood, dragging her up with him, and picked her off her feet, swinging her around like a ragdoll, she still hanging off his back.

"Come here, woman!" he shouted. "Get around here!"

She let go of his shoulders and slid down. He spun around and picked her up again.

"You're home," she said, in between kisses, her words a whispered thank you to the Lord.

"When did you get stateside? How are you? Are you done now?"

'Whoa, pretty lady. One question at a time. How about a drink?"

Abby sprinted to the bar as he sat, poured one for everyone at the table and served them. She stood next to him, touching his shoulder, his back, his hair. She wanted to possess the love and wallow in affection for her husband. Tears stung her eyes, and her lips ached with smiling.

He wrapped his arm around her hip and patted it as he continued a story he'd been telling before she arrived. Bear watched the faces as the tale spun on, all eyes eager to hear about the battle, the victory, the heroism. Frank was intense, focused inward in remembrance, his eyes alight, laughing.

"You wouldn't believe it," he said. "It was glorious, and we were there and part of it all. We were there!"

"Wish you hadn't been," Patrick said. "Sounds bloody awful."

Frank spun to his father-in-law, a frown slamming his eyebrows together.

"You got to be kidding," he said. "And miss all that?"

He pulled Abby onto his lap and wrapped his arms around her.

"You get it, don't you, girl?" he said, bumping his cheek against her chin.

"I don't know. I think I came in at the end of the story."

"It's the thrill of battle. Man against man, and the toughest wins. That's all."

Jackson, standing at the bar, said he understood, and Jesse told him that was because he was a child. A stupid kid.

"So, you saying I'm a kid, Jesse? And stupid to boot?" Frank said, quick anger sparking the words. His jaws bunched and nostrils tightened.

"No. I said Jackson was a kid, and he is. I didn't say a thing about you."

Frank nodded, not sure how to respond. He pulled on his chin and glared at Jesse, letting him know he didn't like the comment, but he was willing to let it go.

Abby searched the faces around the table and glanced at Bear who was watching hers. Cleo stood on his knee, her front paws on his shoulder. A strong hand eased down her back like a nighttime lullaby, and Abby heard the loud, comforting rumble of Cleo's purr. The sound settled her, was mesmerizing, and she jerked back to awareness when Jesse stood to leave.

"Early day tomorrow," he said. "Coming Edna? Welcome home, Frank," he said, turning back as he went through the door to the lobby. "Glad you're in one piece."

Frank stretched and twisted his neck like it was stiff. When he lowered his arms, he patted the decorations pinned on his uniform. The shirt was crisp and creased down the sleeves, the cuffs and collar starched. He looked handsome, like someone Abby knew, but not well, perhaps like a longstanding neighbor, or a third cousin. She tilted her head to peer at his face, to take a closer look.

"You flirting with me?" he asked, a half grin crinkling his cheeks. He squeezed her, and Abby struggled for air. "I've heard about women like you."

She drew back, startled, her eyes wide and fearful.

What did that mean? Had his brother written his horrible lies in a letter? Frank didn't look angry, but how would I know?

"Wh . . . when did you get stateside?" she asked. "You didn't write you were coming. I would have tried to meet you."

"Wanted to surprise you. Did it work?"

"It did. Yes. I'm stunned. Did you ship to New York?"

He nodded. Eyes flickering.

"You won't believe the stories I have. Europe is amazing. The people are . . . well, just strange. Not like us."

"But it's a war zone, Frank. People are likely going to seem different under those circumstances. Don't you think?"

He pulled at his chin again, revisiting scenes she couldn't know.

"Other nations might look different on the surface," Shorty said," but beyond cultural customs and traditions, I'd think we're pretty much the same."

"Wish you'd speak up," Frank said. "That damned whisper gets irritating."

"I said, cultural . . ."

"I heard you," Frank said, waving his words away like they were irritating mosquitoes. "But I don't agree. Some other people are odd, abnormal."

"You don't mean that, Frank," Abby said.

"And how do you know what I mean and what I don't? You weren't there. I was."

"I'm sorry. I know I wasn't there; it's just that . . . Nothing. Never mind. It doesn't matter."

Patrick pushed back his chair and stood, ruffling his already messed curls.

"I'll do the bar tonight, Daughter," he said. "You and Frank get on out of here."

"I'll help do the bar," Shorty added, trying to raise the decibels of his whispering voice. He was a giant of a man, too large to produce such a soft sound, and even he didn't understand it. It simply was.

Bear and Shorty headed for the kitchen to help Patrick.

"Well I'm not ready to go up, yet. I've got space for a couple more drinks first." He smacked Abby on her bottom. "Get your long-lost soldier a whiskey, Abs, and come back and tell me I'm your hero."

Joe Foster came in while Abby was fixing their drinks. He clapped Frank on the back and hooted.

"Damn! Glad you're home. Good thing, too. Get things back in ship shape around here."

"Sit down, Joe. Thanks. Glad to be home."

Joe spun a chair around, straddled it and rested his scruffy chin on the back.

"Whiskey, girl," he shouted without turning his head to look at her. "A double."

Frank leaned back and patted his lap when Abby came with the drinks. She put them on the table and shook her head.

"I'll be right back, Frank. I . . . uh, need to check on dinner preparations, and . . . I'll be back."

She fled to the kitchen and ran into her father.

"Whoa, lass. You're a whirling dervish. Slow down."

"I can't stand that man. I can't sit at the same table with him."

"Frank? Your husband?" he asked, his eyes wide and dazed. "Now isn't a good time to figure that one out, lass."

"Not Frank. Joe. Stupid, nasty, evil Joe Foster. I can't abide him, and he's sitting at Frank's table. I either have to ignore my husband, who's just home from the war, or make nice with a man I can't stomach – I can't! I can't do it."

Patrick wiggled his elbows and turned in a circle. He closed his eyes, counted to three, and opened them.

"You're still here! I don't believe it. It always worked before," he said, sounding disappointed. He cocked a foot against the other ankle, crossed his arms, leaned against the wall, and talked to the air in an obscure Celtic language that most likely didn't exist except in his mind.

"Stop it! I know what you're doing. I'll go. Just behave. Can I trust you to do dinner and tend to things if I talk Frank into leaving the bar?"

"Lass," he said, tilting his head in his most charming, Irish manner. "I'd never let you down."

She rolled her eyes at him, pushed the swinging doors and strode through, determined to convince Joe Foster to leave – nicely convince him. But when she got near the table, she heard words that raised her ire. Enflamed her.

". . . trouble unless you take charge of her, man," Joe said, his whiskey glass halfway to his mouth. He sipped and turned his head to see Abby's furious face.

She knew the 'her' Joe was referring to. Herself. She wanted to pick up his drink and dump it on his head.

"So, is Joe filling you in on your filial duties, Frank?" she said.

"Nope, just stuff about what's gone on in the neighborhood since I 've been gone."

"I'll bet."

Abby smiled as she spoke and pulled out a chair. She leaned toward Joe and patted his dirty hand, knowing he'd hate it.

"Need help recollecting what's gone on, Joe? I could probably help you out."

He smirked at her, showing his yellowed teeth, and she rocked back in her chair. She hated giving up anything to him, but she couldn't tolerate his breath.

"Just talking man stuff. You know," he said and watched Abby bristle.

"Where are your bags, Frank? Did you already take them upstairs?" she asked, trying to ignore Joe's presence.

"Left them at the farm."

"Oh," she said, unable to hide her surprise. 'I didn't realize you'd already been there."

He nodded and sipped, looking over the edge of his glass at her, his blue eyes sparkling.

"Yeah. We're gonna fish for steelhead tomorrow on the Pere Marquette. Should be perfect timing."

"Oh. Good for you. That should be fun."

Abby was still for a moment. She didn't know what to say. Of course, he'd want to see his parents and brothers. They were close, and he must have missed them. Why shouldn't he go fishing if that's what he wants to do? She saw Joe out of the corner of her eye, his smirk growing into a smile and wanted to ram her fist into his few bad teeth.

"You should do that while you can," she added.

"While I can?"

"You know, before you get back into work and all. Take some time to relax and have some fun." She rubbed his arm, felt the tight muscles under his shirt. "You earned it."

"That and some," Joe said, and pointed his empty glass at Abby. "Fill it up."

"Yes, I did," Frank said, "and I'm gonna fish a bit. Maybe sleep in." He gave Abby a look that said more than his words, and she blushed and got up to fix Joe's drink. Frank grabbed for her bottom and only succeeded in giving it a light pat as she scooted out of his reach. She'd seen the look in his eye.

"Why don't we leave the hotel in Da's care tonight, Frank," she said when she brought Joe's drink. "We could take a walk or just go upstairs and catch up?"

In other words, let's dump Joe Foster before I dump his drink on him. Let's go anywhere away from him.

"I think your little wife is making propositions, Frank. Better listen to her."

Frank picked up his drink and stood.

"Think I will," he said, and nodded to Joe. "Let's go, Abs."

When she opened the door to their room, Abby's room, Phantom and Cleo scampered in and leaped onto the bed. Phantom kneaded the quilt, beginning to make his nest next to Abby's pillow, and Cleo stretched out on her lookout-corner, ever the guardian, the watch-cat.

Frank took two giant steps to the bed, lifted Cleo in one hand and Phantom in the other, pulled his arm back like he was bowling and released the cats on the upswing. They flew through the air and landed outside the door which he quickly closed.

The skin of Abby's face tightened, faded to white, and her lips pressed together in an effort to stop herself from saying the words that came instantly to mind. She drew in an uneven breath, like the air in the room had been sucked out.

Frank didn't notice. He sat on the bed and toed off his boots, kicked them aside and started on the buttons of his shirt. When it was open, he shrugged it off and flung it on the dresser. He lay down and patted the bed next to him.

"I'm waiting for you, Abs. What are you doing over there?"

His grin was wide, and his eyes heavy lidded, suggestive.

Abby poured water into the pitcher and splashed it over her face. She dried off slowly, trying to figure out what was happening. Why was he acting like she was his to command? Like she was . . . she didn't know. His whore. Like he'd paid, and now she had to perform. This wasn't her Frank. This wasn't her husband loving her. She didn't know this man.

"You mad because I booted the cats out?"

She didn't want to go there, not right now, but it felt like abuse and troubled her.

"Not happy. This has been their room since you've been gone."

"But now I'm back," he said, stuffing her pillow behind his head to stare at her.

"You threw them," she said as gently as she could. She didn't want to anger him on his first day home. She didn't want to fight.

"I tossed them. Lightly. And they landed on their feet like cats do. They weren't hurt."

"Their feelings were. They aren't used to being tossed around. It's a matter of trust."

He bolted upright.

"Well, damn. I go off to war and come home to learn my wife cares more about her damned cats than she does me. Maybe cares about a lot of things except me. Joe was right."

He grabbed a boot and twisted to shove his foot into it. Abby pulled it out of his hands and wrapped an arm around his shoulder, trying to stop him. Trying to make everything right.

"That's not true, Frank. Please don't be mad."

"Well, it sure enough feels like it."

"I'm sorry. Really."

"Come here then. Show me."

Frank wrapped his arms around her middle, nuzzled her belly and fumbled with the buttons of her dress. It dropped from her shoulders to the floor, and in moments they were naked, and Frank's hands were everywhere. Abby kissed his shoulder, tasted his neck, and heard his groan of pleasure. When he penetrated, she stifled her cry of discomfort, and he lay heavily on her, letting his body ease, his heartbeat slow.

He rolled from her and flung an arm over his face. In moments, she heard breathing too even and deep to be wakeful breath, and she knew he'd fallen asleep. She slipped from the bed, washed at the nightstand, and drew her dress over her head. Tiptoeing from the room, she whispered to Phantom and Cleo who sprawled outside the door, grabbed her coat and left. She didn't want to see anyone. Didn't want to explain why her husband was upstairs and she wasn't, especially not to her father or friends. She couldn't explain what she didn't know, what she didn't understand.

She strolled by the lake, sucking in the smell of spring, feeling it settle on her cheeks and in her tousled hair. She tasted it on her tongue and at the back of her throat, the damp earth, the melting snow, winter growing into something new. The sun would soon set. It hovered at the horizon, and teased as it teetered on the clear line between land and sky.

Phantom and Cleo trailed her, stepping carefully on the damp ground, avoiding muddy patches. Now and then, Phantom streaked into the weeds, pretending to hunt rodents. He rarely caught them, but he liked fantasizing. He came back, sauntering like the great, white king of the jungle and giving Cleo a self-satisfied look.

Behind Phantom, Cassandra materialized leading her clowder and surprising Abby. She hadn't seen her coming, but that wasn't unusual. Cassandra appears like an apparition out of the air or a cloud or . . . nothing. The uniqueness of her presence disturbed some folks, but Abby was growing used to it, even enjoyed its eccentricity.

"How are you this warm evening?" Abby asked.

"Better than you, I think," Cassandra said, peering into Abby's eyes and nodding her shawl-covered head.

"Now, why do you say that, Cassandra?" she said, an unintentional tired sigh escaping her lips.

"Why wouldn't I? It is true."

"I'm going to walk a bit. Join me?" Abby asked.

Cassandra poked her walking stick into the mud, disturbing a frog who was trying to inflate after a winter of hibernation in frigid mud. He croaked and made a feeble attempt to leap.

"It's difficult to become fully awake in a cold world," Cassandra said.

"I imagine. Poor frog."

"What makes you think I was talking about a frog?"

Abby laughed, and the woman winked.

"Want tea?" she said.

"I would. Thank you."

Chapter Eighteen

Frank dumped a duffle bag, tackle box, and several fishing poles on the floor just inside the front door of the hotel. He leaned an Ithaca twelve gauge and a Springfield bolt action in the corner and hollered for Abby.

She leaned her head out an upstairs doorway and smiled at him.

"What are you doing? Moving in?" she asked, teasing but hoping he'd say yes. And he did.

"I'm done at the farm."

She came out and leaned over the banister, dragging the dust mop loaded with Phantom.

"Done? As in you're not going to farm anymore?"

"I repeat. I'm done. They don't need me. There's my dad, my two brothers, Ceci and Ma. What do they need with another two hands?"

Abby wedged the mop against the newel post and skipped down the stairs. She stretched up to kiss him and heard his frustrated sigh.

"You okay with this? I mean, is this what you want?" she asked.

He pulled away from her and grabbed his duffle.

"Sure. More fishing. Our room?" he asked, indicating the bag.

She nodded and eyed the fishing gear and guns.

"Maybe the storeroom for the other stuff."

"Guns aren't going in a storeroom," he said over his shoulder. "Grab them, will you?"

She carefully picked up the rifle in one hand and struggled to carry the heavier shotgun in the other, finally wrapping her fingers around the barrels of both of them, she swung them up and carried them like a baby, together.

In the room, Frank took one look and leaped to save them from her callous embrace.

"What are you doing?" he shouted.

"What you asked me to do."

"You don't bang guns together like they're rutabagas. They're valuable. You have to respect them, treat them with care."

"Sorry. I didn't think I banged them. Did I?"

Frank put them on the bed to inspect them, turned them over to look for scratches, and Abby saw gun oil seep into the wedding ring quilt that was her mother's and sucked in her breath.

"Can we put them on a towel or something, Frank? They're marking up the quilt."

Frank ceased his inspection long enough to give her a look and shook his head in confusion.

"It's a quilt," he said, at a loss about her concern.

"Yes. My mother's."

"It'll wash, Abby. Where should I put them when I've wiped them down?"

She looked around the room. It once seemed large enough for them both, but it was growing smaller by the day. The dresser was on one wall, the bed another. The washstand and armoire
took up the third and the window seat the fourth. A mirror stood in one corner, a chair and reading table another, and that was everything. There was no more space available.

Abby's head spun looking for a place for Franks guns, but was befuddled.

"Can they sit in a corner?"

"So anyone can see them and steal them?"

"Drape a blanket over them?"

When Frank didn't respond, Abby said she needed to get back to work. Betty couldn't clean all the rooms alone.

"Go on then. I'll work it out."

Abby took his fishing tackle and poles to the storeroom before looking for Betty. She found a shelf in the back where she could lay the poles out of the way with enough room for the box that held his supplies.

She chewed the tip of her pinky, ran a hand over her forehead, and smelled the acrid scent of metal lubricant. She rubbed her hands together and wiped them on her apron as if that would make it all go away, rid her mother's quilt and her own mind of the stain. She felt the gun oil between her hands and exhaled annoyance.

He was occupied with issues at the farm. He'd been to war. He didn't mean to be careless about the quilt.

Let it go, Abby. Don't be so picky.

Betty raised her eyebrows when Abby found her, asking if everything was alright without the words. They'd come to that place. Working together every day imbued them with special communication skills, a tilt of the head, a shrug of the shoulders, a flip of the hand was a language others couldn't interpret.

Abby rocked her head from side to side.

Betty said, "Hmmm."

Abby rolled her eyes to the corner of the room and huffed.

Betty slapped her leg, grabbed a sheet, and snapped it open. It floated onto the mattress, and she punched it down, folded and tucked in the corners.

Abby wiped out the bowl, hung new towels, and gripped the dust mop with force. She rammed it under the bed and Phantom shrieked.

Mrow!

"Thought he was probably asleep in a drawer," Abby said.

"No. Cleo is."

"They taking turns?"

"Seems like."

Before heading down to help with the lunch crowd, Abby went to her room to check on Frank. She inched open the door and tiptoed in. He was asleep on the bed in his underwear. His pants were in a pile on the floor next to his boots. The shirt he'd been wearing had been tossed to the dresser and dangled from the corner.

She picked it up to fold and saw the framed picture her father had given her. It was of him and her mother at their wedding, the only picture she had of her mother. It was lying on the floor, knocked over by his tossed shirt. She placed it back on the dresser, further into the corner so it might be safe from flying clothes, and turned to go.

"Hey," she heard. "Come over here and keep me company."

He stretched his long arms over head and then reached out for her. She moved closer, and Frank wrapped an arm around her legs and tumbled her to the bed on top of him. He ran a hand over her hips and bottom, purring like Cleo.

"Nice. I like waking to this," he hummed, finding a nipple and squeezing it.

"I can't stay, Frank," Abby said, trying to rise.

"You don't have to go right now."

"I do."

Frank continued to fondle her with one hand and held on with the other, thinking he could change her mind if he had time and touched her in the right places. But Abby pushed herself away and stood, watched his brow furrow and his jaw bunch in annoyance.

"Later, Frank. Truly. Right now, I have to work."

She looked for the guns and didn't see them, so he must have found a place for their storage. She ran her hands down her skirt, pressing out the wrinkles and smiled at him. "Later?" she asked.

He sat on the edge of the bed and pulled his pants on. His boots followed. She watched him don the cast-off shirt and admired his lean body, the strong torso, the broad shoulders.

"You gonna let your hair grow a little now?" she asked. "I like it curling around your ears."

He flashed her a grin.

"You gonna be friendlier if I do?"

"I have to work, Frank," she said, trying to breeze through the words so he wouldn't be irritated.

"Sure. I'm hungry. Can I get lunch like a paying guest?"

His words hurt, but she shrugged them off. He didn't mean it. Did he? He was in between worlds and confused.

"I'll seat you at my special people table."

"So, you do have special people, huh?" he asked as they left the room. "Special men?"

"People, Frank."

He decided he would work at the hotel with Abby, and bartending would be the best fit for him. He didn't know how to cook, didn't want to clean rooms or launder the linens for them, nor did he want to wait tables.

"I'll be a great bartender," he said. "I can talk to people just like you do, and I know about drinks, so it's a cinch."

It worked for the first couple of nights. They were slow, so it didn't matter that Frank drank as much as the guests did. But by Friday night, when the hotel was full and Jackson needed Frank to fill his orders, it was clear the bar wasn't a good fit. Frank *was* perfect for the bar, but it was on a stool or at a table being waited on by somebody else.

He tried the front desk, greeting people, taking their money, carrying their bags to their rooms, and that lasted about a week. His brother, Terry, dashed in, grabbed Frank's arm, and said, "Steelhead. Let's go."

Frank dropped the bag he was getting ready to tote up the stairs, said, "Sorry," and took off for the storeroom to snatch his equipment, calling for Abby.

Abby saw him dash back through the lobby with his gear as she came down to greet the abandoned guest.

"I'll take your things up, Mr. and Mrs. Peters. I believe you're in seventeen, so just follow me."

"You don't need to carry our bags, young lady," he said, his classically handsome face grinning at the abandonment. "And if the fish are biting, I might throw this in our room and get myself down there, too."

"That would be after you have settled us, Nathan," Mrs. Peters said with a grin.

Frank decided a job with regular, steady hours wasn't to his liking. He preferred handyman work he could schedule more haphazardly. He said he could fix broken things around the property, take care of the yard, replace worn boards on the porch, maybe paint it, make the trips to Baldwin for supplies if he had a list. In the winter, he could shovel snow, haul wood for the fireplaces. He could be useful.

Abby wrapped her arms around his neck and smiled.

"Farm running without you?"

"Yeah. They're trying to expand, though. Terry has some big ideas."

"That's great," she told him. "And I think you doing odd jobs around here is a wonderful plan. And you're useful here; you're needed."

He wiggled an eyebrow suggestively, and Abby scampered away, heading for the kitchen to start breakfast.

"I'll have sausage and eggs for you in about ten minutes," she called back.

Strange Al was already there and had the bacon and sausage in monster cast iron pans. Coffee was beginning to percolate.

"I treasure you, Al," Abby said, her tongue stumbling to keep from putting *Strange* in front of her name.

"Hmm," Al said.

"Where's Frank keeping himself?" Bear asked. He and Shorty held up the end of the bar and sipped their ale. Cleo moved under Bear's chin and crawled up his arm to sprawl over his shoulders.

She filled the tray with drinks Jackson ordered before moving toward her friends.

"I'm not sure. He's been busy with odd jobs around here lately, but I haven't seen him much today. Maybe he's fishing."

"Saw his pa and brothers at Foster's," Shorty said.

Abby shivered as an involuntary repugnance marched over her body.

"Probably selling eggs they won't sell to me. Don't know why it would take all three to peddle a few eggs, though," she said, more to herself than her friend.

"Three tall whiskey and water, Abby," Jackson called, and she walked away and forgot about the Adams men.

Bill Sanders and Jesse Falmouth strolled up to the bar with news Abby had been waiting for. Brigadier General Hoffman couldn't be in Idlewild to award the soldiers at the Chautauqua, but he was sending his second in command to speak for him. And Dr. Dan Williams, the Chicago surgeon, agreed to be the keynote speaker for the weekend ceremonies. The best news, however, was nineteen soldiers who had fought in France for the Allied Forces responded positively to the invitation and were making the trip to Idlewild.

Abby jumped up and down and clapped her hands together like a little girl.

"That's wonderful news! It's coming together! I hope we can accommodate them all."

"Bear and I'll bunk together that weekend," Shorty said. "You can use my room."

Abby put a hand on his.

"Thanks, Shorty. That okay with you, Bear?"

"Only if he promises not to spoon me. I can be as ornery as my namesake."

"Did we hear from the Chambers?" Abby asked.

"You know Micah. They'll be here," Jesse said. "You can double up the soldiers. They won't mind. And a couple of them are staying with Edna and me."

"Good. That's really good. I'm so excited about all of this."

Frank didn't show up until dark, so Abby kept a plate of Patrick's meatloaf, cabbage and potatoes warm for him. She was wiping down the bar after the last guest left and getting ready to head upstairs when he showed up.

"There's my wandering husband," Abby said. "Want dinner or a drink?"

"Food," he said. "I'm starved."

"Be right back."

Abby brought the plate and set it in front of him. He picked up a fork and didn't stop moving it until the plate was empty. He didn't speak or look up, just shoveled until he was finished. He straightened, rubbed his belly, belched and grinned.

"Good stuff. I was hungry."

"I could tell," Abby said with a grin. "Do you even know what you ate?"

He rolled his eyes sideways and gave her a mock frown.

"Steak?"

"Hardly."

"Don't know."

"Was there enough? Are you still hungry?"

"Naw. I'm good. I'll take that drink now."

Abby drew a glass of ale, pushed it toward him, and continued scrubbing the wooden bar.

"Where you been?" she asked.

"Here and there. Everywhere."

"It's been busy here today."

She whirled around and smacked her palms on the bar, her eyes alight with the fire of joy.

"I forgot! It's happening! The Chautauqua honoring our Negro soldiers is going to happen. I'm so excited. Dr. Dan is keynote. Benjamin and Bradley and seventeen other soldiers are coming and Brigadier General Hoffman's second in command. Isn't that great?"

"Sure," he said.

"Aren't you pleased?" she asked.

"You knew you'd make it happen."

His words deflated her enthusiasm. She didn't know what it was she expected from him, what words she wanted to hear, but knew it was something more than those.

"I already heard it, Abby," he said.

She turned with a smile of relief. That explained his words.

"How'd you know?"

"I was in Foster's when Sanders came in. He was spouting off about how Idlewild is going to be the greatest place in the nation. Gonna be famous."

"Could be," she said. "Are you done here? People are gone, and I'm really tired. I'd like to go on up. I mean, you don't have to be done. You can get whatever you want from the bar and kitchen . . . whenever you want. You know that, right?"

"I know, Abs. Go upstairs. I'll be there shortly."

Her step was heavy on the way to their room. Cleo nudged her ankle all the way as if she was helping.

"Thanks, girl."

Green circles stared at her and blinked.

"I do appreciate your help, Cleo. And you can come in, but scoot down to Bear's room when Frank comes up. Hear me?"

She blinked again, a slow closing of her eyes, a movement Cleo made instead of meowing. She opened her mouth, and no noise came out. Maybe Cleo thought Phantom made enough for them both.

Abby laughed when they leaped on the bed.

"Did you hear me, Phantom? When Frank comes up, you guys skedaddle. Okay?"

Mrow.

"I mean it."

Mrow.

"Now you're just sassing."

Mrow a wah-wah.

Cleo blinked.

Abby washed up, slid into her long, cotton gown and sighed. She sat at the window seat and both cats buried her lap in feline warmth.

"Love you guys. It's been a really long day."

She was asleep when Frank came up, but waked with the stomp of his boots and the door banging against the dresser. The cats flew out the instant it opened. They'd learned his footfall and had left the bed to wait by the door.

She rolled over and tried to regain slumber as he undressed. She heard each boot hit the floor, his shirt knock over the same picture frame, and the change in his pants clatter to the wooden floor. She buried her head.

It just sounds loud and inconsiderate because I was sleeping. He doesn't mean to be thoughtless.

The bed bounced when he sat and rolled toward her, and she curled tighter. His arm went around her, and a hand cup her breast and squeezed. His manhood pushed against her back and moved insistently.

"I was sleeping, Frank."

"But you're not now, are you? See how much I need you?"

Abby turned to embrace him, to be the wife he wanted, the wife she wanted to be.

When he slept, she wrapped in a blanket and left the room. Cleo and Phantom, lying just outside the door, followed and cuddled in her lap on the porch. She rocked and watched the night sky blink on and pondered life on another planet, in another world. She believed in the possibility of life up there. She believed in possibilities – period. The unknown was a vast string of potential and likelihoods, and staring at it in the night sky brought it closer.

Nearer home, frogs croaked, now fully awake from their long, cold sleep. A coyote yipped and another responded. She played with the idea that one of the voices was deep and masculine. The other a light, feminine yip. They'd find each other across the miles, maybe all the way across the lake, and they'd make a den together, make a family, and yip happily ever after together. The silly thought made her smile.

A bat skittered through the moon's beam, casting a monstrous shadow with its wings. It darted from side to side as if its erratic movement might frighten predators. And the owl responded.

Who, who, me?

"I don't want to live in space," she told Cleo and Phantom. "Look what I have here. All this and you."

Mrow.

With April's warmth, the island exploded with construction and energy. Echoes of hammers and saws, laughter and orders carried across the water to the hotel. Abby lifted the windows and propped them open to let in spring and the sounds of progress.

The hotel was full, every room holding folks either building or thinking about it. Their eyes burned with excitement, and Abby knew it was for more than owning a vacation home in a Michigan wilderness.

The fervor in their eyes glowed for belonging to something bigger than any single person. They were investing in a lifestyle that had been denied them, not just for *their* lifetimes, but for their parents, their grandparents, for their ancestry all the way back to when an African toe first touched American soil.

Some held breath in dreadful, unspoken expectation their resort wouldn't happen. Something would surely kill the dream. Someone would tell them it was a mistake. Others moved forward, eyes straight ahead, lips pressed together in determination and opened in laughter because they believed in the dream's conclusion.

Abby caught their joy, held it in her hands like a precious gem, and wore it on her sleeve. Her laughter reflected theirs, and she shared in their belief that Idlewild would be their nirvana, their idyllic city of gold where oppression could not live, and freedom thrived.

She and Strange Al cooked giant mounds of pancakes, sausages, bacon and eggs, and fed hungry, eager guests. As quickly as they cleared the breakfast mess, she and Betty raced through cleaning the rooms, boiling the linens, hanging them to dry, and folding them for the next bed. The dirty linen bin filled and emptied so fast, Abby wasn't sure whether she was putting clean sheets on the line or taking them off. Betty laughed when Abby asked her.

"These clean?" she said, sticking a clothes pin over the white fabric.

"Would I put dirty sheets on the line, boss?"

"Not sure. Would you?"

"Only if I could. And you didn't catch me." Betty grinned. "They'd freshen."

She was back to her old self, having gotten used to Strange Al being in the kitchen. She wouldn't be around her if she could help it, but proximity no longer made her go silent and moody all day. Abby wasn't positive about the reasons for Betty's response to Al, but she had a pretty good idea and figured if Betty wanted to discuss it, she would. She was happy her young friend was back.

"When this is done, I need to put my feet up for a few minutes," Abby told her. "We've got a town meeting after supper, so it's going to be a long day. Even longer than usual."

"Here at the hotel?" Betty asked, "cuz I can stay and help Jackson."

"No. The pavilion. It's warm enough, and Jesse figures on a lot of people for some reason."

"Maybe I'll go, if you don't need me here. Could be interesting."

"Sure. Come along with me. Just don't boss me."

"I don't ever boss you, boss lady."

"No, I don't mean you shouldn't boss me – like around, I mean call me boss. Dang it, Betty, you know what I meant. You're pulling my leg again," Abby said, her hands in her hair and messing with the thick curls.

"So, what you're saying is, I can boss you around. I like that."

Betty put on her best lopsided grin, grabbed the laundry basket and trotted away, leaving Abby with her mouth hanging open.

They were late to the meeting, having to finish with the dinner crowd before leaving Jackson to tend bar and wait on the few remaining people. Most had already gone on to the meeting.

Abby saw a wall of backs blocking most of the pavilion. The seats had already filled. She moved toward the front edge so she didn't have to peer around the much taller and broader backs of the men in the crowd. Her first thought when she saw the participants was that someone had cut the group with a jagged knife.

A cluster of farmers, identified by the work clothes sporting signs of their livelihood, sat up front, their faces eager for the meeting to begin and end. Terry and George Adams, along with Frank Sr., were part of their group. So was Joe Foster. The only colored man sitting near enough to the group to be considered a possible part of it was the unlikely Samuel Moore.

Across the center aisle from them sat Jesse and Edna Falmouth, Bill Sanders, Del Branch, Ratty and Flora Branch, the IRC leaders, and Patrick. Sally and Sue pushed into the crowd and plunked themselves on the bench holding Patrick. Sue shoved him over with her hip, and he had no control over where his bottom was going to land, so he grabbed Sue's arm and held on.

Behind the farmers' group and the business folks was the largest of the three groups, the lot owners and the potential owners. They filled benches at the back half under the pavilion roof and spilled out onto the grass behind them all.

Curiosity was high, mistrust apparent, tension tangible. You could smell it, like the musky scent of fear. It seeped from the pores and mingled with sweat and soap from a morning's bath.

Abby's heart thumped in her chest, and her head swung back and forth. She found familiar faces, puzzled over the seat choices, and moved on to the next recognized set of eyes. Frank came into her view, sliding in from behind the standing crowd and squeezing onto the bench holding his brothers and father. Abby stayed standing next to Betty whose parents came up behind them, and, a few minutes later, Bunny and Cassandra joined them.

Jesse stood and tried to bring the meeting to order, but voices rose in objection.

"Then who will lead?" he asked. "I've done this many times in the past. What's the difference today?"

"You're biased," a man shouted from the farmers' corner.

"Then you're welcome to run this meeting."

"I'll do it," Joe Foster said. "I been here longer than anybody."

"That's cuz you're older than my grandpa," a voice said, and laughter followed.

"Than dirt," another said.

Joe stood up to face the crowd.

Abby groaned.

Anybody but him. He's malicious and cruel.

"Let's get this started," he said. "And I'll do it. You're turning this town into a circus. All this Chautauqua claptrap."

He glowered at Abby, and hoarfrost glazed her skin. "Selling off tiny lots so people from Detroit, and Cincinnati, and God knows where can build stinking little cabins and leave 'em sitting empty all winter long. It's the stupidest, lamest brained thing in the whole world. There. I said it. It's done. Everybody that agrees with me raise their hand and we'll put a stop to it right now."

Joe's face was blotchy deep violet by the time he finished talking. He stuck his hand in the air, and what started as murmurs grew to an angry rumble. Several people held their hands in the air, as well, agreeing with Joe and wanting it done.

Bill Sanders stood and moved forward. He glared at Joe and turned to face the audience.

"Joe doesn't know what he's saying, and he can't stop us from selling our land in whatever size pieces we choose. Nor can any of you. I don't know what he's up to, but you folks can't take a vote to stop us. So . . . what is the real problem? Let's talk about it."

Mr. Tatum, Strange Al's father, stood and twisted around to face as many of the group as he could see. He hitched up his filthy pants, cleared his throat and spat at the ground.

"Here it is," he said. "You're taken all the prime ground around the lake, good farm land and givin' it to coloreds. Before you know it, we'll be outnumbered in the whole

247

damn county, and . . . you never know after that. It ain't right."

A clamor rose in the back, and Abby saw a few people turn and walk away. They'd heard enough, and they'd been hearing enough their whole lives. This was supposed to be different. It belonged to them . . . *belongs* to them.

She cringed when she saw Frank Sr. heave himself up. He was an impressive man for his age, large boned, square jawed and a full head of corn and gray colored hair. He took his time turning to face them, letting them all see the smoldering anger on his face.

"My sons and I are trying to expand our holdings; can't feed three sons and their families on what we own." He let his fierce eyes land on Abby. "Ain't that right, Abigail Riley Adams?"

He paused, let it infiltrate and spoke again.

"We need land. Not some little stamp sized piece of crap. Lots of it. Can't get the government owned land. You gonna sell to me, Mr. resort building man?"

"Now, Frank," Ratty Branch said, moving in his direction.

"Stay where you are, Branch. You don't want to be mixin' with the farmers. We know where you stand, and you sure don't want the stink of cow manure to mess up your pretty suit."

"Frank," Ratty repeated. "Resort land is different than farm land. Its beauty should be appreciated by many, shared and enjoyed by many instead of a single family – or cow," he added, trying for humor to stave off the anger boiling in the crowd.

"It's also a way to build the economy in the area," he said, thrusting his hands out, palms up like he was showing them a new economy. "Idlewild can use a shot of money. People couldn't even find work after the lumber left, and construction on cabins is helping with that. It's progress. There aren't any jobs for young folks. Ain't that right, Betty? You looked for months in your last year of school. And Jackson. He got a job with the new hotel, too, which wouldn't even be here if not for the resort folks. And Al Tatum, too."

"Don't you be speaking my girl's name in the same breath as those two Negros, Branch. You'll come to regret it," Tatum shouted, his face mottled with barely controlled fury.

Ratty looked at the tips of his shining, black boots and back out at the crowd. He shook his head. Del Branch joined his brother in front. He put a hand on Ratty's shoulder and nodded to the anxious faces at the back.

"In late April, we're holding the best Chautauqua yet. Music, speakers, literature, dancing. What we're doing in this small town is the envy of big cities all across the nation. We're so fortunate. And we're honoring the colored soldiers who fought for our freedoms in France. They fought with French soldiers because the United States forces didn't want them. After getting to know all of you . . .," he paused and looked toward the back, letting his eyes roam to each dark face, "I'd be proud to stand beside you in battle. I'd be proud to stand beside you in peace, and I'd be proud to be your neighbor, here, at the Idlewild Resort!"

Del's voice had continued to intensify with each phrase, and, at the end, it softened to a deliberate whisper that had people leaning forward to hear. It was meant for the farmers at the front. "Cuz folks . . . this here meeting isn't going to change anything, so I suggest you learn to like it."

People believed Adelbert Branch. He said it. He meant it.

Abby heard one man applause and then two. She turned toward the unhurried sound to see Shorty and Bear making noises of approval as their hands came together with intention. Pretty soon, it was three and five and, finally, many. She glanced to the farmers, met her husband's eye and brought her hands together. He turned red and away.

The Adams men rose like a wave cresting in a storm and strode off, shoulders hunched, heads together.

Chapter Nineteen

Except for Sally and Sue, only men filled the hotel bar following the meeting, and it was a subdued room. No animated talk. No laughter. They gathered in segregated groups, like a flower garden planted according to color. The men stopped to talk and mixed roses with daffodils on their way to tables of their choice, but they sat with their own.

Abby noted the color blocks, but was too busy to give it much thought. Jesse, Sally, and Sue kept up soft chatter at the bar, and Abby listened with half an ear. Even the ladies used their church voices.

"To you, girls," Jesse said, his glass touching his forehead in their honor. "Surprised you aren't working tonight with all the boys in town."

"Naw," Sally said. "When boys are mad they want to hit something, or kick it, and I don't want it to be Sue or me."

"Yeah, if they're thinking lovin' tonight, let 'em go home to their wives," Sue said. "I'll be at our home when their feeling a bit more jolly. That's why we're here 'stead a there."

Jesse laughed, appreciating their raw knowledge of humanity and their acceptance of its shortcomings.

Sue kicked her stubby legs back and forth.

"What's wrong. You want down?" Jesse asked.

"No. Moving blood around. The last time I sat on one of these stools, half of me was almost dead when I got down. No blood in the lower part of me. I swear. Fell to the floor like a drunk man. Or a dead one. Isn't that right, Abby?"

Abby was listening to pieces of Sue's tale and filled in the rest. She chuckled, remembering the debacle with Sue rolling around on the floor like a turtle on its back, flippers flailing.

"You did, Sue."

"I keep saying. You need to put a foot rest here just for me, right in front of one of these stools. I could put my feet on it, and my blood could make its way through my whole body then."

"I'll give it some thought, Sue. I will."

Jesse raised his brows, rolled his eyes, and nudged Sue with a shoulder.

"You're a pip," he said.

"What's a pip? Is that a good thing?" she asked.

"It's a bleep or a beep or a ping or a ding," Sally said.

"How do you know?"

"I'm not illiterate. I read."

"Well, la ti da. A well read, scholarly, colored hooker. Aren't you something."

Sue bopped sideways, bouncing her fleshy breasts back and forth with each word. Jesse's eyes were compelled to follow their path.

"That isn't nice, Sue," Abby said, refreshing their whiskey glasses.

"Well, it's not, not nice," Sally said. "It's pretty damned accurate. I'm well-read, colored and, as I like to put it, a lady of the evening, but hooker's the common terminology. And Sue is common, not scholarly."

Abby snorted and Jesse slapped a hand on his knee and guffawed. Everyone in the bar looked their way, and most wished they were sitting with them, with people having fun. Not talking about the farmers or the resort or the potential problems. The laughing people at the bar had obviously left the town meeting behind and found something amusing to talk about.

"And you, Miss Abigail," Sally said, "have tongues wagging. You gotta be careful."

"Why? What did I do?"

"Only slightly more than Branch and Branch, but they're men and rich," Sally said.

"Yes. And you ain't neither," Sue added.

Sally shook her head and rubbed her forehead in disdain before glaring at her cousin.

"Ain't neither? Jesus, Sue," Sally groaned. "Ain't doesn't exist, and it's especially abhorrent in a double negative."

"Can we get back to why I've made tongues wag?"

Jesse sipped and said he knew what they meant.

"Enlighten me, Jesse."

"You're at the forefront of the Chautauqua events, you promote activities for the colored residents, and you don't act like a *wife*, the traditional kind all the men around here understand and expect."

Abby stiffened, cocked her head and puffed up. She was miffed.

"Sorry," she said, throwing her shoulders back to put more space between them. "I didn't realize you . . ."

Jesse grabbed her hand.

"Wait. I didn't say *I* thought all that stuff about you. *I* think you're great."

"Oh." She turned to the ladies. "What do *you* hear?"

Sue wiggled closer to the bar, breasts spilling even more onto the shiny, wood top and threatening to climb out of her dress like newborn puppies.

"We hear things. People talk like we're not even there, you know. Like we're furniture or a broomstick. Well, that would be Sally, not me. I'd be more like a comfortable, overstuffed sofa they got used to seeing in a room."

"Sue. What are they saying?"

"Oh, yeah. Just that you're not much of a wife to Frank, so busy working here all the time."

Abby scratched her head and lifted her shoulders.

"And that you like colored people better than whites."

"Well, some of them, I do. Why shouldn't I?"

"And that you got two boyfriends." She thumbed sideways down the bar to Shorty and Bear.

"Hmmm. Well, they're boys and friends, so . . . I guess, but they're also my family, and other than my father and husband, all I have." Her words were defensive and weighted with annoyance.

Sue lifted her hands in the air and wiggled them, saying, "Don't shoot the messenger."

"I'm sorry. I asked. And, truthfully, I already knew everything you said. I just refused to say it out loud. I shouldn't have put you on the spot."

Abby's gaze roamed the room and settled on the men having drinks and talking. She did like the people who came to the hotel. She hadn't met one she disliked. Other than Samuel Moore, maybe, and he wasn't really a hotel guest. He was a longtime Idlewild resident. She couldn't stand Joe Foster, and he shared her race. Oh, yeah, and the woman she couldn't please during breakfast that day.

Her glance strayed to Shorty and Bear. She couldn't ask for better brothers. She would trust them with everything, with her life. Why should she have to give them up just because she got married?

Jesse tapped her hand.

"Don't let it get to you. You're alright."

"I forgot," Sue said, "the all-time best reasons you're bad. You drove us to Baldwin, and you have tea sometimes with Cassandra. White women don't do that. You did notice we're not white, right?" She indicated the three of them sitting at the bar. "Tongues flapped good over all those things but mostly the last two. And I think you're okay, too."

Abby clasped Sue's chubby, bare forearm, an Irish white hand on a very black arm. "I noticed." She wrinkled her face in a grin, tossed her auburn mane, and pounded her fist on the bar, garnering wide eyes from Phantom.

"I think you're damned okay, too. All of you."

The bar emptied and Abby was in their room washing up when Frank got home. She toweled her face and hands, turned down the quilt on the bed and climbed in.

"Do you need more water, Frank? I can go down and get some."

"No. This is fine."

"I was hoping your family would join us here for a while since they were in town."

He harrumphed and turned to stare at her.

"Seriously? After the meeting tonight? Weren't you listening? I know you were there – with your friends."

He threw the towel on the dresser and plopped hard on the bed to remove his boots.

"Why not, Frank? Why wouldn't they come in for a drink?"

"You just don't get it, Abby. You're not with us. You're with them."

"Who is us? Your family?"

"Who else?"

Abby yanked the quilt up to her chin and chewed the inside of her cheek.

"I'd like to be part of your family," she said, a nostalgic note in her voice. "They don't want any part of me."

"And why do you think that is? You've made it clear you're on the side of the resort owners and the coloreds."

Frank tossed his pants on the dresser, and the shirt followed. Abby cringed when the picture of her mother crashed to the floor again. Maybe she should just put it away. Take it out of harm's way.

"I didn't think we had sides. I thought we were all working together, toward a single goal for Idlewild," she said, touching his back to get him to look at her.

"Not everybody shares your lofty ideals, Abby. And I just want a wife nobody talks about constantly and looks at like she's a lunatic."

"Frank, I don't know what I'm doing that's so terrible. Why don't you tell me what bothers you, and we can talk about it?"

He lay down, stretched out, scratched his chest, and shoved his arm under Abby's head. She listened to the rhythm of his breathing and knew conversation was over. He fondled her breast with his free hand and reached lower. Had never begun. She squeezed her legs together, trying to let him know she didn't want to be available, but he pushed them apart, and she let him. She pretended it was alright.

She closed her eyes and concentrated on the pleasure Edna had told her about, had said was wonderful, but there was never enough time. It ended before it started. She waited for the light snore, grabbed a quilt and tiptoed to the porch.

The moon had risen white-gold against black satin and lit up wispy cloud threads that held up a sky full of stars. Two moons stared at her, an extra one in the lake. It wiggled when the water rippled, and the stars ran around, twinkling on and off until it was hard to tell up from down.

Abby rested her head at the back of the wooden rocker and stared, wishing the man in the moon would talk to her. Tell her what was right. What wasn't. Or more to the point, what was she *not* doing that she should be? Give her a man's perspective.

"Help me out," she said to the glowing sphere in the sky. She smiled, feeling foolish talking to the moon. "Might better talk to the birds. They at least talk back, Abby," she whispered and sighed. "They're right. I'm nuts."

Hoo. . . came out of the woods skirting the lake, and Abby jumped, her eyes scouring the trees for friend or foe.

"Stop that. Not fair."

Hoo, Whoo . . .?

"You. Stop it."

If you insist, she heard, but knew it was in her mind. At least she hoped it was.

When her eyes began to droop, she went back to her bed, walking softly on the wooden floor so she didn't disturb anyone's slumber. She lifted the covers and slid in, pulled them up to her chin and let herself grow quiet. She lay on her back with her arms crossed over her chest to take up as little space as possible. When it occurred to her she looked like a corpse ready for burial, she moved her arms to her sides and lay quietly until she fell asleep.

Abby saw the sun come up from the kitchen where she was preparing breakfast with Strange Al. When Patrick came to finish up, she heaped a plate with pancakes, sausage, and eggs, threw it on a tray with a cup of coffee and ran it upstairs to surprise her husband. She toed the door open and put the tray on the dresser next to his pants.

"Breakfast, Frank. Just what you like," she sang, kneeling by the bed next to him.

He groaned and threw an arm over his face.

She brushed the hair from his forehead and said, "Wake up sleepy head. Food."

His eyes opened, and he groaned like a grizzly as he reached for her.

"It's early. Why so early?"

"Cuz lots of people are here and more are coming. It's a work day. Get up lazy bones."

She stood up, got the tray, and put it next to him.

"Breakfast in bed just for you. Hungry?" she asked.

"Guess so. Smells good."

Abby waited while he scooped up egg and sausage, took a swig of coffee and swallowed.

"Well . . . I'll go. I could use you for a little while when I'm checking in folks," she said, unsure how he'd respond after last night.

"You mean carrying bags like some . . . bellboy?"

Abby pulled at her bottom lip and wondered how they had come to this place.

"Yes. Like I do, every day we have guests coming in."

"Fine. I'll be down in a bit."

She turned away and whispered, "You're welcome for the breakfast," as she went through the door.

"What?" he yelled.

"Nothing. See you in a few minutes."

A steady stream of people waited to check into the hotel, and Abby pointed bags out to Frank and gave him the room keys, hoping he wasn't hating helping her. He didn't engage in small talk with the guests and refused the tips they tried to give him. The rooms began to fill, and Frank fled. When she looked for him, Al pointed to the storage room where his fishing gear was stored.

"He left?" Abby asked.

Al nodded.

Patrick searched his daughter's eyes and didn't know what he found there.

"You good?"

"Sure, Da. I'm fine. It's going to be a busy day."

"Eat," he said.

"I will."

They hadn't minded waiting in line to register for a room. They smiled and talked, shared information about where they'd come from and their hopes about what they'd find at the Idlewild Resort for Colored People. They'd been told, but weren't sure they believed what the real estate salesmen had claimed.

A lake to fish and swim in? Horses to ride? A club being built on the Island where colored musicians and singers were welcome? No signs reading *coloreds not allowed*? Or *Sundowner Town?*

Many eyes shone with anticipation, and more than a couple in hard-bitten doubt, unconvinced the beauty of northwest Michigan could be theirs to enjoy. Abundant water, forests for hunting and hiking? Freedom from white antagonism and constraints? No oppression?

Folks were excited to tour the area. Jesse, Bill, Del and Ratty led the skeptics and cynics on long walks around the lake. They took them on boat rides across Lake Idlewild and around to the Buckles' home. The couple told how they had come all the way from Medicine Hat, Canada, lived in a shed for several months back in 1916, and waited while their home was being built. The Buckles were the perfect picture of happiness, of peace and serenity. Of freedom.

After they met the Buckles, their belief simmered. They met other families already living in their cabins on the island, even though it was early in the season, and these residents reached hands out to the newcomers as old timers who knew the ropes and validated their dreams. Confidence in the Idlewild resort grew.

By the end of the tours, many bought lots, found contractors to build their cabins, and went back to the hotel full of optimism, eager to bring reality to their visions. Belief began to brew steady bubbles of hope.

The bar filled early that evening, and Abby's feet ached. She hadn't been off them since early morning, but the smiles on the faces of patrons kept her moving. Happy chatter spread like fairy dust blowing with warm winds of transformation.

Not even Joe Foster's face caused a frown when he limped up to the bar and ordered a whiskey. Patrick, hearing his belligerent voice from the kitchen, came out wiping his hands on a long, white apron. He scanned the room for Shorty or Bear and, not seeing either of them, sidled up next to Joe who gave him an angry nod.

"Are ye not feeling good then, Joe?" Patrick asked.

"Sure, I am. Why the hell shouldn't I be?" Joe said, after downing half the whiskey in his glass.

"Thought ye might be having a wee bit a trouble with your memory."

Joe snorted his disdain. "You're the one with his brain off kilter."

"Well, ye keep causing trouble here for Abby girl and me, and we keep asking you to find another place for a drink. Yet, here ye are."

"I'm not the one who's sick, but now you mention it, thousands a others are. I think you and your *guests* ought a know about it." He twisted the word guests as if it was dirty or tainted, and his eyes rolled toward them. "That influenza is back to killing people. If this whole damn town dies, it's on your head, Patrick Riley!"

Joe's voice rose a notch with each word until he was hollering again, and every face in the bar turned his way. They watched with curiosity and looked at each other in nervous glances. Patrick saw their discomfort and grasped the man's arm to drag him to the door – once again. Joe jerked away and turned to the room full of people.

"It's damn true!" he yelled at the curious eyes following him. "It ain't cuz I'm white and yer not that I'm saying it. Spanish flu is back, and it's cuz a you!" He turned to Patrick who was trying again to drag him to the door. "You'll be sorry bringing 'em here, Riley."

Patrick held tight to Joe's arm and pulled it behind him, but the wiry man slipped from his grasp, and Patrick's short body rammed headlong into Bear who strolled in at the same time Joe slid free. Bear stood Patrick upright and deduced the problem. He took a single step, put a hand behind Joe's neck and bounced him toward Shorty who was just then walking in.

The giant lumberjack grabbed Joe by his shirt and marched him to the door, the trouble maker's toes skimming the floor as he went. Angry gurgling came from his throat as he tried to scream invectives through a larynx constricted by his own shirt.

Patrick swiped his hand together as if to rid them of dust and hiked up his pants.

"Well done, lads. I'd have managed, but the three of us made short work of it."

Bear nodded and grinned. Shorty gave him a pat on the back that sent Patrick flying across the room.

"Sorry," he said.

"You forget yourself, ye big oaf," Patrick said coming out of a stumble. "Have one on me. You earned it... maybe."

She was enjoying the night air on the porch when Frank strolled up.

"Take my chair," Bear said. "Think I'll walk a bit."

Shorty said he could use a stroll, too, and joined him.

"Did I scare off your boyfriends?" Frank asked. "Didn't mean to."

"Funny, Frank," she said. "How was your day?"

"Fine. Ready for bed?" he asked.

"In a bit. I'd like to unwind right here in the cool air. It was a busy day. A little crazy, and I just got done."

Frank nodded, and Abby saw a scowl form on his brow. He didn't ask about her day or comment. It was as if it didn't matter or even exist. A flutter of irritation piqued her, and she tried to let it go. Told herself he hadn't gotten used to civilian life yet.

"Thanks for helping me this morning. With the bags," she said.

Frank nodded and thrummed his fingers on the arm of the chair.

Cleo leaped up the steps and landed in Abby's lap. She absently stroked the cat and watched her husband.

"How was fishing? Did you enjoy yourself? Catch anything?"

"Yup. Couple."

But his face showed anything but enjoyment. In fact, it showed no emotion at all. Beneath the scowl, it was blank, an unwritten slate. Abby looked for some clue to how he was feeling, what he was thinking – in his eyes, anywhere, but couldn't find a thing. The jaw muscles twitched, and the Adam's apple moved when he swallowed. That was it.

"Frank, talk with me. Tell me about your day."

He turned in his chair and reached for her. Startled, Cleo swiped, scratched his hand, and he batted the cat off Abby's lap.

She took his hand in hers, turned it to look for a wound, but didn't find any blood.

"Gonna live?" she teased.

"Damned cats."

Abby tried to let it go, but couldn't.

"They're important to me, Frank. I wish you wouldn't mistreat them."

His eyebrows rose as if he was stunned, and Abby wondered if he was, if he truly didn't understand. Or maybe it was her. Maybe she didn't get it.

"It's an animal. And it scratched me. What about that is so cussed difficult? Jesus, Abby. I've said it before. You care more about those damned animals than you do your husband."

"That's not true, Frank. But I *do* care about them."

Both fell silent, neither happy with the evening. Neither willing to delve into it further. Abby was too tired and hurt, and Frank was too angry. Not with the cat, but with his wife who couldn't be what he wanted and needed. He didn't know when she had changed, but she was either a different person than before, or he hadn't known her at all.

Patrick came out with his nightly glass of Irish and groaned as he slid into his chair. He noted the silence, but he didn't feel like talking anyway, so he tilted his head back and toed his chair to a slow, peaceful rock. Sipped his whiskey and closed his eyes. He turned to look when he heard the door open and close as Frank left them.

"No goodnight, sweetheart?" he asked.

"No. No goodnight."

"Hmmm."

One tear escaped and took its time rolling down her cheek. It glistened, and you wouldn't know it was there without the moonlight that lit it.

Chapter Twenty

Summer 1919

Benjamin Chambers felt strange in his dress uniform, an imposter trying to look like a hero, a rusty toy soldier like the tin ones he played with as a boy. Medals covered his chest, and he unconsciously covered them with a hand, not to protect, but to hide. Harrison Wilson walked next to him and was a twin in his decorated jacket, but his chest was puffed with pride. He would have waved it like a flag if he could. He slapped Benjamin on the back.

"You earned those shiny things, Ben. Use 'em. Girls around here are gonna love you. Me, too."

"Man, girls love you wherever you go. In and out of that uniform."

Seventeen other Croix de Guerre soldiers filled dress uniforms in various shapes and sizes. Tall and short, brawny and thin, arms and legs missing, or an eye or worse, they were soldiers with two great similarities. Medals were suspended from all nineteen chests, and they were all Negroes of the 369th.

They knew each other better than most brothers, so meeting in Idlewild was a reunion, and some, like Benjamin, were shy about their war record. Others echoed Harrison in their own praise and garnered smiles and laughter from the people around them: mothers, fathers, and siblings who already knew how great they were.

Dr. Dan Williams gave the keynote address, Jesse Falmouth led the ceremonies, and Colonel Davidson awarded the medals.

Jesse pointed out several residents of the Idlewild resort and asked Mr. and Mrs. Buckles, of Medicine Hat, Canada, to stand.

"This beautiful lady and her husband were the first to take up residence here. They believed in our promises. Have we told the truth, Helen?"

She nodded and grinned, her long earrings shimmering in the glow of the lanterns.

"Stand up all you Branch folks, Wrights, and Lemons. If we just counted all the Branches in the Idlewild census, we'd double in size! These folks gave us the promises. And they've kept their word."

Eight people stood and took bows.

"Have you been swimming? Fishing? Kissing in the woods?"

He got a laugh from his audience. He was vamping them up, getting them excited to hand it over to the Colonel for the important part of the ceremony, but he wasn't done. He talked about what it meant to be colored in 1919.

"It's different now for all of us. We're earning more than ever. We're getting an education, going to college, learning a trade. We do important jobs. We teach, we heal, we uphold the law! We're the *new African Americans*. Don't you ever forget it!"

Hand clapping, foot stomping and shouts raised the roof of the pavilion and spread to the forests and across the water to the island. Joy hung from the stars blinking on one by one and guarding the sliver of moon cocked haphazardly in an ebony sky.

Abby's heart pounded, reverberated with the joyful noise Jesse had generated. She had listened and understood, but something about what he said gave her pause.

Was there something wrong with the old Negroes he talked about? She had liked them. Or didn't she know them? Was it only the new ones she knew? She'd never known any before moving to Idlewild, so she had nothing to go on. Maybe she wouldn't know an old African American if she met one. She laughed at her silliness.

I'll ask Edna or Jesse if they're the old or the new variety. That'll straighten me out.

Then it was Colonel Davidson's turn at the podium. He grinned when Jesse turned it over to him.

"You're a hard man to follow," he told him, "but I've got the heroes on my side. And I've got the ribbons."

He began by saying he didn't know much about the Idlewild resort but that he'd been given a tour by Bill Sanders who tried to sell him a lot, of course, so he knew a little and was pleased at what he saw.

He stuck his hands in his pockets and pulled them inside out as if looking for money.

"Maybe next year. I'm just a poor soldier. Save me a lot?" he teased.

He called each of the soldiers to the platform, one by one. When they stood together behind him and in front of the crowd, he turned to them and saluted, a sharp snap of a hand to his forehead, eyes straight ahead, immobile moments of honor. They acknowledged him in kind. Nineteen hands flew in rigid, hard-armed salute. Applause exploded.

The Colonel found space on each chest to pin the new ribbon next to the Croix de Guerre given by France and talked briefly about each soldier's exploits, their valor, selfless courage and determination under extreme conditions. Tears hovered in the eyes of men and women alike, even though some had heard at least pieces of the tales before.

But this was different. This was new, and it was more than a simple ceremony honoring a group of soldiers, more than being recognized with the Croix de Guerre ribbon. This was about a battle that had been waging in America for generations and had only a little to do with World War I. The great war, while epic in itself, was in this instance merely a vehicle that carried on the Negroes' fight for recognition. For respect.

In Idlewild, a whole town was gathered to honor soldiers, to identify and applaud heroism. Skin color was an issue only because there were no white soldiers in the 369th division. And recognition for valor in combat was a battle won. They knew they'd not won the war. But it was a beginning, and even a small victory felt good.

The soldiers marched off the small stage to thunderous applause and calls for the beer tent to open. Buddy Black's band set up, chairs were moved, and dancers took the floor. Abby's toes tapped to the music, and she kept one eye on the hotel porch, and one on the musicians. She ran back to check on Jackson and Betty who were sitting at the bar with nothing to do because everyone was at the pavilion.

"Don't worry about us," Betty said. "We're having fun cuz you're paying us to sit here and not do anything but tell each other lies while you go broke."

"Was that a lie, Betty Jean?" Jackson asked. "Did you not really swim across the lake? Did you fib?"

"What do you think?"

"You tell me. I don't know. You're a pipsqueak, Betty."

Abby listened to them banter, told Betty to come in later the next day, that she'd be back in an hour or so to take over, and left to listen to the music and visit with friends.

Shorty grabbed her for a dance, and soon she had a line of men waiting to swing her around the pavilion floor. Her feet hurt, but she laughed and smiled so hard her face was stiff with grinning. It occurred to her once or twice to look for Frank, and she did, but couldn't find him or any of his family. It niggled at her that she was probably having a better time alone with her friends than if he was there making her feel like she shouldn't be having any fun at all.

"Where's Frank," her father asked. "You two fight?"

"No. No fight. We don't really do that. Not sure where he is. I haven't seen his brothers either. None of the family."

She wiped a line of sweat trickling down her face and looked around at the people on the outskirts of the large group.

"I think they're the only missing family. Even Strange Al's brothers are here," Patrick said.

"That's a surprise. Where?"

"Way at the back. Standing with Joe Foster."

Abby shuddered hearing his name.

"That man scares me."

"Just keep clear a him, Abby. I can't abide him either."

Patrick wrapped an arm around her back and was about to swing her out onto the dance floor when Sue waddled up and grabbed him. She yanked the leprechaun away from Abby, wrapped both arms around him and dragged him to the middle of the room. There was nothing he could do but comply and get lost in the pillows of her breasts.

Abby's mouth opened in laughter, but her eyes strayed back to the Tatum boys and Joe.

She returned to the hotel to relieve Betty before the band quit playing, figuring folks would head to the bar, not ready to relinquish the night to sleep.

"Wait just a few minutes, Betty, and Bear or Shorty will be along. Someone needs to walk you home. It's really dark, and there's a lot of strangers in town."

"I been walking these trails all my life, Abby Adams. Not gonna start asking for a babysitter now."

"But I feel responsible for you being out so late."

"You're absolved of that responsibility, boss. I'm going. See you around ten. Isn't that what you said?"

"That'll work. Be careful."

Betty opened the door, and a hoard of people came through, forcing her to stand there and hold it like she was the doorman they'd been waiting for. She showed them her beautiful teeth and made sweet comments to the soldiers who either blushed or wise cracked back to the young girl.

Abby watched and wished she would wait for an escort home.

Jackson shouted an order for drinks, and Abby forgot all about Betty. The bar was filled to overflowing. Every seat was taken, and people lined the bar three deep. Shorty came behind to help, and Bear filled in waiting on tables Jackson couldn't get to. Patrick went to the kitchen to make snacks.

Benjamin cracked his knuckles and flexed his fingers, grinned and played a rousing James Reese number that had people tapping their toes. Every soldier in the bar knew the

Reese syncopated rhythm because he had toured with the Hell Fighters at the end of the war. He was a music legend to colored musicians, and Benjamin played like the tune was written for him.

Edna talked Jesse and Bill into clearing space for a small dance floor. She grabbed Jesse's hand, pulled her skirt up with the other and moved into an inviting foxtrot. Her husband grinned and followed. What else could he do? It was all in the feet. Shoulders still. Hips immobile. Eyes on your partner. Loving them with your eyes and nimble feet. Edna's head flipped back at the end, and Jesse kissed her neck. The perfect end to a foxtrot love story. The crowd that had gathered around them cat called and whistled approval.

Shorty nudged Abby behind the bar.

"You do that?"

"Good heavens, no. Two left feet."

"Bet not."

He'd win the bet. Her ten-year-old bedroom had been a stage for filmy, white dresses and ballet shoes; handsome, black-suited adagio partners and dreams. She had danced to the sound of her own voice and painted the bedroom stage in colors of her imagination. Shorty saw it playing in her eyes.

"Fire!"

The word immobilized the room, and all heads spun toward the windows. Orange fragmented the dark sky in multiple locations, both on the island and the mainland. A communal roar of anger set people in motion. Chairs scraped across the wooden floor and boots tramped in a race to the door.

"No, God," Abby said, running to the kitchen to tell her father.

"Bring all the buckets and lock the door behind you, Abs. Jackson, let's go," he said.

They ran to the shed for rakes and shovels and headed to the fire with the fewest people around it.

Sparks flew as water was tossed on the flames, and Abby kept an eye on the woods, watching for a stray ember to light the forest surrounding them. Curses barked and coughs hacked from smoke choked throats, and they had to back away from their work to breathe. As soon as they filled their lungs with a puff of clean air, they went back to waging war against the fire, red ashes and smoke.

Like before, it didn't take long to reduce the flames to water-logged char, but this time rage smoldered in the leftover ashes. Folks weren't as ready to ignore it and hope it wouldn't happen again. They couldn't carry on the delusion that the fires were childish pranks or empty messages. This had the weight of malicious, intentional destruction. That much was clear.

The *new African American* Jesse had lauded today put fists on their hips and spread their feet in fight-ready stances. They weren't going anywhere. They would not be cowed, and the sooner people figured it out, the better everyone was going to be. It was in their eyes, the thrust of their chests, the grim determination of their jaws. It was in them all.

As soon as one fire was doused, fire fighters joined the crew at the next one and the next, until they were one huge group, and all that could be seen in the dark was spiraling, murky steam reaching for the sky. They went from scorched cabins to the untouched, carrying lanterns to look for something the arsonists had dropped, looking for evidence, looking for confidence and courage.

Doors had been painted with the white cross on red some of them had seen before. They washed them and moved on, mumbling invectives, but undeterred.

They found the burned bottles of kerosene bombs that had been thrown at the cabin exteriors or tossed in windows. A paint brush lay in the grass near the foot bridge. One of the soldiers spotted it near the water. He shouted, pointing.

"Let it lay," Jesse said. "Don't go near it, right now. Let the sheriff get it. Find someone to go for him, please."

Henry Piccard, the man Joe Foster tried to run out of his grocery store the year before, stood with an arm around his wife, Georgia. He pulled at his lip and stared across the group of men and women who had fought to save the cabins. They were a good bunch of folks.

He'd gotten to know them pretty well over the past year and couldn't name a bad person, except one. And he saw him now at the edge of the group.

Joe Foster was sidling up to the men at the back of the crowd. He hadn't been around when they were throwing buckets of water on the flames, when they were choking on acrid smoke. He hadn't been around when they were washing paint off the doors. Why was he here? When did he cross the footbridge?

Henry ambled over to Bill Sanders, greeted him and nodded in Joe's direction. Sanders' eyes widened in surprise. Joe's toxic hatred of the resort folks was well known. It wasn't likely he would lift a finger to help save their homes.

"Hmmm," Bill mumbled. "Odd."

"I thought so, too."

Bill headed in Joe's direction.

"What ya doing, Joe?" he asked.

"Just lookin' around."

"Come to help?"

"Sure," Joe said, a snide grin exposing rotted teeth.

Bill winced, as he always did when he saw Joe's mouth, and wondered how the man could stand the smell. He backed up a step or two and tried again.

"Didn't see you cross on the bridge. When did you get here?"

"None a your business when I did. Now ain't that so?"

"Could be my business, Joe. I still own much of the property you're standing on. Could be the sheriff's business."

"You're a horse's ass, Sanders."

"That could be, too. But now you're here, you should stick around till Hicks gets here. He might want to talk to you."

Joe turned and headed toward the bridge.

"He'll know where I live."

Bill watched him cross the lake and go into his store. He couldn't tell if the man smelled like kerosene or not. Joe had too many other competing odors, but he wouldn't put it past him to try driving the lot owners away with fire and paint. Skulking around in the dark would be just Joe's style.

Not far from the store, he watched Cassandra standing motionless facing the island, a row of cats next to her. He swore he saw fire in their eyes. They glowed. They were brilliant orbs blazing across the water, two by two. He turned away.

These people, the folks on the island, needed some protection. He owed them safety.

He spotted Abby with her own personal defense planted on either side of her and smiled. The view gave him an idea. Bear and Shorty. He headed their way.

"I need you two," he said, pointing at them. "You still doing construction?"

"Yes. Work's sporadic, but it's enough," Shorty said, looking down at Sanders' full head of white hair and rubbing his own barren scalp.

"How'd you do it?"

Sanders looked up – close to a full foot higher than himself.

"What'd I do?"

"Grow all that hair."

Sanders smiled, and Shorty wondered if he could ask about his teeth, too. They were the biggest he'd ever seen. He wasn't sure they were real, and someday he wanted to yank on them to find out.

"It's a talent," he said. "And I'm interested in a talent you two have." He pointed to Bear and Shorty again.

"Okay. What?"

"We need a night watch. Men who'll patrol the island and mainland resort areas. Honest ones who'll keep a lookout until things get settled. What do you think? The IRC will pay."

"Both of us?" Bear asked.

Bill nodded and grinned.

"I think two's best. You can watch each other's backs just in case of trouble."

"How long?"

"That, I don't know. Until things settle. We don't have a real police department nearby. Just a county sheriff and his deputy, who . . . well, let's just say he's busy in other parts of the county."

"I don't know if this is a good idea," Abby said. "It could be dangerous. You're not trained to be officers."

"No. But I'm big, Abby."

"Bullets don't care about big."

He hugged her and yanked on her hair like a bratty, little brother.

"We'll watch tonight, Bill, and let you know tomorrow about the next days."

Sanders climbed on a stump and hollered for attention. He explained his plan for their safety and received words of appreciation for his efforts. He introduced Bear and Shorty, and they applauded them, too. Especially Shorty.

"You're safe now," Edna said to the folks around her. "Nobody messes with Shorty. And I hear Bear got his name cuz he tangled with a Mama Bear. He won."

People milled around the site for a time, waiting for something to happen. They talked in whispers as if crime needed the respect of soft voices, or they were afraid to speak too loudly and bring attention to themselves. There was safety in anonymity. And safety in groups. If they went to their cabins, they'd be alone with their families and vulnerable. It wasn't a conscious thought, a mindful fear, but it lurked in the recesses of their brains, and they swallowed the words clogging their dry throats.

Micah Chambers and his wife, Maggie, along with several of the decorated soldiers, made their way to Shorty and Bear. Micah knew them both and wanted to hear directly from them how they planned to keep residents and cabins safe.

"We'll walk the perimeter of the island and the resort area of the mainland," Shorty said. "Beyond that, we're not going to concern ourselves. Except for the hotel, of course. They hit that once already. With paint."

"You carrying guns?" Micah asked.

"No. I played baseball as a boy. Still got my bat," Bear said. "And the gorilla will just pick up a tree if he needs a weapon."

That got a chuckle out of them, and they eyed Shorty with respect.

"We can patrol," Benjamin offered. "We sure know how to do that."

"You staying at the hotel along with Ben, boys?" Micah asked.

When they nodded, he suggested they take turns downstairs on the porch and take a walk around the building every half hour or so. Maybe two at a time. With so many soldiers, they'd only have to do two hour shifts and that would free Shorty and Bear to concentrate on the resort cabins.

"It's likely whoever did this is home in bed by now," Shorty said. "We're probably wasting our time, but . . ."

"Yeah. And that's a big but," Micah said.

"Don't say big butt around me, husband. I'm right here, and I can still pack a wallop."

Micah smiled, squeezed her and whispered something that made her smile. "Good timing, Maggie."

He looked away from their small group and saw others just like them, folks finding solutions to a few hours of peaceful sleep that would be difficult to come by if they didn't have a plan. Some dispersed to their cabins. Others were making their way back to the hotel via the footbridge.

Lanterns swung, lighting up legs or feet and shining down in a yellow-white circle around them if hands held them high enough. Spheres of cold, false daylight illuminated the footbridge. Their low voices were like a moving cloud, a swarm of night insects, whispering its way to the mainland.

Sheriff Hicks made a tour of the burned and painted cabins, rapping on doors and talking with anyone who happened to be there and answered his knock. His next stop was the hotel.

He sat at each table to question people and got answers that sounded like echoes across the room. He was growing irritated. Everyone was at the Chautauqua and then the hotel, but no one saw anything at all, nothing until the flames. He was tired of hearing the same words.

"Look! Somebody lit those fires. Somebody painted those doors!" His voice exploded in volume with each word. "And by the way. You washed the damned evidence. Next time don't do that!"

"You saying there's going to be a next time?" Jesse said. "Why not catch the guy before he does it again, Sheriff?"

Rumbles of agreement vibrated the room, and Hicks held up his hand to settle them down.

"I'm trying, folks. Bear with me."

"It didn't seem like you or that hopeless deputy tried too hard the last time," Bill said, but he offered up a half smile to ease the words. "What's different now?"

The sheriff waited the span of a tick of the clock and rubbed at his chest. He knew Bill spoke the truth, and it was embarrassing. It had been wrong, but he thought the problem would go away. It had been a prank more than real arson, whatever that might be, and however *real arson* could be misconstrued from a cabin burning without apparent reason.

Obviously, he'd guessed wrong. He didn't want to say that for more reasons than his ego, but kerosene and bottles said it for him.

"All I can do, Sanders, is find him now. And with all of your cooperation, I will."

When he had talked to everyone in the room, he went to the bar and sat with his chin on his hand, thinking and looking around the room at the faces he'd just talked with. Abby brought him a whiskey and lifted her eyebrows before setting it down, asking if it was okay for him to have a drink.

"Sure. One or six," he said.

"I gather you didn't get any useful information," she said.

"Nope."

"I didn't think you would. These people aren't the ones you're looking for. Why would they burn their own places? Paint their own doors?"

Officer Hicks leaned back and rubbed his chest, wiping away the heartburn. He picked up the drink, sipped and rubbed again.

"Maybe that drink isn't good for you," she said, hoping it was heartburn and not a heart attack. She liked Sheriff Hicks.

"The drink is fine and dandy, Abby. It's the job that isn't good for me."

"You didn't answer."

"Answer what?"

"Why would these people burn their own homes? You're looking in the wrong place."

He shook his head and glared at her. She poured more in his glass, but just a little because they didn't need a drunk lawman, and waited.

"Okay, Abigail Riley Adams. But they might have seen something, and just where do you think I should I look? You tell me. Point me in the right direction."

"Well, you won't find maple sugar in a butcher shop. The farmers or the residents who don't want change, and .. . people who don't want more Negroes in Idlewild. People who don't want the population to change."

"I suppose you have specific names for me? Other than sugar?" he added, pulling at his earlobe.

"Sorry. That wasn't nice of me. No, I wouldn't say suspect names exactly. More like types."

She crossed her arms, and her fingers tapped a tune on her bicep.

"But, Joe Foster has been quite vocal about keeping people out of town. And so was Mr. Tatum at the last meeting we had. In fact, the farmers banded together to try to keep the Idlewild Resort Company from selling off small pieces of property. Lot kinds of pieces."

The sheriff nodded and watched Abby's face, interest flickering on his.

"You mad at your in-laws?"

Abby's head jerked back.

"Good heavens, no. What a strange question to ask. Why did you?"

"Your husband is a farmer. Quite sure his family would have been part of that farmers' group you talked about. Mad at him?"

Abby went silent. Hicks watched comprehension dawn in her eyes.

"You think his family might have lit these fires? Painted those doors?" he asked.

Jackson came around the bar to fix the drinks he needed seeing Abby deep in conversation with the sheriff.

"That's ridiculous."

"Where is Frank, Abby?"

She backed away and growled at Jackson.

"I'll get it. What do you need?"

Jackson ran back to his side of the bar and waited at the drink station.

Folks were leaving, and Frank came in as Abby was sliding the tray of drinks to Jackson. She forced herself not to run to him and pasted a smile on her face, one she hoped looked better outside than if felt on the inside. It felt stiff and phony.

"Welcome home, Frank," she said. "Missed you at the Chautauqua. Hungry?"

He shook his head and eyed her.

"Drink?" she asked, catching Sheriff Hicks' eye as she turned and wishing she hadn't. He wore a curious expression, and it felt like he was watching her.

"Whiskey," Frank said.

The sheriff moved his empty glass nearer to Frank.

"One more, Mrs. Adams," he said. "You missed all the excitement, Frank. Where you been?"

"Fishing."

"At night?" Hicks said.

"Bull head trotlines. You do that at night."

The sheriff nodded and looked at Abby.

"You a fan of bull head, Abby?"

She shrugged her shoulders.

"Never had them before, so ... I don't know."

"Catch any?" Hicks asked.

"Sure. A bunch."

"I haven't been bull heading since I was a boy. I'd like to see them. Where are they?"

"At the farm. Ma's skinning them and probably still at it."

They both sipped, waiting for the other to trigger more conversation.

"Hear any scuttlebutt about the resort trouble when you were out and about?" the sheriff asked, and hunched over his drink like he was more interested in it than the answer.

"What trouble you talking about?"

He thought Frank was being deliberately obtuse and it irritated him. If he hadn't heard what every person in the area was talking about, he'd just come from the moon.

"Oh, you know. Little things like arson and unauthorized paint jobs. That kind a stuff."

"Nope. But who in hell would I hear anything from? I don't hang around those resort people. Abby does. Ask her."

"I was thinking more like from the farmers," the sheriff said. "Something they might have said in passing."

"You're barking up the wrong tree, Hicks."

Frank tossed back his drink, got to his feet and headed for the stairs. The sheriff's eyebrows lifted as he watched him go without a single word to his wife. He turned to her in time to see the guard pull down over her eyes.

Bill Sanders took Frank's place. He wanted to explain to the sheriff about the patrol they'd set up for the resort property cabins so there would be no misunderstandings. Especially so the sheriff wouldn't arrest the patrol while they were skulking around the grounds in the dark.

"And the soldiers are taking turns patrolling the woods surrounding hotel since it was vandalized, too. First, actually," Sanders said.

The sheriff didn't like the idea, but there wasn't anything he could do about it. It was private property, and they had a right to guard it.

"No guns, right?"

"No. Shorty and Bear don't need guns. And the soldiers didn't think to bring theirs."

Hicks laughed.

"That's good. Well, you got two good men on the resort patrol. You're lucky."

"I know that."

"I'm leaving. I'll be back in the morning to talk to more people. Residents, too. All the folks, Abby."

She didn't respond. Her mind was elsewhere, so she nodded vacantly and made no comment.

Two soldiers came inside from their porch sitting and sentry duty, and Benjamin and another soldier walked up to say they were replacing them.

"You'll remember to leave the door unlocked so we can get back in after you go to bed, right?" Benjamin said.

"I won't leave you out in the dark, my friend. Be safe out there, please."

The sheriff left, and Bill waved goodbye. Only Abby and her father remained in the bar. It was still except for the clink of glasses as she washed them.

"Feels odd without Bear and Shorty at the end of the bar."

"It does, Abby girl."

"God, I miss Nirvana."

"Leave those, and let's join our personal patrol soldiers on the porch."

Chapter Twenty-one

Coffee brewed, filling the air with Patrick's chicory blend. Bacon sizzled and competed with the aroma. Abby was slicing potatoes when Strange Al pushed through the door with an elbow, tying her hair back in the ribbon that was no longer blue. She needed a new one, and Abby gave herself a mental reminder to buy one for her.

Al washed her hands, lifted an onion and said, "chopped or sliced?"

"Sliced, and morning to you, too, Al," Abby said. "Missed you at the Chautauqua yesterday."

Since it wasn't a question, Al didn't feel forced to respond, so she didn't. She turned her face away and stared hard at the onion she worked on.

"It's too bad you weren't able to enjoy it. The ceremony was great, and the music was unbelievable. Buddy Black's band can really make your toes tap."

Al nodded and hacked at the onions.

"How many?" she asked.

"Four. I saw your brothers. You should have come with them."

The door swung open, and Betty came in, splashed coffee in a cup, and turned to leave, but not before Abby saw her swollen cheek and black eye. She dropped the potato which rolled across the floor and stopped at Betty's feet.

"What in the name of God happened to you?" Abby asked, her voice a choked whisper.

Betty's hand flew up to cover her face like she'd forgotten her bruises. She backed out of the kitchen, holding her cup with one hand, her cheek with the other, and glaring at Al as she went. Abby followed.

"Betty! Stop!"

In the bar, Abby put a hand on the girl's shoulder to keep her from running off again and turned her around. She caressed the side of the girl's injured face, disbelief and horror on her own and seeping from her eyes.

"How did this happen? Who did this to you?"

"Nobody," she said, the word harsh and spit from her mouth like it was rotten meat.

Abby glanced back toward the kitchen, knowing she needed to get back to breakfast. The hotel was full, and hungry guests would be down and demanding food. Betty's eyes followed Abby's to the kitchen door, and red-hot anger burned in them.

"Have you seen a doctor? Your poor face. . . it looks terrible."

She grimaced, what might have been a smile on another day.

"Thanks."

With a closer look, she could see a split in Betty's puffy bottom lip, a black and swollen eye, and a purple cheek. She'd clearly been beaten. This was no accident. Abby wondered about bruises she couldn't see, and her blood boiled.

"Well, have you?" she asked.

"No, and I'm not going to."

"But . . ."

"Let me get to work, Abby."

She tried to pull away from her boss, tried not to let her eyes betray how bad she hurt, how pained and humiliated and angry she was. Betty wouldn't say anything. She couldn't. It needed to be buried because no good could come from making a big deal of it. She'd learned that long ago on another dark night. It was better this way. No . . . not just better. It was the only way.

Colored girls can't say no on a dark night, alone on a country road. That was the way of things.

"When you tell me who did this, I'll let you go."

Betty stared at her with defeated, dead eyes.

"Then I quit."

Abby stepped back a pace, stunned by her friend's inflexible stance.

"You can't quit."

"Hell, I can't."

"I mean. Never mind. That's not what I meant, Betty. You are free to do whatever you want."

"Ha! I'm free? Really? One time I thought so." She walked away. "I fell, Abby. That's all."

And that's what everyone would say, anyway. That, or the colored girl asked for what she got.

"You're a liar, Betty. And I'm mad."

"Cuz I'm a liar?"

"No. You know damn well why, but I won't bother you about it, just now. Go to work, and I'll see you in a few. Don't scare the guests."

"Yes, boss," Betty said.

The two words were hollow imitations of Betty's humor and short their normal acidity, but she walked away, head held high. Abby watched her go, a blend of admiration and irritation fumbling around in her brain, struggling for supremacy.

When she shoved through the swinging doors to the kitchen, one half slammed against the wall and bounced off. Al's head spun around, her eyes wide with fear.

"Sorry," Abby said.

Al nodded and went back to the potato she'd been peeling, having taken over Abby's abandoned job. They worked silently, frying the potatoes, turning the bacon and sausages, pouring pancake batter on the griddle. When the platters were piled high, Abby carried them out to the buffet tables and greeted guests who were there and waiting.

Spirits were subdued, like they'd all had restless sleep following the night's vandalism, but, when asked, the soldiers reported no activity during the night patrols. And they supposed that was good. With coffee and breakfast in their bellies, they grew more animated, and smiles took over, riding alongside enthusiasm for the day's Chautauqua events.

"I don't think you boys moved from the porch chairs," Shorty said, coming in with Bear, fresh from their resort patrol. "We could see you from the island. Snoozing in your rocking chairs like a couple of old ladies."

"Talk about old. Can't you talk any louder, old man," Benjamin said around a mouth full of pancake and smirking. "Your voice box too broken-down with age?"

"Don't need to. People listen when I speak."

"Then speak to us," Abby asked, thinking about Betty. "See anything on your watch last night? Any activity at all?"

In Abby's mind, there was no question her friend had been attacked, and she gasped when Shorty said they had seen something. All eyes were on him, and Abby was intent.

"Well?" Micah said.

He shoved out his hand to count on the fingers

"First – some raccoons. Second - Cassandra and her clowder. Twice. Maybe should put her on the watch payroll. Third - opossum, and fourth - a real nice herd of whitetail. Fifth - soldiers on the porch, two by two just like going to the ark. Oh, yeah. He switched hands. And – seventh, or is that sixth. I got confused. Bats."

The room groaned with complaints about comedian sentries.

"Guess you boys had a full night. Maybe tomorrow you'll catch us a skunk or two," Micah said.

Sheriff Hicks strolled in like he had no place to be and took a seat at the bar, looking around at folks as they finished up their breakfasts.

Abby brought him a cup of coffee and offered a plate.

"Already ate, but it sure smells fine."

"We put out a good breakfast most days," she said.

She gnawed at the tip of her pinky finger, brooding over a way to talk with him about Betty without really doing it, without betraying her secret or her trust. Seconds went by with the sheriff watching her trudge down the pathways of her mind. He was used to waiting. It usually gained him information he could use. When Abby turned to leave, he was surprised. Waiting almost always worked.

"Hey," he said, the word unintentionally coming out of his mouth like a bark.

"What?" Abby said, stopping in her tracks.

"Nothing. Thought you wanted to say something."

"No. Did you need me for anything?"

"No. Just gonna talk to these good people to see if they remembered anything new before heading out to see other folks."

"Well, help yourself to food if you want."

Patrick came downstairs to take over the breakfast work, and Abby went up to find Betty who was flipping a sheet onto a bed. Abby took an edge and tugged it tight, folded the corner and tucked it under. She ran the dust mop under the bed, dislodging Phantom, and swept the room while Betty scrubbed out the basin and changed the towels at the washstand.

"Is Cleo in a drawer?" Abby asked.

"The armoire."

"Come on, Cleo," Abby called, and the black cat streaked across the room and out the door like an ebony bolt of lightning. Both cats waited at the door of the next room, one with fur as white as a first snowflake, the other black as the devil's heart. Cleo reached out a paw to catch Abby by the ankle as she walked by. She turned to look at them.

"Aren't they beautiful side by side?" Abby said.

"Yeah. They're cats. Notice they haven't had a litter of kittens?"

"They probably will at some point. Maybe they're smarter than people and want to get to know each other really, really well first," she said and added a melancholy sound that was meant to be a laugh.

In the third room, Abby couldn't help it and asked again. She tried not to, but . . .

"You gonna talk about your face?"

Betty turned away and grabbed the bottom sheet.

"What do you want to know?"

"Did it happen on your way home last night? In the dark."

"Uh-huh. It was dark and I fell."

"Come on. That's not from a fall. That's a hit. Somebody hit you. More than once. Please tell me who. Will you talk to the sheriff?"

"No!"

". . . but you need to."

Betty cocked a hip and slapped her hand on it, looking like a tough girl in a diminutive body, but someone you wouldn't want to tangle with.

"Lookie here, white girl. You don't know a damn thing about me or what I need to do. Just cuz I work for you, doesn't mean you own this black body."

Abby blanched and swallowed. They were friends. Skin color had never been an issue between them – right from the beginning, and tears came to her eyes thinking she'd been wrong all along. It *was* an issue, and she hadn't known it. She'd been a fool. A silly, small town, *white girl* who didn't know anything about the world. Didn't know people at all. Didn't know squat. Not a damned thing.

She widened her eyes and blinked several times. Only one tear escaped and made a path down her cheek to drop from the point of her chin.

She grabbed the sheet Betty flipped and tucked it in. Ran the dust mop and broom while Betty cleaned the bowl and did the towels. She kept swallowing the tears at the back of her throat, but it convulsed and kept producing liquid that sprang to her eyes. How it got to her eyes from her throat was a mystery.

"I'll be back in a minute. Go on to the next room, please," she said in a choked whisper.

She fled to the safety of her room and stood with her back against the door, working to soothe away the hurt, the confusion. Frank stretched and patted the bed next to him. Unable to speak, she shook her head. He patted again.

"Come on over here, Abby. You can spare a few minutes for your husband. I don't ask much."

"No, Frank."

She wanted to run away, and her eyes flicked behind her to the door, but there was no place to hide, nowhere she could be alone, and she was being squeezed. Her chest sucked for air that wouldn't come. Perspiration coated her skin, and she wanted to scream, but there wasn't enough air to make a noise.

"Come here, Abby."

Like she'd been drugged, her feet moved without her brain telling them to, and she found herself standing by the bed. Frank pulled her down and folded her into his arms. His hands fondled her breasts. She felt her dress being pulled up and his hands on her bottom. She rolled from the bed and landed on the floor.

"No. I can't, Frank. I . . . I have work to finish."

"Jesus, Abby. It's just a few minutes."

"Sorry."

She raced from the room, down the stairs and out the door, not seeing wide eyes looking at her, not seeing anything. When she slowed down enough to notice, she found herself in the woods that edged one side of Lake Idlewild.

She sat on a fallen log and grasped her head in her hands. Minutes crept by while her heart drummed a heavy, erratic rhythm. It was broken. She squeezed her eyes shut and curled into an upright fetal position as tiny as she could get, invisible and nonexistent.

In time, she heard the sounds around her, the sharp whistle of nearby quail and the following gentle tu-tu-tu of the female talking to her chicks. It was the sound of love, the voice of nurturing, and it brought more tears to her eyes. How she wished to hear her mother's voice. Now more than ever. More than anything.

The sun streaked in between the trees where the forest met the lake, and Abby watched ruby throated hummingbirds feed at horsemint and lobelia, small bright patches in the sunlight. Her heartbeat evened out, and her shoulders relaxed and dropped back into place.

Had the flowers grown there on their own, and, if not, who had planted them? The vision of Cassandra planting wild flowers nurtured a slow, healing smile.

"It's something she would do," she murmured.

Mrow.

"Took you long enough, my friends."

She walked down Cassandra's overgrown path and saw the open door long before she got there. There was no sign of the owner, and Abby called her name several times before entering.

A brightly decorated tea pot sat in the middle of the table, steam coming from its spout, a matching cup and saucer next to it along with a plate holding two tiny cookies. Abby called again, tilted her head in listening confusion and sat in front of the cup and saucer.

Phantom and Cleo peered inside with round, anxious eyes, cased the room for enemies and sauntered in. They made one careful tour of the area and curled up on the rug in front of the hearth.

She poured the tea and sniffed the sweet, earthy aroma, leaned her back against the chair and sipped. She picked up one of the cookies and nibbled at the edge. Her tears dried, and her heart begin to heal, and she wondered if it was the tea. Had Cassandra put some strange herb in it? Or was it the house? Peace enveloped her when she was here. Maybe Cassandra had cast a spell on it. A good spell. One that helped, not harmed.

She chuckled to herself, and the cats opened their eyes, glanced at her and closed them again.

"Yeah. I feel like a nap, too. I think it's the house. Wonder where Cassandra is?"

She took her time enjoying the tea and cookies, wrote her hostess a note and left, feeling much better than when she had arrived.

Both Frank and Betty were gone when she got back. Her father took one look at her swollen eyes, raised his eyebrows and patted her arm.

"We're not gonna be busy until the Chautauqua is over for the day. Take a rest," he said.

She nodded and went upstairs. The room was a mess with Frank's clothes tossed about. The towel hung half in, half out of the wash bowl. It had siphoned up the water from the bowl, and now it dripped in a steady trickle onto the floor. She wiped it up, got fresh towels, poured water from the pitcher and washed her face. She picked up Frank's shirt and pants, his socks and underwear, and put them in the laundry hamper. Pennies were scattered on the floor, shining in the sunlight. Those she put in her change jar.

Anger stirred when she bent to pick up her mother's picture. She took it with her to the window seat and propped it in the corner by the window. Her gaze went from her beautiful mother to the pavilion where a number of people had already gathered to hear W.E.B. Du Bois talk about social change.

His civil rights arguments enflamed some, calmed others, but always focused on the education of colored men to gain the rights they had been denied. Education was his solution, the answer to curing most ills. Abby applauded his ideas and hoped today he invited calm. Idlewild didn't need flames again tonight.

She made the bed and lay on top of it, trying to rest, but her mind was a jumble. She was tired, but the moment she felt herself drifting off, she jarred herself awake with visions of Betty's broken face. Of Frank. Of Strange Al. Of fires and painted crosses.

She hissed out a disgusted puff of air and got up. She put her boots back on and went down to work. Work always helped. Work was an essential balm to a wounded heart.

She didn't go to the Chautauqua. Her heart wasn't in it. But the windows were all open and music drifted in. Bear and Shorty kept her company at the end of the bar, waiting for their shift on night patrol. They'd decided to continue, at least for the week. After that, they'd talk about it. Phantom and Cleo bookended them.

Abby busied herself in the bar getting ready for the crowd that would swarm in after the music ended.

"How come you're not out there, Abby?" Shorty asked.

"I don't know. Didn't feel like it."

"Hmmm. Doesn't sound like the Abby I know."

"Not tonight. Quiet sounds good."

"You sick?" Bear asked.

She chuckled and put a hand over his.

"You two mother hens . . . Stop clucking. I'm fine."

"Hmmm. Fine is never good."

Shorty ran a hand over his bald head like he was finger-combing hair.

"You think it's gonna magically come back?" Bear teased.

"Ladies tell me they love my bald head."

"Maybe Sue and Sally. And they'd say anything. Love anything, too."

"I think you're beautiful," Abby said. "You, too, Bear."

The bar filled instantly when the music ended, and Abby no longer had time to think. For that she was grateful. Benjamin played blues on the piano, and another soldier pulled out a harmonica and joined him. It was so good, it was hard to keep your eyes off them.

Sally, who sat at the bar next to her cousin, said he was making love to the harmonica, and she might have been right. His heart was poured into every note, every mournful slide, every painful bend.

"Do you know *Old Woman Blues*?" Sally yelled to Benjamin. When he nodded, she made her way to the piano, leaned against it like a diva, and bellowed a tale of woe that had something to do with yesterday's news and day-old squid. Abby hadn't heard the lyrics before, but it fit her dejected mood.

When it thinned out in the bar, Abby left Jackson to finish up and took a drink to the porch. It was warm and sultry, the kind of night that sits on your skin like it was palpable, touchable, and if you wanted . . . you could lift it off and put it on a shelf next to your quilts.

She toed the wooden porch to rock and rested her head against the seat back. Cleo curled on her lap, and Phantom sprawled on one shoulder and arm. It was nice to be alone, serene and soothing but short lived. The piano stopped, and Benjamin and several soldiers joined her, but they must have sensed her need for peace, or needed some themselves, because they rocked in silence.

Heat lightening flashed with a rhythm that was reassuring and mesmerizing and turned the sky fleetingly scarlet. So consistent were the flashes, she came to expect the next one and was jarred when it delayed as if taunting and provoking just because it could. It was bigger, stronger.

Fireflies competed with the heat lightening, filling the night with dancing color. Raccoons foraged at the edge of the water, heralding Cassandra and her cats. Loons yodeled, an eerie tremolo echoing on the water, and frogs croaked their love across the lake. Their nocturnal instruments, their compositions were nature's first symphony and sent warnings and love, invitations and messages, and songs for the simple pleasure of singing.

A sigh escaped Abby's lips, and she tugged at the ribbon holding her hair in place. The mass tumbled over a shoulder and she threw it back and rubbed at her head.

"Are you troubled?" Benjamin asked

She shook her head.

"Sometimes I just wish I was in Nirvana," she said.

He smiled, stretched his long legs out in front of him and leaned his chair way back. He looked sideways at her.

"We all wish for Nirvana, but that state of grace is seldom achieved."

"I meant the town. Where I lived before coming here."

"Interesting. Hard to leave Nirvana, I imagine," he said, with what might have been a chuckle. "I'd like to see a town with that heavenly name."

"Nothing left of it. Maybe someday I'll show you."

She said goodnight and left.

In their room, Frank lay sprawled, uncovered in the heat, with one arm flung across his face. His body glowed white in the light of the moon, and she stood motionless for a moment and stared at him. She hadn't really looked at him before, not naked. The only times they were unclothed were during their intimate moments, and then it was brief. She took her time, now.

He had a splendid body. It was muscled and lean, probably from his time in the service and his work on the farm, she thought. His legs and arms were long, and his shoulders were broad, his chest filled out and leading down to a narrow waist. A birthmark was on his thigh in the shape of a crescent moon. Why hadn't she seen that before? His penis lay flaccid next to it, and she hadn't known about that either. She'd not seen it look like that. What else didn't she know?

She saw his shirt and pants thrown on the dresser and smiled because the picture of her mother sat unmolested in the corner of the window seat. She picked it up and sat, staring alternately at the man in her bed and out the window at the display in the sky. Both unusual sights.

She pondered the things Edna had told her about loving and its pleasure, its joy, and wondered if her friend had lied. It wasn't joyful at all. She had no compass, however, and didn't know who to ask about it.

Chapter Twenty-two

Sunday morning was subdued. It was church under the pavilion, a last talk by Du Bois, and people packing up to head home. They said it was hard to leave, even though some things had happened they didn't want to remember. Still, they had made friends, had heard words that lifted their spirits and music that was part of their heritage and filled them with joy.

Bear and Shorty came back from patrol with no new information. The soldiers, too. It was disturbing not to have any evidence, not to see anything tangible and know it was there, could find it if you knew what to look for and where it was. Without answers, you looked at everyone with suspicion and wondered. Were they truly what they'd always seemed, or were they false? Were they malicious pretenders?

The trouble makers hadn't gone away. Hate still lurked behind doors, around corners and trees – behind a smile. Whoever had sent the fiery message was still here, on the prowl, and that was the only thing everyone was certain of.

Bill asked Shorty and Bear to continue the resort patrol, but, except for Benjamin and a friend, the soldiers had gone home which meant they wouldn't be there to watch the hotel. Abby felt safe, though, knowing Bear and Shorty were out there in the dark, silently watching. They'd never neglect her and her father.

A number of lot owners whose cabins were finished planned to stay in Idlewild, some for the whole summer. Micah and Maggie Chambers went home, leaving Benjamin to care for their cabin, and a group of folks were staying on at the hotel and making a week of it.

Others, however, packed up their tents and belongings and caught trains to various cities around America. Near the pavilion and spreading over to the island, it looked like a ghost town, reminding Abby of Nirvana. After the tents were gone, squares of flattened grass marked the ground, like grave sites or reminders of something gone away, something uncomfortably missing.

With final shouts of farewell, voices went soft, all the way into whispers. The stillness dictated quiet walks or naps, so the unusual peace could prosper and grow. Silence was in the atmosphere, riding on the air. It was Sunday afternoon, a time for thoughtful reflection.

Before Buddy Black left, he asked if he could come back to play some weekends during the summer season – for money, of course, and Abby told him he'd have to share that honor with Benjamin who was staying the summer, and she'd already asked him to set aside some playing nights. She told Buddy they couldn't pay much, yet, but he could have a free room if that worked for him, and his eyes lit with a good kind of fire.

Phantom sprawled on the counter near Buddy who stroked the cat and talked to it. Phantom responded by displaying his pink belly and purring loudly. He grabbed a hand with both his paws, claws out—just a little, when Buddy tried to quit petting.

"You want to go on the road with me, Phantom? We'd be a kickin' duo – Buddy Black and the rockin' white cat."

"Wow! Great name for a musical group! I think he wants you, Buddy. But you can't have him."

He turned his twinkling black eyes on Abby.

"The world isn't ready for us, Phantom."

"I have a black cat, too."

"You think color's the problem?" He shook his head dramatically. "Hell, no. He wants to rock my blues. Way ahead of his time – musically, that is."

Abby laughed, and her eyes shone.

"You need to let me know in advance about needing a room," she said. "We get pretty busy, and I'll need to save one."

"You'd do that for old Buddy?"

"I would. You're my buddy, Buddy. Bet you haven't heard that one before, huh?"

He squeezed her in a hug, and she squeaked with its strength. Frank peered over the railing just then, and Abby couldn't tell his thoughts by the expression on his face. They were hidden. His face a blank.

Buddy picked up his bag and waved his way out the door.

"I'll be back," he said.

"I'll bet you will," Frank mumbled as he came down the stairs.

"Morning," Abby said, and blushed as she remembered gawking at his naked body the night before.

"Morning to you. I'm starved," he said.

"The buffet is still up, Frank. Help yourself. I'll join you when I'm done checking people out."

Abby poured a cup of coffee and joined Frank at his table. He pushed a piece of toast around his plate, sopping up the last of the sausage gravy and eggs.

"More?" Abby asked.

Frank shoved his chair back and shook his head.

"Can I ask you a question, Frank?"

"Sure. Might not answer, but you can ask."

Abby sipped coffee, trying to formulate her thoughts without using words she didn't have the right to say, but she knew what she believed was likely true. She wanted to ask the questions and not implicate anyone.

"Well?" Frank said. "I gotta go, Abby."

She looked up, surprised, but, in the next second, nodded and shrugged.

"Where?"

He stuck his tongue into his cheek and moved it around, a habit he had when he was thinking. It looked like he'd tried to swallow a hamster, and the tiny rodent was running around in his mouth, bulging Frank's cheeks, trying to find a way out.

"Check the trot lines," he said. "Meeting George and Terry in an hour."

Abby nodded and leaned forward, determined to ask what she needed to know.

"If you were positive a young girl had been assaulted, and maybe, probably, raped, and you were also pretty sure who had done it, what would you do?"

He shrugged and tugged an earlobe.

"It would be up to the girl to do something, I guess. So, I'd do nothing."

"But what if she wouldn't? What if she felt like she couldn't?"

"Well, then, that's her choice, and there's your answer. Stay out of things that aren't any of your business, Abby."

She rubbed her hands over her jaw. The muscles were tight, like she'd been clenching her teeth together and grinding for a decade.

"But, Frank, she needs help, justice . . . and the person . . . people who did this need to go to jail."

Frank sighed and stood to leave, but turned back and leaned down with his hands on the table, his face next to hers. She thought he was going to kiss her and was astonished and pleased. She puckered her lips and closed her eyes.

"She shouldn't have been alone in a place where she could get attacked. What do you think people will say if you get involved in this? They already talk about you constantly. Leave it alone, Abby."

"But . . . she needs somebody . . ."

Frank was already half way across the floor and heading for his trot lines.

"Go catch a bullhead, Frank, you bullheaded man," she said to herself, and looked around to see if she was still alone.

She checked on her father and Strange Al in the kitchen to make sure they were getting ready for lunch and supper. Al turned away from Abby as she'd been doing all weekend, and Abby shrugged her shoulders and gave her da a hug.

"Going upstairs to clean. It'll take a while."

"I'll be here with Al. Although sometimes I think I'm just talking to myself. She's just not a good conversationalist." He twinkled when he spoke and poked the girl in the back with his wooden spoon. "Are you, girl."

"Nope," she said without moving her head a smidgeon in any direction.

Abby remembered the ribbon she'd stuck in her pocket for Al and pulled it out.

"I brought you a new ribbon for tying back your hair. I hope pink is okay, Al. It's all I had. I'll leave it on the table for you."

"I don't need another ribbon. I have one," she said.

"Well, every woman can use two."

"You don't need to do that," Al said, a peevish tinge coating her stubborn words.

"Hmmm, well . . . I'm going up now."

Upstairs, she met another wall. Abby had decided not to say anything more to the young woman. Not now. She was going to try a more upbeat approach, so she went in humming a tune.

Betty's face looked even worse than on Saturday. Her eye was less swollen, but the purple and black was more vivid, deeper hued, and the marks on her cheek were growing purple now, too.

Betty had finished changing the linens on the bed and was using the dust mop under it, dislodging both cats who scampered to the door and perched there like furry porcelain statues.

Abby scoured the washbowl and hung new towels, hummed and poured fresh water into the pitcher, hummed and dusted the dresser. Betty swept the floor and ran the polishing cloth around it with the dust mop. They were ready to move on. She sang in the next room. Not a hum, but vocals with actual words and notes. Not loud, either, but with enough sound that her friend could hear it.

"*Hey, friend, I needed you,*" she sang.

Betty rolled her eyes and kept on working. They made the bed together. It was easier that way, and she watched Abby as she avoided eye contact. She pursed her lips and furrowed her brows. Two lines appeared between her eyes, marking her otherwise flawless, satin skin.

"I'll do the bowl this time," Betty said. "You sweep and dust mop."

Abby interrupted her singing long enough to say, "Sure thing, boss," and went back to her song.

"*Hey, friend, you never ask of me more than I can offer you.*"

"You just make up that song? Cuz I never heard it before."

"Maybe I did. Just maybe it's a song about friends being there for one another. Doing for one another."

"Forget I asked," Betty said. "You got an agenda, woman, and I don't want it being me."

Abby let out a huff of frustrated air and stared hard at her.

"I was determined not to talk about this today," Abby said, stretching her neck and twisting her head to the side, trying to relieve the stiffness, keep herself busy *not* talking.

"You're not doing a real good job of *not* talking about it. The singing was creative, though," she said with a chuckle and slapping the dust cloth over the small dresser.

"Come on, Betty. Talk to the sheriff. Please. I'd be there with you every second. I would hold your hand."

"I don't need you to hold my hand." She faced Abby with rigid eyes. "What I need is to be left alone. And I need a gun."

Betty walked out of the room, and Abby heard her repeat herself, like the idea was a revelation, an epiphany she was elated by. "I need a gun," sounded like she was thanking someone for a precious gift.

Abby sucked in air and followed, fear twisting her stomach. She had visions of a gunshot wound, a bleeding chest, a funeral, and Betty being hauled off in manacles, sent to a federal prison where she was fed bread and water and made to scrub the concrete prison hall floors on her hands and knees. Or maybe pound rock out of a big mountain, for whatever reason they made prisoners pulverize rocks, if they really did.

"No!" she shouted. "No gun. You can't do that. Someone will get hurt."

"That's what guns do, boss lady. That's why I need one. But I'm not gonna do it. I just want to. They probably wouldn't let me buy one even if I had the money."

Betty stopped talking and went to the window. The sun was high overhead, and a brisk wind was pushing the water around Lake Idlewild. Little waves picked up flashes of light and sparkled, like diamonds had dropped from the sky, pieces of a broken necklace.

"Probably not," she added, "because I'm colored, nobody's gonna sell me a gun, and I wouldn't need one if I wasn't colored. Isn't that entertaining?"

The sorrow in her voice was a spike in Abby's heart. She moved to her side and tried to offer the comfort of a hand on her arm. Betty jerked away, and Abby didn't try again. She stood still and looked outside at the same things Betty saw. The same lake with the same diamonds dancing on the water. The same breathtaking picture. But she sensed they didn't see it the same.

She wouldn't have said that before coming to Idlewild. Wouldn't have believed it if someone had told her, but she could say it now. They looked through different lenses, and as much as Abby tried to understand her friend, she couldn't borrow Betty's glasses and see what she saw, or her shoes and walk in her world.

She couldn't even say she understood. How simple and unfathomable was that? She didn't. She could only listen and feel her sorrow, and she could only do that if her friend would speak.

"It *isn't* entertaining," Abby said. "And you wouldn't need a gun if you put whoever pummeled you in jail."

"You're still in Nirvana, Abby. Don't think you ever left it and probably never will."

"What are you talking about? I left Nirvana years ago."

"No, you didn't. I'm not talking about that ghost town you lived in before here. You're still in that heavenly state of bliss, that other Nirvana none of us colored folks ever been to. Maybe not most whites either. Just you. And you'll never accept that I've never lived there, but I don't hate you for it."

She smiled, and for a moment, Abby was the child whose wound was being kissed and bandaged by an older woman. Maybe Betty *was* old. Maybe she had generations of collective age and memory and learning packed into her brain, into her soul. And Abby would never comprehend what her friend intrinsically knew because . . . because Abby had white skin. And Betty had inheritance, genetics, African ancestry and dark skin.

"So . . . you're going to let him . . . or them get away with hurting you? Maybe let them hurt the next girl. Maybe your sister?"

Betty whirled around, her black eyes glittering fury.

"You leave my sister out of this!" She growled the words, and her chest heaved.

Abby had pricked the wound, and Betty bled. Tears formed in Abby's eyes. She didn't want to hurt her friend more than she already was. Didn't want to add to her pain.

Betty threw the dust mop on the floor and strode to the door. Abby grabbed her arm and held on. Neither was willing to give up. Betty pulled, and Abby tugged back, begging her not to leave.

"Please. Please, don't go. I'm sorry, Betty. Really. I'm sorry. Don't go."

Betty stopped pulling away from her, but Abby didn't let go. She draped her other arm around the girl in a tight embrace, a dual effort to comfort and restrain.

"I care about you, Betty," she whispered.

"I know." The words came out late and soft. "Get to work. I know the boss. She's a slave driver."

Abby gave her a splintered half grin.

"Was that an intentional word choice?"

"Naw. Wish it had been. It was good, wasn't it?"

"Yes . . . and no."

Betty's wry effort at humor hurt in hidden places, like she'd been punched where no bruises would show. Abby could do nothing about their differences, nothing except try to appreciate them when more and more, day after day, she knew comprehension was a futile effort. She couldn't feel Betty's life, but she couldn't quit trying. The more she knew her friend, the harder it was to realize she'd never know her. She could only love her.

Abby remembered Bunny's harsh words.

Sheriff Hicks stopped by after the light supper crowd had dispersed. She poured him his favorite whiskey and set it in front of him. He sipped, his eyes on the wooden bar a foot from his face, deep in thought.

Abby left him alone for half an hour and figured that was enough. She tipped the bottle, refilling his glass, and forced him to meet her eyes.

"Well?" she said.

"Well, what?"

"Well – as in what have you discovered?"

"You know I can't talk about that, Abigail Adams."

"Why not?"

"Because . . . I can't."

Abby leaned her forearms on the bar close to him and tilted her head up. She wanted his full focus. She wanted him trapped by her eyes. She hesitated, forming the words carefully.

"If you knew a young woman had been assaulted, beaten and maybe raped, what would you do about it? Where would you begin?"

"Who?" he said, his shoulders thrusting back, an angry frown forming on his weathered face. "Who got beat up?"

"A hypothetical person. Nobody. Anyway, what would you do?"

"Abby. If someone has been hurt, you have to tell me."

"Um . . . There's no one. I was just wondering."

Hicks rubbed his chest, his lips clenched in a pained grimace.

"You okay, Sheriff?"

"Just this damned heartburn. And Abby . . . she needs to tells somebody . . . like me. It needs to be reported or it'll just happen again."

Abby glanced across the room and pinched her teeth over her bottom lip.

"I think it already has. This time is the *again*."

"To the hypothetical person who doesn't exist?"

Abby nodded. "What can I do?"

He deflated. "Talk her into talking, or tell me who it is. I'll talk her into it. Other than that, you have to let it go."

Abby's eyes hardened. Anger simmered.

"You have no other options, Abby. I'm sorry."

"What are you doing here, Sheriff?"

He stretched and ran a forearm over the badge pinned to his shirt pocket and polished it.

"Showing off my pretty, shiny star. Either makes folks happy or afraid. Never happens at the same time or to the same person."

Frank came in as Hicks was leaving, and Abby went around the bar to give him a hug that didn't get the response she had hoped for, needed.

"What did he want?" Frank said, pointing his thumb at Sheriff Hicks.

"To show off his star."

Frank squinted and looked disbelieving and disgruntled. "Come on."

"It's what he said."

"You two were head to head for a long time. What else did you talk about?"

Abby dragged fingers through her curls and tilted her head.

"How do you know that?"

"I was on the porch."

"Why didn't you come in?"

"It's a nice night. I was cooling off."

"Oh. How were the trot lines? Full of bullheads?"

"Yup. Something to do."

"Everything good out at the farm?"

"Sure. Why wouldn't it be?"

Abby shrugged and went to pour him a beer.

He glugged half of it and sighed, irritation in the set of his shoulders. He rubbed his forehead and gulped the second half.

"You were talking to the sheriff about the girl who got attacked, weren't you?"

299

Abby swallowed and reached for his glass to refill it, but he grabbed her arm and held her there.

"I thought we discussed this already," he said, frustration increasing the grip on her arm.

"We did."

"Well, then?"

"You're hurting me, Frank," she whispered, looking around the room, her neck growing hot and red.

Sitting with her husband, Edna watched the exchange, and her eyes met Abby's until she glanced away, embarrassed.

Frank dropped her arm, and she rubbed at the red finger marks.

"Sorry. But why'd you go ahead and do what we already decided you wouldn't? Why'd you do that?"

"I didn't, Frank. I asked him a couple of questions, and that's all. It doesn't mean anything."

She glanced over to see if Edna was still watching them, but her friend was deep into conversation with her husband. Probably about her and Frank.

"You just can't stay out of things, can you?" he said, startling her out of her musing.

"Yes, I can, and we didn't decide anything. You may have, but you and I were just talking."

He got up from the stool and stood staring at her. "I'm going up. Gonna get some sleep before we run the lines tonight."

"You're going out for more bullheads?"

"Sure." He looked everywhere but at her. "Is that a problem?"

"No. Not at all. Get some sleep. Good night, Frank," she said, wondering how things could go so wrong, like a train going downhill on the wrong track.

She picked up his glass and saw the marks on her arm, still red where his fingers had squeezed. She washed the glass, dried it and rubbed her arm again, not knowing why he'd been so upset. Not knowing bothered her the most. She didn't know how to avoid disappointing him if she didn't know the cause before the crime.

It didn't feel like she was doing anything offensive or wrong, but Frank thought differently, and when she saw disapproval on his face, she questioned herself. It seemed he didn't like much about her anymore.

Maybe it was a *man* thing. She huffed in exasperation. Maybe women couldn't understand. Had her father been an enigma to her mother, too? Did he look at her with disappointed eyes, like he didn't approve of anything about her? Maybe it was like being colored and white, man and woman. Nobody was expected to understand anybody.

I don't believe that. Da worshiped her. Still does.

Bear and Shorty came down for coffee before heading out for the night patrol. She gave them each coffee and a piece of left over apple pie, happy to make two men smile. They were easy to please, and it made her feel good doing it.

While they ate and moaned in pleasure over the pie, Edna came to the bar to pay their bill. She eyed Abby, said she'd be by tomorrow, and asked what was a good time.

"For what?" Abby asked.

"To have a chat."

"Why?"

"You a Philadelphia lawyer all of a sudden? A friend can't come by for a visit?"

"Yes. No. I mean yes, come by. And, no, I'm no lawyer." She huffed. "You're confusing me."

Edna's dark eyes bored into Abby's, imprinting her brain with the image Edna had seen moments ago.

"After lunch and before supper," Abby said.

"I'll be here then.

Abby watched her all the way to the door.

"You okay?" Bear asked.

"Sure," she said, hiding her arm from his perceptive, caring eyes.

Chapter Twenty-three

Abby put off going upstairs. She made two cups of chamomile tea and took them to the porch. Her father was asleep in one of the rockers, so she put the cup on the floor by him and lowered herself into a chair without making a creak or a squeak. She sipped the steaming liquid and rocked.

The breath escaping her lips was long and slow, releasing the pressure of the day. Perched on the steps, Cleo and Phantom turned at the sound of her sigh. Like marionettes and owls, their heads pivoted on immobile shoulders.

In the distance, Cassandra's spectral form captured their attention, visible periodically as wisps of cloud floated across the sky and revealed the quarter moon's light.

Not for the first time, Abby wondered what drew the woman to the water's edge every night. A healing root growing in the mud? A crab scuttling about in the dark but hiding beneath the muck with the daylight? A simple walk in the privacy of night, away from prying eyes and the cruel tongue of misconception?

Abby stood and moved in her direction, holding her cup of tea. Cassandra turned toward her and waited.

"Thank you for the tea the other day, Cassandra, and for sharing your home. I wish you had stayed to enjoy them with me."

"They were not to be shared on that day. Another time."

Abby held up her cup.

"It's not as good as yours," she said with a smile. "Will you share your secret with me some day?"

"Secrets proliferate. Yours leave you wanting."

"I won't even ask how you know. They do. It does. Sometimes I want to fly far, far away."

"No distant treetop beacons you with lure of springs' new bud. You would play with clouds and uncertain winds. Fly you must."

Here we go.

"You're confusing me again, Cassandra. Can you just tell me what you mean?"

Abby peered at the lake, listened to the sound of darkness come alive with an excitement not heard in daylight. Different. Enchanting. This murky world belonged to them, the insects, the owls and bats, the nocturnal predator and prey, creatures freed by dark.

Abby lapped up the fragrance of a summer night, tasted it. Damp and musty, it clung to her bare skin and nestled in her hair. "I *would* play with a cloud," she said, her words a wisp on the air. "And a thunderstorm. Storms make me want to dance and my heart beat fast."

"I know." Cassandra touched her hand so lightly Abby wondered if she had imagined it and continued on her walk. Her clowder followed single file behind her.

"Come on, Phantom. Cleo."

She hadn't seen her cats join them by the lake. Didn't know they were there until Cassandra left and she felt their soft fur brush against her ankles.

"Let's go home."

Her father was awake when she got back to the porch.

"Secret assignations with the town necromancer?" he asked, dimples showing and eyes squinting in humor.

"Yes. Cassandra and I are boiling up some trouble in a big black cauldron. Got any toad wart? A few bat eyes? I need six."

He chuckled and stuck a hand in his pocket, pulled it out, and showed her the lint in his palm like he did when she was a child.

"Just some fairy dust. Need any?"

Abby snorted.

"Boy, I could use some. I could use a pot full."

She said goodnight and went upstairs on tiptoes. Frank's light snore met her at the door, reminding her to use stealth and not wake him. He only had a few hours to sleep.

She poured water in the basin and rinsed her face and hands, slipped out of her dress and laid it over the back of the chair so it wouldn't wrinkle and washed her arms and neck. Still feeling clammy from the hot day, she stepped out of her slip and undergarments, dipped a cloth in the water and ran it over her body, sighing with the pleasure of clean, cool skin.

She pulled her thinnest nightgown over her head and slid into bed. She didn't want the sheet over her; it was too warm, and when Frank turned on his side and flung an arm over her, she tried to carefully push its heavy warmth aside.

"You're late," he mumbled.

"Sorry. I didn't mean to wake you."

"That, I believe."

He clutched a breast, squeezed it, pulled up her nightgown and reached lower. He moved his body over hers and thrust himself between her legs.

Tears leaked from her eyes, slid down the sides of her face and wet the pillow beneath her head. She closed her eyes and tried not to cry out from the discomfort. She tried to enjoy lovemaking, but it didn't feel like loving. She didn't feel anything except hurt and stupid.

She felt him begin to quiver and moved against him so he would finish more quickly and collapse on her, roll over and go back to sleep. She'd learned that much about their lovemaking. When he did, she went back to the washstand and cleansed his seed from her thighs. He was snoring before she went back to bed.

She lay with her eyes squeezed shut for the better part of the night.

What had she done?

Her stomach churned. This wasn't what she thought marriage would be. In her dreams, they'd laugh together, walk hand in hand, smiling and talking about their future. They'd make wonderful plans, and he would kiss her lips tenderly, hold her, touch her with love. He would adore her . . . and like her. She would see it in his eyes, in his affectionate caress.

Loving with Frank was never what Edna had described with her and Jesse, but this night was even less, or more, depending on the perspective. It was unlike all the other times when she was left feeling empty and indifferent. This was harsh and angry, and it seemed intentionally so, like he was punishing her with his right to her body. She felt rebuked, chastised . . . because he didn't like what she'd done in talking with the sheriff.

She wanted to know passion, but it seemed far, far away from their bed.

Abby went through the motions making breakfast with Al. She found herself getting angry at the girl over nothing. She did her work silently, as always. She avoided looking at Abby and fled to the walk-in pantry when she heard Betty' footsteps near the kitchen door.

"Morning Betty. You're looking better today. Better Betty," Abby said with a tap on the girl's arm.

Betty did a quick scan of the kitchen looking for Al and poured coffee. She raised her cup in the air like it was a toast.

"To better Betty, the beauty queen. See you upstairs." She headed back through the swinging doors.

When they squeaked shut, Al came back, picked up her butcher knife, and continued slicing bacon.

Silence fell like a cold November rain. It wasn't a companionable quiet as it should have been by this time in their relationship. It was uncomfortable and itchy on the skin, as if they'd rolled in poison ivy.

"What makes you run away when Betty comes in?" Abby said.

"I don't run."

"You do. You just went to the pantry for nothing." Abby was being peevish and knew it.

She heard Strange Al's annoyed puff of air and watched her search for an answer.

"I changed ribbons."

"No, you didn't, Al."

"Yes. I did. The pink."

"Why in the pantry?"

"Hair in the food."

Abby's shoulders slumped, and she grimaced and chewed her lip. Getting mad at the Tatums' sister would do no good. She didn't even know for certain it had been the Tatum boys who'd hurt her friend, or that Al knew anything about it if they had. She was putting together a set of disconnected actions and coming up with a conviction.

... because she was sure they'd done it before.

... because they were different.

... because somebody beat her friend.

... and because Betty feared and hated Al.

She was glad when her father showed up to take over breakfast preparation and scooted out.

"Tail on fire?" he asked as the door swung back.

"Sorry. Morning, Da."

She and Betty worked like two hens pecking at the same corncob getting the rooms back to pristine cleanliness. They whisper-talked in monosyllabic sentences about everything except her face and the attack. That didn't mean Abby wasn't thinking about it, but she was trying to keep it to herself – for Betty.

Edna was in the bar waiting for her when they finished the last room.

"You're early. Coffee?" she asked.

"I'll get it. You relax for a minute."

"I should see if Da needs me before I sit."

Edna, walking toward the coffee urn, whispered, "Need anything, Patrick?" She poured coffee into two cups and looked at Abby. "He doesn't need you. Cream and sugar?"

Abby laughed. "Just cream. Lots."

She sipped, waiting and watching Edna's eyes, contemplating but knowing the reason for this visit. Not that she wasn't always welcome. Abby enjoyed her company, respected her brusque manner.

They covered weather and healthy small talk, Daisy's newest tooth loss and artistic skills, Jesse's irritations, Patrick, Cassandra, Sally and Sue, Shorty and Bear, and fell silent. The reason for the visit stuck in their brains like porcupine quills in a coon dog's mouth. Neither one could spit it out, and their tongues maneuvered around it painfully.

One long breath after another came to an end when Edna grasped Abby's arm and shoved up her sleeve. The red marks from the night before had turned a light pinkish purple, but were undeniably there. Edna scowled and yanked the sleeve back down.

"What in hell is going on?" she said.

"It's nothing. Really."

"Nothing? Really? Come on, Abby."

"Truly, my friend. I bruise easily. My lily white, Irish skin, you know." She grabbed her auburn curls and pulled them over her shoulder to rake her fingers through them. She shook the tail at her friend as a reminder of her Irish heritage.

"You should never have a reason to bruise, Abby. Never. Ever. Especially not by your husband. Your best friend."

"He's been frustrated lately. Just home from the war. Not needed at the farm. And me."

"What about you?"

The puffs of air from between Abby's lips made them flutter together, sounding like startled quail lifting into the air.

"What not? I seem unable to be the kind of wife Frank needs. But I'll learn. I'm new at this," she said with a half-hearted chuckle.

"Bull . . . loney," Edna said and snorted at her escape from cussing again in public. "You work your butt off and wear a smile doing it. What else does he want?"

Abby fidgeted, unsure about sharing their private lives.

"Me not to do that, I guess. He doesn't talk a lot, especially if you can't talk bullhead. That's another language, you know," she said, working on a smile from Edna or a change of topic.

"I guess it would be. I can't talk it either."

"I – I don't think he likes me being involved with the resort events, or working here, or . . . not being at the farm."

Edna rolled her eyes.

"What does he think you can do about all of that? Leave your father to handle all this by himself? This is who you are."

She paused and stared intently into Abby's eyes.

"Would you want that? To live at the farm with all the rest of the Adams clan?"

Abby shook her head.

"No. I wouldn't. I love the hotel. And I love the Chautauqua events and all the people, the excitement of meeting new folks and learning new things. The music. And I couldn't leave Da."

"If I remember correctly, the Chautauqua was your idea. So was the pavilion. We need you and your ideas, Abby. Idlewild needs you."

"I don't think Frank sees it that way. He sees it as . . . interference."

"Balderdash and poppycock. Tell him to grow up."

"He liked the way Idlewild was before the resort."

"Yeah, well, a few people did, and it isn't that way anymore. They need to get used to it."

Edna frowned and cracked her knuckles. It looked like she was getting ready to punch somebody, and it wasn't hard to figure what her friend was thinking at that moment.

"Transitions aren't easy, and Idlewild is in one right now. Will be for some time as more people come. Growth and change is hard, but it's gonna happen, and most of us believe that's a good thing."

She turned to Abby, her face inches away and wearing a serious expression. It made Abby sit up and take note.

"Idlewild is in development. It's a toddler taking its first steps toward becoming a place colored people can be proud of. A place for us to relax, play, sing, just *be* when no other place will have us. Some people can't stand to see growth and change in things they think belong to them. It scares them because they can't control it. Makes them feel left behind and inadequate. Makes them do stupid things."

Edna drained her cup and set it back on the saucer, pulled Abby's hand toward her and shoved her sleeve up again.

"You and Idlewild have a lot in common. You've grown and changed a bunch since you came here. But nobody owns you, girl. Nobody. Remember that."

"He didn't mean to hurt me."

Edna stood up and squeezed Abby's shoulders.

"They never do. And if he doesn't mean to again, I'll show him some hurt myself."

She smiled on her way out, and Abby didn't know how to respond. She couldn't find the words to convince Edna because she didn't know what they were.

Jackson came in and Abby told him he was on his own. She was leaving for a few hours. She let her father know where she'd be, saddled Marie, tied on a couple bags, and headed home. She needed Nirvana.

The sun was high and warmed her head and shoulders. Lilac scent mixed with the dust on the road and shouted summer. No other fragrance did it quite so well. She let Marie amble.

The shabby sight of the old place could have brought tears to her eyes, but it didn't. She knew it would be overgrown with scrub brush and vines, so she'd been prepared and wasn't surprised or saddened by it. Abby wondered if she was growing impervious to the call of Nirvana.

Ivy covered the porch columns and climbed to the roof, and brambles and thorns tugged at her skirt as she waded through the weeds to the door. It was still locked, and she closed her eyes in a silent prayer of thanks, knowing vandals could easily have entered and damaged her old home. Hobos could've lived in it, and no one would have been the wiser.

The inside was dusty, and traces of mice and bats were plentiful, but it looked the same as when she had locked the door. She pulled open some windows and let the air have its way with the dust, choking back sneezes and coughs.

She wandered through the aged building, touched the scarred, wooden bar with affection, remembering the last night they'd had guests: Shorty, Bear, and Yancy. They drank till the wee hours, and carried Abby around on their shoulders. Yancy had even proposed marriage. She smiled remembering the touching farewell they'd given her.

She looked in every room. She didn't know why, what she was searching for, but the empty spaces drew her. When she had been everywhere, in every nook and cranny, she drew water from the well and poured it into a tub the birds bathed in and drank from. She gave Marie water, unpacked one of the bags the mare had carried and filled the bird feeders with seed. She sat on the porch steps and watched.

It didn't take the blue jays long to find the food, and their raucous chatter brought the chickadees, sparrows, and robins. Doves gathered beneath the feeders, picking up seeds dropped in the feeding frenzy.

A whitetail came to the edge of the woods and stared at her. Two spotted fawns followed, staying out of harm's way a few feet behind the doe.

"Hey, Momma," Abby whispered so she didn't startle her. "Do you remember me? I brought a present for you, too."

Walking slowly so they wouldn't run off, she retrieved the second bag and spread beets and apples on the ground just inside the copse in the shelter of the trees where the whitetail would feel safe. When Abby was once again seated on the steps, the doe led her fawns to the goodies and helped herself.

Abby's smile began in her heart and made its way to her eyes. This was what life should be – no stress trying to be something you weren't – no tension trying to live up to someone else's ideal. The flora and fauna whose world she shared had no expectations. Life without expectations was serene.

She found the trail that rambled through the small thicket of woods on one side of the hotel and behind it. It was overgrown but still visible, and Abby picked her way to the end of it, coming out again on the other side of the building. Like she'd frequently done as a young girl, she talked with her mother on the way and asked questions she would have asked if her mother had been walking next to her, holding her hand. Questions she might have asked about marriage. About Frank. About Betty.

Only the birds answered.

Back in the saddle, she absorbed the sight of her old home with a strange blend of feelings. She painted a picture of the hotel, the woods, the homely front porch, and tucked it inside her mind – to take to her bed – to sleep and dream with, to carry around like a child does a favorite, tattered blanket.

She missed the home she knew as a child, when it was busy with rowdy lumbermen and Nirvana neighbors, but they were gone, and the town stood as dusty and barren as the hotel. She missed the place that was, the one that bloomed when her father was young and virile, and she was carefree and innocent.

She nickered to Marie and turned her toward Idlewild.

Chapter Twenty-four

She spent some time with Marie when she got back to their stable, rubbed her down, and gave her a good brushing and extra oats. She kissed her velvet muzzle and caressed her ears.

"Appreciate your efforts today, old girl," she said. "We'll go more often if that's okay with you. It'll be good for us both."

The horse whinnied.

"Thanks. You're right, and I love you, too."

A few patrons were in the bar when she went in. She put an arm around her father, kissed his cheek and wallowed in his warm affection. He squeezed her waist and eyed her with unspoken questions. Eyebrows raised. Head tilted in Irish interrogation.

"Later," she said. "I have to wash up, change clothes and get back out here to help Jackson."

"I'll be holding you to the later thing, lass."

She took the stairs two at a time, feeling better than she had for several days. Once inside their room, she whisked her husband's pants, shirt and underwear from the floor and flung them into the laundry basket, making an effort not to care they were tossed around the room. Two dirty socks were on the dresser, and she grinned as she sailed them through the air, landing them in the basket with the rest. She smoothed the quilt that held the indented shape of his body and removed her skirt and shirt to wash up.

She pulled a clean dress over her head, brushed her wayward curls and left them hanging down her back. Her mother's picture still rested in the corner of the window seat, safe from Frank's flying clothes. Abby picked it up and stared at the beautiful face, the warm eyes, the sweet smile.

"I fed your critters today, Mama. Thought you'd like that." She nestled it back into its safe place in the corner by the window. She could look out and see the lake.

Enjoy the sunshine.

The bar was half full by the time she went back downstairs. Benjamin was at the piano, and Abby smiled, waved a hello and went behind the bar.

"Everything alright while I was gone?" she asked Jackson.

"Sure. I made some great tips. You should leave more often."

"Maybe I will."

Patrick came out of the kitchen bearing bowls of steaming Irish stew and plates of soda bread for Bear and Shorty who were perched on their favorite stools. He joined them, asking Abby to pour a shot of Irish.

"Ye seem a mite discombobulated," Patrick said to the two men. "What's got you feeling down? Night hooligans out and about?"

"To tell the truth," Bear said. "We're not sure."

Abby's ears perked up and she sidled closer.

"Explain because either they are or they aren't. There's no in between with hooligans," Patrick said.

"Did you see somebody?" Abby asked. "Who?"

"No. We didn't see anyone. We never do," Shorty said.

Jackson came with a drink order, and Abby left to fill it, trying to keep an ear on what her friends were saying. Sally and Sue came in and plopped next to Patrick, Sue engulfing his small frame in a mushy, cushioned hug. He gave his customary charming grin and went back to the conversation with Bear and Shorty who nodded and smiled to the two ladies.

"Then what's the problem if you don't see anyone prowling around in the dark? That's a good thing. That's what you want, right?" Patrick asked.

"Oh. I know what you're talking about," Sally said. "The pictures they've been finding here and there around the island. That's what it is, isn't it?" she said, the wide grin on her face saying 'Bingo! I won!'

"What pictures?" Abby asked. "Someone's leaving pictures . . . like photographs?"

Shorty shook his head and rubbed his jaw.

"No. Ugly pencil or ink drawings of hateful things. We were trying to keep it quiet. Let the person leaving them think we weren't looking for them or him. Hell, maybe it's a her."

"It's not quiet, Sweetheart," Sally said. "Every colored man and woman in Idlewild knows about the KKK pictures, even if they didn't get one personally. You don't know us. We're connected. Like a spider web, one strand leading to another." She wiggled her fingers in the air indicating mysterious connections.

"KKK? That's awful! But if you never see anyone at night, Shorty, how do the pictures get around . . ." Abby said.

"It would be an easy thing to do during the day. A small piece of paper unobtrusively dropped from a hand coming out of a pocket," Shorty said. "They're not that big, and who'd notice when folks are out enjoying themselves in the water or the woods. Or in their cabins relaxing."

Benjamin's fingers were light on the keys, creating a mellow background so soft and unobtrusive the melody was like night air drifting over the lake. Or a morning fog painting the landscape. Abby breathed with the music, trying to feel its stillness, stay in there instead of in the madness they were discussing. Sue's demanding voice brought her back.

"Speak up. I can't hear you," she said. "I never knew such a big man could talk so small. You whisper quieter than a man hiding from his wife."

Shorty grinned and rubbed his head.

"Sorry, Miss Sue. I'll try."

"How long has this been going on?" Patrick asked.

"Since the last fire. Folks find them during the day and hand them over at night during our patrol. They watch for us to do our rounds and greet us with a new picture or two. We have quite a stack of them."

"Does the sheriff know about this?" Abby asked.

"He will tomorrow. One of us is riding to get him," Bear said.

"See, that's how you need to talk. The Bear man can speak. Not often, but loud enough," Sue said, reaching around Patrick to rub Bear's shoulder.

The lines in his beard grew red, and his eyes closed in a grin, but his lips turned down when he saw Abby's face go granite. He followed her gaze to find Joe Foster ambling toward the bar, the crooked leg marking his gate. Abby lifted an eyebrow to her da.

"How many times do I have to kick him out," Patrick groaned under his breath.

Sue, next to him, heard his lament, touched a pudgy finger to her temple and made little circles.

"There's nothing in Joe's head, Patrick, my fine Irish sweetheart. Not even a teeny, tiny lick of a brain."

"We'll try again. Mebbe he'll be good this day."

He nodded to Abby, saying serve the man, and watched Joe slug back his shot of whiskey and ask for more. On his third, he must have decided he'd drunk enough courage to be himself again.

"What you two doing in here? Shouldn't you be out there babysittin' the cabins?"

"We're heading out in a bit, Joe. Soon as it's dark," Shorty said.

"Yeah," Sue piped up. "That's usually when the skunks come out." She turned to Patrick again. "See, he didn't get it. I was talking about him. You got it, didn't you?"

Patrick patted her hand.

"Hear you got a stack a pictures of our fine colored residents," Joe said, a nasty grin on his face that Bear would like to rearrange with his fist. Maybe put his nose right next to his ear.

"That's not your business, Joe," Shorty said.

"Mine as much as yours. You're not the law."

"If you want to discuss it, I'll send Sheriff Hicks to your place tomorrow. Discuss it with him."

Shorty's quiet words left no room for barter, but Joe just couldn't leave it alone.

"Was one a picture of your maid? What's her name? Betty?"

"Betty isn't any body's maid, Joe. And why are you talking about her?" Abby said, anger simmering and threatening to spill.

He tilted his head down, looked up at her through bushy gray eyebrows, and stared at her, his wicked eyes making her spine prickle in discomfort, like a cactus was rolling up it. He looked through her eyes and into her brain and found her deficient, saw her abhorrence of him, and nailed her to the cross for it, smiling as he pounded each one. He reveled in the distress he created, watched as it twitched across her face.

"Everybody knows about Betty, Abigail. She asks for it. Sticking 'em out in front of her like a whore. Wantin' men to look at 'em." He wiped spittle from his mouth. His chest heaved and nostrils flared. "Ain't the first time, either."

"Shut your mouth, Joe Foster, and get out. You're disgusting and not welcome here. I don't know why you can't get that through your thick, stupid, damned head," Abby spouted. "Get out!"

She shook with rage.

Bear and Shorty had left their stools before Joe finished speaking and were standing on either side of him when Abby finished.

"Let's go, Joe," he whispered.

"Bye, Joe. Nice seeing you again," Sue yelled, and Sally nudged her arm.

"Behave yourself, Sue. Go sing a song with that nice colored boy at the piano."

Sue went to sing, leaving Patrick and Sally to stare at Abigail.

Sally put her long fingered hand over Abby's and murmured "Muh muh muh, girl. You're gonna have to grow some skin. No man's worth shaking over. Specially not that ignorant Neanderthal."

316

She flipped her head, tilted it sideways and back and looked around the room for any other possible listeners she could impress.

"Yeah," she grinned. "I know what it means to be a Neanderthal. I read. Sub human. That's Joe Foster."

"Come on, Benjamin," Patrick said when the place cleared out. "Give your fingers a rest and join us on the porch for a toddy. Call it a day, Abigail."

"When these glasses are washed. What's your pleasure, Benjamin?"

She poured a tall one for them both, and they left her in the semi-dark room, watching the two men walk out.

They were an unusual pair, Benjamin as dark and clean cut as her father was shaggy and white – from his pale Irish skin to his curly hair. Benjamin was tall and broad shouldered, and Patrick was bandy-legged, making him appear even shorter than his actual height. Benjamin was soft spoken and serious, and Patrick would joke with a corpse if he thought he'd come up with a good one and maybe get a laugh.

Patrick liked the young man, had taken the soldier under his wing when his parents returned to their home, left Idlewild and their son who was still recovering from war injuries. He saw Benjamin's struggle with wounds of the mind and wanted to help him heal, at least hold out a supporting hand for him to take if he chose to, a listening ear if he wanted to talk.

Most nights, after Benjamin's stint at the piano, Patrick led him to a chair on the porch, rocked and talked about the day or about nothing. Or didn't talk at all.

"His worst wound is in the heart, Abby," her father had told her. "And it's been carved up pretty bad. He's a good lad."

"He's no lad, Da," Abby had said.

"Aye, and you're no lass, but I still call you one."

Abby told Jackson to go on home and took her time cleaning up the bar, seeing scenes of horror in every corner

– evil pictures right next to Joe Foster's face. Phantom and Cleo eyed her as she moved around, washing down the countertop, sweeping up, mumbling.

"You think I'm pretty stupid, don't you? I can tell by the way you're looking at me."

She put the chairs up on the tables so she could sweep under them and looked back at the cats.

"Do you dislike Cleo because she's a black cat, Phantom? Is that why you two don't make a litter of cute little kittens?"

Mrow, wah.

Prrrr . . . kow, Cleo said in answer to him.

Abby spun around.

"You talked! I didn't think you had a voice box. Yea! Cleo! And I knew the answer all along. I didn't even need to ask."

The cat opened her mouth wide like words should come out again, but they didn't.

"It's okay. I understand," Abby told her. "Some of us don't need to talk a lot."

Abby finished the sweeping, poured herself a glass of sherry, and joined the rockers on the porch. She took the advice of her cats and let it go. The world was not lost to suspicion and hatred, just some people.

A few hotel guests had found chairs lined up on the porch to sit and watch the sun sink into the water, a mythical phoenix dying in flames. Stars winked on, tiny candles lighting the moon's way through the dark so it could hang in magical stillness, a beacon for lovers, raccoons, and owls. And Cassandra.

She took the open chair next to her father, lowered herself into it and stretched like Phantom. All would be well. It had to be. She couldn't let men like Joe Foster change who she was, the way she wanted to live. The way she saw life.

She caught a glimpse of long legs through half-closed eyes and looked up to see Frank walking across the yard. She held out her hand to him and asked how he was, like he was a familiar face, maybe a neighbor she'd come to know fairly well, or someone she knew long ago.

He ignored the hand, and she let it drop in her lap.

"Hungry?" she asked.

"No. Ate with George and Terry."

"Have a chair. Want something to drink?"

"Sure. Whiskey. A tall one."

She got up to get it, and Frank took her chair and rocked back. He didn't say anything. Didn't acknowledge his father-in-law in the chair next to him.

She handed him the drink and dragged another chair close to his, sat and considered what to say, what to talk about that would interest him. Not Joe Foster. She wanted to forget he existed. Not Sue and Sally. Frank didn't like it when they came to the hotel for drinks. Didn't think it looked right.

"How was your day, Frank? Did you catch fish? Maybe you could bring Papa some to fry up."

"Do that. Next batch," he said.

"Did you see Ceci? How is she? I miss her."

A sound like half a laugh-half a snort came from his throat, but he didn't look at her.

"She's fine."

"And Chunk and Bailey? I probably wouldn't know them it's been so long."

"Probably."

Abby sipped her sherry and pushed to rock her chair, her head against the back slats. The stars had done their job well, because the moon was making its way steadily toward the spot where it would spend the night.

She could make out craters and mountains on it; at least, she believed she could and pretended she knew what it would be like to walk on the moon, explore the vastness of an uninhabited world. Or maybe it wasn't uninhabited. Maybe it was a more civilized place than earth, more evolved. Peaceful and loving.

"I rode out to Nirvana today," she said, reminded of her visit by thoughts of peace.

Frank turned his head to look at her for the first time.

"Why?"

"I just wanted to."

"Obviously. But why?"

"Feed the birds and deer. I loved Nirvana, Frank. I still do. It is my childhood home."

"It's dead, Abby. Nothing's there."

Abby toed the floor to rock, sorrow and irritation stirring together like thick wallpaper paste. She glanced at Frank's profile and thought him handsome, but dressed in a dark cloak of dissatisfaction, a garment sewn of metal fabric, like armor. Had he always been this way or was it new? Was it the war? Or was it something she had done to make him . . . distant . . . detached.

"My mother's there, Frank."

"She's gone, Abby. For a long time now."

On the other side of Frank, her father's chair stilled. She knew he listened and wished he didn't have to hear their words.

She didn't have a response, and Patrick, too, remained silent. Minutes dragged by filled only with the sound of insects, frogs, and larger night creatures foraging near the edge of the woods. A periodic splash drew their eyes, and concentric circles picked up the moon's glow where a fish had broken through the water's once glassy surface. Abby imagined a beautiful speckled brown trout leaping for glee, not fleeing from a predator, and painted a smile on its fish lips. It brought a smile to her own.

"I'm going up," Frank said, and vacated his chair. The screen door banged shut and bounced against the wood frame, and Abby's fingers tangled in her hair. She closed her eyes and held her breath, waiting for the banging to stop reverberating in her brain.

"Nirvana is a beautiful place to visit," Abby said, as if she needed to defend her trip.

"It is, Abigail. And it's filled with life. Ye need not feel sad about going there."

"It's peaceful, especially now. No people to muck it up. Just critters . . . and Ma."

"Tis true. And a beautiful trail through the copse your ma made so she could get away from the likes of me and the rowdy lumberjacks. Then . . . you came along and took the same path. You both knew when the trout lilies were out and the Indian turnips."

"And trilliums and bluebells," Abby said, her eyes closed and seeing the landscape of her mind. "And the morels. Don't forget the mushrooms."

Patrick chuckled. "Never, lass. I wouldn't be forgettin' the mushrooms."

"It sounds lovely," Benjamin said, and Abby started.

"I forgot you were there. Sorry," she said. "We were in the past and most likely maudlin."

"No. Sorry I interrupted. I remember you telling me about Nirvana. One day, I'd like to see it for myself."

"That's right. I did, didn't I? I'll take you there some day. It really is a bit of a ghost town."

"Some ghosts are good company," Benjamin said. "I live with many, I do."

His words hovered in the air like campfire smoke on a wet day and dispersed around each of them, one by one, to sit on an arm or lay across a shoulder. Abby shivered and moved into the vacated chair next to her da.

"You know many ghosts?" she asked, her words whispered in awe and hope. "Why? Where?"

Benjamin filled his chest with night air, and they heard him release it bit by bit, taking time to reflect before sharing his thoughts. He knew some might consider him crazy. He might, too. And on certain days, he did. But mostly, he believed his way of dealing with death worked.

He couldn't let his brothers go just yet. They had died for him - as he would have for them, and he was following by their sides into death when the medic forced him to come back. He hadn't wanted to.

Benjamin leaned forward, his elbows on his knees, and stared out at the still water. So much tranquility wasn't fitting. Not now, not after the brutality of France.

"The sun rises and sets, storms pelt the earth, and rivers flow, winters come, and summers follow with green grass and flowers made into wreaths to decorate soldiers' graves. But no soldiers live there. Their graves are empty because the pieces of their bodies lay in blood drenched fields, and the ghosts follow me, not haunting, but keeping me company."

Long, hushed minutes passed, and Abby leaned across her father's knees and touched Benjamin's shoulder.

"I'm sorry," she said. "I was just interested."

He turned his midnight eyes to her, taking in his friend Patrick, as well.

"My apologies for being so grisly. I got lost in time for a moment. I keep my fellow soldiers by my side. They're my best friends, my brothers, even though they no longer have use of flesh and blood."

"The soldiers . . ." Abby asked. "Can you see them?"

"Sometimes. I always know when they're here, hanging out with me."

Abby looked around, trying to spy a wisp of white that would indicate another presence, a lurking soldier, a ghost. Her eyes flickered from one side of the porch to another, searching, but found nothing she could be sure of.

"Are they here now?"

"Somewhat. In a way, they're always with me."

He chuckled. He'd been somber long enough, and he didn't want to scare his friends.

"You've been pulling my leg, haven't you?"

Patrick chuckled and Benjamin's sweet baritone filled the night.

"Only a little. I don't mind ghosts. They're good company considering some of the choices we have."

"I agree," Patrick said, still rumbling with gleeful chortles.

Chapter Twenty-five

Abby was placing a bowl of fried potatoes on the buffet when the sheriff poked her in the back and said, "Put your hands up. You're under arrest."

Without turning around, she said, "If you want breakfast, that's not the way to get it."

"Darn. Did you know it was me? Or were you talking to just any old fool who'd poke you in the back?"

"Any old fool," Abby said, turning to shine a smile at him. "But I could smell you and knew."

Hicks backed up, his hands palms out like he was warding off an attack.

"Surely not. I don't smell. I take baths, Miss Abby. Honest."

"Pipe tobacco, Sheriff Hicks. Sweet cherry. I love it. Take a plate."

He did, piled it high and headed for a table.

"Join me?"

Abby poured coffee and followed him.

"I gather either Bear or Shorty was banging on your door by dawn this morning."

"You got that right. Big fist, too. Bout made me fall outta bed."

"Must have been Shorty," she said with a grin and a nod. "He's the biggest man I've ever seen. Sweetest, too. Kind of like an apple dumpling."

Abby sipped, waiting for a revelation from him, but he'd decided eating was more important. She sipped again at her coffee and couldn't wait any longer.

"So, what do you make of the pictures, Sheriff? Does someone mean to do harm?"

"Hard to say. Could be maybe; could be not."

She tapped the edge of her saucer with a fingernail.

"Okay. How can you find who is doing this? It's a terrible thing. Scaring people, I mean. Or at the very least, making folks a bit nervous."

Sheriff Hicks forked a mound of fried potato into his mouth and turned to watch several guests fill their own plates and sit at nearby tables.

"It's a sick thing to do, but . . . Abby, I don't know that it's within my jurisdiction to stop. Don't think it's illegal to draw pictures and put 'em around for people to look at. It's hateful, but hating isn't against the law."

"Well, it should be. What's happening isn't right."

"I agree."

Hicks shoveled more food on his fork, and Abby looked around the room to keep an eye on the guests and their needs. Betty came in, returning the broom to the storage area, and Abby saw her eyes widen and fill with instant anger. She stood still, her fingers tightening around the broom handle, and stared at Abby sitting with the Sheriff. She turned and fled, her black boots beating the wooden floor.

Abby followed, calling her name. She caught her at the door, ready to leave the hotel.

"You asked him to come here, didn't you? You lied to me," she said, her words streaked with disappointment.

"No. Yes. We asked him, but it's not what you think."

Betty looked sideways at her boss, her eyes hard and unyielding.

"What do you mean?"

"Shorty and Bear brought him here because of the pictures, you know, the drawings that have been scattered all over the island."

"Yeah. I know about them."

She still held the broom, but her fingers began to relax, and she blew snorts of air from her flared nostrils, getting rid of her hot anger.

"So, he's not here about me?" she asked.

"No. I told you I wouldn't. But I still wish *you* would."

"No."

Betty glared at Abby one last time, making a point, and walked toward the stairs.

"I'll get started," she said.

"I'll be up in a minute," Abby said, turning back to continue her chat with Sheriff Hicks who was being entertained by her father when she got there. She refilled their coffee and called to Frank who'd sauntered in.

"Make me a plate?" he asked.

"Glad to. Have a seat."

Patrick shoved a chair out for him.

"You know my son-in-law, Frank," he said to Hicks.

"Sure. Big farm just north of town. Butts up to the Tatum's. How you doing, Frank?"

"Not too bad. What're you doing in town today?" Frank asked.

"Just checking on things. A little art work going on, scaring people."

"Yeah. Heard that."

"Where'd you hear it?"

"Around," he said.

"Want to tell me about it?"

Frank pushed his spine against the slats of the chair back and slanted his head at the sheriff.

"You accusing me of something, Hicks?"

"Just looking for information, Frank. Don't get excited."

"Well, it sounded like questioning a suspect."

Patrick sipped his coffee and watched the interplay, curious about Frank's reaction.

"I can't do my job without asking questions. Comes with the territory. Do you remember where you heard it?"

Abby set a full plate in front of him, and he took a bite before answering.

"Think it was Foster's. Somebody found a couple and showed them to Joe. He laughed."

"Joe Foster's an obnoxious fool," Abby said. "Who brought in the pictures?"

"I didn't pay any attention who. They just left them there on the counter. Ask Joe."

Hicks rubbed his chin and glanced from Frank to the doorway as if waiting for answers to walk in. Abby watched his face and knew he was processing the scene at Fosters, visualizing it. She didn't wait to see if he asked more questions.

"I'm heading upstairs to clean. Nice seeing you, Sheriff. Stop up before you leave, Frank?"

They were making up the second room when Frank found them.

"You wanted something?" he asked.

Abby took his arm and led him to their room.

"Feeling like some loving?" he asked, wrapping an arm around her and pulling her against him. "I'm fine with that. I can meet George later."

"No, Frank. I just wanted to talk a minute."

"Course. Knew it," he said, and Abby wished she could put a smile on his face, wished she had brought him to their room for a different reason, one he would have liked.

"What do you want, Abigail?"

She fidgeted for a moment, not sure how to ask, not wanting to see anger and disappointment darken his eyes once again.

"It seemed to me you knew more than you told the sheriff. Was I right?"

"What makes you say that?"

"Just the way you looked."

"I looked hungry. That's all. Now *you* sound like you're accusing me."

"No, honest, Frank. I'm not accusing you of doing anything. I'm just asking you to tell what you know, if you know anything. This is serious stuff. People could get hurt. It makes them afraid and . . ."

He leaned against the closed door and stared at her, rolled his head around like it was stiff or hurt, kneaded his neck, and crossed his arms over his chest.

"It's always going to be this way, isn't it?" His eyes were hard, unyielding ice. Abby searched for a glimmer of affection in them and couldn't find it.

"What way?" She tugged at the mane curling over her shoulder with one hand and stuck the other in her mouth to chew at a ragged nail. She felt guilty of something. She wasn't sure what, and that was annoying, frustrating her to no end.

"You and your resort people against me and my family. What did we do to you?" Frank said.

"Nothing. And it isn't like that. It's not about choosing sides as if we're at war or playing a game. Why must you always look at it that way?"

She tried to put an arm around him, to soften his anger, but, for once, he resisted and didn't reach to fondle her. He stood stiff and inflexible.

"I'm not against you," she added, "or your family. And what do they have to do with any of this?"

"It certainly seems that way. I'm going."

"Can't we talk about this, please?"

"Nothing to discuss, Abby."

Frank left, and Abby didn't know if he was gone for good, for an hour, or for the day. She didn't know a lot about her husband, and she didn't know how she ever would. If he wouldn't talk with her, how would she learn who he was?

She yanked at the nail she'd been nibbling on and watched blood surface where it had torn into the quick.

"Damn. That hurts," she said, and her eyes filled with tears she blinked away.

She poured water over the finger and squeezed it until it quit bleeding.

"Life should be so simple," she murmured. "A little water, a little squeeze, and we're good to go. Slap a bandage on, give it a kiss, and wham, we're mended."

She kissed the offended finger and tried out a smile.

Hicks interviewed nearly everyone on the island, and not a soul had seen a single scrap of paper in the process of being dropped or delivered. Nor could anyone guess who the artist might be.

Between Shorty, Bear and the Idlewild residents, the sheriff had collected well over a hundred hand drawn pictures and had them spread out on Jesse's desk. They sorted them by content: burning crosses, Negroes hanging from tree limbs, dark figures cowering from white hoods, fearful faces with mouths open wide, indicating screaming.

On the other side of the desk, they made piles of pictures with angry dark faces holding torches to barns and white people running around with their hands in the air wearing wide eyes and opened mouths.

Some of the pictures resembled cave drawings in their simplicity and were a variety of stick figures in horrific situations. Others showed some minor imaginative detailing. This obvious difference in creative talent said more than one artist had been recently creative. A review of the pictures convinced them all.

Bear was more concerned by what seemed to be conflicting themes than the fact there were at least two artists. He said so as he poked at the piles with a thick finger.

"These images, the ones of angry dark faces look like colored folks maybe drew them."

"Spit it out, Bear," Shorty said.

"Just . . . the stories in them are different than the ones with people hanging from trees. That's all."

"Appears drawn by folks with different purposes, doesn't it?" Shorty said.

Jesse nodded and scraped a hand across new stubble on his chin.

"This pile, the ones with hanging coloreds, I assume was done by a white hand," Bear said. "The ones with the torches against the barns, look like colored folks did the drawing."

"You can't tell the artist by the drawing," Shorty said. "But if we assume they are making a point, then, yes. I agree."

"Does that get us any closer to answers?" Sheriff Hicks pulled the piles toward him and went through them again, one by one. The other three men in the room waited and watched as he finished and pushed them all back into a single pile in the middle of the desk.

"Well?" Jesse asked.

"Some folks are tired of the cabin fires and KKK painted doors and are demanding it stop. Wouldn't you say?" he asked, turning to look at each man in the room. "Some of these pictures shout, 'leave us alone or we'll burn your barns... or worse.'"

The sheriff looked at Jesse for confirmation. The usually upbeat lawyer squeezed his eyes with a thumb and index finger and ran the hand through his hair.

"I'd agree," he said.

"The others look like they were drawn by a white hand and were meant to strike fear in the hearts of the colored lot owners, make them leave, or, at the very least, make them look over their shoulders and behind them in the dark."

"But who?" Jesse asked. "And are they doing this together, for some idiotic reason, or is someone doing it in retaliation against the other's pictures?"

"I don't know. And this is all speculation based on the pictures themselves," he said to the two men. "We've got nothing to go on. It doesn't make sense to think they could have been drawn by one person, and we don't know anything else."

"What now, Sheriff?" Shorty asked.

"Keep doing what you're doing. Get in touch with me if anything changes – a new kind of picture – anything. I'll be around daily to be a presence. Let 'em know we mean business."

Jesse stood and held his hand out to the sheriff. He moved in close to the lawman, closer than either was comfortable with, and looked into his eyes.

"Are these threats real? I need to know," he said. "Should I take special precautions with Edna and Daisy? Like move them somewhere else?"

Hicks held the man's hand moments longer than a handshake would normally allow while he considered his response. Jesse deserved honesty. So did his wife and child.

"Wouldn't hurt. I don't believe there's an intentional serious danger, but you've read the newspapers. Lincoln didn't end the Negro plight. I don't need to tell you. You

coloreds know that. And you know people still get hurt.
Some die."

"Yes. We surely do know that. And I'm not a fearful
man, but I'm glad these two are walking around at night,"
Jesse said. "I hope Bill and the rest of the Resort Company
respect that and can afford to keep them on."

Jesse put his hand on Sheriff Hicks shoulder, letting him
know he didn't hold him responsible for the problems they
were having in Idlewild and walked him to the door.

"You're welcome here," Jesse told him.

"Got that," Hicks said, and from the doorway watched
an old, colored woman walk down the footbridge to the
island. Several cats followed her in single file, not looking
right nor left, not noticing the birds that fluttered nearby,
but heads up and straight ahead, following like they'd been
hypnotized, and she was a snake charmer – or in this case,
cat charmer.

"What is that?" he asked.

"That is Cassandra and her clowder."

"Clowder?"

"Flock of cats," Bear said. "Miss Cassandra has lots of
cats."

"I'll bet Idlewild is the only place in the whole world
that uses the proper name for a bunch of cats," Shorty said
with a firmly installed small grin, glad for a reason to smile.

"I haven't interviewed her. Does she live here?"

"Sure does. And she doesn't miss much. You might
want to," Jesse said.

"Where?"

"You'd miss her place if you didn't know where it was.
Follow her now. You'll like her," Bear told him.

Chapter Twenty-six

Fall swathed Idlewild in intense sights and sounds: leaves in gaudy shades of orange and red, the irritating squawk of Canadian geese terrorizing other fowl and fishermen, brisk winds whipping up white caps on the water, and wood smoke spiraling into the air from hearths and campfires. Summer's gentle nature was a memory.

Frank had come home after their brief squabble and acted as if nothing had occurred. For him, fall was hunting and business as usual, and as long as breakfast, supper and Abby were available when he wanted them, he went about life in general content. Abby didn't know what he did all day, but his time was his own, and she didn't ask. He made repairs around the place if they were needed and if she requested it, but he didn't volunteer for anything.

There were few guests at the hotel, but most of the cabins on the island were full. People, like Micah and Maggie Chambers, had built hearths in their small cottages and stayed late into the cold weather. Benjamin moved into the hotel when his parents reclaimed their place, and Patrick let him play for his rent.

With fewer guests, Abby found time to travel to Nirvana. She hauled tools and cleaning supplies to their old place and spent comfortable and delightful hours putting the hotel back into some semblance of shape.

She cleared the encroaching scrub brush that had made its way up to the building and swept the wide expanse of covered porch. She sat on the steps soaking in the late day sun, letting it warm her face. She cleared the cobwebs from the small bar and reminisced about the many lumberjacks she'd known, and some she'd loved, from the time she was a toddler to the time she left Nirvana.

She pumped water into a bucket from the old hand pump out back by the kitchen and scrubbed down the wood bar. It had dried in spots and needed oil, but that was for another day. In the sunbeams leaking through dust covered windows, it still glowed with the deep radiance wood wears from years of loving care.

By mid-November, she had the bar, the kitchen and most of the rooms cleaned. If anyone had asked her why, she wouldn't have known what to tell them. It needed to be done, sort of.

Taking care of their old place was cathartic and right. Homes shouldn't be left to decay, to fall down in disrepair. These rooms held memories. Her mother and father had stared out of these windows in longing and in joy; they'd laughed and cried. Their lives had been breathed into the walls, and then she came along and repeated the living and memory making with her father.

It was right to have everything sparkling and shiny, taken care of and cherished.

Only a few people were in the bar when she got back, so she let Jackson go early and donned her work apron. Patrick held up one end of the long bar, next to Bear, Shorty and Jesse.

"Welcome home, lass," he said. "You thinking about moving back to Nirvana?"

"Just taking care of it. That's all. You should see how nice it looks now."

"I'll do that someday," Shorty said. "I'll take a ride with you."

"Me, too," Benjamin said from the piano bench. His fingers moved gently over the keys making music soft enough to talk over. "You promised me a tour."

Abby smiled at the quiet man. Quiet made her happy.

"It would be my pleasure, and it's ready to be enjoyed. Name the day – as long as we're not too busy here."

"Tomorrow," Benjamin said.

"Perfect," Abby answered, but Shorty and Bear said they'd have to wait for another time. They had a meeting with Bill Sanders.

"What's that about?" Patrick asked. "You getting fired?"

"Don't know, but that's a possibility. Nothing bad is going on," Bear said. "Just the pictures being strewn about."

"That may be because of your presence," Abby said. "Without you two wandering around at night, who knows what could be happening."

"It's all guess work. We don't know anything and might not know until too late, until it happens," Bear said.

"God, don't say that." She shuddered and turned to the piano player. "We can go, Benjamin. Afternoon? About two? Just us."

"I'll hire a buggy," he said.

"You can ride with me. Marie can take us both. She's strong for her age and we'll go slow."

"Nope. I'll hire."

Frank came in as Bear and Shorty left for their night patrol, and Abby told him about her afternoon in Nirvana and about her plans to share it with Benjamin the next day.

"Want to go with us?" she asked. "I'm finally gonna show him the place I've been talking his ear off about."

He shook his head, looked at the man at the piano and asked for a whiskey.

"Did you hunt today?" she asked.

He nodded and told her he got his buck. It was hanging at the farm. She was glad they kept it there. She didn't want to see a dead deer even though she recognized the value of venison. She couldn't stand seeing it with eyes, feet and fur. She didn't want to think about it wandering through the woods a short time ago, nibbling at foliage and living in peace.

"Argh." She slapped her leg to rid her mind of the troubling thoughts. It wasn't fair to Frank. He was a hunter, a good, careful one. He never left a wounded animal in the woods, and he never took aim unless he was certain the shot would kill.

Leave it alone, Abby. Let it go. You don't understand hunting or the hunters.

"Why don't you close up? Nobody's here," he said.

"I can go up. See you tomorrow, Benjamin. Two o'clock."

He nodded and they left.

"Sure you don't want to go tomorrow, Frank? Might be fun. You already got your buck," she said on the way to their room.

He shook his head and took the stairs two at a time. As soon as he pushed the door open, Phantom and Cleo bolted from the room and scooted between his legs, making a dash for Bear's open door and his bed.

"Damned cats. Gonna knock me over the railing someday."

The tread of his boots indicated Frank's dour attitude, and she had come to dread nights when his disposition fell around them like a steady, cold rain, dampening everything it settled on.

"They already tried. Remember when we moved in here?" she said, trying to tease him into good humor. "They get nervous around you, Frank. That's all, so they run."

"Bullshit."

Frank was out of his clothes and into bed before she'd finished washing her face and brushing her hair. She turned from him to remove her clothes, never having gotten used to disrobing in front of him, and pulled her gown over her head.

"Don't know why you think you need that granny gown every night," he said, watching her with half closed lids.

"It feels right, Frank. Naked doesn't. And it's pretty, not granny-ish."

She pirouetted and turned to him, pointing to the pink lace inserted along the front.

"Look at it," she said. "I didn't know my granny, but I don't think she had a nightgown this pretty."

Frank tugged at the hem, pulling her closer, and wrapped his arm around her legs.

"I'm just gonna take it off, Abby. Come on to bed."

He scooted over and she climbed in and lay still. When Frank rolled toward her and tugged at the gown, she caressed his back and neck and was pleased to hear his groan of pleasure. She took his hand from where it grasped her breast and pulled it to her face, cupping it with her own to keep it there, trying to ask him to kiss her without telling him what to do. Talking about it was just too hard, but she was trying.

When Frank lay on his back, one arm cocked over his face and the other out sideways, she knew in a moment she'd hear his light snore. It was always immediate. He didn't suffer waiting for sleep. His head hit the pillow, and he was gone. She wanted to drive her elbow into his side .. . accidently and gently, of course, just to see if he could fall asleep in six seconds again. Her eyes were wide open.

She yanked her nightgown down around her legs and lay immobile, thinking, willing her mind to be as still as her body. She gave up, went to the washstand, dipped a cloth into the cool water, and washed herself. When she was clean, she moved to the window and saw her reflection.

The woman staring back at her was virginal in the long white gown, and a soft, satirical laugh escaped.

Maybe that's who I am. I'm a spiritual virgin. I just don't want to be and don't know what to do about it.

She smiled at her image, a half-hearted effort, and tried to see the lake beyond her reflection, but she became a part of it as the images blended. It appeared as though she was standing in the water, the hem of her granny gown dipping into it. Abby waited to see if she would sink into the depths of Lake Idlewild and raised her brows, wondering if it was prophetic.

At two o'clock, Benjamin pulled up in front of the hotel in a shiny, black, two seater trap. He wrapped a rein around the post and went in to look for Abby. She hadn't seen anyone climb out and had her nose pressed against the window pane, eyeing the buggy. She jumped when he spoke from behind her.

"Come on, Abigail. Your carriage awaits," he said, laughing at her reaction. "Get a wrap. It's chilly."

He went out to wait, and she came down the steps with a basket on her arm and tugging at the white shawl Bunny had crocheted for her at Christmas time.

"You want the sides put on? It'll be warmer," he asked.

"No. It's a glorious day."

He helped her up, went around to get in, and nickered to the black mare.

"This is beautiful," she said. "Where did you get it?"

"The livery in Baldwin. Actually, I'm thinking of buying it and the horse, so the owner let me take them for the day. I like both."

"I love it!" Abby said. "It's spectacular. I feel like a princess."

She waved and called out to everyone they passed, a huge grin plastered on her face, like a little girl on her birthday. They waved back, some with smiles and some with expressions of curiosity that Abby didn't bother to analyze – or even spare a moment's thought.

"You're gonna love Nirvana, Benjamin. I just know it. And I've got a surprise for you."

They were there long before Abby was ready to stop. She'd enjoyed the sunshine, the easy ride, the companionship. When he turned the mare onto the lengthy driveway, he stopped some ways from the hotel and stared, taking in the peaceful porch, the gray, weathered building, the signs of Abby's recent upkeep. He sat perfectly still, looking at her old home.

"This is perfect. You were right, Abby. It is Nirvana."

"Well, the town is called Nirvana, but I think it applies to this spot, too, in a great many ways. It's actually called the Aishcum Hotel because for a few years this was Aishcum county."

He nodded and looked a few moments longer before clicking to the mare and pulling closer to the building. He jumped down, wrapped the rein around the porch rail, and went around to help Abby, but she'd already leaped from the trap step and was heading to the porch.

"Come on in," she yelled. "I'm excited to show it to you."

Abby dragged Benjamin from room to room, pointing and talking, describing the people who had stayed there, going on about anything that popped into her head. Benjamin smiled and at least pretended to listen. She finally dragged him to the bar and told him of their last night there with her father, Bear, Shorty, and a lumberjack named Yancy who had proposed to her.

"I tended Bear in an upstairs room when he tangled with a real bear," she said. "He was horribly hurt."

"You're a good woman, Abigail."

She glanced at his face to see if he was teasing or serious.

"You want to see the trail my mother and I walked? At different time periods, of course."

"Sure would. Lead on."

The sun was warm in the shelter of the trees, and they followed the familiar path worn through a small thicket growing near the building.

Bird chatter led and followed them, and squirrels ran up the sides of trees to scamper a few feet away and watch from the safety of their sideways perch.

"I usually bring food for the critters when I come. I didn't today. They're going to be mad at me."

"I can bring some back for them," he said. "Wouldn't want them to be angry at you."

"And you're a good man, Benjamin. Really kind."

They came out at the opposite side of the hotel and walked around to rest on the front porch steps, both lost in thought and watching the wildlife.

"Is that the town of Nirvana I'm looking at beyond the trees?"

She nodded. "What's left. Few people live there since the lumberjacks left."

"I like that. It's quiet."

"We can take that route back if you want, and you can conjure up some Nirvana ghosts. There should be plenty."

Abby strolled to the trap and returned with the basket. She spread a small cloth between them and set out a block of cheese, a half loaf of bread, two glasses and a small decanter of sherry.

"Which do you want first? The sherry?" she asked.

"This is quite a treat. I don't know what to say."

"Say sherry," Abby said, her eyes alight with fun. She was enjoying herself – more than she thought she would. Benjamin was easy to be around.

"Is this okay?" he asked.

"What? The sherry or the trip? Why wouldn't it be?" she said, handing him a glass half full of a deep amber liquid. "You're my friend – my piano friend. And I knew you would love this place. I'm happy to share it with someone I thought might appreciate it even a little bit as much as I do."

He took the glass and they sipped in silence, looking out at the vivid panorama nature had provided. In time, Abby cut a few chunks of the cheese and bread and nibbled.

"Help yourself, Benjamin."

He did. When they'd finished their repast, he asked if he could take another look at the bar and kitchen. Abby was packing the basket and rolled her eyes his way.

"Sure. Any special reason?"

"I have an idea." A smile inched across his face and sat in his eyes. He went in and she joined him, wandering through the now dusky rooms.

When they came out, Abby turned the key to lock up, grabbed the basket sitting on the step, and said, "Okay. Speak."

"In a minute."

They were half way back to Idlewild when she punched him on the arm.

"You've had your minute. Lots of them. What's going on inside that handsome head?"

"Hmmm. Thinking. I love your Nirvana. I want to live there."

Abby was more than stunned. Somebody else in her home? Somebody else making it their place?

"Are you serious? What would you do there?"

"Live. Same thing I'm doing at your current hotel."

"But . . ." Abby didn't know what else to say. She went quiet, wondering if she was ready to give up *her* place to a stranger. Well, not a stranger, but not family, either.

"I've had enough noise, Abigail. I'm ready for peace. And for just the sound of my piano and the critters."

"None of my business, but how would you live?"

"Small pension and a trust. Not much, but I don't need much. I could pay your dad a little to lease it, maybe open up the bar to whoever is left in town and wants a drink. I'd buy a piano and play for them if they wanted."

She could picture him playing his melancholy music in the empty bar, wandering through the empty rooms, dusting the sparse furniture – living in a ghost hotel in a ghost town. Sometimes she would like that herself. She'd like to get away from people she didn't want to see, things she didn't want to watch happen. She'd miss her friends, the resort people, noise and laughter, though, and asked Benjamin about longing for those very things he wanted to escape.

"Have you thought this all out?"

He grinned at her.

"Doing that while I talk. Didn't know I'd love the place before I went. I just suspected it when I listened to you talk about your Nirvana."

Abby turned sad eyes his way.

"I don't want the place sold, Benjamin. Da doesn't either, so maybe this is just the thing. You, I mean. You're just the thing. Can you swing a hammer?"

"A bit." He glanced sideways at her. "Not very well, but I'm capable of learning. Why?"

"Instead of lease money, what about a trade? You'd just take care of the place. You know, keep it up. If there's anything major, of course, like a new roof, we'd pay for supplies and we'd help. What do you think?"

"I like it, but what about your father? What will Patrick say?"

"He'll say whatever I tell him to say. He's my little parrot papa," she said, a sparkle lighting her eyes. "I'm being silly," she said when doubt clouded his expression. "He likes you, Benjamin. I know him, and I know he'll like the idea. And the place is empty. It needs care."

Benjamin dropped her off at the steps of the hotel, and she bounced out, eager to tell her father of their tentative plans. She ran through the door and into the lobby, skidding to a stop in front of Frank who stood in the middle of the room, a monolith barring her way and glaring at her like she was rabid vermin. His jaws quivered in anger; his eyes burned.

"What in hell do you think you're doing?" The words were staccato, like bullets from multiple guns.

Abby stepped back from the blaze of his fury and held the basket in front of her like a shield.

"What do you mean?"

"That was a straightforward question, Abby. I think you know the answer unless you're too false to answer it."

"Stop shouting, Frank," she said, "and let go of my arm, please."

"Answer me. Where were the two of you?"

"You know where I was because I told you last night. In Nirvana. Showing Benjamin our old place."

With the thought of Nirvana, her earlier happiness tried to seep in around Frank's anger, and she yearned to tell him about it, share it with him, but knew it wasn't to happen.

"You were gallivanting around with . . . him, just you and him . . . all afternoon." He looked away from her and his nostrils flared. "What's wrong with you Abby? You're a white woman. A white, married woman, in case you've forgotten, and he's colored and a man. What are you thinking? What will everyone think?"

Abby stepped back, stunned.

If he thought it was wrong, why didn't he say anything last night when she told him about their plans? And asked him to go with them? Why keep his feelings to himself until it was too late? Until now? Until she'd done the thing he didn't want her to do?

"I don't know what I was thinking, Frank, other than sharing a place I love with a friend. You could've gone. I asked you. Nothing was wrong with what I did. What we did."

"Do you think my mother would run around with another man? Let alone a Negro?"

Abby set the basket on the lobby counter and removed her shawl. Her hand shook, and her mind went blank. It was too much to comprehend. She looked around to see who might be listening to her husband's condemnation.

She clutched at her chest. Her pounding heart pumped blood to the rest of her body, but it was breaking. She was sure of it. The blade of his accusations embedded there, twisted, and she bled with each cruel cut of his words.

Where was the man she'd married, and who was this one?

"I don't know what you mean by *run around*, but is that what infuriates you, or is it the color of Benjamin's skin?"

The inside of her lip was raw where she gnawed as she waited for a response, waited to hear this was all a mistake, a horrible joke gone awry.

"Will you answer?" she asked.

Frank spun away and stalked out.

"Nope," he said, at the door just before he slammed it.

Abby's shoulders slumped, and she stood watching the door, hoping it would open again and he'd come back, think better of his harsh words and apologize. Wrap her in his arms.

Her breath hitched in her chest and her throat ached with unshed tears. Her eyes blinked and burned. Stiff legs dragged her to the window, and she watched Frank stride to the corner of the building, heading back toward the stable.

She could catch him there. She could be there before he saddled his gelding and rode off, but she pressed her forehead against the cool pane and tried to grow tranquil, still her pounding pulse. If she stayed there long enough, she'd become part of the landscape. She'd become invisible, and no one would see her or talk to her, demand she be someone she wasn't, someone she didn't even know how to be or who it was.

Cold from the window pane seeped into her forehead, soothing the hot ache behind her eyes. She closed them, and when she opened them he was gone. How many times would she fear he'd left forever? She sniffed, blinked, and banged her head against the pane several times, rattling it in the frame.

She pushed her hands against it and spun around, tilted her chin up and walked into the bar. Next to her father's glass of whiskey was a smaller one filled with clear, amber sherry. When she climbed on the stool next to him, he shoved it toward her.

"Drink up, lass," he said, and turned away to finish a conversation with Bear and Shorty, one she was certain hadn't ever been started.

She was grateful for the time to herself and watched them chatting as she sipped at her drink. When her father turned back to her, she was as composed as she was going to be.

"Good trip to Nirvana?" he asked.

"Yes. It truly was. Benjamin loved it, as I thought he might, even the dead old town. Ghosts and all. In fact..."

And she told them about their idea, looking at her father for approval in his twinkling Irish eyes. It was there, and she drowned herself in it.

Chapter Twenty-seven

"We're gonna have the right to vote," she told Strange Al, "and I'm gonna be the first in line."

Al sawed at the bacon slab. She didn't look up or respond, just kept on making thick slices of the fat, smoky meat and throwing them into the pan.

"Don't you care, Al?" Abby asked. "It's good for the entire country to have women's input. We have a unique way of looking at things, different from men's, but just as good."

"Pa wouldn't like it," Al said.

Abby's head spun around, and she stared at the young woman. She was stunned. Every morning since Al had been working at the hotel, Abby talked to her while they prepared breakfast, and she had come to expect dead silence in return. What had prompted a response from Strange Al to this particular question?

"Why wouldn't he?" she asked.

"Just wouldn't."

"He doesn't own you, Al. It's important to honor your father, but you have some rights." She turned, looking for a reaction from the girl. "Well, don't you?"

You're being a witch, Abby. Stop it.

Al wrapped up the slab she'd been cutting and walked out of the room. It was several minutes before she came back, and Abby got the point.

"I'm sorry, Al. Please forgive me. It's none of my business. I'll be back in a minute."

Abby ran upstairs to her room and threw herself on the empty bed. It had been that way for two weeks – since her trip to Nirvana with Benjamin. She pounded her fist on the mattress, growled an unintelligible noise, sat up, and laughed at herself.

"I sound like a wild animal," she said.

Cleo opened her eyes and moved to settle on her lap. Phantom rubbed his head against her shoulder, purring.

"Well, you guys like my bed all neat and pretty, don't you?"

Mrow.

"And you like sleeping with me."

Mrow.

"Got any other words?"

Wah-wah.

"Knew you could do it."

She snuggled with her cats and mulled over her words to Al. She was ashamed of herself for butting into Al's life. She'd gotten miffed that the girl wouldn't stand up for herself, wouldn't do something that was her right to do – even if it went against her father. Or her brothers, or who knew whatever other family member had a hold on her.

She stroked Cleo's sleek, black coat and felt herself relax. It always worked. Caressing her cats was therapeutic, a healing salve for the wounded soul, and the gentle rumble of Cleo's purr was a lullaby.

"Thanks, my friends. Why is it so easy to see what someone else should do? I have to go back to work and try to mind my own business."

She splashed water into the bowl and rinsed her face, took a last look at the neatly made bed, and ran out the door and into Betty coming to get her.

"I was looking for you. Al's putting the food out, so you want to start up here now?"

"Guess so. We're full. Folks are thinking about Christmas already. You sure she doesn't need me?"

"Your pa is in the kitchen with her, so no."

They made the bed, dusted the dresser, and swept the floor. Betty looked especially pretty in the morning's sunshine, and her big brown eyes held a fire Abby didn't always see there. Her skin was clear and glowing like burnished bronze, and rosy as if she'd just come in from frolicking in the snow. Abby took note of her friend while she ran the dust mop under the bed, ready for Phantom to be riding it when she brought it out.

Betty glanced Abby's way, aware she was being observed.

"What?" she said.

"What, what?"

"You know," Betty said.

"No. Guess I don't."

"You ready to go on to the next one?"

"Sure."

They were half-way through making the bed when Betty tugged at the quilt and said, "So, is he gonna move there?"

"Who is he and where is there?" Abby said, a glint in her eye that said she already knew.

"You know. Benjamin," Betty said, the rose on her cheeks growing deeper.

Abby tilted her head up to look at her.

"You got a soft spot for that man, Betty Gerard?"

She let out a puff of air like Abby had said something ridiculous.

"Course not. He's old. He just plays pretty music, and I know you'd miss that. Just thinking of you, boss."

"I see." She grinned like she saw it all and didn't believe Betty for an instant. "Yes. I think he's going to do just that. His parents are coming in this week, and he's going to get their approval – not that he needs it. He's a grown man, an ex-soldier, and he can do what he wants. But he respects his ma and da."

They worked in silence through the rest of that room, and in the middle of the next bed-making, Betty blurted out the thing that was bugging her.

"Is it true Frank left you because of Benjamin?"

Abby tugged on the auburn braid hanging down her back.

"Where'd you hear that?"

"Everywhere. That's what people are saying."

"Well, they don't know anything. Frank and I had a disagreement, but it had nothing to do with Benjamin. It was a misunderstanding. He'll think it over and come back."

"You sure?"

"About which?"

"About Benjamin."

"Betty," Abby said, intent on making the girl believe her. "I should say it's none of your business because – well, it isn't, but I certainly get into yours sometimes – so I'll tell you. Frank is angry because Benjamin and I went to Nirvana together, but he shouldn't be. There was nothing wrong with what we did. Frank was invited to go, too."

"It's Benjamin who should be upset," Betty said.

Abby grabbed the broom and stood with her hand on the top of it and her chin on her hand, trying to figure out what Betty might mean. She couldn't.

"I don't understand. Why should Benjamin be mad?"

"Seriously? You don't know?"

Abby slowly shook her head back and forth.

"I like you, boss, but you come from another planet or under a cabbage leaf, or you been living under a bed with the dust bunnies all your life. Ben is a colored man. You're white. You put him in a dangerous place being with a white woman, off in no-man's-land by yourself for half the day. That's why he should be upset. Get it? People will make him out to be a bad Negro just like they do all over the country, and he isn't."

"I know he isn't, but he didn't have to go with me. He wanted to. He asked me take him, and he knew I was white then, too."

Betty shook her head and looked at Abby like she was a stupid two-year-old. She paced to the window and back and tried to shake out the bit of frustration that was creeping over her.

"Boss. I know you're trying to make a little joke, but people are saying things, white people, and that's dangerous for Benjamin."

"God . . ." Abby kicked at the broom and watched as it clattered across the floor. "What can I do about it? Seriously. Help me."

"You can't change the world, Abby. It's the way it is. I'm just warning you."

"I don't agree. People can change it. That's the only way it'll get changed. And as long as we're talking about that, you can help do it by bringing charges against the men who attacked you. I'll be with you every step of the way."

"We're going there again, huh?"

"Yes, and this isn't subterfuge to get the talk off me. I'll keep bringing it up until you agree to do it."

"How is that going to help change the world? They're just gonna say I'm a whore and asked for it. You know it, Abby. That's what happens to raped girls . . . specially colored ones. It's gonna be all over town, and what man will want me then? I'm soiled. Dirty. And a whore. You're asking me to put that out there for everyone to see."

Abby expected to see tears gathering in her friend's eyes, but when she looked up, Betty's eyes were hammered steel, and Abby couldn't fathom how she managed it. How was she able to gather the strength around her, stand up straight under the onslaught of bias and injustice?

She smiled at Betty and flung an arm around her shoulders.

"You're gonna say yes one day, my friend, and you're gonna be happy when you do."

"Maybe I will. Maybe someday I'll put those men in jail. But not likely and not now."

Abby, her arm still around Betty, opened the door to find Al standing there. The three women stepped back in surprise, and Betty jerked from Abby's arm and went back into the room for their supplies.

"What did you need, Al?"

"You said you'd be back, but I'm going home."

"I'm sorry. I meant to, but then Da was there, and Betty and I got busy and . . . I'll see you tomorrow."

Al's eyes went beyond Abby to where Betty was gathering supplies. Her expression was blank as she stared, and Abby couldn't help but wonder what was inside the girl's head, if much of anything. She'd like to keep her at the hotel and give her a home, refuse to let her be abused by the father and brothers who used her as a slave, cook and laundress, housekeeper and doormat. Abby hoped that was all, but she feared for her.

"Is there anything else, Al?"

She shook her head and left, her shoes a whisper on the bare steps. How long had Strange Al been standing there, and how much she'd heard? For Betty's sake, she hoped it hadn't been long. Al was . . . well, strange.

When the rooms were finished, Betty said goodbye and headed for the shortcut through the woods to her house.

In the darkest thicket, she felt an arm go around her neck and squeeze. She couldn't scream or even suck in a breath. She clawed at the arm, and it tightened more. She was afraid her neck would snap and she would die.

She grabbed for the man's head, but he was tall, and she felt her nails dig into his cheek. It infuriated him, and he pitched her around like a rag. Her neck stretched and twisted, and her body hit the ground. His hand squeezed her throat as he bent over her.

"You!" she choked out, spitting enough venom to kill him once and for all.

"Stop fighting me or you're gonna die," he said.

But she couldn't stop because she thought she was going to die anyway. She kicked at his shins, and he cursed her. She kicked again, and he put a boot on her chest up next to her throat and removed his hand.

Another man ambled out of the bushes and put his boot on her face. She turned her head so he wouldn't smash her nose, and he pushed harder. She could feel her head sinking into the marshy dirt of the forest ground. If he pushed too hard, she'd get a lungful of muck instead of air. She quit fighting.

"What do you want?" she said, her voice like the dead leaves around her.

"You know what we want. Pull up your skirt."

"I'm not your whore."

The boot lifted from her face and kicked her side. Ribs cracked.

"That's not what I hear. I heard even *you* said you are."

"Liar."

"That's the story at the hotel."

Bells went off in Betty's brain, and she saw red, blazing, agonizing fury. Al.

"Let this be a lesson. You don't want to talk about us to Abigail. Not to anyone. Ever. Think you'd know that by now."

He bent down and ripped her blouse open while the other one readied himself. She dragged her nails across his face and tried to kick him between the legs. His flesh and blood stained the tips of her fingers, and the need to look at them, to see his gore, was strong. She needed to know she'd wounded him.

He punched her jaw, and she blacked out, but not for long enough. She prayed to be unconscious, to sleep through it and wake when it was over – or not wake at all. She prayed hard for it.

God isn't listening. He never listens.

Abby walked in the crisp December air with no particular place to go, no place to be for an hour or so. Jackson was taking care of the bar, and Patrick had supper well under way.

Cleo and Phantom followed, making her feel like Cassandra, pied piper of the cat world, and it occurred to her others saw her that way. Crazy white woman and her baby clowder, baby by Cassandra's standards.

She giggled. She should get a few more cats, prove them right. Go into competition with the *witch woman*. If Frank was going to stay away, maybe she would. Fill the bed with cats so she wouldn't be cold or lonely.

As she was about to pass the lane to Cassandra's house, she paused and sensed the woman's special tea on the taste buds of her mind. The idea of her pleasant home and miracle brew teased her, and, before she had time to think about it, her feet were walking down the lane, cats following.

Even the woody path to Cassandra's place was peaceful. While the deciduous trees were mere angular sticks with tufts of brown leaves stuck on like a bald man's head, the firs and pines gave life with their greenery. Every now and then, bursts of red showed up as determined sumac shrubs reared their fiery heads, and holly bushes battled the critters to save a few red berries for the holidays.

Abby smiled at her Irish faerie imaginings and hummed a made-up tune to go along with them. She looked forward to seeing her friend, to enjoying the peace that came with Cassandra and her home. As she neared the door, it opened, and the woman drew a shawl over her head and beckoned Abby to follow.

"Where are we going, Cassandra?" Abby called, trying to keep up with the older woman's amazing speed as she darted into the woods.

"Come. I've waited for you."

It wasn't long before Abby heard the whimpering. She raced toward the sound and knelt at Betty's side. She lay in a fetal position, her eyes closed, arms wrapped around her stomach.

Abby pulled the skirt down over her naked limbs and draped her own shawl over her bruised torso.

"Betty," she said. "Betty, it's me. Abby. Look at me, please."

There was no response, no movement, no change in the consistent low sobs coming from her throat. The side of her face was bloodied, swollen and filthy. Her hair was tangled and matted with mud and blood. Angry tears fell from Abby's eyes and burned the back of her throat. Her chest ached with her friend's pain.

"Betty. Listen to me. We're going to carry you to Cassandra's house. It's right near here. We'll take care of you there."

Between the two of them, they half dragged-half carried Betty to the cottage and lay her on a blue satin fainting couch in Cassandra's living space. It sat in front of two floor-to-ceiling windows that looked out on several bird feeders. Cassandra handed Abby a thin quilt and said, "Undress her."

Betty didn't put up a fight when Abby removed her tattered shirt and skirt. She lay unmoving, eyes unseeing, unresponsive. Cassandra came back with a basin of fragrant water and several clean towels that Abby used to bathe her face, arms, hands and legs.

She rinsed the cloth, turned her to the side and removed the forest mud from her backside. Her poor body was already purpling with bruises, and Abby growled with the need to kill whoever had done this.

She covered her with the quilt and talked to her, smoothing the hair back from her face, cooling her bruised skin with the aromatic water.

"Tea, Devil's Claw and Birch leaf. A little Kava kava. Make her drink."

Cassandra handed Abby the steaming cup and moved behind the couch. She held her shoulders up and let her head drop back. Abby spooned as much as she could between the swollen lips.

Within minutes, tears leaked from the corners of Betty's squeezed eyes. In a few more, she opened them, and Abby's own pain intensified when she looked into the deep, despairing hollows.

She knelt by the couch and held Betty's hand. She didn't talk. There was nothing to say to make it better, nothing to do but this – hold her hand and let her know how much she cared.

Together, they dressed her in one of Cassandra's lavender nightgowns, and she rested silently again.

"I need to get the sheriff, Betty. You know that, don't you?"

Betty reared up from the couch, ready to charge from the room. Cassandra pushed her back down, her head shaking from side to side.

"This must be reported," Abby said in a harsh whisper.

"He'll not find me if you do," Betty said turning her face away from Abby.

"Okay, Betty. I won't. I promise. Just rest. Please? But we have to let your parents know where you are."

"I'll go," Cassandra said.

"Don't tell Pa . . . anything," Betty said. "Just say . . . something."

"I'll tell them I need you for a few days, Betty." She turned to Abby and stared hard. "Stay quietly until I get back."

"She's my friend, Cassandra."

"I know."

When Cassandra left, the house drew in around her, close. Abby twisted around to see if the walls had moved and rolled her eyes at her foolishness. She checked to see if Betty was stressed by it, but she seemed content, oddly so. Her body was relaxed and her features soft, eyes were closed and still, without tears seeping out as before. Maybe she could ask Cassandra for a cup of that special tea. She could use it about now.

She wanted to talk to Betty, to ask who had done this to her, to beg her to see the sheriff, but she didn't want to upset her again. She had promised Cassandra.

"Tomorrow," she said. "We'll talk tomorrow."

Betty gave a small nod to indicate she had heard and squeezed Abby's fingers.

Abby took the long way home and avoided the woods, just in case. She was convinced her friend would recover from her wounds – physically – but was concerned she would never be the same inside where it mattered. How could she? How could anyone?

Betty had been beaten but more. She'd been defiled. She'd been violated and robbed of something so personally possessed, so privately owned that no one had the right to claim it belonged to them to do with as they chose. Taking her – because they could and wanted to – was an act against nature, against God.

It was the highest form of crime, and Abby's mind screamed the words.

Her fury walked with her, and she tried to dwell on something else. A sob tore at her chest as she thought about her relationship with Betty. She loved her, but couldn't know her. And Betty thought she was a stupid white girl. She snorted.

When it all boiled down to burnt gravy, maybe friendship couldn't hold up to color. Damn.

She sniffed and felt like a spoiled brat.

Tears tried to collect, but Abby widened her eyes and took a firmer step, lifted her knees higher, and shoved her shoulders back. Heaven help an attacker who thought she was fair game. She wished one would come.

Try! She'd like a chance to ram a fist in his face – like her father told her – thumb outside the mole tunnel, flat fist in the face first, then the knee.

The bar was full when Abby got back. She donned her apron, and Jackson gave her a 'glad you're here' smile as he went out among the customers. She tossed her braid over a shoulder and went to work. Patrick was running bowls of cabbage soup to hungry folks, and the cousins were regaling Bear and Shorty with stories they probably shouldn't be telling in public.

Abby heard Bear's hearty laugh and Sally's girlish giggle and it slid over her like a cool mist on a hot day. It was good to be back. She loved these people, dark or light, hooker or lumberjack. She loved them and needed them surrounding her, especially today.

She looked up when the door opened, and her stomach landed by her knees. Just when she was affirming love for them all, in sauntered Samuel Moore to make her rethink her silent declaration.

"Mr. Moore," she said with a cautious smile as he walked directly toward her, exuding too much coiled energy to be packed into his slender body. His self-confidence bordered on arrogance and seeped from every pore of his body. Appearing unaware of himself was a useful commodity and one of the things that made people shy away from him. Abby included.

Except for a narrow mustache, he was clean shaven, and his black curly hair was trimmed close to his head. She couldn't help but admire his lean good looks even if his attitude grated on her nerves.

"Ale, please, Abigail," he said with a weak answering smile.

She brought his drink and set it down in front of him.

"Supper is cabbage soup with Father's famous soda bread," she said.

"Not tonight. I didn't come to eat."

He drew his immaculate suit jacket open and pulled several five by five inch pieces of paper from the inside pocket. He flipped through them one by one and looked up at Abby.

"I came to give these to the resort patrol." He nodded toward Bear and Shorty. "I hear they've been collecting them and looking for the artists."

He put the small stack on the bar and patted it as if the contents were precious and might fly away or be stolen.

"And what are . . . oh! More pictures? Where did you find them?"

"I didn't find them."

He sipped his ale and glanced around the room, appearing bored, one hand still protecting the pile of paper.

"Someone gave them to you?"

He shook his head.

Jackson came with a drink order, and she moved away from Samuel, fixed the drinks, and went back.

"Then, where did you get them? I don't understand."

A large gold ring on his right hand clunked as he thumped it on the edge of the bar, an extraneous movement he would deny making if it was pointed out to him. His mind traveled somewhere else, and Abby watched, waiting.

"Did you know I wanted to be an artist? Live in a garret or loft, whatever they call it, someone's dusty old attic, and draw by the light streaming in through a single, grimy, cobwebbed window. Even starve because to be a true artist, one must be hungry and poor. Scorn the majority of the populace because they don't understand art or starving."

"You got the scorn part down."

He laughed, and Abby was startled to think it might be possible to tolerate this Samuel Moore someday, maybe even like him.

"Quick, aren't you."

"Not usually. Are you telling me you drew these pictures, Mr. Moore?"

"Samuel, Abigail. I'm not your father."

"Well?"

"Yes. I am the artist."

"Why?"

"I was tired of the one-sided conversation."

"I understand. Gets tiresome, doesn't it?" Abby stopped moving away from him and swiveled back. "No. I don't understand. What conversation?"

"The one some undoubtedly white, horribly bad artist was having with the colored folks in Idlewild."

She nodded, a glimmer of truth dawning in her eyes.

"So, you drew back at them. You sassed."

He smiled, for the second time.

"Yes. You could say I drew back."

Samuel picked up his glass and peered into the yellow liquid. He sipped twice before setting it back down. At the piano, Benjamin's sweet notes filtered through the still, warm air and Abby glanced his way. Samuel's eyes followed and came back to hers. She tugged at her bottom lip with her teeth.

"What's the white equivalent of Uncle Tom?" he said.

She gasped and choked on the water she'd sipped. Jackson called to her, and she filled his order, coughing all the while as she tried to get air into her lungs, and went back to stand in front of Samuel, feet spread, hands on hips, chin in the air.

"What are you implying?"

"It was a simple question. Remember when I told you there was no Uncle Tom in me? It was at the Gerard's home. They were holding services that day."

"How could I possibly forget. You were quite rude."

"It's not rude to speak the truth."

"You're wrong. Sometimes it is, and courtesy deems some words better left unsaid."

He nodded his head, acknowledging the accuracy of her statement. And she was thinking, *deems?* Since when do I say *deems?* She made herself move away from him and silently tried to prepare a final comment. She'd join Bear and Shorty after her concluding word. Just be herself. No more *deeming.*

When she returned to Samuel, she said, "I'm sad there is no Uncle Tom in you because he was a hero. He defended his people, worked for them while endangering himself, and stayed true to what he believed in. He's a role model you might hold to the light and strive to become."

Samuel's laugh startled her. He opened his mouth wide, and the sound rumbled from his chest, rousing others from their quiet pondering and light conversations, whatever they were doing. She stared at him, his narrow face, his white teeth, his erect posture, and wondered why she hadn't noticed it before. He was beautiful.

"You're funny, Abigail. Would you mind asking Bear or Shorty to abandon the Misses Sally and Sue and join me for a moment?"

Chapter Twenty-eight

Abby went downstairs, put the coffee on to perk and breakfast meat in the iron skillets. When Al got there, she grabbed the thick hank of hair hanging down her back and tied it with the dingy pink ribbon. She eyed the sizzling bacon and sausage, thinking she must be late.

"I'm early," Abby said, reading Al's eyes. "I couldn't sleep."

"Potatoes?" Al asked.

Abby nodded, poured them both a cup of coffee, and set one near the girl. Abby was having trouble concentrating on what needed to be done and thought more caffeine might help. She poured in a hefty dollop of cream and swirled it around, the spoon making rhythmic tics against the side of the cup long after cream had turned the coffee solid beige.

Al looked sideways at Abby and continued to peel long lines of skin from the potato in her hand, her face void of expression as always.

"I need help upstairs today, Al," Abby said. "After we have the buffet set up, I'd like you to fill in there for Betty. Pa will have to make do without you."

Al nodded, and Abby noted she didn't ask where Betty was or if anything was wrong. Maybe that was normal for her and suspected that could be the case. She was always oddly silent, but it occurred to Abby that Al could know something about what happened to Betty.

"It was a beautiful day yesterday, wasn't it, Al?"

"Uh, huh."

"Did you find a way to be out enjoying it?"

"No."

"You sure do work hard. Sometime you should take a break. Get those brothers of yours to make supper for themselves and make their own beds. They're big boys."

Abby didn't expect a response and didn't get one. She kept prattling on, hoping to spark something. She didn't know what – a reaction, a word, a bolt of lightning from the cloud of knowledge.

"Were they working at home?" she asked.

"Sure."

"All of them?"

"Why?"

"I just wondered. We don't talk much. I'm curious, and I'd like to know you better."

Al continued to peel.

"How many brothers do you have, Al?"

Al's face went deeper into her work, her shoulders moved forward.

"I don't want to talk about them."

"Why not? It must be great to have brothers. Wish I did. It would be fun. They'd protect me from the world of evil monsters."

She laughed as she tried to paint a picture she didn't believe was true for Al.

"Is it like that for you? Having brothers, I mean?" Abby asked, probing, pushing.

Al ignored her questions and wouldn't look at her. She sliced the peeled potatoes and threw them in a skillet with some of the bacon grease.

Abby moved next to her, turned the bacon and flipped the sausage patties to the other side. She huffed, frustrated.

"I need to know something, Al. When you came upstairs yesterday, did you overhear any conversation between Betty and me?"

No response. Abby made her voice soothing, like warm milk just before bedtime.

"I just wondered."

"I don't eavesdrop."

"Of course, you don't. I didn't mean to imply you did. Maybe just by accident you heard some of our conversation?"

"No."

Abby gave up. She didn't know why she thought Al might be involved in the attack on Betty, or what Al could tell her that would help her friend. It was a gut feeling, intuition and pieces of circumstance.

They finished cooking breakfast, filled the buffet platters, and took them out to the bar. People were already leaving their bedrooms and filing downstairs, drawn by the unique scent breakfast food sifts into the air through walls and doors and into the unconscious mind.

She greeted the guests by name and received hugs from several. It was good to be hugged, especially this day.

Patrick took over with a frown when she said she was stealing Al for a while. She could have cleaned the rooms alone, but she wanted – no, she needed to get done early so she could go to Cassandra's to visit Betty.

"I'm really sorry, Papa. I need her today," she said.

"I'm pulling your wee leg, Abby girl. Go on. I'm here and ready to cook a storm."

"You have recipes for a storm?"

"What?"

Her father shook his head. It was too early for him to be witty.

Upstairs, shaking out sheets and sweeping floors, she kept up a constant barrage of instructions to Al, realizing how nice it was to work with Betty who knew exactly what to do without being told, had since her first day on the job They were like Siamese twins connected at the sheet ar broom. They didn't need words, but she couldn't blame She'd not done it before.

In the third room, Abby confronted her.

"Do your brothers protect you, like you protect t'

Al's head jerked up, and her eyes went wide in '

She didn't answer, and Abby grew frustrat planted her feet wide and threw back her shoulde it brought courage into her heart as well as appe and determined.

"Al, I think you overheard the conversatic were having yesterday and told your brot' Didn't you?"

Al's eyes were planted on Abby's, her hands a twisted knot in front of her chest, her head moving vigorously from side to side. The pink ribbon came loose and fell to the floor. They both watched it drift and curl like a dusty, flat snake skin, discarded once the new one was grown. Abby shivered as the image crossed her mind and called herself a fool.

"Never mind. It doesn't matter. I don't know why you would tell them what you heard, but I'm sure there's a reason. I can't make Betty press charges, and I can't make you tell what you know. Maybe you all have the right idea, and I'm just butting in and living in a fantasy world where right and wrong are things people fight for."

Abby's dead voice sounded strange even to her own ears. She had failed. She thought of Nirvana, and a sigh slipped from her lips.

"It's a fairy tale, Al, and all damsels in distress get rescued because all the men in the forest are knights, not brutal beasts."

She picked up the cleaning supplies and moved toward the next room, her feet dragging like she was slogging through mud. Her legs had no strength. Her spine was broken.

She heard a small voice behind her.

"Yes. Because I can't be there alone with him. Not without my brothers."

"What did you say?"

Al turned away, and Abby repeated the question.

"My brothers can't go to jail. Pa would kill me."

"Why on earth would your father hurt you?"

Abby had to lean close to hear Al's whispering voice.

"He beats me if they're not there. Because I'm not my ma."

"What? That's ridiculous."

Al glared at her, eyes piercing and disappointed. Just like always, she'd been prodded to speak, and now she was sorry she'd said anything. People didn't believe her. They didn't care. She'd learned that a long time ago. She should've known. Words were wasted.

Abby realized her error too late.

"My God, Al. Why do you stay? You could go somewhere . . . or report him."

Al's face had gone blank. The brief glimmer of light had fled her eyes, and once again they were cold gray stone. Like graveyard monuments.

"Are we done?"

"I'll finish up, Al. And . . . I'm sorry. I'm really sorry."

She reached out to touch the girl on the shoulder, to give some reassurance, but Al moved away, and the hand intended to give comfort waved uncertainly in the air, an unrecognized and unreturned flag of truce. It went to Abby's face where the fingers massaged her eyes and temples.

Al left the room, and Abby sat on the unfinished bed, stunned at what the girl had told her. Horrified that she thought her father would kill her. Even more horrified by her own tactless response.

Abby wondered about the truth of her words but knew Al believed it was a fact, and it gave sense to some of Al's questionable behavior. No wonder she was withdrawn and remote, inaccessible.

But she had answered. She had recognized right and wrong. She was glad for Al and grateful, even if there was nothing she could do with her information.

The first flakes came down as she was walking to Cassandra's. The sky played its snowy role well. It was gray-white from horizon to horizon. Cold looking, like ice frozen over abandoned fishing holes, all bumpy and crusted. She pulled her thick shawl tighter and blessed Bunny once again for her nimble fingers.

She startled a rabbit when she turned onto the pathway and watched it dart back and forth, get almost to the trees and out of Abby's line of sight and dart back again, confused. Her presence made it nervous and unable to make a concrete decision about the best direction to flee.

"I appreciate your dilemma, but make a choice, cottontail," she said.

"You're so good at it?" the rabbit replied, darted her pink eyes to the woods and scampered off.

"You don't have to be snide," she said, moving on down the path. "For crying out loud, Abby. You're talking to a rabbit. And what's worse, you heard it respond!"

She hurried the rest of the way and met Cassandra standing outside her house.

"Don't worry. That one always talks," she said.

Abby laughed and caught herself. She'd thought Cassandra was teasing, but now she wasn't sure. Her face didn't show emotion; her eyes didn't change. She'd make a perfect gambler.

"How is Betty doing today? Better, I hope."

"She is resting."

"Before I go in, may I ask you something?"

She nodded and bent to caress the gray, purring mass weaving in and out between her ankles.

"Do you really believe Betty shouldn't talk with the sheriff? She should let whoever did this get away with it?"

"This isn't about my beliefs."

Abby kicked the dead grass at her feet and blew hot air from her nostrils.

The devil danced at the edge of Cassandra's lips.

"You make dragon noise. Want tea?"

"Yes, please, Cassandra. Can I go in to see her now? I know you were guarding the gate – just like another fairytale dragon."

They linked arms as they went, friends – just. Their attachment to each always spun in and out of reach because backgrounds, experience, whatever it was, stretched the boundaries of their communication.

Betty looked worse. Her face and lips were swollen and discolored. Cassandra must have put salve on her cracked lips because they glistened red and purple in a grotesque parody of lush beauty.

Abby tried not to gasp when Betty turned toward her.

"I know," she whispered. "I'm lovely."

Abby kneeled down and put her hand on Betty's.

"It's not so bad."

"Liar. She gave me a mirror."

"Oh." Abby's eyes went to the window, escaping Betty's perceptive stare and raised eyebrows. There was nothing else to say other than healing takes time but usually happens, all the platitudes that never help and frequently serve to irritate.

Cassandra brought tea for all of them and helped Betty sit up enough to take her cup.

"Are you okay?" Abby asked.

Betty snorted.

"I can't laugh, boss. It hurts and my lips bleed."

"Your beautiful lips . . . God."

"Stop."

In between silences and sips of tea, Abby decided to tell Betty what Al had said. Let her make of it what she will. She hoped it would push her to do something about the attack, but she wasn't going to badger her. She was done with that. Maybe she'd use a little gentle persuasion, but that's all.

"I talked to Al this morning."

"Bet she didn't talk back," Betty said, making Abby laugh and choke on the sip of tea she'd just taken.

"Funny. Glad to see you still have your sense of humor."

"And?"

"I'm just giving you information, not pushing you. So . . . well . . . she overheard the conversation we were having yesterday morning about pressing charges over the last attack, and . . . she told her brothers. I'm so sorry. This is my fault."

"I already knew . . . that she told her brothers, not that it's your fault."

"But how? Who told you?"

"Them." Betty spat the word like it had a vile taste. "They said something about the story at the hotel, and me admitting I'm a whore. They'd been told I said something like that."

Both Cassandra and Abby stared at her, the idea clutching at them with clawed fingers. While not absolute, in Abby's mind her words confirmed the identity of her attackers. At least one was a Tatum.

"Oh, my God, Betty. What can we do?"

"We can do nothing," Betty said, the harsh gravel of her voice punctuating each word, pounding at the meaning.

"But..."

"This," Betty waved her hand over her face and bruised body. "This was a warning. They made that clear."

"Al's afraid of her father. She told me."

"And I'm afraid of her brothers."

Now it was confirmed.

Samuel knew something had happened. The village bristled with anger, and shame lay in the set of shoulders and distrust in the quick glance of eyes. It was in the air, like a mist from nowhere. They didn't know what made it or what it was made of, but they knew it was there. They felt it. They smelled it.

He didn't think it was the pictures. They'd been around too long to create this much angst, but something recent had spiked tempers.

Church service that week was at the Gerard home, and Samuel decided to go. It was heavily attended and, except for Abby, all colored. His mustache twitched when he saw her, and he twisted his gold ring.

She had courage – or ignorance – and it crossed his mind that he should back her into a corner again and mention Uncle Tom just for the fun of it. The thought quirked his lips, but slightly. He was careful to maintain his artfully created reputation.

He moved to Abby's side and greeted her, looking away and around the room as he awaited a response. She was either ignoring him or was too captivated by his presence to speak. He didn't know which.

"Surprised to see me?" he asked.

"Um . . . I guess I am. I didn't think you attended regularly."

"Nor you, I guess."

She shook her head.

"True."

"Why today?" he asked.

"Just felt the need."

He perused the crowd and noted a pivotal missing piece. Betty.

"Where's your young Gerard."

"Isn't Betty here?" she asked, feigning ignorance.

"I don't see her. Was she at work this week?"

"Why do you ask?"

"Why do you answer my questions with questions?"

"Why do you ask questions? Feels like you're a lawyer."

He tilted his head toward her.

"I am."

"That's right. I forgot."

Abby felt like a fool. Samuel Moore had been disconcerting lately, actually always, and it made her stumble over her tongue and portions of her brain freeze.

He stuck his hand in a front pocket and removed a shiny pocket watch, flipped it open and closed.

"Odd she'd miss service in her own house," he said.

Abby ran her hands over her hips, straightening her skirt and her shoulders.

"You should ask the Gerards about it. I'm going to take a seat because it looks like the reverend is about to begin." She moved to a chair and was unsettled to see him right behind her. "Are you following me, Mr. Moore?"

"Samuel. And no. I'm sitting, just like you. Where do you think Betty might be?"

"I . . . I don't . . ."

"You can't lie in church, can you?"

She was glad the pastor picked up the hymnal and began the first song. Abby glanced sideways in surprise as Moore's big baritone filled her ears. He'd surprised her again.

At the last amen, Abby sprinted out of the house, eager to flee any more of Samuel's questions. He'd have to get his information from someone else. Anyone but her.

Mildred Gerard told him her daughter had been ill and was recuperating, but her eyes said something more. He was being lied to, and he knew it. He wasn't a lawyer for nothing. A question here and there led him to the knowledge that Abby had been spending time every day at Cassandra's house, and that led him to the woman's door.

When he knocked, several cats were hanging around, rubbing against his legs, and they followed him inside. Cassandra gave him tea in her small home and watched with humor as he tried to manage his cup amidst all the felines vying for his attention. One was on his lap. Another on his shoulder. A couple clawed at his leg looking for a friendly scratch behind the ear. He liked the cats, but so many was a . . . a lot.

"How do you do it?" he asked. "And why don't you teach them to take turns?"

"I don't teach. They do."

"You have a nice place. Pleasant and cozy."

"Thank you."

Samuel Moore was not used to stillness in people, other than himself, and Cassandra's motionless was total tranquility. She didn't fidget. Her hands lay in her lap unmoving. She was at peace in the absence of words as she watched Samuel and made no attempt at chatter to fill the empty space.

He found her enjoyable and interesting and looked around at his ease as he listened for the sound of another person in the house.

"Is Betty here?" he said, thinking with Cassandra a simple question might not get a simple answer, but it could be the best route to one.

She said, "Yes," and he raised an eyebrow.

"Might I talk with her?"

"I'll ask."

She left the room and didn't return. Instead, Betty walked in and sat at the table across from him. He saw bruises on her face beginning to yellow, and his stomach burned with acid. Someone had used Betty as a punching bag and perhaps more.

He clasped his hands together, knuckles whitening with the force, so he didn't pound the table. He waited for his heart to stop hammering before he spoke.

"Want to talk about this?"

She shook her head, but changed her mind.

"I walked into a tree?"

She put a hand over her mouth to stop a grin he could see beginning in her eyes and trying to spread to her broken lips.

"Does it hurt?"

"Only when I laugh. And I think that old oak broke a couple of ribs."

"They'll do that. Damned old oak trees."

They were silent for a minute, each assessing the other, looking for a crack in the other's armor where truth could seep through and hurt.

"Do you know what I do, Betty?"

She shook her head.

"I'm a lawyer. And I don't prosecute people, but I know the person who does. I can help give your assailants some jail time. I can at least help you decide what to do and how to do it."

"Did Abby send you?" she asked, her voice hard.

"No. She protected you. But you've been hiding, and she's been visiting here, and . . . I remember before."

She turned away from him, embarrassed and ashamed she couldn't stop it from happening, couldn't protect herself. She was a victim, and it infuriated her.

"I'm not saying they did, but if they violated you, you don't have to say so. You can press charges for the attack, for the beating. Get people to see these monsters for at least a little bit of what they are."

A fist came to her mouth and she pressed it gently against her lips to still the trembling.

"You didn't do anything, Betty. This isn't your fault."

"That isn't what people would say if they knew."

"They don't have to know everything. Just consider what I've said. I can help you."

"They'll get away with it. I know they will. How often do you see white boys go to jail for beating a Negro? When does that happen?"

Tears filled her eyes along with too much despair and knowledge for her years.

He couldn't lie and meet her haunted eyes. She spoke the truth, but he wanted so much for it to be different. They *needed* it to change. They *all* did. His voice was deep satin as he pleaded.

"It'll take strength and conviction to have the first feet on that path, Betty, to be the first to stand up and say, 'You can't do this to me!' But you can do it. I know you can. You have guts, and you have friends."

She fiddled with her teacup and looked to Cassandra for support, but she wasn't there. She lifted a black and white cat from the floor where he sat staring at her and folded it in her arms. His comforting purr rumbled through her chest.

"You know I'll get beaten up again. I'll have to look behind me every time I go home from work. Every time I leave the house."

"You do now, and they'll be in jail."

"And if they aren't? I'll get beaten. And if they are, others will find me. Don't you get it? Whatever happens – I get hurt. Or dead."

He wanted to wrap the girl in his arms, rock her troubles away, but that wouldn't be doing her any favors. If she was going to do anything about the assault, she needed strength, not coddling. And if she wasn't going to, she needed strength, not coddling. He thumped the table with his gold ring. She needed logic, not sympathy. She needed a different world.

"See a doctor, Betty, just in case."

He watched her argue with herself.

"Why did you agree to see me?" he asked.

"Cassandra didn't give me a choice. She said go talk with Mr. Moore, girl."

He smiled and patted her hand.

"She's a smart woman."

"She's nice to me."

"You're a lucky lady to have two such good friends."

"Abby?"

He nodded and said he'd be back the next day for her answer, called goodbye to Cassandra and left, surprised to see her waiting for him at the end of the path, a clowder spread out around her.

He stopped at the hotel before heading home and ordered his favorite ale. The room was full, and Jackson ran back and forth between customers, delivering orders to Abby, and racing to another table while he waited for her to pour. Abby's focus was on filling his orders and watching tables to make sure Jackson got to all of them.

Patrick brought food and cleared the empty bowls, letting his impish charm loose as he worked. It was a seamless waltz, and they stepped well together, outwardly unconscious of the friction simmering around them like hot water about to boil.

But Samuel knew – at least as far as Abby was concerned – she had more on her mind than pouring drinks. He watched, knowing it would be awhile before he'd get a chance to talk with her. Benjamin played a tune that sounded like a lullaby in its sweetness, and Samuel felt the stress of his meeting with Betty pull at his limbs. He was tired. His eyelids drooped and wanted to close.

Seeing women beaten – and worse – made him question if people would ever get along, ever learn acceptance. Hell, he'd settle for people just not beating on each other. They could hate all they wanted if they'd just keep their damned hands to themselves.

He waited for Benjamin to take a break and waved him over.

"Can I buy you a drink?"

He said sure and took the next stool.

"You settling in here for the winter?" Samuel said.

"Looks like I will."

They meandered around all the superficial talk Samuel could think of; he wasn't very good at it. Benjamin jumped in to help because he understood.

"What is it you want, Samuel?"

He explained, watching for signs of disagreement. There weren't any, and Benjamin said his friends would come whenever he asked, men who had served with him in France.

"I'll be in touch. Do nothing unless I give the nod."

"Understood."

"If the young woman agrees to charge, we'll let the law do its work."

"Again. Understood."

When Benjamin's fingers caressed the piano keys once again, Samuel moved down near Shorty and Bear. He touched his nearly full glass to theirs and raised his narrow black eyebrows in question.

"Before work?" he asked.

"Not really working Sunday nights," Bear said. "But we will. We'll take a couple of tours around."

"This your new haunt?" Shorty asked, a scowl wanting to form between his eyes. "Been here a bit lately."

He glanced Abby's direction, his meaning clear and intentionally intimidating.

"Don't mean any harm," Samuel said. "I'm just taking care of some business. That's why I'm sitting here with you two."

"And what business is that?"

Shorty's whisper, while unnerving to many, was just a voice to Samuel who traded on making others uncomfortable. He leaned in so he didn't have to ask Shorty to repeat himself.

"My business is taking care of business."

"That's hokum," Bear said, the tracks in his black beard growing pink. "Not looking for a twenty-dollar line of bullshit. What do you want?"

"Protection for your friend, Abby."

Both heads turned sideways and their chins protruded in deliberate defiance. Samuel would have found the picture funny if there had been any humor in this mess. As it was, he tried to squelch the threatening smile. They wouldn't have liked it.

"Why?" they asked together.

"Because she's walking alone, and she shouldn't . . . not right now."

"Can you be a bit more explicit," Shorty asked, running a hand over his shiny head.

Samuel tilted an ear toward the music, his sharply angular face at odds with his eyes as he listened to the peaceful melody coming from the soft touch of Benjamin's fingers. He'd like to do that, and he'd like to feel the kind of peace it took to make that music.

You don't have that in you, Samuel. You don't own that kind of harmony.

"Excuse me. Why?" Shorty said, nudging Samuel's arm.

"What?" Samuel said.

"Why shouldn't Abby walk alone?"

"All I can say, unless she confides in you, is that the woods are dark, and they're not lovely, just deep at this particular time. The grapevine is tingling, and she is stubborn."

Aggravated, Shorty rasped his fingers over his skull, hard, and Bear scratched at his beard.

"You talk in riddles. Why don't you just come out and say it?" Bear said.

"I hear rumbling among the colored folks, and I see angry eyes in white faces. Just take care of her. That's all."

He left without having a chance to speak with Abby but made sure he'd bump into her at Cassandra's the next day.

He was at the cloth covered table drinking tea from cups with handles so tiny only the tip of his finger went in. He squeezed his thumb and finger together to keep the cup from tilting down and spilling the hot, fragrant liquid in his lap.

Cassandra's lips quirked at the corners.

"Want a bigger cup?"

His eyebrows arched into vivid points at the centers.

"Is this a test?"

"Why do you ask?"

"I suspect you do lots of things with tea cups. Even test my manual dexterity."

"I think you mean tea *leaves*," she said, "and your information is based on inference and faulty interpretations of my love of tea."

Samuel gave up and wrapped his hand around the outside of the small cup, managing to maneuver it with just the long fingers of one hand.

"Better?" she grinned.

"Infinitely. Is your charge joining us?"

"If you wish."

Betty came to the table just as he spotted Shorty and Abby coming around the pathway's bend. He stepped outside, surprising her, and thanked Shorty, saying he'd escort her back.

"I don't need a chaperone, boys. I'm a big girl, and I can take a walk by myself."

"Same thing she told me when I asked to come with her," Shorty said.

"Now is not a good time for a stroll in the woods, Abby."

She kicked at the grass and growled disapproval.

"You're both irritating, and I thought better of you, Shorty."

"Implying not of me," Samuel said. "I'd offer you tea, Shorty, but it's not mine to give."

He waved them both away like they were inconsequential gnats.

"Get some rest, Shorty," Abby called after him and turned to Samuel. "How did you know where she was?"

"You. You're a creature of habit, and I followed you."

"You're a slug."

"Come on in. I'll bet Cassandra has more tea in toy cups."

"I love her tea," Abby said, raising her hand to knock on the door as it swung open.

"Did you think about what I said, Betty?" Samuel asked after they had tea and pleasantries out of the way.

Betty spoke to her hands, refusing to meet his eyes.

"I can't. I'm sorry. I just can't."

Abby covered her hands with her own.

"We'd be there for you. Every step of the way," she said. "You can't let them get away with this brutality, Betty. Don't let them."

"I'm sorry. I can't be the first feet."

"What? What are you talking about?"

"On the road . . . or path."

She searched Abby for a glimmer of understanding in her eyes and didn't find it.

"Mr. Moore said it. Ask him."

Betty rose from her chair and shoved it up to the table.

"I'll be going home now, and I'll be at work tomorrow, boss, if I still have a job. Please don't be mad at me."

Her brown eyes floated in unshed tears, and her thick, black eyelashes flapped up and down as she tried to rid them of the salty liquid.

"We're not mad, and, of course, you have your job. I've missed you more than you'll ever know. You're my Siamese twin."

Betty raised an eyebrow in confusion, and gave up with a shrug. "Mmmmhum. We're twins."

Abby waved her hand in dismissal. "Later. I'll explain later. Are you sure you're ready to come back to work? You can take more time, you know."

"I'm ready." She sniffed and thrust back her shoulders. "I'm not dead. Until then, I'm not beaten. Just beaten up. There's a difference, you know."

Her lips turned up at the last bit, like she was done with the conversation and wanted them to know and to end it on a light note.

"There's our Betty," Samuel said. "And if you're certain about leaving here, Abby and I will wait and walk with you."

"You don't have to do that."

"Yes, we do," Abby said. "I've been told I can't walk alone, too. Like I'm a two-year old, for crying out loud. Want to warm a bottle for me? Give me a rag doll?"

Samuel's chuckle sweetened the air, and Abby smiled.

"Go get your things, Betty," he said.

"What things? This wasn't a planned vacation."

"She's back. Betty's back," Abby said and put an arm through hers. "Let's go, guard dog. Thank you, Cassandra. For everything."

They discussed avoiding the shortcut where Betty had been assaulted, and she scoffed at them, sarcastically asking if they were afraid the boogiemen were still there, waiting for her to go home through the woods.

"Well, no," Abby said, giving her a roll of the eyes. "But it might bring some painful memories for you, so we could walk around it."

"Those memories are already in here," she said, pointing to her head and dropping her finger to her heart. "They're all mine, and they're not going anywhere. That's something nobody can take away from me."

Chapter Twenty-nine

Samuel made it sound like a racial issue, saying the ending to her story would be different if Betty had been white, but Abby wasn't convinced.

"Do you still insist this is about color?" she said after dropping Betty off at her home and continuing on to the hotel.

She held a hand out to catch a fat snowflake. It melted against her warm hand, and she did it again. They walked a wide foot-worn path through the woods back toward town, and snow began to whiten it and cling to the trees on either side. The trail squeezed them in green and white parallel arms.

"Of course, it is. Anything else is nonsense."

"She's also a woman. They attacked her because they could. They didn't choose to beat a man."

"True. But they also didn't choose to knock around a white girl."

Abby cocked her head and rolled her eyes up, stared at the sky. Snowflakes stuck to her lashes. Samuel's eyes were warm, liking that she thoughtfully measured his words.

"Whatever color," she said, "a molested woman is always beaten up twice, once during the attack and again in court. Somehow it becomes her fault, and, afterwards, she lives with the ruin of it for the rest of her life. So, I guess she's flogged many times, and that doesn't even count all the times she does it to herself."

Samuel stopped her with a hand on her shoulder and looked directly into her eyes.

"Not everyone shares those views. Some of us respect women." He tilted his head, waiting for Abby's reaction. "We even hold some of them in high regard."

She didn't know why, but having his respect warmed her. It was significant. She swallowed hard and walked taller because of it.

They came out of the woods near Foster's store. Abby blanched when she saw Joe standing in the open door, watching them move down the road. He shuffled outside and waited.

"Traipsing through the woods with white women now, Samuel? Not enough colored girls in town for you?"

"You're an obscene creature, Joe Foster. Slither back under your log," Samuel said as they drew closer. Joe backed through the door without responding.

Abby shivered at the iron in Samuel's voice and black steel in his eyes. Tiny hairs tickled the back of her neck. Samuel Moore frightened her every once in a while, as though he harbored fury, held it hidden and quiet like the calm before the tempest. The tempest was in him.

They moved down the road, and Abby felt her toes begin to stiffen in cold. Winter was here. Beautiful, but Michigan cold.

"So, what do we do now? If Betty refuses to charge her attackers?" she asked.

"She *has* refused. Didn't you hear her?"

"I did. I just keep believing she'll change her mind. She won't, will she?"

He shook his head and stared straight ahead. He didn't want to tell her there were other means to certain ends, had been other pathways to justice since the beginning of time. Punishment would be dealt and communications sent.

They should have sent one the first time, tacked a note on a door, whispered harshly in the night. But they had let it go – hoped for peace, and it had happened again.

At some point, this incident would have to be different because doing nothing was an invitation for more. It was approbation, acknowledgment *their* message had been received and accepted.

It was time they responded. Sent a declining RSVP.

Frank flung the door open as soon as Samuel's foot hit the first step to the porch. A pace behind him, Abby bumped into his back and yelped. She didn't see her husband, but she heard him and swallowed.

"Nice of you to come home," he said, his face expressionless other than for the two deep lines creasing his brow.

"Mr. Adams," Samuel said, reaching a hand out to Frank who pretended not to see it.

Samuel left his arm extended long enough to make a point before dropping it to his side.

"Hello, Sam. Where've you been, Abby?"

"Visiting Cassandra, Frank. I'm happy to see you. Let's go in. It's cold out here. My toes are about to snap off."

Samuel moved up the steps directly in line with Frank, making him move aside or be walked over. He'd be damned if the insufferable man would force him to walk around.

He moved.

"Why is *he* with you?" Frank asked.

"He was kind enough to escort me home. Shorty insisted," she said, trying to pour water on the flames of his ire. "Can we talk about this later, please?"

"Thank you, again, Samuel," she said as he opened the door to enter the hotel.

"You're welcome, Abigail," he said, nodding to her and purposely ignoring Frank. He knew an explanation would do no good.

"I don't like it when I come to see you and can't find you anywhere. It isn't right."

Abby's mouth flew open. She was staggered by his words. He spoke like she'd done something wrong.

"If I'd known you were coming, I would have been here, and I'm here now, but I have to get behind the bar."

She peered through the door and grimaced. She'd been gone longer than intended, and Jackson was swamped. She tucked her hand around his stiff arm and tried to lead him to the bar, but he dragged his feet.

"Please stay, Frank, and we'll talk later. Please?"

"Always something, Abby."

She was torn. Moisture clogged her throat. She didn't know what to say and couldn't say it anyway through threatening tears.

It annoyed her when she choked up, and she knew if she tried to speak, the flood gates would open. She also knew when she lay in bed tonight, not sleeping, all the things she should have said would come to her and slide off her tongue like butter on a flapjack.

She would be erudite and logical. Emotions wouldn't interfere with her ability to speak, and Frank would want to hear what she had to say. But that was later, tonight, when he was gone, when she really didn't have to open her mouth and speak. If she didn't care, if she didn't love him, she'd be able to swat him like a fly when he was being a thoughtless irritant . . . but she did, and she couldn't.

She let go of his arm, and a few words squeaked out, something like, "I'm sorry. I have to get to work."

He followed her in, drank the beer she poured for him and ate the plate of pot roast Patrick gave him. Samuel chose to sit at a table near Benjamin, who joined him during a break in his music. Abby watched them talk with their heads together. Their sudden friendship was interesting and, for Samuel, unusual.

She finished as early as possible, letting Jackson close up, and followed Frank upstairs, eager to try to make peace with her husband. She wanted to see him smile again. It had been a long time, and she missed it. Missed him.

But he was mad. He flopped into the overstuffed chair and swung a leg over one lace covered arm, propped his elbow on the other and his chin on a fist. His eyes squinted to half mast, and he looked ready to do battle. She wasn't. She never was. She wanted harmony.

"Why are you running around with that colored man, Abby? Why were you at Cassandra's with him? In the woods, no less. You know how that looks, what I think about it."

"I wasn't with him. It wasn't like that. And would it matter if I was at Cassandra's with Samuel? What would be wrong with that?"

Frank slapped his palm on the table next to him, making her and both cats jump. Cleo's black back bristled, and Phantom's blue eyes glared.

"What's wrong with you? You're not stupid, Abby, and I'm beginning to think you're doing this deliberately. You already said you were there together."

Frank unfolded himself from the chair and stood in front of her, making her look up at him from her seat on the edge of the bed. Making her feel small. Ineffectual.

"Are you lying to me now?"

She rubbed her neck where it kinked from tilting her head upward and ran her hands down Cleo and Phantom who'd come to sit on either side of her. She heard their warbling purr and took a small comfort in the sound.

"No, Frank. It's just . . . he was there when Shorty and I got there, and Samuel said he'd walk me home so Shorty could leave . . . and it took a while because we had to walk Betty home . . ."

"Betty! What in hell does she have to do with all this?"

"Please sit, Frank. Settle down. It's Betty I went there to see."

He flung an arm through the air in frustration.

"Damn. Everybody in town gets more of you than I do. You can't help it, can you?"

"She needed me, Frank."

"Yeah. And so does everyone in this town. Hell, even the Idlewild fancy ladies get more of you than I do. The whole damn village does. You know the word 'no?' This is how you spell it. N. O. No."

His words slapped her, and she flinched when he shouted the last one. Her eyes filled, but she widened them until they quit leaking, and it felt like she'd held them open for so long they were stuck that way. The tears had dried, and her eyes were packed with sand paper.

"I can't tell you about Betty, Frank, but she truly needed my help. I wouldn't lie to you about that. About anything, I mean. I wish you'd believe me, try to understand."

He tilted his head and stared at his wife. His breathing was ragged, like he'd run a mile, and his nostrils flared.

"You won't tell your husband about an employee that you spend time with, along with Samuel Moore, another man, and the witch woman. And you think that's okay?"

"Yes. I'm sorry. Betty was hurt and needed me. Somebody hurt her. I can tell you that much. I wish you would trust me . . . just a little." She shook her head and rubbed her arms like she was searching for warmth. "I can't . . . I can't say more."

A smile tilted the corners of his mouth, but it didn't reach his eyes. It wasn't real.

"So. You really can say no. To *me*. Hah! And I thought you couldn't do it. Congratulations, Abby."

He sat again, his arms crossed over his chest and looked at the space around him. Not much remained in the room that belonged to him. He'd removed most of it, little by little as need arose. Living this way wasn't what he wanted. And he knew it.

"Are you really as color blind as you act?" he asked.

"I'm not color blind. Why do you say that?"

"Because you act like there's no difference between a Negro and a white man. That's why."

"Well, there isn't . . . except for skin color," she said with a half-hearted laugh. "It isn't that I don't see it. It's that I don't care about it. Why do you?"

"Care?"

She nodded. Frank rubbed his forehead and left his head in his hand, looking down at the floor. He was quiet for several moments, and Abby watched, wishing she could be in his brain, see his thoughts, ease his pain.

"I care what folks think. You don't. And right now, I'm pretty sure they're thinking things I wouldn't like."

"And if they're thinking things that aren't true?"

He looked into her eyes with unwavering penetration.

"They're still thinking them."

He stood again, and Abby stood with him. The cats scrambled under the bed.

"Don't go, Frank. We can work this out."

"Gotta go, Abby."

"When will you be back?"

"Don't know."

She heard him take the stairs two at a time and, from the window, watched him walk away in the dark, his form a shadow with long legs loping around the corner to the barn to get his horse. He was going home.

His home. This had never been one for him, and she understood. The farm, with the brothers and parents and nephews, couldn't be hers. This was. She was selfish, and she knew it. A wife was supposed to go where her husband led.

Abby threw herself into work. Cooking and cleaning rooms were always waiting there to drive unwelcome thoughts from her mind. Work was a remedy for whatever ailed you. It didn't change from moment to moment or day to day. Fry potatoes and make pancakes. Let the bacon crisp and cook the sausage so it was no longer pink. Easy as pie.

Betty was back at the hotel the next morning, a dusting of corn starch on her face to disguise her multi-colored bruises. She collected her coffee with as much bravado as she could muster and even walked near Al to pour it.

Al's face never lifted from the skillet she was tending, and Abby chewed her lip and watched both women skirt each other like they were each avoiding a venomous snake. If they only knew the other's story, they could find common ground, might even come to a friendship based on inequities and injustices in common. But she couldn't make that happen, and she knew it.

It was wrong. Stupid. Senseless.

Betty swung into the job like she'd never left it, and Abby was happy to have her back. When the bruises faded and were no longer vicious reminders, they began to drift through the days as if the devil had never stepped his cloven hoof into paradise.

The grapevine still prickled every now and then, and pictures still floated around. Word of Betty's assault filtered into common suspicion and made folks look behind them when they were out and about.

Sue and Sally kept them informed of anything newsworthy throughout the winter months. They heard everything even remotely true or dramatically created from their bedmates who talked just to make themselves more interesting.

"They'll tell everything. Especially if their cheeks are nestled in these soft pillows," Sue said in a loud whisper, patting the generous cleavage spilling out of a purple silk dress.

"They don't need pillows to talk. I get as much information as you, Sue, and I don't even have fried eggs in that region."

"You could use a dozen. Put em in your bodice. Make you look more like a girl. I could help you."

Sally tapped her cousin on the back of the head.

"I like myself just fine, and so do my friends. Wiggle your legs so they don't fall asleep."

Frank worked through his anger, at least enough to come back and spend nights with her in their room at the hotel, but he no longer pretended to work there. Abby didn't know what occupied his time during the day and hoped it was doing something he enjoyed. He didn't talk about it. He didn't communicate, period. Abby tried to think back to a time when they did talk with each other, and couldn't remember one.

He refused to revisit the issues briefly discussed when he accused her of not being able to say no. He acted as if it hadn't happened, and she let him. It was easier than arguing about a matter both knew had no good resolution, even had opposing values. Their lives ran on railroad tracks, never meeting, but not colliding either. Like train Pullmans, they were only loosely connected.

He was at the end of the bar when the resort people came to see Abby. His eyes rolled when they called her name, and he sighed loud enough for her to hear. He gulped his beer and strolled out of the bar and up the steps without a word.

It was March, and Bill Sanders, Ratty Branch and brother Del came back to town set on hosting another Chautauqua. They were eager for spring and the influx of lot owners they knew would be sprinkling the area with new cabins and economic prosperity.

Property sales had been substantial over the winter months as real estate representatives worked Chicago, Cincinnati, Detroit and many other metropolitan areas, locating people with money in their pockets and desire for what Idlewild had to offer. A place to play with others who looked like them. A place they were welcomed.

Jesse Falmouth slapped the table and shoved out a chair for Abby.

"For just a minute," she said, looking around and taking a seat.

"These shindigs were your idea," he said. "So, what do you think? Mid-April? Can we get Du Bois again? Folks really liked him."

"It's kind of late, but we can try," Abby said.

"Pull up a chair, Samuel," Jesse said. "Join us."

Abby's head spun around. She hadn't heard him come in.

"Yeah. We could use some fresh ideas. We're pondering on Du Bois again. What do you think?" Sanders said, leaning back in the chair, his hands smoothing a crisp black vest, a watch chain glowing golden and swinging from its pocket to a buttonhole.

Bill Sanders competed with Samuel in snappy dress. Both could have stepped from the pages of Harper's Bazaar, and neither gave the impression it mattered. Their chic and sophistication were as natural as a sun rise.

"Du Bois, but he should recite selections from *The Souls of Black Folks*," Samuel said and watched for Abby's response. "I'd bet not many in this town have read it."

"I haven't," she said. "Should I?"

A smile lit his eyes, but didn't reach his lips.

"Only if you want to know your neighbors," he said.

"I do. Who's the author?"

"He is."

She hid behind her hands, hoping the dim lights might hide her growing blush.

"I'm so embarrassed. How could I not know that?"

Jesse came to her rescue, saying he hadn't read the work either, but it only helped a little.

"I've got to get back to work," she said, seeing Jackson whiz by and giving her an excuse to escape. "Just let me know what I can do to help. Whoever speaks at the Chautauqua can stay here. I'll save a room."

When Betty reached the porch, her face was red under deep russet, and she bent over with her hands on her knees, trying to catch her breath. She stood that way for several moments, sucking air in harsh gasps, before straightening and preparing to saunter to the hotel. It wouldn't do for Abby to see her like this, to know she'd been running from them.

They'd been following her for days. Sometimes in the morning and sometimes at night and not every day. She never knew when they'd be there or what they were planning. She still didn't, but she suspected, and she carried a long, heavy limb with her, using it like it was a walking stick so no one would question her woody companion.

It was them – the Tatums. Not all of them, maybe two or three at a time, or maybe even just one. It didn't matter. They were huge, and they were men, and she wasn't either of those things. But she'd use her stick, and they wouldn't get away without feeling the weight of it on their heads or wherever she could swing it and connect. This time, she would leave them with something more than scratches to remember her by.

The worst part was not knowing when they'd appear and not knowing when they'd do more than stalk her. Hatred swelled in her gut – right next to the fear and nausea, and it took all her strength to leave the house every day – and to keep it from her father. People talked about her and *it*, but not to him. Never to him, because they knew better.

Betty watched her mother's eyes flicker across the room to her husband and back to her daughter, a nervous foxtrot between the two of them. The plea was silent. She'd never tell Betty to keep it to herself, and she wrapped her arms around her daughter in comfort when she could, but they both recognized the awful price James Gerard would pay if his daughter ever told him the truth. So, she was silent.

Samuel walked by and saw her on the porch.

"You look winded, Betty."

"Yeah. I ran to work. It's good for me. Getting healthy."

"Especially if someone is chasing you. Is that the way of it?"

"Naw. That's not it, Mr. Moore."

He nodded and fingered his neat mustache while he watched the lie squirm across her face.

"It's just that. It surely is," she added, trying to convince him.

"You gonna run all your life, Betty?"

Moments passed while she considered his words and he considered her options. There weren't any good ones, and he knew that as well as she did. There damned well weren't any good ones, that's for sure. Just options. And this was one of them.

She turned to leave, and he told her to be safe and be smart.

"I'm smart, Mr. Moore," she whispered, "but I haven't been safe in years."

He'd kept an eye on the girl since her time at Cassandra's, and came to the conclusion other measures would have to be taken. She was being harassed. Even if they didn't strike this week – they would. Eventually. When the game they were playing got old and they wanted a little more excitement. That much he knew with certainty. In their minds, the girl belonged to them, to do with as they would. It was a matter of their pleasure, not of right or wrong. She was their toy.

Now, they would get to play with the boys.

Chapter Thirty

Within a week, five tall, broad shouldered men showed up in town. Clean shaven, brawny, and soft spoken, they sat at a corner table of the hotel bar. When Benjamin came in, they slapped his back with hearty goodwill. They were fellow soldiers, men he would trust with his life, had trusted with it. He would be living for eternity in French soil if not for them, and when he had contacted them, they had responded. Without question or comment.

They sipped at their drinks, watched the faces around them and learned . . . by the eyes, the movement of hands and the set of shoulders. Reconnaissance wasn't new to them. It had been a fact of life. When Samuel came in, he nodded in their direction and sat at the bar. Benjamin joined him when he took a break but left him at the bar to go sit with his soldier buddies.

The day came when the men who'd been following Betty sauntered in for drinks, and Samuel watched the soldiers from the corner of his eye. They paid no more notice to them than anyone else, possibly even less.

The soldiers ran into Betty several times when she and Abby cleaned their rooms, and Abby noted the esteem they gave her. She smiled, thinking they were flirting with a pretty girl.

"They might be sweet on you," she'd told her.

"What? All of them at once? That'd be a work of magic," Betty said with a giggle.

"We're going for a walk," Charles hollered, banging on doors to the two rooms that held his companions and calling them to breakfast early one morning. He was the oldest of the group of soldiers. When he said, "Let's go," they did.

Abby filled their cups with fresh coffee when they filed downstairs and waved at the empty buffet.

"It's not ready yet," she said, "and it's still chilly outside. You need warm food."

He smiled at her, thinking about lying on a French hillside in the cold rain. This was paradise.

"You all thinking about becoming lot owners?" she asked.

"Could be," Charles said.

Mick, the youngest, bubbled with enthusiasm when he nodded toward Abby.

"Yeah. We're gonna take a look around the woods for sure. We like hunting . . . and fishing," he added when a foot connected with his shin.

They did scout the woods and checked out the Tatum farm. They sat in the small grove of trees beside the house and watched the men come and go, noting their looks, remembering one from another.

One hitched a pair of oxen to a plow and snapped a black whip over their backs to get them moving. Another threw feed on the ground for a passel of chickens who scrambled and, in the confusion, pecked at his boot. He kicked at the bird, and it squawked and flew into to air and back to the ground.

"Ass," Mick grunted.

"Al shoulda done this," chicken man growled.

"In the dark?" a third man said. He had put a bowl of food on the step and was ruffling the ears of a mangy, old hound dog and talking to it.

They watched a fourth man dump a bucket of slop into the pigpen and laugh when the huge animals scrambled over the top of one another to get at it.

"How many Tatums are there?" Luke asked in a muted whisper.

"Four. Three bastards. One boy. With the dog," Charles said.

"How do you know?" Mick asked.

"He didn't kick it. He petted it. Pay attention."

They followed Betty as she went to work and returned home.

Her head jerked from side to side with each sound, each crack of a twig, each hoot of an owl. Her heart banged in her chest, and her wide brown eyes stared into the woods as she tried to see behind trees, under fallen brush.

"Why can't we tell her we're here?" Mick whispered. "She's terrified."

"Want to go to jail?" Charles asked.

He shook his head, knowing the answer before he'd asked the question. He grimaced, hating her fright. Despising the men who made her feel that way. Loathing the world that let it happen. His stomach clenched and he grew queasy watching her tense in dread at each sound.

"When?" Mick asked.

"Now," Charles said, leaping from his crouch to land on Skunk's back, his hand over his mouth to keep him silent. He waited to release the man until Betty was well away from them, and, when he did, Skunk spun around, ready to throw a punch.

His face fell and his Adam's apple bobbed when he saw the five tall black men scowling at him. He swallowed and sidled away, but Mick dragged him back.

Four of the soldiers stepped a few feet away, leaving Skunk and Charles facing each other. Charles took a swing, and his fist met Skunk's jaw, snapping his head back. Skunk retreated a step to keep his balance, but didn't fall.

"What the hell?" he said, pain making his words an angry whine.

"This is for Betty," Charles said, and swung again, this time with a left. The third landed in his stomach and hurled Skunk to the ground. Charles picked him up and punched again, hurling him to the ground once more. He grabbed the man's shirt and ripped it down the front, pulling it from his shoulders.

"Is this how you do it?" he asked, yanking Skunk's pants off and tossing them. Charles kicked him when he tried to get up.

"Stop! Dammit! What are you doing?"

"Just having the same kind of *fun* you have with Betty. Roll onto your stomach."

"Wait. I . . ."

Charles kicked him hard in the ribs. Skunk rolled over.

"Now, get on your hands and knees."

When he didn't move, another hard kick found its mark. Skunk pulled himself up, and panic started to creep into his mind, stalking the stray thought that he could escape and nothing worse would happen.

Charles looked over to Moses and said, "Get me that stick over there, the thick one."

Skunk watched the man walk in front of him and pick up a thick limb. Panic rose up and attacked.

"No! Don't! Please! I'm sorry, I'm sorry. Please! I'm . . ."

His pleas were suddenly cut short when a foot found its target between his legs.

Skunk curled into a fetal position, knees meeting his forehead, and lay frozen in pain and fear.

"I have friends in Idlewild," Charles said, "and I'll know if you hurt her again. If you harm *any* woman, I'll . . ." He swallowed his words in disgust. "I suggest you don't. I don't make idle threats."

He stood back, flexed his hands and leaned against the trunk of an old oak.

"Would have served him right if you had used that stick. Would have seemed fair," Mick said quietly.

Charles watched the whining man groan and try to uncurl.

"I know. I get it. But this is Du Bois' justice and common sense in action. I don't want to let it become revenge. It's a necessary lesson. That's all." His words were harsh, chopped short with bitterness and salted with sorrow.

Charles let his gaze roam the spring forest. What should have been a place of peace was tainted by the hate and ignorance controlling the man on the ground.

He thought he was hallucinating when a woman in a long purple gown appeared next to several cats. She stood motionless, watching, and he blinked, waiting to see if she would disappear as quickly as she came. They'd been seen.

She disappeared before he could catch her, but they stumbled onto Cassandra's pathway where she waited for them.

"Charles, Mick, Andrew, Moses, David," she said, nodding to each of the men in turn.

Charles scratched his neck, puzzled.

"And you are?" he said.

"Almost satisfied," she said. "Would you like tea?"

She led them to her house and fed them tea, along with freshly made biscuits and boysenberry jam. Like all big boys, they shoveled it into their mouths and tried to hold the tiny cups without dropping them onto the saucers or breaking off the handles.

"You still haven't told us who you are," Charles said.

"I am many people: Cassandra, prophet, clowder tender."

"What did you see in the woods today?" Andrew said.

"Enough."

"Enough for what?"

"To be partially satisfied."

"Will you tell?" Charles asked.

"Tell what?"

Charles nodded, satisfied they were safe.

"Well . . . that . . .you know," Mick said, flinging a loose hand in the air.

"Leave it alone, Mick," Charles said. "Our host is a wise woman."

"Yes. I left that one out." Her eyes dazzled them all.

"What?" Mick asked.

"A wise woman." She patted Mick's hand and turned to Charles. "You must finish what *they* began. One is not enough to learn what they must know."

He nodded. He didn't like beating people. He was good at it, but it was only a necessity, not a sport, and he already knew what she said was the truth.

Betty didn't know she had five escorts to work and home each day. She knew eyes were on her, and being watched prickled her skin. She felt them but heard nothing. They had learned how to move across the ground without making a sound.

On the third day, every head turned toward the sound of feet moving clumsily over the ground. Twigs snapped, a squirrel's angry chatter followed and a blue jay screeched annoyance. There was no attempt to be silent. They were arrogant in their supremacy, their fragile power. They invited interference.

Three men burst through the trees, Moose and Jonah Tatum, and a man they didn't know. The soldiers circled them from their outer positions and stood with their hands on their hips, watching.

"Got us outnumbered, boys. Too chicken to go one on one?" Moose asked, his lips a goading sneer. "Did you all gang up on Skunk? That how you beat him so bad?"

"Only took one of us," Charles said. "That's what we'll do today." He looked at Andrew, Moses, and David. "Take your pick, gentlemen."

They squared off, David with the unknown man. He noticed deep scratches on the man's face that were healing but not healed.

Might leave a scar, he thought.

"Got a name? I like to know who I'm beating."

"Name is George," the man said, his chin shoved forward, his arms hanging by his sides in insolence like he hadn't a care in the world. "George Adams, and you can kiss my ass goodbye on your way out of town."

"Go, George."

The soldiers, knowing their own abilities, waited for the others to throw the first punch, but after a few seconds, they were done waiting.

It didn't take long before George and the brothers were on the ground bruised and bloodied with broken ribs, their knuckles unmarked because they hadn't landed a single blow. They lay much like Skunk had, curled in fetal positions moaning and shaking their heads in pain and confusion, waiting for the stars to stop blinking on and off in front of their eyes.

"If you touch Betty again or ever harm another woman, we'll find you, and we will end you," Charles said, toeing Moose Tatum to make sure he heard and understood. He didn't get a response, so he poked a more energetic toe in brother Jonah's side.

"Nod, if you understand."

Jonah nodded between gulps of air.

"Be better for you if the sheriff didn't get involved. Better for all of you."

The visible wounds and bruises were intentional. They wanted everyone to see it, wanted the whole town to know what happened to Betty wasn't going to be tolerated ever again, not in Idlewild. It wouldn't be discussed out in the open, but the grapevine would know, and it would spread. The statement would be loud and clear.

This town was Betty's and Cassandra's and Sue's and Sally's and Samuel's and the Girard's and the Parker's and the Falmouth's and any other Negro looking for a peaceful retreat.

They share it as they choose with other good folks.

Cassandra tilted her head and stared at George lying on the ground with the other two. His brothers would not take this well. There would be repercussions somewhere, for someone. She nodded her head toward Charles, mimed drinking tea, and he nodded back.

They walked away from the battleground feeling, if not good about their work, at least confident it had been right and honest and necessary. Du Bois would uphold their intervention. There was no other way to accomplish what this did, and they knew it. It wasn't their first brush with hateful prejudice. They'd lived with it their entire lives – for decades and centuries and generations. Being targets of bias seeped from their pores and when they bled, you could smell it. It was in the salt of their tears.

It would not taint Idlewild.

They wiped their hands on their trousers and looked forward to tea with the delightful and uncommonly intimidating Cassandra and her clowder.

At dusk, near the Tatum house, Jonah and Moose held their ribs and limped around back, hoping their father would be passed out and they could avoid him. They waited outside the back door, listening for his ornery voice and, not hearing it, tried to get the attention of their little brother or Al so one of them could sneak out some food. They were tired, sore and starving, having left to trail Betty before breakfast.

They scratched at the back door like a dog, hoping she'd think to let the mutt in and find them. They ran when the door opened and they saw their father – with a belt in his hand.

"Get your sorry asses back here, or you'll be sorrier!" he bellowed and went after them, waving the long belt in the air around his head like a lasso.

They stopped running at the edge of the woods and turned back to stare at him. Rancid, fear-laced sweat dripped from their skin. They sucked air into their lungs in ragged spurts, and cries like tiny yips squeaked from their lips. They were three and four again.

"You lily livered punks! You let yourselves get beat up just like Skunk, just like weak little girls. I'll show you what beat up looks like!"

Spittle ran down his chin, and he staggered as he ran after them. He fell, got up and kept on coming. Moose and Jonah were frozen in place and watched with dread and loathing. He was drunk, but that didn't mean the belt would be lighter or would hurt less. The old man's rages intensified with each mouthful of liquor.

And if they ran, they might just as well keep on running because the madder they made him, the more days it would take them to heal, to recover from his blind rage.

They dropped their heads and moved toward him, their hands clasped together in front, their eyes lowered. Eye contact made him worse.

They walked to the shed in silence and hugged the center post, one on either side like they'd been doing since they were children, since their mother had died. They locked eyes, giving one another strength, and then slammed them shut and worked on blocking out the pain and the sounds of the belt buckle and leather slapping their backs.

Their old man took turns, first one back, then the other, making sure the buckle did its job. Neither would add to the noise with a scream or a moan. For years, they survived on their hatred of the man with the belt and the prideful fact that they took it in silence. In a small way, their stillness beat him.

The voice they heard before passing out was their pa's screaming invectives, shaming them for losing in a fight with colored men. That was unforgiveable, and Skunk had made the mistake of explaining.

George lay on his bed fully clothed, still wearing his boots, while his mother swabbed his face and chest with warm water. Tears ran down her leathery cheeks as she looked at her baby boy's bruised and bloody face. His eyes were swollen shut, his lips split, his cheeks and sides beginning to purple. He tried to shove her hand away, but she pushed his arm down and spoke sharply.

"You let your mother tend your wounds, Georgie. Who did this to you? You tell me, now."

When he tried to talk, the pain in his split lips drew his hand over them, and he pushed her away with a hard shove. She plopped on the floor and glared at him.

"I'm going for the sheriff," she said.

When she tried to rise from the floor, he grabbed her arm.

"Don't," he said with a grimace through unmoving lips.

Boots stomped at the kitchen door, and she heard Frank and Terry bickering about some stupid field and when it should be plowed. How could they care about that right now? It didn't matter. The farm didn't matter or the damn cows either. Somebody had hurt George!

"Get up here," she called.

"Where?"

"George's room."

Heavy boots thudded on the stairs, and the doorway filled with her other two sons.

"What the hell?" Terry shouted. "You run into a train?"

"Yeah," George mumbled. "G'out."

He turned his head to the wall and tried to ignore them, but they wouldn't go away. They talked about him as if he wasn't there, speculated, grew angry and suspicious.

"He needs a doctor," she said.

"Naw. He'll mend. Just a few cuts and bruises," Terry said.

"You a doc, now?" Frank asked with a grin, but he wasn't too concerned, either. Young men fought. They got themselves into scrapes and out.

"Same thing happened to Skunk a few days ago," Terry said. "Joe told me. You hear about that, George? Your Tatum friends tell you about their kin?" He nudged his brother's boot with his own.

Frank's ears perked.

This wasn't just a single friendly brawl?

"Yeah. Jonah and Moose look like me. Maybe worse."

Frank blew hot air through his nostrils, and his ears reddened.

Who in hell was going around beating men up?

"You want me to explain to Frank, George? Tell him why?" Terry said, prodding his little brother.

Emily Adams stuck her face in front of Terry's, two inches from his nose.

"You better tell me, now. What's going on here?"

When he didn't speak, she thumped a finger in his chest, making him take a step back. "I'm done fooling, boy. You tell me what's going on."

"Shut up, Terry," George said, anger and fear threatening his voice.

"If she gets the sheriff, you're in trouble. You know that?" Terry said. "Some folks might just care a little about what you did. In fact, seems to me somebody cares quite a bit by the looks of you."

Emily grabbed George's chin and made him look at her. "What'd you do, boy?"

"We were playing with one of the colored girls. Just having some fun. That's all."

"What kind of fun?" she asked, her voice a harsh, rasping whisper.

But she didn't need to be told. She visualized it, already knew it, and wished like hell she didn't. She wanted it hidden, as it should be. Buried in the garbage dump where all vile stuff should stay.

"The Tatums been having fun with her for years. Everybody knows that," Terry said.

"Everybody doesn't know it. I don't know it. Does she know it? This colored girl? Did you ask her if she was having fun?"

Emily was screeching, heart breaking in two. She looked at her three sons and didn't know them. They were strangers, one beaten and bloodied, and one swallowing hard, Adam's apple bobbing up and down. Another wore a smirk she didn't understand and didn't like.

She rubbed her hands together, the knuckles turning from red to tortured white, and spun around to leave.

"Somebody beat you. I'm getting the sheriff."

"Your son might end up in jail," Frank said, a quiet voice of reason following her down the hall.

She raced away from his words, and Frank found her sitting with her elbows on the kitchen table and her face in her hands. Her shoulders shook, but no sound came out. Frank poured brandy into a glass and set it on the table. When she looked up at him, eyes red rimmed and haunted, he nudged the glass toward her.

"Drink it."

She sipped, shuddered and drank again, draining the glass and slamming it back down.

"What a mess. What a stupid mess. Your father is going to kill him."

Frank nodded, knew it for the truth.

"He doesn't need to know all of it," she said, pleading with bleary, worn eyes. "Maybe, he just got in a fight?"

"He's probably gonna hear something around town."

"Could be, could be not. Those other boys won't want it around either."

Frank headed for the door. His mind was in a whirl. How many people already knew about this?

"Where you going?" she asked.

"Town. Need to talk with my wife."

His mother turned from him, got up and pulled her apron down over her head, doing what mothers did, what farm wives did. They fed their families. Patched dungarees and wounds. Cared for them. Protected them. And cried, not knowing them.

"Go to your wife."

Chapter Thirty-one

The two deep lines etched between Frank's eyes should have warned her, but she was happy to see him, so she went around the bar and tried to wrap her arms around him before he took a seat. His hands stayed by his sides, and she hugged a ramrod stiff back. She tilted her head to peer into his face.

"Frank?"

"What? I'd like a whiskey, Abby."

She dropped her arms, hurt, and went back to her place behind the bar. She poured a generous amount in a glass and set it in front of him, going down the laundry list of how she could have disappointed him this time.

Frank swiveled on his stool and eyed the men who sat and talked and drank at various tables. He knew most of them and recognized all of the faces, having seen them at one time or another, mostly here at the hotel. From a distance, he checked them over for bruises or scratches and didn't see any. Maybe the men who beat up the Tatums and his little brother weren't here. He couldn't believe at least one Tatum hadn't been able to land a punch, even if George couldn't, but not a man in the place looked like he'd been in a fight.

He gulped his whiskey and pushed the glass toward his wife.

"Anybody new in town?" he asked her when she neared.

"Here? Now?"

"Yes."

"I don't think so. All the guests have been here awhile."

He nodded, and Abby watched his jaw muscles bunch and jump. She knew that movement. He was mad or frustrated. She understood the look, just not the why.

She turned to wait on Samuel Moore who had taken a seat at the other end of the bar and was stopped by Frank's hand grasping her arm.

"What do you know about George?" he asked.

"Your brother, George?"

"Don't play stupid, Abby. Of course, my brother, George."

"What about him? What do you mean by what do I know?"

Frank glared at her, positive she knew what he was talking about but refusing to admit it. She was playacting, and she was good at it.

"I need to go, Frank. I have customers," she said, looking intentionally at his hand on her arm.

He released her, and Abby walked away to wait on Samuel.

"Got any coffee on, Abigail?"

His hands played ghost piano on the bar, long tapered fingers tapping different notes, one by one.

"Really? Coffee?"

"I think it's a good night to stay alert. Where are your buddies?"

"Bear and Shorty?"

He nodded.

"Told me they were taking some extra walks. I don't know why."

"That's good," he said, tapping away while she stood motionless, pondering. "Coffee?" he added.

She came to with a twitch and watched Phantom stalk down the bar toward him, his blue eyes wide. Samuel stroked the cat's back and listened to the peaceful purr.

"He'll get white hair all over your beautiful jacket."

"I know. Coffee?"

Abby smirked and spoke over her shoulder on the way to the kitchen.

"I guess I don't hear if it isn't alcohol."

Frank watched the exchange, the tops of his ears growing warm as she stood there chatting. She acted like they were old friends, good friends. He finished his drink and slammed it on the bar hard enough to get her attention as she came from the kitchen with Samuel's coffee.

"I'm going upstairs. I'd like to talk with you if you can leave your friends for a few minutes," he said.

She got her father from the kitchen to cover for her and went up. Frank was sitting in the chair waiting for her.

"What's wrong, Frank?"

"George was beaten up."

Abby's eyes widened and she stepped back, her shoulders knocking against the door.

"My God, no. What happened?"

"I figured you could tell me."

"But . . . how would I know?"

"Figured your friends might have told you."

Abby couldn't respond, didn't have anything to say. She was stunned.

He leaned back in his chair and studied her as she moved to sit on the edge of the bed.

"Which friends?" she said. "And why would my friends beat up George?"

"This is what I think. Your little Betty gets herself assaulted – so she says – by some white boys, and she won't press charges because she might make a name for herself. So, she calls in some muscle to beat them up instead."

Abby was confused. "What does that have to do with . . ."

"George said they were just playing with her, having some fun."

She got it. Abby leaped from the bed and stood poised for a fight in front of her husband.

"George did that to Betty? George helped those Tatum monsters rape her? Beat her?"

Fire flew from Abby's eyes, and her nostrils flared. She wanted to strike him, to burst his contented, ego filled bubble.

"You didn't see her, Frank," she said, her voice a dangerous whisper. "She was beaten. Her eyes blackened. Her ribs cracked. Her sides purple. Her lips split. She was lying curled in a fetal ball where they ... *played with her.* She couldn't even walk. I'm sickened by your words. By your brother ... by you."

"Well, you should see him. He's a mess."

"Good. He deserves it and more. Did anyone rape him? If not, he only got half of what he had coming to him, and I pray someday he gets the other half."

Abby's chest heaved. Her anger had no place to go, no outlet. She knew she had to get out of the room, away from him, and said she was going back to work. He grabbed her arm to stop her.

"Don't touch me," she said, and twisted away from him.

"I need an answer. Do you know who did it? Did you know it was going to happen?"

"Why?"

"It's important."

"No. And I didn't know."

Frank slumped in the chair.

"If you had known, would you have told me? Would you have stopped it?"

Abby chewed her lip. She wanted to be honest with him, and she wanted to say what he needed to hear, but the two ideals were at war with one another. They were polar opposite answers. He wanted a yes, but she didn't think that was the truth. She didn't think it could be.

She chose a middle ground and hated herself for it.

"I don't know, Frank."

His huffed as he stood.

"You care about everybody in this town but us, your family. People talk about you like you're colored, or you think you are. Or you want to be. You weren't like this in Nirvana. You didn't pick colored people over your own."

"I didn't know any ... or that this was a choosing kind of situation, like kids playing games. I'm not picking any *group* of people. Just good people. And I'm choosing right. Not wrong."

"And you think you know coloreds now?" He laughed, a scornful sound that cut, a knife dicing up her feelings like chopped onions. "You don't know them."

"No, I don't. I haven't lived their oppression, so I'll never know that. I haven't been the object of derision and scorn because of the skin I wear. I haven't known a whip or been used as a mule, or made to bear a child from a man I hated. I have taken drinks from any well I wanted and bought a cup of coffee at any counter I chose. I have not been made to question my own value . . . except by you, Frank."

She didn't think he heard her last words, and that was fine. She'd whispered them as an afterthought, not because it wasn't true, but because she hadn't known it as a truth before this moment.

But it was accurate, and the realization smelled of the forest after a storm, fetid undergrowth freshened by the rain. Her hand held the doorknob.

"You're right about one thing, Frank. I don't know them . . . but I want to. And I will, if they will let me."

His jaw muscles twitched, and he leaped to his feet, hands clenched into fists. Abby flinched from him and wondered if he'd wanted that response from her, if it was intentional. Did he want her to fear him? Just a little?

"You don't know what you're doing. You need to make a choice, Abby. Come to the farm with me or stay here without me. You need to choose."

Abby's throat closed with thick moisture, and she tried to swallow it away. She stood as tall as she could, straightened her back and lifted her chin, opened the door and stepped through.

"I'm going to work, Frank. You can let yourself out."

"You'll be sorry about your choice."

"You made it, Frank."

She blinked away the tears before they rolled down her face and rocked back and forth as she stood at the landing, hands gripping the wooden railing. She listened to the voices, some in debate, some in laughter, and tried to hang on to the sounds of normalcy.

She knew she'd review the entire episode, over and over, when she was in bed, trying to sleep. She knew she'd find the right words, and he'd not be angry, not give her ultimatums. Later. When it was too late.

She had failed at marriage. She didn't know what she should have done differently or how to do it. She loved him, cared about his welfare and knew he wasn't a bad man. She didn't know how to open his eyes to the world around him, and she didn't know how to live with his blindness. She didn't know how to make him happy.

Daytime hours filled with work, and Abby had no time to hurt, no empty moments to dwell on her loss. Having her da and friends beside her helped.

The Chautauqua was in two days, and the hotel erupted with guests and activity. Tents sprouted all over the Island and around the pavilion. Idlewild was a sea of new faces. Impromptu music rang across the water from groups sitting outside the cabins. Folks with guitars and banjos, dobroes and mandolins, strummed and picked. Those who hadn't learned an instrument, played the spoons, and everybody made music.

Sweet notes wafted in through the open windows on warm spring air as they cleaned rooms and Abby hummed along. Her feet tapped from the time the music began in late morning to nightfall when she fell into bed.

She loved the Chautauqua, the speakers, the comradery, putting aside differences and coming together to enjoy what Idlewild had to offer. It gave her hope.

It was too cold to swim, but she saw boats on the water with long bamboo poles sticking into the blue sky and eager faces watching them. Every now and then, the tip of one jerked down and then back toward the sky, and a voice yelled, *Got em*, and *Nice one. He'll make dinner.* It was hard to leave the window scene.

"Come on, boss. Want to get done before the speakers start talking tonight?" Betty said, pulling her away.

Abby dragged the dust mop down the hallway, taking Cleo for a ride on the way. Phantom followed, batting at the black cat, trying to get a rise out of the tranquil feline. She peered over the railing to see Sheriff Hicks walk in with Samuel Moore close behind.

"Hello Sheriff," she called. "Mr. Moore. I don't think anyone's in the bar. Need something?"

"A couple of coffees would be great, if you wouldn't mind," the sheriff said.

Abby told Betty she'd be right back and sprinted down the stairs.

"You're gonna break your neck on those steps one of these days, Abigail," he said as she took his hand,

"Good to see you, Sheriff. Any particular reason you're here?"

"Just here to see your pretty face," he said, his lips curving into a gap-toothed grin.

"Fancy talker. I'll get those coffees."

She set two cups on their table and stepped back, watching their faces.

"Yes?" Samuel said, his eyebrows lifting.

"Uh, yes," she said, shifting her feet and feeling nosy. "Why *are* you here? Did something happen?"

"Precautionary, Abby," the sheriff said. "Want to make sure nothing *does* happen."

"How are you going to do that?"

Samuel leaned back in his chair and tugged at his mustache, waiting to see how the sheriff would handle the curious Abby. He saw a glint in the man's eyes and concern in Abby's.

"Wa'al little lady," Hicks said, pretending to be the noted sheriff of small town dime novels. Abby booted his leg with the toe of her shoe.

"You're making fun of me now."

"We plan on shuttin' down this here Chautakie," he said.

She grinned. "You mean, Chautauqua?"

"That what it is? Anyway, no people? No problems. That'll work, don't you think?"

"Alright, Sheriff Hicks. I got the point." She batted her eyelashes and folded her hands in front of her. "I won't worry my little head about men's business."

When she turned to leave them, he relented and told her they were deputizing some men for the weekend, and increasing patrols all night long.

"It's long past time to end this nonsense that's been going on."

"I agree. Thank you, Sheriff. I'll leave you to your meeting. Nice to see you again, Mr. Moore."

"Samuel. And you, Abigail."

She ran to the kitchen to tell her father to check on the two men and refill their cups, and back up the stairs to finish the rooms, content knowing Idlewild was in good hands.

Reverend Hammond opened the Chautauqua on Friday evening with a sermon on loving yourself and loving others more – all others – angels and sinners alike. Some faces grinned in glee, and others frowned, when he called Sue's name to be the first in line to accept the blood and body of Christ.

"My favorite convert!" he shouted. "Where are you?"

Way in the back of the crowd under the pavilion, people stood and shuffled backwards to let her wide body through. She yanked on her dress, smoothing imaginary wrinkles, until the low neckline was about to reveal the breasts that some dreams are made of. The congregation collectively stopped breathing and sighed with relief when she let the dress go and waddled forward.

She took her time, turned her head to nod at each row of faces, her chin high, her grin enigmatic and indecipherable. She left every person curious about what was going on in her mind to be the object of everyone's attention, and most importantly, the reverend's. Did she pretend to be a bride walking the aisle? Was she truly feeling the call of the Lord? Or was she an actress?

When she reached Reverend Hammond at the front of the pavilion, she looked up from her four-foot something height and winked at him. The chalice he held jiggled, and a drop of red wine ran down the side of it. He wiped it with an index finger and held it to her lips. When she took it eagerly, he returned her wink, shocking people in the first few rows who were close enough to see it. He put the wafer on her tongue and blessed her.

Sue turned and stood still, looking over the faces painted with eager bewilderment over what she'd do next. She curtseyed and extended her arm, palm up, inviting them to the makeshift altar.

"It's your turn now," she said. "I'm done."

Du Bois spoke next, and the shuffling of boots on the concrete continued until he lowered his voice and they had to be silent to hear him. Abby stood outside the pavilion, having left the hotel too late to get a seat. She craned her neck to see him.

He was a handsome man with lightly thinning hair and a short, carefully groomed beard. To Abby, it felt that he was looking directly at her, and she wondered if he was or if all members of his audience thought that. Was it a trick of his to make people feel drawn into his words?

She moved to the side, and his eyes followed. She stepped back to see if it continued, and bumped into Samuel Moore who grabbed her arms to keep her from tumbling into someone else. It was crowded.

"What are you doing, Abigail?"

"Watching his eyes. They're following me."

Samuel grinned. He knew what she meant. That was Du Bois' gift. His eyes captured people, helped convince them of the truth in his words.

"Do you believe him, Abigail?"

"What? Which?"

"The idea that rule-following and laws don't take precedence over right. I haven't said it correctly, but I think you get the gist."

His words were low, not to interfere with the speaker's, and Abby leaned in to hear.

"Yes, but . . ."

"But, what?"

"That leads to vigilantism which has no boundaries. No order."

Samuel's eyes peered off into the dark, and Abby saw deep sorrow hiding there, knowledge and grief she hadn't seen before. Or hadn't taken the time to notice.

"That is true," he said, bringing his eyes back to her. "It's a conundrum. That's why Du Bois says justice and common sense must sit in the same hand as right. All three are essential if one is going to ignore legal precedence."

She turned to face him.

"This sounds serious. Like you've been thinking about the subject for a while."

"I *am* a lawyer, Abigail. And I *am* a Negro."

She didn't respond for many moments. She didn't know who or what she was anymore. Worse, she felt like she was nothing that could be defined or described, nothing anyone could put in a niche and say 'this is who you are.' She envied Samuel. He knew exactly who he was.

Applause exploded around them as Du Bois finished his address. People were on their feet, stomping, clapping hands and shouting. She wished she knew what he'd said that had prompted the display of approval.

Samuel shrugged and apologized.

"I shouldn't have distracted you," he said.

"I was interested in what you were saying, Samuel. And here comes my favorite guitarist."

"You know many?"

"Nope," she grinned. "But I know him, and I love Buddy Black. He sings my kind of blues."

"You wear your heart on your sleeve, girl."

He walked away from her, but turned back.

"Stick close to home tonight, Abigail."

She tilted her head and raised her eyebrows.

"Please," he said, and walked on.

Flames shot into the sky during Buddy Black's music. Abby was just thinking she should head back to the hotel because it was nearing the end of his session, when she heard shouts from the island and looked up to see orange licking at the dark like the devil's tongues. Every head under and around the pavilion turned toward it.

It took seconds for the pavilion to empty and mere minutes for the footbridge to fill with people, buckets, rakes and shovels.

Several cabins were burning when they got there, and they formed water lines from the lake to the fires, with full buckets passing from hand to hand to be thrown on the flames and empty pails going back again.

Arms swung back and forth knowing the bucket bail would be placed squarely in their hands – without looking – without doubt. They knew it would be there. They had faith, and it didn't occur to them to doubt the next in line would do the job they'd stepped up to do. Their arms ached with the effort.

Folks threw dirt with shovels until blisters formed and raked hot coals to be buried in sand. They tossed wet blankets, slapped at burning embers, coughed in the black smoke and ran from it to gasp for clean air and back again to fight the flames.

When the fires were out, blackened men and women slumped to the ground, exhausted. Tired of fighting fires. Tired of fighting, period. They had come here with hope, and it was going up in ashes. In beatings. In fear and suspicion.

Abby pulled her father's arm, dragged him over to where Jesse was sitting and collapsed next to him. He rubbed his forehead, not looking at them.

"This can't continue," Jesse growled. "It has to stop."

"They're going to catch them this time, Jesse. I know it," she said.

"What makes you think it will change anything if they do, Abby? You gonna change a hundred years of hate?"

"Yes. We are. Are you giving up?"

Her face was streaked with ash, and long straggles of auburn hair hung limp and grimy. She looked at her hands and saw blisters forming and broken nails imbedded with black.

Jesse swiped a hand over his soot streaked face and groaned.

"Jesus, girl. Don't you see what's happening?"

"Yes. I see you leaving your daughter something better than you found when you came here. Daisy deserves it."

"You play dirty."

"Yes, I do. When I need to."

Across the island, she saw Benjamin and three of his soldier friends fall to the grass to rest. Bill Sanders, looking grubby for the first time since Abby had known him, dropped down beside her and passed a flask to Jesse. Pastor Hammond, Buddy Black and James Gerard joined them, eyeing the flask with desire.

This time, the flames had reached far into the sky, and the Gerards had spotted it from their farm. They were late getting there, but they'd pitched in.

"Where's your friends, Abby?" Jesse asked.

"Who? You're all here."

He squinted his eyes and raised his hand in the air to indicate really tall.

"Oh. You mean Bear and Shorty?"

Jesse nodded, not believing the two would shirk this work, but concerned over their whereabouts.

"I imagine they're out there," she said, pointing to the dark edges of the trees that circled parts of the island.

"Hiding? I can't believe that."

"Stalking. Come on. Let's go home, Da."

"Let's go get a nice, wet, wee drink. On me," Patrick said.

She rose, took her father's hand and pulled. He groaned as he stood, and his bandy legs bowed so far out he waddled from side to side like a duck as he walked back to the footbridge.

Patrick called out to the rest to join them, and they trudged across the bridge, a soot covered, somber group.

Chapter Thirty-two

Abby dragged up the stairs to wash her face and get out of her smoke-stained clothes. She toweled her hair, trying to remove some of the soot, and grimaced when she looked at the blackened towel. After a quick brushing, she braided the mess and went to pour drinks for the thirsty crowd.

"Go wash your hands and face, Jackson. In the kitchen. You look like a chimney sweep."

He scowled and grumbled. Abby smirked, pretended to stomp her foot and pointed the way.

Voices were subdued and folks hunched over the tables, talking in rumbling, low tones. Smoldering anger underscored their words, and shoulders sagged in defeat. Abby poured drinks, hefty ones, and watched. She cursed arson as an evil thief. It struck in the dark and fed on optimism.

The atmosphere in the room was tense, leaden with quiet. It was like waiting for a storm, and faces were intent on the unspoken ferocity around them. There was no banter, no teasing, and Abby feared many of these folks might not return to Idlewild. They'd go to their safe homes where their lives were, if not perfect, predictable; if not hopeful, rational. She despaired for them all.

But as she watched, she saw an occasional lip curving in a half grin, a hand raise to pat a shoulder, and she bounced on her toes and clutched her belly. Hope grew. Someone laughed and someone else cursed goodheartedly. She closed her eyes and thanked God.

You're tough, my friends, and I'm so glad.

She looked over the full tables, checking for empty glasses, and watched Jackson head in the direction of one. He brought it to her and she was filling it with whiskey when Shorty's large frame filled the doorway. He looked behind him, talking to someone, and strode across the room, leaned into her and spoke next to her ear.

"We've arrested the four Tatum boys. Taking them to town. Thought we should just go and tell everyone when we get back. Don't want... well, you know."

"Why? How do you know they did it?"

"Found them running from the cabins with the evidence on them. Kerosene and bottles. Paint they didn't have time to use. It's them. They tried to hide in the woods, and they're going to jail this time."

Abby nodded, eyes wide. She hated to think of anyone going to jail, but they deserved it – for much, much more than just burning the cabins.

"Should I not say anything?"

"Let us get down the road a piece. Just in case. Don't want an uprising."

She watched him leave and tried to forget about it as she got busy serving the crowd. Patrick had heated the leftover stew and put it on the buffet tables with slices of soda bread and butter. People helped themselves, happy, at least, to be filling their bellies.

"Can ye pour one for your tuckered da, sweet Abigail?" he asked, sitting down gratefully.

"I can. A big one. You earned it today, Da. Are you okay?"

"I'm gonna live, lass. So, you gonna tell me what the big one said to you in secret?"

"Shorty?" she asked, stalling.

He pursed his lips and squinted his eyes. He knew how to make his daughter speak the truth.

"He told me they were taking all the Tatum boys... oh, my God! They can't take all of them!"

"Why not? What's got you so flummoxed?"

"They're taking them to jail – away from the farm. They can't take all the brothers and leave Al. You don't understand. I have to go."

She untied her apron and threw it on the bar.

"You gotta tend the bar. I'm taking the mare," she said.

"Where you going all by yourself? It's dark."

"The Tatums. I have to. She can't be alone."

"Her Pa's there."

"Yeah. That's the problem."

Abby ran from the room with Patrick following behind her as fast as his toddle would allow. She came close to running smack over the top of Samuel Moore who grabbed her arm, once again, to keep her from knocking him down the steps.

"You off to a fire, Abigail?"

He took one look at her face and stepped back.

"Not funny, huh?"

"I don't have time to explain. I have to go to the Tatum farm. Right now. Al's brothers aren't there because they've been arrested, and I need to bring her here."

"Why?" Samuel said.

"She needs me. I know it sounds crazy, but I need to go."

Abby's fearful eyes convinced him. Even if she was wrong, and Al didn't need her help, Abby believed she did. She was going there – in the dark – by herself.

"My buggy's tied over there," Samuel said pointing. "It's still hitched. Get in."

Patrick thumped his shoulder.

"Thank you, Samuel. She'd go off on her own."

"Probably right about that."

"So, you want to tell me what's going on?" he asked when they were rolling down the road toward the Tatum's.

"It's a long story."

"As you can see, I've got some time."

Abby cleared her throat and tugged her braid, unsure how much she should say. It was Al's story to tell. But Samuel needed to know. He was here and putting himself in possible harm's way.

She looked sideways at him. He must have gone home to clean up after fighting the fires because his suit jacket and shirt were spotless. The gold chain hanging from its pocket gleamed in the moonlight. His hands holding the reins looked as they always did, nails white, clipped short and clean. She looked at her own and frowned.

"Kind of grubby, aren't they?" he teased, without smiling.

She tucked her hands away out of sight.

"I'm waiting."

Samuel was helping. He had earned truth.

"This goes no further, especially if all is well. Al is afraid of her father. I believe he beats his children. And . . . especially her."

"Any special reason to beat her?"

"According to Al," Abby said, her voice little more than a whisper, "because she isn't her mother."

"A bit more, please."

Abby snuffled, and a teardrop streaking her cheek.

"I think Strange Al's brothers somehow protect her from her their father."

"Strange Al?"

She closed her eyes. "Sorry. It's a silly name I gave her. I shouldn't have, but she is an enigma."

"It suits her. She'd probably like it if she heard it. Anyway. Continue."

Hooves hit the dirt and bats skittered across the road.

"Without her brothers around, she believes he'll kill her."

Samuel turned to stare.

"You're not serious."

"I am. Al believes it."

"But what father would do that?"

"A crazy one. A monster. And a young woman has little recourse. Al believes she has no other choice. Women like Al don't have options! But today, she's getting one."

Samuel flicked the reins and the mare picked up speed. They didn't speak again until the buggy turned down the lane to the Tatum house.

Samuel hopped to the ground and looped the reins around a rickety railing. Abby was up the steps and banging on the door before he was done. She banged again and nudged the door open to call for someone.

"Al? Are you here? Please say something."

Terrible silence answered. Abby turned and looked into the yard and beyond, trying to see movement, hear a footstep, anything. She jumped when a whine brought her attention to the corner of the house. A scraggly hound dog limped up the porch and pushed against her leg.

"Hello, boy," she said. "Where's your family, fellow? Where's Al?"

She swallowed the thick lump in her throat and pushed the door further open.

"Step aside, Abby. Let me in."

Samuel walked into the kitchen, and she and the dog followed. They called for Al and Mr. Tatum. Nothing.

"Nobody's home," she said, fear crackling her voice. "Where could they be? I don't think they go anywhere."

They left the house and followed a well-worn path to the barn. Cows moved about and chickens clucked a nighttime serenade. Samuel slid back the barn door, stepped inside and stopped dead still. Abby heard the harsh intake of his breath.

"Bastard," he said. "Get in here, Abigail."

Al was slumped on the floor, her hands tied around a post. She was bare to the waist, and blood streaked her back. Her head lolled to the side, and her eyes were squeezed shut. Her bare legs stuck out on either side of the post and were streaked with bloody welts.

Abby swallowed back the bile at her throat and rubbed her face.

You will not throw up. You will not cry. You will not.

Samuel took a knife from his pocket and cut the ropes that held Al against the post. She collapsed against him and he laid her down in the filthy straw, pressed fingers to her neck, looking for a pulse.

"She's alive."

"Thank you, God."

"Get blankets, behind the seat."

Abby flew to the buggy and back. She spread out a blanket, and Samuel lay the broken, bleeding girl on it and covered her with the other one.

"We'll have to take her back to the hotel, Samuel. We can't help her here. Her father may be hiding out. He'll show up, and . . . well, we need to be away."

"Let's go. You're going to have to drive or hold her, Abigail."

"I'll hold her. If she wakes up, at least she'll know me."

She didn't want to say Al might be afraid of his dark skin and maleness. So much had gone on in the young girl's life, Abby didn't know how she'd react. What she might fear.

She climbed into the buggy, and Samuel placed the lifeless girl on her lap. Al was so small, she fit like a baby in her arms, with her legs dangling and her head resting on Abby's shoulder. Abby tried to hold her gently, to not hurt her any more than she already was, and was glad the girl was still unconscious.

"I'm sorry I doubted you," Samuel said.

Abby chewed her lip.

"And I doubted her."

They made record time getting back, and Al never opened her eyes.

The bar was still full when Samuel carried Al through the lobby and up the stairs. Heads craned to see what was going on, and questions flew.

"Later," Samuel said.

"Hot water and salve, Da. And bandages," she shouted down to Patrick when he poked his head out.

Abby flung open the door to her room and pulled down the quilt.

"Put her here, please. I'll light the lamp."

Al groaned when he laid her down, and tears rolled from her closed eyes. In the lamplight, both of them gasped at the horror Al had been through. Someone had beaten her poor face. Her eyes were swollen shut and black, her cheeks puffed and purple, her lips split and distended. What they could see of the rest of her had been whipped with a wide strap, probably the bastard's leather belt.

Abby dampened a cloth in the basin and wiped Al's face.

415

"I need to remove the rest of her clothes. Help me."

"Maybe I shouldn't be here for this," Samuel said. "You need a woman."

"Do you see another woman here? Anywhere in the building?" Abby growled, staring with hard, bitter eyes.

"No."

Together they got her ripped skirt and pantaloons off, and tried to swallow back their anger and disgust.

Patrick brought hot water, handed Samuel the bandages and salve, and turned to go.

"You good, here?"

"Yes, Da. We're fine. Thank you."

She covered Al with a couple of towels and bathed the wounds on her face and chest as gently as possible, hoping what she tended was the worst she'd find. She spread salve on the open cuts and loosely bandage her chest, then uncovered her legs and worked on them. She smeared them with salve, bandaged them as well as she could, and asked Samuel to help turn her over.

"You can leave after that, Samuel, and thank you."

Samuel cursed and twisted away when the damage to her back was unveiled.

"Bastard. If she survives this, she'll have my regard," he said. "We need a doctor."

"Yes, we do. But we're all we've got."

"I want to kill that man, so help me, God," he whispered. "I've got to go. I'll see you downstairs."

She emptied the bloody water into a bucket, poured clean into the basin, and grimaced as she moved the cloth over raw, broken skin. She sobbed as she worked and remembered the number of times she'd been short with Al, the number of times she wanted to yell at her. *Speak up, girl. Talk a little. Join the rest of the world.*

Well, now, she understood. The world wasn't a great place for Al. Why would she want to be a part of any of it? Why would she want to be friendly with anybody? Now, she didn't blame her. She blamed herself.

She didn't know what else she could do to make the girl more comfortable, what to do to help her survive, to make

416

her want to live, besides pray. She knelt on the floor next to Al's head and whispered close to her ear.

"I'm praying for you. I'm here for you, my friend, and I'll never let that man near you again. You have a home with me for as long as you want it. Hear me, Al? You *never* need see your father again. I promise you. I promise."

She stood with a hand on her aching head, turned the lamp low, but not out. She wanted Al to have some light, needed her to know she wasn't still in the barn waiting for the next swing of the strap.

"I'll be back up in a few minutes, Al. I need to take care of something."

She dragged down the stairs and stood at the entrance to the bar watching the men as they talked. Heads shook back and forth in denial of another's words, and other heads nodded agreement. She heard the words *leaving* and *done here* and *knew it was too good to be true.*

She saw Jesse, looking defeated, and Bill, still uncharacteristically filthy, but waving his arms enthusiastically. She heard voices arguing *this is still Eden and worth fighting for.*

Abby absorbed it as if she was all-knowing, all-seeing, and it crossed her mind to wonder if both she and Al had died, but this couldn't be heaven. Colored and white people still sat at separate tables. That wouldn't happen in heaven. There was no harp, no music period. And Joe Foster was here.

Nope. Not heaven. Maybe I'm not going to heaven.

Benjamin sat with his soldier buddies instead of at the piano, and Abby hoped he hadn't burned his precious hands. His fingers should only touch the cool ivory of the keys on a Baldwin piano or caress a beautiful woman. They weren't meant to battle blazes.

Joe Foster sat at the bar, his clothes, while dusty and grimy as usual, were free of soot. He'd stayed far from the blaze, watching from a distance with a sneer of satisfaction on his face, as it was still. Abby glared at him when she moved around his back.

"What?" he asked, as if her eyes had charred his skin. She would if she could. A hint of a smile quirked her lips when Cassandra crossed her mind.

Maybe she could make a potion . . . Naw. Wouldn't work, would it?

She ignored Joe's question and walked over to Samuel.

"I need one more thing from you, please."

"Sure."

"I need Cassandra. Will you ask her to come?"

He nodded. "On my way."

He left the room and many eyes followed him, wondered about his abrupt departure and how it was connected to Abby.

Abby went into the kitchen for a pot and long handled spoon, and came out banging it. Every head turned toward her, eyes wide.

"I have something to tell you, so please listen."

She waited until the clamor of their surprise died down and looked around the room, noting each face, each pair of eyes that sought a reason for the noise she was making. She knew them all, some well, some a little, but she mostly liked what she knew of them all – except for Joe. She hoped she could convince them that this was their home – or their place to rest and play.

"You won't have to fear fire any more. They caught the men red handed and all four Tatum boys are at the Baldwin jail by now. They were the artists of the little pictures that floated around Idlewild, too. Well, some of them."

She pictured Samuel.

Hands came together in loud applause and shouts filled the room. Palms slapped the tables and drinks spilled. Jackson flew around the room, cleaning spills and refilling glasses. Patrick tended him at the bar.

Abby banged the pot again.

"I'm not done," she shouted.

"What else could there be, darlin','" Bill shouted. "That's the best news ever."

"This. Idlewild is never going to become what we dream unless we come together and take care of one another, trust and respect each other, help each other. If we don't do that, we're just gonna limp along pretending to be special, pretending to be a place like no other in the entire nation."

Abby hung her head, disgusted with herself, tears trying their best to defeat her, but she wasn't going to allow it.

"A young girl lies upstairs, half dead, beaten by her father. Did any of you know Al Tatum had been whipped with his belt before? Did you suspect he beat his children and not say anything, not do anything about it?"

She sobbed and swallowed hard, shoving back the sick bile that flooded her throat, rising from the ashes of her guilt.

"I did. And I'll live with that awful knowledge about myself for a long, long time. A while back another young girl was assaulted, and we all knew it and hid it instead of doing something, instead of hunting down the wicked men who did it to her and seeing them punished."

Eyes looked away. Hands rubbed at bristly chins. Heads nodded.

She put the pan on the bar and tugged at the auburn braid hanging over her shoulder. Stiff, sooty curls stuck out of it along the entire length, making it look more like a long chimney brush than a sleek braid. Abby stared at them.

"That's all."

She didn't know what else to say but knew there was more. She was tired clear through her bones, and her heart was broken. For one more day . . . she'd kept George's name a secret.

I am part of the problem.

She flipped back the frayed braid and left the room.

Chapter Thirty-three

Al twisted and moaned in her sleep. Her skin was hot to touch, and Abby worried she would die, that her wounds were too deep. In the pale light of the moon, she swabbed the young girl with cool water, marveling such a slight body could shoulder the heavy burden she had borne. It was too much to imagine.

She moved to the window seat, listening to Al's shallow breath, terrified for the young girl and praying for Cassandra to hurry when her form materialized. She stood alone, without her clowder.

Abby pressed her cheek against the cool pane of the window and motioned to the witch woman, who nodded and glided toward the hotel door. Abby met her there and led her to Al.

Cassandra pulled the sheet back from Al's wretched body, closed her eyes, and turned her head away. For the first time since Abby had known her, she was without perfect serenity. She uttered an oath and clutched at Abby's arm. She looked ancient.

"I need hot water," she whispered. "In a basin and in a teapot. Bring it, please."

Abby brought the teapot first and left to get the basin of hot water. Cassandra had the pot steeping with a fragrant tea when she returned.

"Smells like what you gave Betty."

"Tis. Devil's claw, Birch leaf and Kava kava."

She handed a packet to Abby and ordered her to stir it into the basin of water.

"What is it?"

"Five-flower. Yarrow for the deep wounds. Turn her. Do her back first. Front after, then the tea."

Abby did as she was told and saw morning spread across the sky as she finished bathing Al in the aromatic water. She had yet to regain consciousness, but tossed and moaned when Abby pulled the sheet back over her.

Tea now. She handed Abby a tied cloth and told her to dip it in the tea.

"Now squeeze it into her mouth."

Cassandra tilted Al's head and held a towel at her neck to catch errant drizzles. When her features softened and body relaxed, they quit forcing the liquid into her mouth and sat listening to her peaceful breath. She slept, and that was the best they could do for her now.

"Tea?" Abby asked.

"Please. I'll make it," Cassandra said with a light in her eyes.

She left the room, and Abby wandered around picking up towels. With nothing left to do but wait, she sat in the window seat and stared at her mother's picture.

"This is a mess. I've made a mess of things. And I'm gonna make more. I have to."

You'll do what's right, Abby. I know you.

Cassandra returned with a tray, and Abby salivated at the aroma.

"I'll stay," Cassandra said. She poured the tea and handed Abby a cup. "When you've finished your cup."

"Where am I going?"

"Many places. You know."

And she was right.

Her first stop was to wake her father, Bear and Shorty. Bear needed to make breakfast with Patrick, and Shorty needed to get Sheriff Hicks. It all came to her.

Patrick came to the door looking like he couldn't focus his eyes, his hand out, making sure he didn't crash into anything.

"What's the ruckus, lass? Why are you banging on me door so early?"

"I need you to cook this morning. I'll get Bear to help. He'll be exhausted from his late night, but it can't be helped."

"What? Why?"

"I'll explain later. Sorry, Da. I'll be taking Marie."

She moved from her father's door to bang on Bear's and break the news to him. He took it as he did everything – with grace. Shorty did, too, when she asked him to get the sheriff.

"I was wondering how long it would take you. I'm dressed to go."

She didn't bother to unsaddle her mare when she got to the farm, just tied her to the porch rail and climbed the steps. Through the window, she saw the entire family around the breakfast table and faltered, took a step backwards and pictured herself sitting with them, part of the family.

She was about to destroy their lives. She swallowed and rapped hard on the door. All faces turned her way and she waited.

"You," Frank's father said, not moving aside to invite her in.

"Could I speak with Frank, please, Mr. Adams?"

"Frank. Get out here," he yelled.

He shut the door behind him and moved down the steps to the yard, his long legs making giant strides toward the barn. She skipped across the dirt until she could pull at his arm and slow him down.

"What do you want, Abby?"

Frank's eyes were flint hard. His jaws twitched, and he rubbed a hand across his unshaven chin.

"Can we talk a minute, Frank?"

"I'm out here, aren't I?"

She filled her chest with courage. Her eyes turned glassy and she blinked.

"I'm just going to say this fast, before I can't say it. I've asked Sheriff Hicks to come to Idlewild. For a couple of reasons. One is he needs to know about George's part in Betty's assault. That's why I'm here. I needed to tell you first. To let you know. I didn't want you blindsided."

He grimaced and turned away. She saw his shoulders bunch and his head moved back and forth in what she took as disbelief or disgust.

"So . . . you're gonna do it. You're gonna turn in your own family, send your brother-in-law to jail. But I guess this never was your family, was it?"

"We don't know that he'll go to jail, Frank, but he deserves to. What he did was wrong. It was despicable. And you know that. Deep down, I know you do."

Frank leaned against the side of the barn and kicked at the dirt.

"It wasn't right, and he shouldn't have done it. But it's done."

"Not yet, it isn't. He hasn't paid for it."

"He was beaten. He paid."

"I'm not going through this again, Frank. Nobody raped him. He had no right to her body! No one has the right to another's body – just their own!"

Frank flinched and backed away from the force of Abby's anger.

"So, you said George was one of the reasons you were bringing the sheriff to town. What's the other?"

Abby chewed at her pinky and checked out the sky. Clouds skittered across the rising sun, alternately blocking it and allowing its rays to warm her, but she shivered and wondered if she'd ever be warm again and if Al would ever see the sun rise again, if she would even want to.

"You missed it all, Frank. More fires at the resort. Sheriff Hicks arrested the Tatum brothers, and Mr. Tatum beat Al, maybe to death."

She whispered the last words with a prayer that death wouldn't come. She had a promise to keep. She would be a better friend. To Al and to Betty, even if the girl hated her for it.

He lowered his head to look in her eyes.

"Seriously? They arrested the Tatums? And her father beat up Al?"

"I'm sure of it. She told me he would. I didn't believe her."

Abby started to tear up, and Frank shuffled his feet.

"You should see her, Frank. I don't know if she'll make it." She shifted her shoulders back and fisted her hands. "I have to get home. Cassandra is with her now."

"That bastard. I always knew he was rotten. Is the old man hiding out with his bottle?"

"I don't know. But I'm hoping the sheriff finds him and they put him away for a long time."

"I've know that little girl forever. She didn't deserve that family."

"She'll never go back to it either. Not if I have anything to say about it."

Abby walked away from him feeling like she would never see him again, like she'd broken the final tie with her husband and left a man standing there who she couldn't even call a good friend. It was someone she didn't know. But if that was true, why did she want to weep? Why did she feel broken in two?

"I'm really sorry, Frank. For everything," she said as she climbed into the saddle.

He nodded and took the steps two at a time. He was in the kitchen, giving his family the news before she made it to the end of the driveway, and it occurred to her that George might be on a fast horse to another town before she made it home.

Abby checked on Al as soon as she got back to the hotel, made sure Cassandra could stay with her for a while longer, and went to look for Betty. She found her cleaning one of the rooms, went in and shut the door.

Betty's eyes widened, and she stopped what she was doing, sensing the intensity in Abby's wide stance.

"What?"

"I need to talk to you."

"Okay. Did I do something?"

"No. You *didn't* do something."

"You better explain, boss. You're scaring me."

The long sigh coming from Abby said it all. She was exhausted. She hadn't slept all night. She was sick at heart, and she didn't want to do this. She didn't want her friend to feel betrayed, but knew she would.

"Sit, please, Betty."

Abby pulled her down to sit beside her on the bed she'd been making.

"I've sent for the sheriff because of Al. Guess you might have already heard her father beat her, tied her to a post and whipped her. She's a mess, a horrible, bloody, swollen mess, and I pray she'll live."

She paused and watched Betty's face. She wanted her to be horrified, wanted Al's nightmare to have an impact. Betty knew what it was to be beaten bloody.

"But I also want the sheriff because of you, my friend. The Tatums are in custody, caught in the act of arson, but you need to add to those charges, and you need to make sure George Adams joins them."

Betty jerked upright and went to the door, and Abby leaped to lean into it, the flat of her hand against it to stop it from opening. Betty's eyes were fierce in anger, her lips drawn back and her body rigid.

"Let me out."

"Please. Please listen to me."

"You have nothing to say I want to hear. You said it all."

"Betty, you have to take a stand. Don't you see? What has been happening in Idlewild, to you, to Al, the fires, the pictures. It all has to stop. You can free yourself from those men who abused you. They'll keep it up unless you stop them. You can do it, but only you. You can lift your chin and say *Nobody hurts me again. I refuse to be used by anybody. . . ever again.*"

Betty snorted, and the look in her eyes accused. Abby wanted to flinch, to crawl away from her eyes. But she had made a promise to herself. To be a friend.

"You don't know what you're talking about, white woman. You don't know what being used means. Don't know about being a receptacle, a whore for a man cuz he wants it, and you're colored and he's white. You damn well don't know a damned thing."

Betty's anger bit through the words, snapped them in half and hurled them, and Abby felt them on her skin, stinging with each thrust. She rubbed them away and tried to hold on to her resolve, to her love for the young girl.

And then it occurred to her that she deserved the truth. Abby lifted her head and stared into Betty's fury.

"I do. Not like you, because you've lived a life I can't possibly know. Your shoes won't fit me, Betty, so I can't walk in them, ever. But I know when someone else treats me like they own my body. No one beat me. I never had to recover from being battered and bruised like you, but I know what it means to feel like a receptacle. Every damned day."

Abby put her hand on her heart, hand clenched as if she could feel it throb.

"It hurts. It demeans. It dissolves you inch by inch until you question your ability to be a perceptive, thinking person because you're not treated like one. You no longer value yourself because you're just a bushel basket or a wash tub or a cup. You have just that much worth. So, you wait to be filled up and hope it's with something that *has* value. Like affection. Like love. Like respect."

She nodded, chewed the tip of her finger for a moment, and continued.

"I know all about being used. I'm good at it. What's even worse – I let it happen. I thought it was ... I don't know, but I allowed it. I never once did anything to stop it, and that makes it my fault."

A door closed somewhere. A footfall echoed down the hallway. A voice murmured. Life continued, but in the small room where Abby and Betty stood, it had stopped and was waiting.

"Well, now I'm making it stop," Abby said. "And I want you to do that, too. If you don't ... it's your fault."

"I am telling the sheriff, today. It'd be better if you did it. With me. I'll be there for you every step of the way if you want me to. Please, please say you will."

Tears streamed down Abby's face and soaked her breast as she spoke her final words, and she didn't realize it, but at some point, they had moved from the door to sit on the bed, and Betty had her arm around Abby's shoulders.

"I didn't know. You know? I'll go." Tears choked her voice.

"Not for me, Betty. For you. For women. For colored women. Hell, for colored men, too. For people, period."

"For us, Abby." Betty wiped a lone tear that slid down her cheek. "I'll do it."

Sheriff Hicks was at a table in the bar drinking coffee with Shorty. He nodded to Abby and stood.

"You wanted to see me, Abigail?"

"Plan on spending awhile Sheriff. I need to speak with you about Al Tatum who's upstairs being cared for by Cassandra. She was beaten. First, though, Betty is waiting for you in the third room on the left. She has a long story to tell, and I can vouch for its truth. Others can, as well."

The sheriff looked as if he'd been punched in the gut when he came back downstairs. He squeezed the brim of his hat in one hand and ruffled his messed-up hair with the other. He went straight to the bar and leaned against it, dazed with the information he'd been given. It didn't sound fabricated to him. It had the ring of truth, and he didn't peg Betty as a liar.

"You found her this last time?" he said to Abby and rubbed at the pain in his chest, squinting.

"Cassandra and I did, in a fetal position in the woods. She couldn't even crawl. And others can verify her bruises. Talk with Cassandra and Samuel Moore."

"I'll be talking with them both . . . and more with you. Now what about the Tatum girl?"

Abby explained it all, and once again told him to validate her story with Samuel Moore.

"Moore again? He seems to be connected to a lot of activity around here."

"He drove me to the Tatum house. We found her tied to the post in the barn, bloody and unconscious. We couldn't find Mr. Tatum. The house was empty and we didn't want to waste time looking for him. We actually didn't want to find him. She is terribly hurt, Sheriff. You can see for yourself upstairs. But she isn't in any shape to talk with you right now."

"Jesus. This just keeps getting better and better."

Abby worried her lip, wanting to be done with it all.

"Al believed her father would kill her. That's why I went when I did. I think she believed her brothers protected her from him – by taking the beatings."

"That bastard. That son of a bitch."

"It's the third time I've heard that in less than twenty-four hours. Find him Sheriff. He needs to be put away. He's dangerous. Evil."

He poked his head into Al's room, took a look at her swollen face, and spoke briefly with Cassandra out in the hallway. Abby sat with Al and watched through the open door. Hicks' head nodded up and down, up and down, and lines deepened his scowl. His eyes were ferocious, and Abby was glad she wasn't on the receiving end of his wrath.

Abby planned to sit by Al's bed the rest of the day and let Cassandra go to her home to take care of the cats. She said she'd be back for the night shift, that she was always better at night than during the daylight. She twinkled when she said it, watching to see if her words had the desired effect, and they did. Abby looked sideways at her and raised her eyebrows.

"Tell me what to do while you're gone, Cassandra. I'm not the healer you are."

"When she wakes, put this yarrow paste into her deepest cuts. More of the five-flower water on the rest of her body and the same tea we gave her earlier. She can have it every few hours. We want her to rest."

"I don't know how to thank you," Abby said. "I would be lost if you weren't here. Al would be, too."

"Al has never been lost. You were for a time."

Abby squinted at her.

"Are you being witchy with me again?"

Cassandra's chuckle went through the door with her.

"I'll be back before the moon."

Shorty's knock startled her. She'd finished the tasks Cassandra set for her and was watching Al sleep from the window seat.

"Come in, but whisper, please," she said, and chuckled. "As if you could do else?"

"Betty and I've finished the rooms. Bear and your papa are well into making supper. What else can we do?"

"Get some rest, Shorty. You've earned it."

"I can sit with Al if you need a break."

"I could use it. Just for a few minutes. I'd like to check on Betty."

He waved her away, and the big man sat watching the tiny girl, Goliath and David, except they weren't enemies. Shorty's eyes grew soft watching her small form move in sleep.

She found Betty as she was preparing to leave, tugged her hand, and walked out on the porch with her.

"I was thinking of something, Betty."

"Lordy, can you quit thinking for a while? I've had all of your pondering I can take for one day."

Abby gave her an I-know-you're -tired-of-me smile. "Just a little more, please?"

Betty pinched her thumb and forefinger together and widened them by a quarter inch.

"That much."

"Have you thought about how to talk with your da, I mean father, about what you are doing? I know you were worried he'd do something to get himself killed or put into jail if he found out what they did."

She nodded. Betty looked at peace with her plans, and Abby saw and relaxed just a little.

"I have. It's gonna go like this."

'A few decades ago, we quit being slaves. Except we didn't. I've been a slave to my fears for you, Papa, and for myself. I feared the Tatums and gossip, too. I'm gonna get rid of one fear at a time. Cuz I'm not a slave.'

"That's what I'm gonna tell him. And this."

'And it's you first, Papa. You let me deal with this, and you don't go killing anyone because they'll kill you for sure. And I'm not gonna be a slave to that fear. It's the fear that let them do it to me three times! Shame on me! I let it happen twice! They didn't kill me, and gossip can't kill me, so that one's easy. But when the Tatums come back . . . well, I'll deal with it. Maybe I'll get that gun. But I'm through hiding. I didn't do anything wrong. They did.'

"I love you, Betty. You are something." Her voice cracked, and she flung an arm around Betty's shoulder and squeezed.

"And you, boss. I gotta go."

Abby squeezed her hand and watched as she hopped down the steps and headed for the woodland path she took home. Samuel Moore waited out of sight at the edge of the woods and followed.

Chapter Thirty-four

Hicks admired the Adams farm as he rode up. It was clean and maintained with freshly painted fences and a wide front porch. He climbed the steps like he was walking to a prison cell. That's what it felt like. He hated doing this to the family. George deserved whatever jail time he got, but the family will pay, too, and that hurt.

"I'd like to talk with all of you," he told Frank Sr. after explaining his purpose. "One at a time."

"Why?" he said, the single word shooting out like bullet from a rifle. "We don't know anything."

His chin pushed out. His lips turned down. Frank Sr. wasn't going to make his job easy. The sheriff would have to work for it if he wanted this man's youngest son.

"Because that's the way we do things, Frank. We ask questions. Where are your boys? Get them in here, please."

"Terry's in the barn and George is upstairs."

"And Frank?"

"Don't know. He lit outta here after that bitch left this morning."

"And who would that be?"

He snarled. "That miserable excuse for a wife. Abigail Riley. Not using the Adams name. She ain't one. Came to tell us how she was going to kill this family."

"Well, I'll want to see the women, too."

"What on earth would they know?"

The sheriff shook his head.

"Just get George, please. I'll talk to the others after."

He questioned George about his part in the assault on Betty and came away convinced the boy had participated. He figured George hadn't instigated it, but he'd gone along and had an active role.

"You'll be charged, George. I'll see to that, but it'll be up to a jury to settle it. And if you run, it'll just go harder on you. Hear me?"

"I hear, but you don't. I told you, she was having a good time."

"And I'm the king of England. Stay put, or I'll find you and throw your ass in jail with the Tatums."

He talked with Cecily and heard nothing new, but Emily Adams knew the whole story. She tried not to say anything incriminating about her son, but the truth became clearer with each of her efforts to hide it.

He talked with Terry as he continued feeding the calves and heard the same story George had told. The girl was an eager player in their little game.

He left George at the Adams' house with orders to stay put and was on Tatum land before he had time to make the pain in his chest stop hurting. He sat his horse and took a couple of minutes, waiting. He saw the dilapidated porch, a rail missing along one edge, and the front door hanging cocked like the house had been empty for a long time and still was. An old, graying hound dog limped down the steps and ambled toward him.

"Looking pretty scruffy, old boy. Your old man here?"

Chickens squawked when they heard his voice and scrambled out of the shed. They pecked at the dirt looking for food and tumbled over each other in their frenzied search.

Hicks nickered to his mare and moved her to the porch, wrapped the rein around the only solid rail and hollered for Mr. Tatum. No one answered when he pushed the door open, so he tried again, but the silence greeting him was absolute. It became clear the house was empty.

He walked through each room, just in case, and let himself out the back door, the dog following. He went to the barn and pushed back the rising bile when he saw the blood-stained straw around the center pole, just as Abby had said.

He didn't know how many horses Tatum owned, but the only animals nearby were a few pigs, a flock of chickens, an oxen team and the old mutt. He'd gone. Tatum had fled the farm.

He found some chicken feed and dumped it on the ground, threw some grain to the pigs and hoped that would keep them for a time. He didn't believe Tatum was coming home.

Edna came by the hotel with a pot of chicken broth. She clucked her tongue over Al, patted Abby's hand and whispered in her ear.

"Don't know how you knew, but surely glad you did. Poor little thing."

"Me, too, Edna. Wish I'd done something about it before this."

"You're helping now. That counts. Let me know if you need anything. Hear?"

Abby nodded and closed the door behind her.

Sally and Sue hollered from outside the hotel after bouncing pebbles off the window. Abby opened it and leaned out.

"What are you doing, ladies?" she whispered.

"Just saying hello, Abby. That's all. Come on, Sue. Let's go so she can get back to her patient."

"Thank you, Sue, Sally."

Isabelle and Flora showed up, but Patrick waylaid them, bought them drinks and said he'd let Abby know they'd stopped by. It seemed to Abby the entire town wanted to talk with her. She had trouble focusing her eyes, making her brain work, and wished she could crawl into bed beside Al and go to sleep.

"Soon," she said as another knock wiggled the door.

Bunny Parker stood in the doorway, regal as ever, and looked past Abby to the girl in the bed. She walked near and put her hand on Al's pale cheek.

"I will pray for her."

The beautiful woman went silent, still watching Al, and Abby waited. She didn't know what to say besides 'thank you.'

"Service is at my house this week," Bunny said. "Family gathering. I'll expect you."

Abby closed her eyes. Her throat tightened, and she couldn't speak. She was going to cry, and she couldn't do anything about it.

Bunny put an arm around her and made soothing sounds at the back of her throat, like a mother does with her child when she scuffs a knee. She patted Abby's back and murmured, turned and left.

Abby fell to the window seat and sobbed, quietly so she wouldn't wake Al. Almost nothing could compare, almost nothing felt so good. Her heart thrummed. Her chest filled. Bunny had invited her to church, to her home, to her family.

Cassandra spent the next three nights with Al, and Abby stayed with her during the day. Al grew well enough to spoon soup into her own mouth and was strong enough to sit up and eventually move around the room.

On the fifth day, Al asked about her brothers, Abby told her the truth. She nodded and her eyes went to the window, avoiding Abby who saw worry consume Al's face.

"You're not going back home, Al. No one knows where your father is. He's missing. But that doesn't matter because you're not going there."

"Really?" she said, but it didn't come out a question. It was more a statement concerning Abby's bossiness, about Abby telling her what she was going to do.

"I didn't mean it like that, Al."

Abby fidgeted with the sheet she was straightening on Al's bed.

"Then what?"

"You have a home here, at the hotel. You can work in the kitchen and live in one of the rooms, and be safe, be part of the hotel family. For as long as you want. I hope you'll say yes, Al. Please, I want you here."

"Yes."

"You'll stay then? Live here?"

"Til I go."

Abby smiled, knowing that was as much as she was going to get out of Strange Al, and she was happy to get that. "I'll leave you, Al. I need to get back to work. I'm so glad you're feeling better."

It was good to be back behind the bar and even better to take a toddy to the porch and sit with her da, Shorty and Bear. The air was warm, and night critters serenaded them. They rocked in rhythm with little talk.

Her eyes widened when Samuel Moore walked up. He asked permission to sit with his eyes, and Abby nodded.

"Would you like a drink? I was going to refill ours."

"I would. Thank you."

He kept his silence when she came back with the tray and handed out the drinks. They sipped and rocked in time with the frogs' croaks and loons' calls until curiosity forced her tongue.

"Did you want to speak with us, Samuel?"

"I did."

"Well?"

"Just giving information. Betty is no longer being followed -- by anyone. Her father is calm and will abide by her requests to stay out of her business. I am assured of both. The Tatums and George have been formally charged, and the old man is . . . gone. His horse returned to the barn without a rider. They've looked, but there's no trace of him."

Abby rocked, visualizing the farm, the horror of Al's life.

"What will happen to the farm animals?" Patrick asked.

"They're being fed, at least until the trial results. After that, we'll see. They won't go hungry."

Heads nodded and chairs rocked – a slow night-waltz. They breathed in the stillness, reveled in the scent of summer darkness, the taste of lake water at the back of their throats.

"Was there something else?" she asked when he turned her way, thinking he looked like he wanted to say more.

He opened his mouth to ask about Frank moving away, but thought better of it and shook his head.

Stars blinked on in a black sky. Diamonds sparkled in the still water, sizzling like hot sparks on the breeze.

"Thank you. For taking care of Abigail," Patrick said.

He leaned back and his gold chain gleamed in the starlight, flickering with each beat of his pulse.

"That old fool Foster said I've been sucking up to a white girl. Told me I was an Uncle Tom," he said, his eyes lighting with humor.

"Really? And what did you say?" Abby said.

"I said, 'Thank you. I've been told by a very good source that Uncle Tom has been misrepresented, that he was a hero, a valiant fighter for the oppressed.'"

She grinned at him but didn't respond.

"Thank you, Abigail, for opening my eyes."

"You're welcome. I found out opening one's eyes is often painful. And then I found that doing something about what you see eases the ache."

Cassandra moved along the edge of the lake, the clowder following. She turned to salute with her walking stick, and a rush of warmth flooded Abby's body – affection for her witchy woman, for Idlewild.

Arising

The rose is not asleep
It only waits
Anticipates a full awakening
There amid its thorny branches
Standing guard
Protecting
Chaste petals sense the touch of dawn
Earth's adolescent kiss of dew
Moistens the tender bud

It reaches to embrace
The gift of morning sun's caress
Accepting nature's touch
Aroused in sensual velvet scent
In instinct
It awaits with stardust pollen in its eyes
Probe of insect
Lovers
Casting buds against tomorrow

Dusk in dying passion
Enfolds the rose in gentle arms
Sorrowed stars lament
While moon drops
Halo the withered rose
And speak in silent voice
Of the mystery of its scent
Having been in full bloom
The rose in sated dying knows.

By JuliAnne Sisung

TO MY READERS

Thank you for reading. I hope you enjoyed learning about Idlewild, Michigan. Little history is available, but I've tried to be true to what I could find. I created characters and events from my imagination, events I thought might have happened given the results of my research.

I would love to know your thoughts. You can go to www.julisisung.com. From there, you can talk to me, leave an email address so I can talk to you, or click over to Amazon or another book store to leave a review.

Struggling authors need reviews, so I thank you.

I'm already working on *Looking for Nirvana,* so if you like this novel, look for the second in the series next year – maybe sooner.